Novels by
C. S. Friedman
available from DAW Books

THE MADNESS SEASON

THIS ALIEN SHORE

IN CONQUEST BORN
THE WILDING

The Coldfire Trilogy
BLACK SUN RISING
WHEN TRUE NIGHT FALLS
CROWN OF SHADOWS

THE
WILDING

C. S. FRIEDMAN

DAW BOOKS, INC.

DONALD A. WOLLHEIM, FOUNDER
375 Hudson Street, New York, NY 10014
ELIZABETH R. WOLLHEIM
SHEILA E. GILBERT
PUBLISHERS
http://www.dawbooks.com

First Printing, July 2004
1   2   3   4   5   6   7   8   9

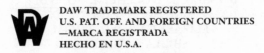

DEDICATION

To Carmen C. Clarke and David Walddon,
without whose gentle but insistent support this
book might never have been completed.

THE
WILDING

One cannot predict with certainty the future course of any man.

How then can one hope to predict the future course of his empires?

—From the writings of ZATAR THE MAGNIFICENT, first Pri'tiera of the Braxin Holding

ONE

Is IT ON? Should I start now?

Yes, we're recording. Go ahead.

I guess you want to know about him. (Pause.) I don't remember much. It's strange when I look back, I can't see his face clearly. Like someone took an eraser and smudged all the colors there. The rest is fine but I can't see that.

(Pause.)

I don't know that I'm going to be able to do much good here . . .

Why don't you just start at the beginning?

. . . All right. All right. I can do that.

The beginning? (Pause.) I came to work for Aleys and Kel right after the birth. They were a prosperous couple, I knew that from the start. Had a nice house on Chandra Prime and a private berth at the spaceport. Really nice. You could tell they both made good money and didn't mind spending it on the things that mattered. That was a good sign. I also figured that was why they were willing to hire me, because neither of them wanted to give up their nice income. I mean, it was kind of odd for Chandrans; usually that race won't let strangers help raise their children no matter what. But I figured that was it, they just needed a little hand here and there to let them stay in the work force while the kids grew up. Not unheard of. Other races do it all the time.

So anyway, I got there five days after the birth. You could see right away that the parents were really glad to have me there. They were a young couple, hardly old enough to be having children, I thought. But then, you never know. I've heard some of the Scattered Races start with conception while they're still kids themselves, some kind of hormone preparation thing. Never worked for one of those races myself, but I've heard tales from nurturers who have. They were pretty critical of the practice, but the way I see it, it's none of our business to tell another race when to reproduce, you know? "Human is as human does," or so they say.

Why don't you tell us about the children?

All right. Well, the first thing you noticed of course was that there were two of them. Two! I mean, it happens all the time with other races, but when was the last time you heard of a multiple birth with Chandrans? They like controlling things so much, it's amazing they'd even think about letting an egg split up all on its own. Or let both halves grow up if it did.

And they were real twins, too. Little girls. (Pause.) Pretty little things. (Pause.) I remember. . . .

(Long pause.)

Go on.

The girls were absolutely identical, a real split-egg pair. And you could see their parents hadn't been ready to take on two, whatever they might have thought before the birth. So they called me in to help. That was fine. I settled in fast and pretty much took over, and they were happy with that. The kids were well behaved, didn't cry much, not unless you separated them. They were bright enough, but they spent a lot of time just staring at each other. I guess identicals are like that. It's kind of like they only have one brain, you know, just split up into two parts. I guess there's some part of them that knows what the other is. You could almost sense that sometimes, when you were watching them. Really eerie.

Did you know about the security issues?

(Pause.) Kel said that because of their genetic code they were at high risk for . . . what was his phrase? . . . "lifestyle interruption." He never explained what that meant. I know the parents had special security all over the place, like this system linked to Chandra Prime's Central Ops that would send people running to help if there was the least sign of trouble.

You could tell they really wanted to explain things to me, especially Aleys. But they said they couldn't. Said the facts couldn't be in my brain, or something like that. (Pause. In a whisper:) Poor little kids. You think if I'd known what was really going on I could have helped more? Oh, the poor babies. He almost got them, you know?

(Gently:) Please go on.

Not much more to tell, for about six pasats. I don't think you want details of child care, do you? (Pause.) Anyway, you don't get much variety with Chandran babies. It's all preprogrammed. You know when they'll have a full head of hair, you know when their first tooth will come in, you pretty much know when they're going to say their first word. Not much is left to chance, in that race. It's the genetics thing. They don't trust Nature much.

Tell us about that night.

(Pause.) I was alone with them, you know? Both of their parents were out. I had the alarm system on—I really did, they've asked me about that a hundred times, you know, but I made sure of it!—Anyway, things were quiet until about midnight. I had them in bed long before then, of course.

And then I—

(Pause.)

Kallesi?

I'm sorry . . . it's hard to remember this part . . . I don't know why. . . .

Take your time.

(With obvious effort:) I . . . I think I went into the library to read. Funny, how even that memory is hazy now, it's all going away, like it never really happened . . . I went in there and called up a book. I don't remember what book it was. They've asked me that over and over again, you know, but I just can't remember. It seems a stupid thing to forget, doesn't it? But how much can it matter, what book I was reading?

(Gently:) Go on.

Anyway, I must have been there a while. Then . . . it was strange . . . I thought I heard the portal chime. But it didn't, did it? The records say no one used it in that time, at least that's what the others told me, when they investigated.

Just tell us what you remember, Kallesi. Don't worry about the others.

My first thought was—and this was odd, I thought that even at the time—"Ah, *he's* here." Like I had been expecting someone all along. But I wasn't, I've told you all that. Aleys and Kel didn't like me entertaining when no one was home. It was all that security stuff, you know. Something about the kids. So even then I knew it was a pretty strange reaction to have. Like, I felt. . . . (Pause.) . . . it was almost like I was inside my own head, watching my thoughts. You know? Observing them from the outside. Very strange.

What did you do then?

I . . . I . . . (Long pause.) I think I went to the portal. I'm sorry I can't be sure . . . this whole thing, I can't remember it clearly. Like half of me wasn't there at the time. I think I went to see who was there. I figured I would just tell them to go away and come back later, but I ought to see first who it was. . . .

The portal has a message recorder.

Yes. Yes. I know that. (Pause.) I don't know why I didn't just tell him to use it. That would have been the right thing to do. That's what I usually did. (Pause.) How much trouble am I going to be in? I mean, the children—

(Gently:) We'll worry about that later. For now just go on with the story.

Anyway I . . . I guess I opened the portal. To see who it was.

You couldn't see him through the viewport?

(Long pause.) I guess I could have. I felt . . . like that wasn't enough. Somehow. It was strange. . . .

Can you describe him?

He was Azean. At least, I thought he was Azean. They tell me now the security images don't match that, that he didn't look Azean at all. But that's what I saw. And it seemed to me at the time that he was familiar to me, and I knew from past experience that he was a regular visitor.

So you let him in.

Yes. I let him in.

It's strange, I remember us talking for a while . . . but again, there are no records of that, are there? Just of him sort of staring into my eyes for a few minutes. If not for that I'd have said we spent a long time talking, about all sorts of things. That's what I remember, you see, even though they tell me now it never happened. I mean, could the records be wrong? (Pause.)

Anyway, after that . . . he went down the hall to look in on the children. I wasn't going to follow him there at first, because I knew he'd visited the babies many times, so all that was okay. But at the same time, I felt really strange about it. Can't say why. Like something inside me was worried, worried enough that I didn't want him to be alone with the girls. At first I felt really bad about having that reaction, and I was afraid that if I followed him and he thought I didn't trust him he might get angry and . . . well, angering your employer's friends is not the best way to get references, you know? But then I thought, you know, these parents are so *careful* with their babies, like they continually expect something to go wrong, so if you have any bad feeling about this, any bad feeling at all, you really ought to go in there and check it out. Just to be sure.

So that's when I went down the hall to go into the nursery myself. And I saw him—

I saw him . . .

(Long pause.)

Take your time, Kallesi. Try to remember.

He . . . he had one of the babies. The little thing was all wrapped up in something, a kind of bag with long straps. There was something else . . . another bag maybe . . . laid out on the dresser. Like he was getting ready to wrap up the other one too, and take them both.

What did you think when you saw all this?

(Pause.) I thought . . . (Pause.) It was all okay. It just was, you know? Like . . . like their parents had planned this all along. I mean, that doesn't make any sense now, but back then it seemed to. This man knew the girls' parents, and he had come to take the babies for a while, and that was all right. I knew that.

And then what happened?

I . . . I don't really know.

(Pause.)

I really don't.

(Pause.)

I'm sorry.

He looked at you again. Like before.

I guess. The security images show that, don't they? I don't remember it. I'm sorry. That part's just a blank. Next thing I remember is him reaching for the other little girl. And somehow . . . that wasn't right. Like some part of me had suddenly come awake, and knew this whole thing was wrong. I remember starting to scream. It wasn't because I *wanted* to scream, but that was the only thing I could do. It was like all the other stuff in my brain had been shut down, so that I couldn't remember how to make the security system call for help, or where the panic switches were located, or . . . anything. It just all welled up inside me, all this fear without any way to let it out, and finally I just screamed. Really loud.

Well, he looked at me as if I had gone crazy—and maybe I had, for a moment—and maybe he would have done something to stop me from screaming, but I guess the house had some kind of sensor set to respond to loud noises, because the warning light on the control pad near the door lit up suddenly. Bright green, which meant that help was on its way. He took one look at that and I guess he decided to run for it. And maybe he figured he couldn't run with a baby in his arms, or maybe in his panic he just forgot them, but anyway, he bolted for the door without either of the little girls. And I guess he just beat your people there, because they came only minutes later, but he was already gone. —You didn't ever catch him, did you?

(Gently:) No. No, we didn't ever catch him.

Are the . . . are the babies okay? They won't let me see them. I really don't know what he was doing in there with them, but he didn't have enough time to hurt them. Did he? Are they all right? Can I please see them?

No harm was done. (Pause.) Please try to be calm.

I loved them, you know? I know that doesn't make any sense, they weren't my babies, but when you live day and night with such little ones, when you're like a mother to them, that's how it is. You would tell me if they were hurt, wouldn't you?

You would be told if they were injured.

I couldn't bear it if I was responsible for that. Those little girls. Such beautiful babies.

I am sure they will be fine, Kallesi. And your answering all these questions helps a lot.

You're going to catch the man who came after them?

(Brief pause.) Yes. Yes we are.

I'm so glad. He shouldn't have come in, should he? He wasn't really a friend of the girls' parents, was he?

We'll know all that in time, Kallesi. For now, thank you for coming. There are a few more questions you will need to answer for our files; the secretary outside can take care of that. . . .

Of course. Of course. Please let me know if anything changes, will you? Or . . . or if I can see the babies again. . . .

Of course.

(Sound of furniture scraping softly across the floor. Footsteps, tentative and uneven. The whisper of a portal turning off and on.)

(Long silence.)

She doesn't know.

No. No, she doesn't.

But you said she was told—

She was told. Several times.

And she's seen the child?

Yes, right after the kidnapping. She talked to them as if they were both still there. Quite unnerving, I'm told. Even reached out to touch the missing child, before someone stopped her. The mother couldn't handle it, said she won't risk her one remaining child in the presence of a madwoman.

Do you think the kidnapper did that to her? Deliberately?

(Pause.) Who knows? From her story it sounds as if he had remarkable powers, maybe he could alter memories like that. But it seems to me more likely that her mind just snapped. Couldn't handle the guilt of knowing that she was responsible for the disappearance of one of her precious babies.

You think we may see others with his capacity coming into the Empire?

No way to tell. But if we do, we're going to lose a lot more children, I'll tell you that. There's no way to defend against something like this. Not that we know about, anyway.

How many have we lost this year, so far?

(Long pause.)

(Sound of a chair scraping back. Hard, angry footsteps. Whisper of a portal field being dissipated.)

Too damn many.

If you would learn the true spirit of a culture, observe what it does when change is forced upon it.

—from the writings of ANZHA LYU MITETHE

TWO

THERE WAS TENSION in the air. Tathas could taste it as he entered the inn, a heady cloud of pheromones borne aloft on the scented smoke that filled the D'arkob, underscored by the faint tang of sweat and the stinging aroma of Braxin beer.

He stood in the doorway for a moment and just drank it in, an ancient cocktail of smells suitable for such a night as this. It made his blood sing in his veins.

No one noticed him. Of course. On a night like this it was vital he go unnoticed, lest some passing Central Guard ask who it was that drew such attention, and learn too many things about his business. Accordingly, as Tathas walked into the common room, he met no eyes, offered no greeting. Others did the same. A dozen women who might normally have flocked to his side kept their distance. Two dozen men who knew him by name pretended that he was a stranger to them. Yet he could feel the tension in the air, he could taste it as he walked. They knew. They *knew*.

They were Kesserit, of course, every one of them. He could see the tribal heritage in the set of their eyes, the olive hue of their skin, the strong arched nose set above a narrow, determined mouth. Let other tribes interbreed until all their physical characteristics were lost in a sea of mediocrity, drowned out by those qualities which the Braxaná labeled "common." The Kesserit had never done so. Nor did they allow their women to be victimized by more common tribes, as Braxin law encouraged. Each woman in the room wore some sign on her person that she was owned by another, giving her the right to refuse to serve as a random receptacle of lust. Never mind that most of those signs were false. The Kesserit took care of their own.

All illegal, of course. So very illegal. The Braxaná had no tolerance for tribal traditions outside of their own, and had made every effort to see them obliterated. Through laws, through custom, and of course through the most ancient formula of all, genetic dilution. Oh, there were Braxins who thought that the laws of sexual access had been enacted for pleasure alone, some grand Braxaná indulgence that had been offered as a bribe to the men of other tribes to win their favor. The Kesserit knew better. Ten thousand years of being forced to bear random seed had made Braxin women the mothers of a new race, one without clear tribal distinctions. Few Braxins today knew what their true heritage was. Few showed any sign of tribal heritage in their features. Fewer still had managed to preserve any shadow of tribal custom down through the ages, against the tide of Braxaná dominance.

But there was a core of those who remembered. One tribe that had preserved its memories, in spirit and flesh both.

And they were here tonight.

They had come from all over, drawn by whispers of the Viak'ket. Kesserit from all across the globe . . . perhaps from other planets as well. He could feel their eyes upon him as he walked across the great room, their scrutiny like a buzz along his skin. *His* people. The words had power, he could taste it.

The bar's owner reached over and flicked a switch behind the bar. Windows opaqued, shutting out any view of the street. A sign that announced "CLOSED" filled the portal, thrumming in the sudden silence. *Now, now the time has come,* the gesture said. *Now we are alone, and no one can interfere.*

"Downstairs," he said gruffly.

Tathas let the crowd precede him. Which one among them was his adversary, that young upstart who had decided that the crown of the tribe suited him? Whose blood would he spill tonight? He felt a wild hunger course through his veins, not just for killing, but for power. There were other hungers that would follow in time, and he knew that any woman present would serve him without question, perhaps even praying that his seed would take root. There was great honor to be had in bearing the child of a Kesserit prince.

As if she could sense his thoughts, one woman drew back from the crowd, and her eyes met his across the room. Black hair framed her face, cascaded down her back: pure black, the mark of the Braxaná. It was always hard with women to tell if the color was natural or not, for cosmetic drugs made it easy enough to change such a thing, but with this one he knew it was. Pale skin, with just a hint of Kesserit gold to it. Deep green eyes, the same color as his own. The mix of elements in her was always a rush, and he could feel a stirring in his loins as he gazed at her, half-breed child of the two most aggressive tribes on the planet. One played its games in the open, observed by all humanity. One held its contests in secret, and chose its leaders according to a formula centuries old. In her both were reflected, a cultural war that might find peace only in this woman's features.

She smiled knowingly when she had his eye, then turned and followed the others into the inner sanctum.

Deep within the bowels of the inn was a chamber carved out of the rock beneath, from which neither sound nor light could escape. Into this the crowd descended and instinctively pressed back against the walls of the room to clear the space in the center.

A circular stage was raised up there, so that all might see it. About it the tribal elders were already seated, five men and one woman whose wisdom and dedication to tribal concerns had set them apart from the common blood. The woman wore male clothing, of course, and bore a male name; such was the custom when a woman was raised to elder status. Thus was the Goddess of Chaos kept at arm's length, and the prophecies of old defied.

Tathas came down the stairs last and looked at them, studying them all. His people. They were here to share this moment with him, this secret and forbidden moment, and to feel their Kesserit blood stir once more as they watched the ancient dance. In that moment, as he gazed upon them, he could feel himself connected to a thousand generations—to tens of thousands—a line of blood and custom stretching back farther than the Braxaná could even remember. No, the Kesserit had not forgotten their tribal roots. No simple law could make them forget what was in their very blood.

He could feel the hushed silence like a shiver upon his skin as he strode through the room and stepped up to the central platform. No doubt there were some who had never seen him before; well, now they would have their chance. He felt their gaze upon him: curious, demanding. What would they see when they looked at him? A Kesserit warrior in the prime of life, who had claimed the tribal crown more than ten years ago and still held it. A Kesserit prince, in every sense of the word. He glanced down at the elders, but did not meet their eyes. He must not court their favor now, not visibly. Whatever choice they were to make tonight had long since been decided. To imply that a few special words or a passing glance might sway their decision at this point would be an insult to them all.

He scanned the crowd, wondering who it was that meant to challenge him. All he knew is that it was a man from Aldous, who rarely visited the mother planet. After a moment there was movement at the far side of the room, and the crowd of spectators parted to reveal a man not much older than himself, whose bare arms were taut with muscle, whose green eyes gleamed with a variety of lusts. He would be strong, of course. And skilled in combat. And hungry for power . . . that above all else. Tathas studied him as he moved forward, trying to read meaning into each tiny movement. Hints of weakness, arrogance, fear . . . anything that might affect his performance. Swordplay alone did not make a Kesserit prince, though it was a vehicle by which other things were judged.

As Tathas had, the man gazed out upon the crowd. Then he, too, ascended to the stage.

Tathas waited until the man seemed ready—a courtesy certainly due one who was about to risk his life in the name of ambition—and then said, in a voice that was strong and unwavering, "I am Tathas, son of Zheret, Viak'im of the Kesserit. By death I claimed my crown, by death I keep it, and by death, when the time is right, I will relinquish it." He bowed a respectful head toward the elders where they sat, but though they gazed back at him, he could read nothing in their eyes. "I submit myself to the will of the Elders."

Not until his words had settled in the vast room, and all their implications subsided, did his opponent speak. "I am Sharik, son of Menest. I am of Kesserit blood, of Kesserit upbringing, of Kesserit soul. I have come to claim leadership of our tribe in the ancient tradition, and to unify the Kesserit of many planets into a nation greater than what it has been, a nation truly worthy of our great tribal heritage." His gaze upon the elders challenged them to find fault in him, or any fault in his offerings. "The Braxaná have ruled long enough. They are weak now, and in weakness they abandon the traditions that brought them to power. It is time for the other tribes to rise up and claim what is rightfully their own."

So that's his gambit, Tathas thought, as the elders rose up from their seats. Of course those ancient judges already knew Sharik's agenda, and many other things besides. Though the elders approached the two men now, and made a show of inspecting them, Tathas knew that they had already judged the matter, balanced Sharik's agenda against his past record of leadership, and decided who, in their opinion, should lead the tribe.

Who that was, and how strongly they felt about the matter . . . ah, that was something no man could guess.

It was the female elder who mixed the wine, pouring it into glasses that were already lined with a dust of herbs and drugs. Not the same, from glass to glass; even from where he stood Tathas could see the difference in content between the two. In that dust resided a volume of judgement: their assessment of the tribe's current state, its past trials, its future glories. In it, most important of all, resided their judgement of these two men.

She brought him a glass and held it silently out to him, even as one of the male elders did the same for his opponent. For all that he had grown accustomed to mortal combat, this was the one moment that always unnerved Tathas. What was in that glass? There was no way to know for sure. If they approved of him it might be some drug to bolster his strength, or his endurance, or perhaps acuity of mind. If they thought that his time for leadership had passed it might be some subtle poison: perhaps a formula that would delay the coagulation of the blood, or prevent his body from processing its energies properly, or make the pain of each blow he suffered more acute. Or perhaps the elders had decided that both men had good cause to claim leadership of the tribe, and all they had added were spices, masking the fact that the decision had been left to simple combat.

Whatever it was, the effect would be subtle enough that he knew he would never detect it. Only once had he seen a man so weakened by the elders' offering that he knew himself doomed, and that man in shame had fallen to his knees then, and offered up his throat to the Viak'im's sword. The Viak'im back then had been his father, and Tathas remembered him explaining later why the ritual was the thing it was, and how the fiery passion of young men must be tempered by the wisdom of age and experience.

In time, of course, the man had fallen to his son's own sword. Such was the way of things.

With a steady hand Tathas took the glass from her and quickly downed its contents, accepting the will of his elders. The drugged wine burned his throat going down, and he immediately began to imagine all sorts of sensations spreading through his body. That was his own agitation making itself known, he told himself. Whatever the elders might give him, it was subtle enough in its effect that he would never be able to sense it. The purpose of the ritual libation was to skew the odds of combat ever so slightly, not to mandate a winner outright.

Balance. Balance. All things in balance. That was the one thing the Braxaná had never learned, and why they were dying out now.

He handed the empty glass back to the elder, not meeting her eyes. A young girl stepped up to the platform then and offered him a circlet woven of human hair, the so-called crown of combat. In the old days the Kesserit warriors would have twisted up their own long hair into tight coils about their skulls, offering some protection against blows; in these days, when long hair on men was against the prevailing fashion, such tresses made the Kesserit warriors dangerously conspicuous. So this custom had taken its place. He took the tightly braided band into his hand, savoring the feel of the twisted hair, fingering the complex pattern of the weave. Each strand had been donated by a woman who favored him, thus making it as much a talisman of luck and a sign of virility as a simple piece of armor. He even caught sight of some black hairs among the shades of brown and he smiled despite himself, pleased that *she* had contributed.

Ah, how they would celebrate when this day was done! Nothing in all the world was sweeter than that, the pleasure which came after combat.

When the crown was in place he shrugged off his shirt, baring himself to the waist. Whispers accompanied the act as a nearby woman caught up the garment, and he heard fragments of wagers being made, admiration and anticipation being voiced. His opponent did the same, and he could see at once that the man had been in many duels. Scoring his chest and arms were the tight puckered lines of ancient wounds, which had been encouraged to scar rather than being healed cleanly, as Tathas' were. Clearly whatever group this man belonged to valued the tokens of past combat as a sign of virility, or perhaps simply a token of luck. Tathas much preferred the effect that came from appearing as though no enemy's sword had ever touched him . . . even if that was as much the result of modern medicine as his own martial expertise.

The female elder remained upon the platform between them during all of this, and if the sight of two Braxin warriors in their prime stirred any female instincts to life within her, she kept it carefully hidden. When they both seemed ready she handed each of them a sword: matched weapons, finely honed. Illegal for anyone but a Braxaná to wield.

"This fight is to the death," she announced. As if it needed to be said. Any man who didn't know the tradition must surely be able to smell it in the air, the sharp tang of bloodlust and death-hunger mixed in with the scent of sweat. She stepped down from the platform then, and turned back to face the combatants. Studying first one then the other, biding her time as if to see if they had the patience she required, the self-control . . . or perhaps searching for signs in them of the elders' drugs working, a faint flush or glistening sweat that would tell her their will was now manifest in the men's flesh.

At last she seemed satisfied, and nodded to one of the male elders. Of course. No woman could give a direct command, not even here.

That man stood, and in a voice that rang with authority cried out, "Begin!"

The newcomer wasted no time, but began his approach immediately. Tathas assessed him with a practiced eye even as the distance closed, noting every flick of muscle, every twitch of facial expression. Twenty years of dueling for the seat of Kesserit power had taught him that men often thought the path to victory would be that which he expected least. They didn't realize that he had seen nearly every trick in the book. A man doesn't take down his own father without hundreds of duels to prepare.

He watched as the man glanced ever so quickly to the audience and back, a mere heartbeat of distraction, and judged him instantly to be the kind who fought as much for show as for victory. Good, that was good. Such men could be dangerous opponents but they were often unnerved by subtlety. So he would play the less obvious game.

He could feel his muscles tense as he took one step forward, then two, but despite the coiled readiness of his body, on the surface he held himself still, utterly still. Eerily still. Against the quivering sword of his opponent his stillness was like a cold wind, and he knew from a flicker of surprise in the other man's eyes that it wasn't what he had expected. Good. Good. Before the first blow then, the battle was already engaged. Mind before flesh. It was what his father had taught him, back in the days when they still had the luxury of casual lessons. Before the former Viak'im had realized that his son might prove a threat to him, and driven him from the house. . . .

A flicker of movement came toward him, lightning-swift. He parried the opening move with a steady blade, feeling his wrist absorb the shock as steel struck steel. That the man's strength matched his own was immediately apparent, and for a moment he could see respectful acknowledgement of it flicker in his opponent's eyes as well; then the momentum of the attack carried them beyond that point, into an exchange that moved so swiftly it allowed for no further reverie. Each time their blades made contact he could feel the other man testing him, gauging his strength, his reaction time, even his strategy . . . and he did the same.

Then: stillness for a moment. He could feel the sweat gathering on his skin as he forced his muscles to be still, the heat of combat still singing in his veins, crying out for motion. But the gambit was going to pay off. He could see the momentary hesitation in the other man's eyes, as he sought in vain for any clue as to Tathas' intentions. All he saw was stillness. Utter stillness. While deep inside the Viak'im muscles tensed like a coiled snake, preparing to strike. . . .

And he struck. His opponent's parry was strong but it was wide, and like a snake Tathas twisted into position about his blade and drove forward. The man leaned sideways to dodge the blow, but a moment too late for safety; Tathas could feel it in his hands as the sharp blade cut through flesh at the man's waist, scoring deep into the muscle there. At times like this he could sense the bloodthirst in that cold steel, which traveled up his arm to take root in his soul. Nothing mattered now but the combat, nothing counted but the kill. Nothing mattered but the dance of blood and power, as ancient as the Kesserit themselves, by which their leaders had always been chosen.

And always would be. No matter what the God-blessed Braxaná had to say about it. Outlaw ancient weapons? Punish dueling among the "lesser" tribes? It would never change things. The Kesserit had not forgotten the days when they wore their own weapons openly, and had never ceased to hate the tribe which outlawed such things for all but their own race.

Tathas swore softly to himself as his opponent engaged him again, this time with a swift combination of moves that allowed for no opening. The man was learning, and very quickly. It seemed to him, as he responded, that his reflexes were even faster than usual. Was that possible? Had the elders favored his reign with a drug that would give him such advantage? If so, then his victory was all but assured.

I am Viak'im! he thought triumphantly, and he pressed forward in a new engagement. Steel against steel rang in the humid chamber as blade scraped along blade towards its target. Then his sword bit into flesh once more, and a thin stream of red began to trickle forth from the other man's shoulder. Tathas could see that his entire leg was streaked with scarlet now, from where the blood flowed freely from his first wound, and soon the loss would begin to slow his reflexes. Bright red footprints had begun to appear on the floor of the platform, dangerously slick. The man tried to maneuver away from the wettest ones, but Tathas didn't allow it. He waited until his opponent's foot came down squarely in a pool of his own blood and then drove forward. Not enough to trip him up. Maybe enough to distract him. It seemed to him for a moment that the man's sword wavered, and when he drove his own downward towards his opponent's head, lending the strength of both arms to the blow, such was the raw power of the move that he nearly reached that arrogant skull. But at the last minute the blade beneath his twisted and angled and the force of his own momentum carried him inches to the side of his target. Then he was on the defensive again—

A worthy opponent. Rare, for him. On another night he might have counted it a pleasure. On this night, with his throne at stake, it was merely one more challenge to be overcome.

Sparks played along steel as their blades met again and again, and soon his own flesh felt the bite of that foreign blade. The floor was slick with blood now, treacherous for them both. Again and again their swords engaged, and the crimson tally of their efforts began to score both bodies, streaks of red that leaked strength down their limbs and onto the floor. Yet still the strength rang in Tathas' veins, and with it the sureness of his elders' favor. His opponent was weakening now, he could sense it; in each attack there was a microsecond of hesitation, in each parry there was a shadow of weakness. Tathas called upon the uttermost reserves of his strength to drive the advantage home—and then there was a parry that fell short in execution, and the full weight of his body was behind his blade, and he forced his opponent's sword to give way and lay the target bare—

Sword into flesh. Deep, deep, beneath the surface muscle, into the soft organs beneath. He could feel the vibration through his arms as the sword grazed a rib, then pierced that precious prize which the ribs were made to guard. Blood gushed out of the wound, hot blood, scarlet blood, the flavor and smell of victory. The body fell; he went down with it. On the floor of the platform he knelt over his enemy, feeling the pulse of his life shiver against the blade that had impaled it. His opponent tried to strike at him, but already the strength had left his limbs, and his sword arm flopped to the side like a dying fish.

I am Viak'im! Tathas' spirit literally sang the words, a chorus of triumph to accompany his kill. Not until the flow of blood had ceased to trickle, not until the flailing limbs had ceased to move, the eyes glazed over, the muscles gone limp with lifelessness, did he withdraw his blade, and dare to breathe an unguarded breath at last.

It was then that he noticed the silence.

Silence? There should be cheers now, howls and curses from the opponent's side, money changing hands as betting concluded noisily, women jostling for a better position from which to win his attention . . . he had been through this before, often enough to know the sound of such things. And this was wrong, this silence. Completely wrong.

He rose to his feet, streaks of red adorning his flesh like some barbaric adornment. And he gazed about the chamber, and followed the gaze of the people surrounding him, to the chamber's one entrance. Where *they* stood.

Central Guard.

They were armed, all of them, heavily armed, and it was impossible to see how many of them there were, for the entranceway was narrow and beyond it lay darkness. But it was clear enough that they had come in force, and as the eyes of the leader met Tathas' own for an instant, he could sense the triumph in that steely black gaze.

Then: chaos erupted. As if emboldened by his very stillness, the spectators nearest the guards began to move toward them. Others turned to run—though where they meant to run to, in a chamber with only one exit, one could only guess. Battle screams were voiced by some, cries of terror by others, and as a backdrop to all that was the repeated hum of a neural stun as body after body was paralyzed in mid-motion, the connection between brain and flesh neatly and painfully severed.

My people, my people!

For an instant he could do no more than stand frozen. His position on the fighting platform gave him an almost surreal view of the fight, and in that second he did not even feel a part of it. What could he do? He would not run. He could not fight. There were too many people between him and the enemy, he would have to cut his way through a wall of Kesserit flesh to even make it to the fray.

—Then the warrior's soul inside him rose to the surface, screaming its rage at this final indignity. Ten thousand years of hatred and outrage, boiling up into a single cry, a single motion. He could feel it erupt from his throat in a primal scream of fury, could feel the heat of it burning along his lacerated flesh. *I am your enemy, not them!* Over the helpless bodes of his fallen people the wordless howl resounded, and the lead guard turned from his killing to face Tathas. Cold eyes he had, black eyes, utterly deserving of death.

Then the guard lifted his weapon and Tathas knew there was nowhere to go, no shelter he could reach from the center of the platform in time. So he did the only thing he could do, and screamed his defiance as he charged forward toward the enemy, willing all his courage into his people, willing all his hatred into the heart of that one pale, smug god-lover—

And then there was pain. Such pain. It reverberated along every nerve, a symphony of agony. He grit his teeth and tried to ignore it, but it was not rooted in any place he had control of, and he could feel his body overloading, shutting down. *NO!* he screamed inwardly. His throat would no longer obey him, his voice would not make a sound. *BLESS YOU ALL, I WILL NOT SUBMIT—*

The last thing he saw before darkness claimed him was his sword striking home in its target.

Darkness. Not numbness. Darkness and a symphony of pain, notes scraped along his raw nerves, chords searing into his flesh. The kind of pain a body cannot endure, unless it exists in the mind alone. Electrodes, drugs, the pricking of gray matter with semi-sentient probes. *Here, this will hurt. That neuron, there, it will hurt more.*

Maybe he screamed. Maybe they pricked the neurons of screaming, so that he had no other option. Maybe it pleased them, to make him do things his conscious mind would never choose to do.

Bless you all!

The weight of the ages. History, embodied in a single man.

Too much. Too much . . .

Black eyes staring at him, thousands of them, hated black Braxaná eyes, blood washing floodlight screaming—

Pain again.

Maybe they woke him now and then, and asked him questions.

Maybe he spit in their faces.

Darkness. Pain receding like an ocean tide, slowly. Siren's song in the distance. Consciousness unearthed like fine sand beneath the surf, grain by grain, trembling in pain's dampness.

Hours to realize that he was awake. Hours more to realize that his eyes were under his own control, that they could in fact open. Or so it seemed. He sent them the proper signals and yes, the muscles trembled with weakness, but they responded. His whole body trembled, expecting another onslaught of pain. Yet there was nothing, save the throbbing memory of past agonies. By the unfeeling gods, did this mean they were done with him? At last?

Ha. He should be so lucky.

For a moment he could hardly focus on what was around him, and he feared that in the many assaults upon his brain his vision had been irreparably damaged. But no, he realized shortly, there were simply no details to see. Just blank walls, and a blank ceiling, and a light that seemed to come from nowhere. Even that much light burned him like the sun would burn him, if he stared into it at high noon, and with a moan of pain he tried to turn away from it—

—and sickness welled up inside him with a suddenness he could not control. He managed to roll over just far enough not to vomit on himself, as the contents of his stomach spewed forth into the featureless whiteness. It smelled even more foul than vomit should, or was that just his own perception, his senses overwhelmed by the sudden overload? What had they been feeding him? He reached up to wipe the slime from his mouth and could feel how much his beard had grown in the time they'd had him, bristling hairs no longer neatly clipped, but a ragged mane suitable for his new estate.

Anger flared inside him, a single defiant spark, and he used his sleeve to wipe every last trace of vomit from his face, refusing to wear such a badge of shame even for a tenth. His shirt was an unfamiliar fabric, stiff with the sweat of pain-induced fevers. How long had he been here? Did the fact that he was awake and cognizant now mean that something was changing?

"Tathas."

It was a whisper, and barely that. A thought, no more, that drifted across the surface of his mind, gentling the damaged neurons in its path. And yet . . . how like that siren's song it was, calling to him from across the oceans of pain. Was that a real voice he had heard? It seemed real enough now.

With a muffled groan he turned to the source of the voice, and blinked his eyes heavily as they struggled to focus upon this new object. Slowly the form of a woman came into view, hazed by the shimmering force field that guarded the portal of his prison.

"Tathas?"

He struggled for speech, disbelieving. His throat was dry and tender and the sound which came forth was cracked and brittle, a weak simulacrum of human speech. "Who . . ."

This misty figure said, "K'teva."

He blinked heavily, trying to clear his eyes, fighting to focus. By the gods who abandoned Braxi, it *was* K'teva. He stumbled to his feet, his legs shaking with unaccustomed weakness as he forced them to support him. It was frustrating, more than anything; he was not accustomed to being helpless.

He managed to stand, and then managed to walk, though the room spun dizzily around him. Strings of damp hair swung in his eyes and he pushed them back to see more clearly; it was long, distressingly long, the kind of length it would take zhents to grow. *Best not to think about that.* Then he was at the force field, close enough to hear its whispered hum, close enough to *her* that if he could reach out past that barrier his hand would touch her hair, the heat of her body a caress upon his tortured skin. . . .

"How?" he choked out. "How did you get here?"

She looked about carefully before answering, and when she spoke it was in a whisper that bore witness to the secrecy of her visit. "Zedras got me false papers. They thought I was one of them." She opened her eyes wide as if to display the cosmetic alteration that had turned her eyes as black as night, framed by skin layered in the palest of powders. "I've passed before, you know that."

"Yes." Members of the first class could go just about anywhere, and she knew how to play the part to perfection. He'd seen her get in impossible places before, and so this one didn't surprise him.

"How long—" The words were out before he could stop them.

She bit her lip before answering, as if trying to decide how to tell him. "Nearly three zhents."

He winced. "The others?"

"Some were taken. Many escaped. They had no real interest in the spectators, only you and . . . and the elders."

He didn't have to ask what happened to the elders. He could hear it in her voice.

Bless them! God-loving Braxaná. Bless them all!

"Listen." Her whisper was fevered now, and she looked to both sides of her as if expecting a guard to show up at any moment. "They're going to bring you to a hearing. It's just a sham, you understand? They're going to bring you before the Pri'tiera's Council and they're going to read the charges against you, and there's nothing you can do to defend yourself . . . because it's all true, isn't it?"

True, yes, true. He shut his eyes for a moment and the whole of his life seemed to pass before him, replete with its myriad illegalities. Possession and use of bladed weapons. Dueling. Propagation of non-Braxaná tribal identity. Participation in illegal tribal government.

Treason, plain and simple. And they had caught him bare-handed.

And now she had come here to tell him that. Why?

"K'teva . . ." The name felt odd on his tongue, a fragment of some former life that was strangely unfamiliar. "You didn't come here just to tell me what they would say before they killed me."

For a moment it seemed like she hesitated. "There is a way," she whispered at last. "A Braxaná custom you can invoke. I researched it."

"Braxaná?" It must have been the zhents of torture that made his head ache so; he couldn't make sense of her words. "But I'm not Braxaná. What do their customs have to do with me?"

"It's called the Wilding. Do you know it?"

He tried to remember, but his memories were all a jumbled mess. Finally he shook his head, frustrated. "No. No . . . the word is familiar, but I can't recall. . . ."

"They don't talk about it a lot outside their tribe. But I found it in their law books. It's . . . it's a ritual, sort of. They started it back in the days of the first Pri'tiera. It's based on some ancient Braxaná practice, mate-capture from their early tribal period, and they updated it and prettified it and wrote it into law. So now anyone from their bloodlines who wants to go out and prove himself, he comes before the Council and he swears off all his property and obligations, and the Holding lets him go. Anywhere he wants. If he comes back with genetic material worthy of being adopted into the Pale One's race, he's accorded all sorts of honors and breeding rights. If he doesn't . . . well, there are those who do it just to escape from a less than savory past, I guess. It seems to work." She paused, watching him closely; her eyes were pleading with him. "Don't you see? They swear off *everything*. The law allows it. A fresh start—"

"But I'm not Braxaná. It's meant for them, isn't it? Their god-blessed bloodlines—"

"*Not on the rings.* I've read it all through, ten times over. Nowhere does it specify what tribe you have to belong to. *Nowhere.* Oh, I'm sure they meant it just for their race, but the point is, *the law doesn't say that.*"

It sank in slowly. With the understanding came a faint flicker of pride, and fleeting memory of what he once had been. "You want me . . . to run away?"

She blessed him under her breath and stepped back, dark eyes narrow with frustration.

"That's what it would be, to our people. Running away to stay alive."

"And this is better? Being butchered like an animal?"

He shut his eyes. So hard, so hard to think clearly. Even standing on his feet this long was taking its toll. But the words had energized him, reminded him of who and what he truly was. "I am Viak'im, yes? Perhaps . . . perhaps the last. If I run now, if I end my days in cowardice . . . what will the Kesserit become? What chance is there then of them ever recovering from this blow?"

"You think that your dying will help them?"

He stared into her eyes. Black eyes, lenses, so different from her own. It pained him that the last time he would see her she would look like one of *them*.

With effort he drew himself up, and he could hear the pride come into his voice as he told her, "Better a martyr than a coward."

"Tathas. Tathas. Please listen to me." There was anger in her voice now, just a tremor of it, and ten thousand other emotions he was too sick and weak to read. "We *have* martyrs. Do you understand? The elders. Your challenger. All dead now, brutally, horribly dead. *Publicly* dead, martyrs to the last one of them. What good will it do the tribe now if you just add your name to that list?" She stepped close to the force field, so close that a white glow gathered around her face as she leaned toward him. "You must live. You must recoup. You can return in time. The Kesserit need to know that not all was destroyed; you *owe* it to them to survive."

A sudden noise in the distance alerted her to the fact that her voice had risen; with a whispered curse she moved a few steps beyond the limits of his portal, then returned. "Someone's coming. I have to go. This is the only way, Tathas. Please believe me. The tribe will need your leadership again, this is the only way. You have to do this."

He was about to answer when he heard the first footsteps. She swore beneath her breath and offered him one last glance with those alien eyes, then slipped away into the featureless white expanse beyond his portal. No way to talk to her any more. No way to ask, or argue, or . . .

. . . hope?

He stepped back from the forcefield, choking back on his pride, knowing that if the Braxaná saw any spark of it that would only anger them more. There was a reason to live now, at least long enough to appear before the Council. One tiny hope.

Was she right? Would it work?

There were four guards in all. It was strangely flattering, that they should need so many for this pale and wasted prisoner.

He could worry later about where all this would lead. Right now all that mattered was his freedom.

Your tribe will need your leadership again. . . .

Two guards flanked the portal. One shut the force field down. One stood directly before him, assessing him with ice-cold eyes, much as one might assess a bottled insect.

"It's time," he said gruffly.

They let him walk unbound, at least. That was something.

The Citadel chamber was large and sterile, and they put him right in the middle of it. Like a bug pinned down for inspection. About him sat nearly a hundred men, all of them Braxaná. The ones nearest him wore the medallion of the Kaim'eri, while those seated behind them wore similar seals as clasps on shortcloaks, tunics, scabbards. It had meant real power once, that sign, when the Kaim'eri had ruled the Holding in a political free-for-all. Now things were different. Now the true power lay elsewhere.

Tathas pushed the greasy hair out of his face and faced them, trying to imbue his posture with a confidence he did not truly feel. It was hard to stand before these men and not be unnerved, for their mere physicality set them apart from everything that was normal and human. Stark white faces layered in paint looked more like masks than like flesh. Short black curled hair was sculpted so precisely that one could imagine each perfect curl lacquered into position, or even a wig made of some entirely nonliving substance. They all wore the traditional sword, of course, even here, and the ubiquitous black and gray uniform in its microscopically distinct variations. On the whole they looked more like mannequins than men, and the fact that there was so little variation between them in facial structure or even expression added an especially eerie note to the illusion. That was the result of inbreeding, of course. Tathas had heard of it, but he had never before seen so many of the Pale Ones in one place together that he could observe the phenomenon for himself.

No wonder they needed fresh genetic material. Their gene pool was clearly in its last gasps. No wonder they'd had to come up with some warped and complicated ritual to get that material . . . since the Master Race of Braxi could hardly be expected to let the blood of commoners mix with its own, could it?

Gods, how he hated them. More in that instant than ever before. And it must have showed in his face, because one of them narrowed his gaze somewhat, and it seemed to Tathas that a spark of answering hatred gleamed in those black, inscrutable eyes. Strangely refreshing.

Then one man who wore the medallion of the Kaim'erate stood, and he used the voice mode of disdain as he said:

"Tathas, son of Zheret. You stand before this Council accused of high treason against the Holding. Of encouraging tribal factionalism. Of participating in proscribed tribal rituals. Of illegal possession of arms and use of those arms in proscribed activities. Of encouraging dissent with intent to destabilize the united Braxin government." For a moment he paused, and the dark eyes seemed to drill through Tathas. Cold eyes, cold hate; he could taste it. "Do you affirm the charges or deny them?"

For a brief, mad instant he actually considered answering the question. After all, the worst of the charges—and the one most likely to lead to a death sentence—could hardly be proven. For a moment he even entertained the fantasy that evidence might matter here, and that justice might be brought to bear in this case.

Ah, that must have been his battered brain crying out for help, to think something like that. The Braxaná might be accused of many things, but "justice" had never been one of them.

With pride he drew himself up, muscles aching at the unaccustomed strain. He could see himself reflected in a hundred eyes, sweat-stained and battered, and knew with sudden certainty that they believed him beaten. Three zhents of neural torture would break anyone, wouldn't it?

Anyone but a Kesserit. Anyone but the Viak'im.

The knowledge put strength in his voice, and for the first time since his awakening the words came out clearly and easily. "I invoke the Wilding."

For a moment there was only silence. His heart pounded inside his chest as he waited, deafeningly loud in the emptiness. Though their expressions were carefully controlled, it seemed to him that shadows of emotions flickered across them. Surprise, of course. Dismay? Anger? It seemed to him one or two were mildly amused, but it was hard to be sure of that. And Braxaná amusement was not necessarily a good thing.

At last one of the Kaim'eri said, "That law is for the Braxaná."

"The law does not specify a tribe," he answered.

Whispers flitted about the room. He kept his gaze focused on the first man, but from the corners of his eyes he could see the Pale Ones stirring. His words had not pleased them.

They can kill you if they want to. Any one of them, on a whim. That's one power they didn't give up when the Pri'tiera took over.

"A minor omission," one man said. Tathas wasn't sure of the voice mode he used—that damned Braxaná dialect was so complicated it was hard to make out sometimes—but he was pretty sure it was part of the condemnation complex. Not a good sign.

"A *legal* omission," he challenged.

He saw heads leaning toward one another, heard echoes of whispered conferences. There was a strange intensity in the room now, and not all of it was focused on him. Braxaná politics. A council chamber full of men with agendas of their own, public ones and secret ones, each one assessing how this moment played into his own private plans. He felt a sudden fury at these men who could play with human lives in such a trivial way, not even pretending that *justice* or *legality* had any meaning to them. What on Braxi were they doing running the Holding? It was time another tribe took over.

Don't think that. Not here, not now. Too dangerous.

At last one man, an older man with streaks of silver in his beard, offered, "It is an interesting concept."

"It is an offense to our Race," another retorted.

"Did our ancestors use outsiders to find mates for them?"

"They would have if it got them results," one said curtly.

"It's a dangerous precedent," another interjected.

"Yes, shall we have all the common folk crying 'wilding' to shrug off their debts?"

"Enough of our own blood are doing it now," one muttered.

It seemed to him there was amusement at that. Grim and cold amusement, that barely cracked the porcelain masks. Whatever passed for emotion in this crowd, it was a different beast than he was used to.

The man who stood before him seemed about to speak again, and from his expression Tathas guessed it was not going to be good—but a sudden hush fell over the chamber, and one by one all of the Kaim'eri and their guests turned toward the chamber's single entrance. Tathas followed suit. Even before he saw the man who stood there, even before the details of his black and gray formal costume sank in, he could *feel* his presence in the room. A tingling along his neck. A cold, clammy crawling sensation up his spine. As if something had entered besides a man, and that *something* had its hands all over him.

"Pri'tiera." The Kaim'era before Tathas bowed. The others stood, that they might do the same.

He was young, if such a creature might ever be said to be truly young. His face was a perfect mask of powder and paint, and when he was still he looked more like a statue than a human being. Yet there was about him such an aura of power, such an absolute presence, that as he came toward Tathas, his long black and gray robes sweeping the floor behind him, the proud Viak'im had to fight the sudden desire to go down on one knee and offer him obeisance.

He had heard legends of such power, of course. The Pri'tiera's line was rumored to be many things, most of them related to ancient tribal demons or vindictive spirits. He had always imagined that a strong enough man might cling to pride even in such a presence. But it was impossible. The essence of the man enveloped him, invaded him, and seeped into his very brain. He had to lock his legs in place to keep them from folding. It was as if a vast hand was pressing him downward, exerting pressure upon each and every cell in his body, and he bit his lip so hard in his struggle to resist its power that blood began to trickle down his chin.

"Strong," the Pri'tiera murmured. He was young, so young! Barely past the start of manhood, and yet he wore the Pri'tiera's robes. How could such a youth gain power among the Braxaná, much less wield it effectively? The concept of a hereditary title was so alien to Tathas that even this close to the man, enveloped by his presence, he could not quite fathom it.

Then the Pri'tiera touched him—one gloved finger to the side of his face—and his legs folded utterly. It was as if his body answered to the youth rather than its owner. The sensation was terrifying, and it did not abate until he knelt, head bowed, before him. His hands balled into fists by his side, Tathas trembled with rage . . . and with fear as well.

For an eternity, it seemed, the Pri'tiera gazed down at him in silence. Tathas concentrated on the taste of blood in his mouth, refusing to acknowledge the submission that had been forced upon him. Again a cold and alien presence seemed to prick at the edges of his brain. He felt like vomiting.

"Let him go."

He looked up. The dark eyes met his own. The strange grip on his soul eased up a bit, but he stayed on his knees, knowing now that if he tried to rise up, if he defied this man in any way, it would only grab hold more tightly the next time.

"The Wilding," the Pri'tiera said. "Let him go." He looked up at the Kaim'eri, scanning the chamber slowly, meeting the eyes of each in turn. "It is my will."

With a sweeping movement he turned his back on Tathas, and the strange force which had driven the Viak'im to his knees was gone. The suddenness of it made his head reel, and as he tried to rise up to his feet again it took all his strength not to stumble.

The Kaim'eri waited until their leader was gone, then turned their attention back to Tathas. His vision was blurred and it was hard to see their faces, but he was willing to guess they weren't pleased.

Braxaná never do anything without a reason. Without a hundred reasons, sometimes conflicting. What does he want of me?

"Get him clothes." It was the first Kaim'era who had spoken to him, who seemed to hold some sort of rank among them. "And a ticket out of here. The nearest border. And see that he gets a copy of the Law as well, so that he knows exactly what he has taken upon himself. And how foolish it is for any commoner to choose such a path."

Slowly the Kaim'era left his seat and descended to the floor of the chamber. Slowly he walked to where Tathas stood, but though his presence might have driven a lesser man to his knees, it lacked the preternatural power of the Pri'tiera's own, and Tathas stood his ground.

"Your life here is ended," the older man pronounced. "Come back when you think you have the price to reclaim it." His tone made it clear he did not think that would ever happen.

Then guards came forward once again and took him roughly by the arms. He heard someone declaring the session closed as they dragged him forth from the chamber. He heard voices murmur comments upon the proceedings, too quietly for him to make out words. He heard the heavy door shut behind him, marking the end of one whole portion of his life. And the beginning of Ar knew what.

I'll be back! he swore.

How strange, the concept of a soul divided. How intriguing, the question of whether the spirit within is thereby divided . . . or multiplied.

Our ancestors feared the matter so greatly that, rather than seeking answers, they destroyed the source of the question.

These days we are more civilized.

—Zatar the Magnificent

THREE

Something was wrong.

Zara could feel it on her skin, a cold chill that crept up her spine vertebra by vertebra. Not fear, exactly. Fear was a response, which implied there was something to respond to. Her feeling wasn't that concrete. More like . . . a nameless dread, doubly unnerving because its stimulus was unknown.

She drew in a deep breath and took stock of her surroundings. Certainly the setting was one which would give any Mediator the shakes. Her Kaldori patron was sitting still as a rock, and she knew enough of his species to recognize that as an ominous sign. The two Han had finally folded their combat ruffs, which was a step in the right direction, but their eyes were still glazed with dark crimson, by which sign she knew that one wrong word could still set them off. And the T'san . . . well, she knew how to interpret the extra stress in its sibilant comments, even if the others could not.

But that was why they had hired her, right? If everybody was friendly, what use would there be for Mediators?

She looked about the room—serviceable white, streamlined fittings, the kind of room that might be transported to any planet without looking out of place—and wondered where the feeling was coming from. Right now it was so strong it was almost tangible, a cold knot in her gut that refused to go away. She hesitated to delay such an important meeting for a feeling she couldn't define . . . but damn it, something was *wrong*.

"S'kar Zara?"

They had noticed her distraction. That wasn't good. With effort she shook herself out of her reverie (shook herself mentally, that is, for no Mediator would make extraneous movements in such a setting) and said, "I was musing upon the benefits that might accrue to all parties if this agreement were to cover not only the current disputed shipments, but future activity as well."

The lead Han puffed himself up in indignation. "There will be no future activity!" But his ruff was still folded, Zara noted, and when he blinked it seemed to her the color in his eyes became a shade paler. Good. Good. Greed was a powerful tool in dealing with the Han, and she was glad to see it had not failed her now. Even the Kaldori seemed intrigued, and the T'san raised itself up on its forelegs a good foot off the ground, a rare sign of open-mindedness. Good. If they were *all* willing to see this current dispute as but one stumbling block on the road to a greater business alliance, this matter might be settled amicably after all.

She went to the far end of the room, behind the desk there, to retrieve the chip which contained all her financial projections—

And that was when the bomb went off.

It must have been one of the Han. That thought was the first and only thing to make it through her brain before it hit her. Then a wave of fire roared toward her, slamming the desk into her broadside, and both of them into the wall. Her head hit the wall with force enough to crack the acoustic tiles, and she could feel the sticky smear of blood she left as she slid down along it . . . but the pain seemed odd, as if it were happening to someone other than herself. Even the flames at the far end of the room were weirdly distant, and when the room responded with a rain of fire repellent, its stinging drops fell on her burned skin like the distant patter of rain in some far-off country. Not her body. Not her pain.

Medics rushed in as the darkness claimed her. Darkness, and a single, terrifying thought:

I knew that was going to happen. I KNEW.
How?????

Medcenter. Soothing drugs. Consciousness reclaimed slowly, from beneath layers of painkillers, peeled back like blankets from her new-grown skin.

Nothing permanent, voices assured her. *A few days for the bones to be healed. Damaged organs being regrown now. Burns were superficial. Nothing broken that can't be fixed. Have patience.*

Other voices: *You were lucky.*

"What happened?" she asked them. They didn't answer. There wasn't enough of her brain functioning, through the veil of drugs, for an answer to have any meaning.

Yes, her brain. That had been hurt too. They didn't tell her that but she heard it whispered through the haze of drugs and treatments, like some bad dream that wouldn't go away. They'd be forcing regeneration now, testing synapses, assessing damage. There was no point in telling her the results until she was capable of comprehending them, of course. But not to worry. Azean medicine was the best, and the Chandrans were standard enough in their biology to benefit from the best of it.

Sleep then. Sleep. Not eternal darkness, but something shorter, better.

How did I know?

She felt odd, walking into the conference chamber on her own two feet. She'd only been flat on her back for days, but she wasn't used to being sick at all.

To her surprise there was only one person in the room. The Director nodded to her as she entered, and indicated a seat at the far end of the table from himself. It was an odd seating arrangement, with no one else there, and she hesitated before she sat down. Like being at a banquet for twenty, at which only two guests had shown up.

He wants a table between you. The knowledge came as if some voice had whispered inside her. *Something about you makes him nervous. Something about this whole affair that he knows is not quite right.*

The clarity of the observation unnerved her. It wasn't that she was unaccustomed to analyzing people—she was trained to read body language in two dozen species, at master level in three of them—but rather, it was the certainty with which she assigned meaning to the gesture. As if she wasn't just testing a hypothesis, but knew without any doubt exactly what the man was feeling.

Strange. Very strange.

She wondered if something had happened to her while she was in the medcenter that could explain his response to her. Perhaps she had said something strange while under the effects of regeneration drugs? Certainly he was looking at her as if she was not quite right, and when he cleared his throat to begin talking—an uncharacteristic gesture for him—she had the distinct impression he was sorting through words in his head, wondering exactly how to approach her.

Mechanically she went through the motions of observing his posture, muscle tension, skin texture, blink pattern, and the thousand and one tiny details of human kinesthetics that allowed one to read a man. Inside, on a much more primal level, a gut fear began to blossom.

Something is wrong here, a tiny voice whispered. *Very, very wrong.*

"Mediator Zara." The Director's voice was steady, wholly confident, and as he folded his hands before him it echoed a lifetime of similar gestures. "You are well, I hope?"

She nodded. "So I am told."

"Clean bill of health, regeneration successful, all tests confirm complete recovery." He sounded like he was reading it right from the medical form. "I'm relieved, quite frankly. When I heard the original diagnosis . . . well, let's just say brain damage isn't a pretty thing, even with all our science. You're a lucky woman, Zara."

She managed a smile. He was skilled enough, no doubt, to see the strain behind it. That couldn't be helped. "I guess." What was so very wrong in this scene? She could sense it, but couldn't identify it. "I'll be glad to get back on the job."

He paused for a moment, an eloquent silence. Her Mediator senses went on high alert.

"Yes. Well. That is what I wanted to speak to you about."

She found she was holding her breath.

He coughed softly. "It's been suggested that after such a trauma one should . . . take time for oneself. Make sure recovery is complete, in every sense of the word." He paused again and shifted his position slightly, leaning forward on the desk. His steepled fingers were a statement of dominance, of authority, of greater comprehension of the situation than a mere Mediator could manage. "I think you should take some time off, Zara. A vacation. You're certainly due one, after this last assignment." When she didn't answer immediately he added, "I really think that would be best for you."

False. False. False. He was good enough to mask all the overt signs of deception, but she was aware of it anyway. It was as if someone had placed the knowledge directly in her brain and then set off hot flares to mark its presence. There was a *reason* he wanted her to leave work for a while, and it had nothing to do with the explosion. Or any real concern for her health.

She felt dizzy, suddenly. Too many thoughts were crowding her head and she didn't know where half of them came from. Her first instinct was to put her hand up to her forehead and rub it lightly—as if such thoughts could be massaged away—but the Mediator in her stopped the all-too-human gesture before it began. *You'll only confirm his diagnosis,* her professional instinct warned her. *Don't do anything that looks weak. Not now.*

By the Golden, this was crazy. The man was her Director, her ally, her colleague. Why was she feeling as if she were facing off against a member of a hostile species? There was nothing wrong here. Nothing. No reason to be feeling as if disaster was right around the corner. No reason why there should be a cold knot in her gut, a feeling that at any moment now things were going to go all wrong.

I felt this way just before the explosion, she realized. A chilling thought.

The room seemed to dip and reel. She put a hand on the table to steady herself.

"Mediator?"

No. It wasn't the same. These feelings were new to her, but even so she could tell that much. This was something more subtle than the last time. The threat was not a bomb this time, rather something . . . more elusive. Less focused.

"Maybe you're right," she whispered. Time, she needed time. Things weren't right inside her; she needed time to figure it all out. If she stayed here they'd be watching her, and then they'd know what was happening to her, and then—

What?

What?

She tried to hang on to the feeling, to analyze it . . . but it slithered out of her mental grasp, until even the nebulous sense of warning was gone. Suddenly she felt exhausted. Overwhelmed. Something was wrong in her brain, and that was clearly what he was responding to. And although it was all too tempting to blame the whole thing on her injury, she knew better. It had started before. *They* didn't know that, but she did.

She should have confided in him, right then and there. She should have trusted him. That was how their profession worked, that was the kind of man he was, that was what their relationship had been in the past. But she couldn't do it. The words got stuck in her throat, and instead of letting him know that something was so wrong inside her that it was scaring her half to death, she only reiterated, "Maybe you're right."

He knew it was an evasion. Of course. He was a Mediator too, trained to read every subtle signal of human interaction. You couldn't hide emotions from people like that.

"Very well then." He shuffled through some hard copies before him as if their exchange didn't even matter all that much . . . but she could see the truth in the set of his shoulders, and she could hear the edge of it in his voice. "I'll have a leave of absence ordered, return date unspecified . . . you take your time, Zara. And come see a staff medic if anything feels wrong." A faint emphasis on the last words revealed just how much he expected some problem to arise. Suddenly she wasn't sure that the medcenter was where she should go, if that happened. *By the Golden, am I afraid of my own people now?*

Numbly she signed the proper tablets for her leave of absence. With pay, the Director assured her, and she managed to smile back at him and look appropriately grateful. *It had damn well better be with pay,* she thought, *after this many Standard Years of exemplary service.* She was among the best in her profession and they both knew it. They wouldn't discard her lightly. They wouldn't make trouble for her unless the cause was something very, very serious.

That's what she told herself, at least. Why was it so hard to make herself believe it?

Dreams. Strange dreams.

Gazing into eyes, golden eyes, so familiar . . . reach out and touch the stranger, for she is yourself. Call her by your own name, see if she answers. . . .

. . . weeping in the depths of night, a mother's voice, a mother's pain: I should have been there! I should have stopped it!

. . . whispers of a secret tongue, gurgles and hiccups and secret sniffles, that only one other can understand . . .

. . . emptiness where a face should be! Where have the golden eyes gone? Where is the voice? Where is the presence so warm and comforting, that has never been absent before?

. . . be quiet, be quiet, or the child will guess . . . pretend there is nothing wrong. . . .

The Records Office of the Institute for the Advancement of Inter-Species Mediation was in the third ring of the administration satellite.

She'd been there once before, to set her thumbprint to some documents, but that had been so long ago she barely remembered the way.
Certainly the office where dated records were catalogued and filed
away wasn't located where a Mediator was likely to trip over it.

The outer office was a small room, as befit one designed for simple
data requests. Of course. Any file in current use was likely to be du-
plicated elsewhere; the people who came here were mostly looking for
past documentation, a simple enough administrative request. You
asked for something, they gave you a copy, end of story.

The secretary was clearly of the Scattered Races, but not a variety of
the human somatotype that Zara could identify. Had some new world
been brought into the Empire recently? Or was she just not as up-to-
date in her knowledge of species and races as one would hope? It
seemed there was a new race being absorbed into the Empire every
time she turned around, these days.

"Can I help you?"

She passed over her I.D. chip and waited while her identity was
scanned and verified. "I'd like a copy of my medfile, please."

The secretary raised an eyebrow. She had four, each accompanying
an eye outlined in a different shade of blue.

"Going on a trip," Zara explained. "I'd like to take it with me."

"I'll see what I can do. Have a seat for a minute?"

She forced herself to do so out of politeness, though the woman's
face was interesting enough that she would have liked to study it
more. The eyes moved independently, pairing off to gaze at changing
focal points as she worked. The blink rate varied as well, Zara noted,
reflecting the same combinations. What a marvelous species that
would be to read! The eyes were always the most eloquent communicator in visual-dominant species. She'd have to find out where this
woman was from and see if there were any research documents on orbital display among her people. Perhaps that would even be a good
way to spend this leisure time she seemed to be saddled with . . . resting on some beach on Ikn with a good research paper and a strong
drink. . . .

She waited. Longer than she should have, it seemed. Azean law
guaranteed any citizen full access to his/her/its medical records, so her
request was a pretty simple one. Download a single file onto the chip
and give it to her. A matter of minutes, at the most.

It seemed to her she waited a very, very long time.

It seemed to her—again—that something was very wrong.

Finally the secretary called her over. Her tone was frankly apologetic, even embarrassed. "I'm sorry, Mediator, there seems to be a datalock on this file. Most unusual. I can process a request for override, if you like."

Now, who in the Eight Hells of Zaiti would put a lock on her medical file? Such an act would be in defiance of the Empire's most basic Covenant. Zara's confusion must have shown on her face, and the secretary moved to fill the awkward silence.

"I'm really sorry. This *is* most unusual. I'm sure that if you apply for an override it will all be taken care of. I can walk the forms through myself, make sure they get proper consideration. . . ."

Zara tried to think it through. There was a lock on her medfiles. That meant that something was in there the Institute didn't want others to see. Of course they had not meant to lock *her* out. That would make no sense. You didn't keep a citizen of the Empire from seeing her own files. That was . . . that was . . . well . . . *crazy.*

"Forward the form to my mail, all right?" By the Golden, her head hurt. She needed time to think. "Just run off a copy of my genfile for now, would you please? At least I can take that with me."

The secretary nodded, and her eyebrows relaxed into what was clearly their natural position. Relief, no doubt. Zara watched as the woman fed her request to the Institute's computer, using a language that was half alien tongue and half Standard abbreviations. Some private code, no doubt.

An answer appeared on the monitor before her. The eyebrows dipped again, and all four eyes narrowed.

"What?" She gave the request again, and again was not pleased at the answer. "That's not right." She seemed to be talking more to herself than to Zara.

"What is it?"

The secretary shook her head. "It says your genome records are under lock, too. But that makes no sense. Genfiles aren't Institute property, they'd have no right to—"

She stopped speaking, but not before Zara had caught the gist of what she'd meant to say. *Someone else did this,* her silence proclaimed. *Someone with the power to override all the Institute's legal safeguards, and ignore an Imperial Covenant besides.*

"Mediator Zara, I am so very sorry." The strain in the woman's voice was obvious now. "I'll look into this, I promise you. In the meantime, is there anything else I can do for you?"

"No." There was no point, was there? If all that was locked away, what was left that was worth asking about?

Zara shook her head numbly and managed to go through the proper motions of a polite leave-taking. It was reflex, no more. Her mind was elsewhere, trying to make sense of all this. But she couldn't. Just couldn't. If she strained to the utmost she could perhaps come up with some reason why the records from her accident might be under security seal—maybe she'd revealed something in her hours of pain that someone didn't think should be made public—but that wouldn't explain the lock on her genome file. Or why they were keeping *her* from accessing those records.

It took no inner voice this time to tell her that something was wrong. And no cold knot in her gut to tell her that it was wrong enough, and strange enough, that she needed to find out what it was.

. . . looking in a mirror, but it's not a mirror. Gazing at herself, but not herself. Golden eyes, short-cropped hair, infectious smile. Tall and lean, familiar frame, hers but not hers. Reach out, touch the mirror, fingertip touches fingertip, no barrier between . . .

Joy fills her. Joy, to be so close.

Pain fills her. Pain, that the moment is so fleeting

Anger fills her. Anger, at those who would rob her of this joy.

The figure becomes a child, then vanishes in a flash of light. From a distance she hears her name cried out, and the voice that speaks it is her own.

Zara!

The Season of Rains on Chandra was renowned throughout the Empire, a time when the waterlogged trees gave up their first set of leaves and hardy rainblossoms bloomed in their absence. Mountains and plains alike were banded with color and the flooded channels swirled with curling eddies, made visible by fallen petals floating upon the water's surface. A thick fragrance filled the air, shifting with every breeze, and insects with iridescent wings arose from the flooded earth to partake of the season's special nectar. The result was a panorama that *Baro's Tourism Guide* called "one of the ten top seasonal displays in the Empire," and millions of tourists flocked to Chandra's shores and mountains each year to see it happen.

All it meant to Zara right now was that public transportation was operating at a crawl and it would cost an arm and a leg to get anywhere. The public platforms were so crowded that finally, with a sigh, she called for a private taxi, and braced herself to pay whatever ungodly sum it charged her. Even so she had nearly an hour's wait before one could come to pick her up.

Her mother lived in the Outlands, thank the Golden, which was far enough from the tourist lanes that there was some hope of peace. She tried to relax as the taxi flew up high into the express altitudes, dodging tourist traffic all the way. Normally she tried to stay ten star systems away from Chandra in its peak tourist season, but this time . . . this time, well, there were things that had to be done.

In truth she might have approached her father instead, but that probably wouldn't be very productive. He was a strange man, oddly distant, and though he claimed to love her, the words were always said as if some vital qualifier was missing. *I love you because . . .*, or maybe, *I would love you if. . . .* She doubted he would have the answers she sought, and if he did, she wasn't all that sure he would share them with her.

Her mother's house was set in the side of a mountain overlooking a small lake, a peaceful setting mercifully removed from the hubbub of the tourist sector. The taxi brought her up to the parking platform and waited patiently while she disembarked, then flashed her an exorbitant fee which was easily three times what the trip was worth. Oh well. With a sigh she took out her bank chip and fed it into the meter, wincing at the cost. That was her father's nature, counting every credit. Her mother would have laughed at her discomfort, and reminded her that a Mediator's salary was good enough to cover such luxuries ten times over.

She wondered sometimes how her parents had ever gotten together. She often wondered why, with all the effort they had gone to make the odd pairing work, they had finally broken up. The only thing she knew for sure was that the breakup had been postponed at least a decade so that she could grow to adulthood before it happened, a choice she either blessed or cursed according to her mood. Nothing was ever said to her about the reasons for it, and any questions she had were deftly evaded. The whole house seemed a place of shadows and secrets, sometimes. So maybe it was no surprise that she should come back here when the whole world around her seemed to take on that same quality.

Her mother greeted her with the requisite maternal enthusiasm, chattering on about how long it had been since she had last seen her, while she took her coat and offered her food and did all the things that mothers do to make their grown children comfortable in a home that was no longer theirs. Zara endured it patiently, using her professional skills to mask her unease while the proper rituals of greeting were completed. Only then did she sit down with her mother and try to broach the subject which had brought her halfway across the Empire for counsel.

"They said that my medical records were sealed up tight," she concluded at the end of the story. "Not only the current documents, but even my genome survey." When the older woman said nothing, she pressed, "That seems wrong. Doesn't it?"

Her mother's expression was strange. For all of her skill at reading people, Zara was at a loss to interpret it. Finally she answered, in an oddly strained tone, "I have your genfile; I can make you a copy."

She exhaled a slow breath, exasperated. "Look, the problem isn't that I need the survey, or any other file. It's just . . . all this *isn't right*. A lock on my private medfiles? That even *I* can't override? What kind of sense does that make?"

She expected her mother to look equally concerned. Or confused. Or . . . something. But the emotions reflected in her eyes, albeit intense, weren't anything that made sense to her.

Pain.

Fear.

Sorrow.

At last her mother whispered, "Gods." Just that. And turned away. The set of her shoulders was tense—no, beyond tense. Zara could see the muscles bunching beneath the thin blouse, so hard she knew it hurt. She wanted to ask what was going on, but she sensed the best thing she could do right now was wait her out. Let her pick her own words and her own time. That's how her mother worked.

The fact that it frustrated the Eight Hells out of her didn't play into things.

"By the Golden," the older woman said at last, "I'd hoped this day would never come. . . ."

"Mom. Tell me." When that wasn't enough she added, *"Please."*

Her mother sighed heavily. She seemed almost to be gazing at something in the distance, not in this place and maybe not even in this time. Zara could see her start to tremble, first her hands, and then her

entire body. Her voice shook as well when she spoke, as if she was fighting an urge to cry. "I'm so sorry, Zara, so sorry . . . we couldn't tell
you . . . we tried, a hundred times we tried, but we just couldn't. . . ."

"Tell me *what*, Mom?" Despite her professional composure, she was
beginning to feel fear herself. It wasn't anything her mother had said,
it was rather . . . rather. . . .

. . . What she was *feeling*. As if that was somehow being transferred
to Zara's brain, directly. She could taste the woman's pain on her lips,
it seemed. The fear.

What in hells was going on?

Her mother turned back to her. The look of utter misery in her eyes
said she would rather be anywhere but here. "Your . . . medical information . . . has always been secured."

"From ME?"

"No. That part's new. But . . . oh Gods, where do I start?"

"How about at the beginning?" she dared, softly. And then on an
impulse added, "Isn't it time?"

Her mother shuddered.

A soft rain began to patter against the house.

Her mother got up and walked to the window. For a few minutes
she just gazed out at the mist-shrouded landscape, mountains in the
distance swathed in colors, muted by the shimmering fog. Zara realized she was trying to order her thoughts, trying to figure out how to
tell her something she'd hoped never to have to reveal, and so she let
her take her time. It was one of the hardest things Zara'd ever had to
do. Fear and frustration were twin knots in her gut, and it took all her
effort to deny their existence, to look peaceful and patient when in fact
she was a storm inside.

Finally her mother said, "You know you had a sister once."

"Yes. You told me. She died when I was very young, right? Less
than a year old, I think you said."

"Less than a year." She whispered it. Her pain was a palpable thing,
as visible to Zara as the mists outside the window. The taste of it was
like a bitter mint. "She's . . . not dead, Zara. At least . . . she didn't die
back then. We don't think."

"You don't think." Zara breathed in sharply. "You don't *know*?"

Her mother turned back to her. A flush of color had risen to her
cheeks, the hue of shame. "No," she whispered. "We don't know. We
searched for years and years . . . we had help from . . . people in high
places. Very high places. There wasn't a sign."

"What happened?" Zara asked. "And why did you wait so long to tell me this?"

Her mother looked older, all of a sudden. More . . . fragile.

"We thought . . . your father and I . . . we wanted to protect you. That's all. So the people who had . . . who might hurt you . . . so they wouldn't. . . ." Again a heavy sigh. A tear began to trickle down from her eye, soon joined by a second. "Gods, I have dreaded this day. . . ."

Zara bit back on her own emotions. Hard. She knew her mother well enough to know that the minute she started yelling at her—the minute there was even a hint of the agitation she felt inside—the woman would shut down, immure herself in silence, and wait out the storm. And that wasn't going to get her any answers. So instead she forced herself to get up slowly, steadily, and went to her mother's side. Close, so close that she could touch her. It took all her strength to talk to her calmly, when what she wanted was to take her by the shoulders and shake her, hard, until all the secrets spilled out. Instead she just said, "You need to tell me everything, Mom. You need to tell me *now*."

With a pained sigh her mother turned away again, and walked into the adjoining office. A few minutes later she returned with a sheaf of hard copies, which she gave to Zara in silence.

Genome survey.

Birth records.

Hers.

She glanced at the cover pages, trying not to voice the torrent of frustration inside her. She'd seen her genfile before, of course. She didn't understand ninety percent of it, but she knew where the genes were that had to be watched, and knew that her medics checked up on them regularly. Not everything could be neatly corrected inwomb. The chemical signals of the human body were such an interactive tapestry that sometimes it wasn't possible to alter a sequence without disturbing other vital functions. Was that what was going on? She had some genetic weakness that couldn't be corrected? If so, she should have been in preparatory counseling for that years ago, and been working with a team of doctors to see that the rogue codons never expressed themselves.

And then she saw it. And she understood.

Oh my gods. . . .

It wasn't in the genome printout. It was a note in the birth records, front and center. Right under her name.

She looked up at her mother. For a moment she couldn't manage the word. At last she mouthed it, but the sound remained a knot in her throat. "Twins? We were . . . twins?"

. . . looking in a mirror, but it's not a mirror. Gazing at herself, but not herself. Familiar frame, hers but not hers. Reach out, touch the mirror, fingertip touches fingertip, no barrier between. . . .

She sat down heavily. She was lucky there was a chair behind her; she couldn't have reached far to get one if there hadn't been.

"Split egg," her mother said quietly. "Identicals."

She shook her head, as if somehow that would clear the memories from it. It only made them stronger. "Gods . . . the dreams . . . that all makes sense now. . . ."

"You've dreamed about this?"

She drew in a deep breath, remembering. "Sometimes. I think. More when I was a child than now, hard to remember. But since the accident it's happened every night."

"Your heart remembers," her mother said softly. "On some level it must."

She lowered her face into her hands, trying to absorb it all. The sister who had been missing all these years had been a part of her, identical, rooted in the same act of creation. For a year she had lain beside her, hearts beating in sync, mental growth following the same ingrained paths. For a moment she wanted to look up at her mother and demand, *why didn't you tell me before?* But she knew instinctively what had happened. At first they had thought the concept too upsetting for a child. And then, years later, there had simply never been the right moment. It had faded into the mists of time, just as the mountains were now fading behind a veil of silver rain.

Except this wasn't just past history. If what her mother was saying was true, the other girl was still alive. Somewhere. Her *twin.*

She looked up at the older woman. With all her professional self-control she still couldn't keep the edge from her voice as she said to her, "Tell me. Everything. *Now.*"

The little color remaining in her mother's face drained. "Zara . . . we did it to protect you. . . ."

"And now it isn't working. The government is involved in this, somehow. I need to know what's going on." With gut-wrenching effort she managed to make the next word sound more like a plea than a command: "Please . . ."

For a moment her mother was silent. Then, with a heavy sigh, she began to speak.

"They did the survey inwomb. We fixed a few minor things. They told us there was one genetic sequence that was of some concern, that they couldn't correct, and they'd send us a counselor to discuss it.

"He came right after you were born. A government man. Said that you had the Kevesi sequence. He explained to us what that meant."

She lowered her face into her hands for a moment. Not crying now, so much as trying to organize her thoughts. Sensing that, Zara waited patiently.

At last she looked up at her daughter again. "What do you know of Llornu?"

Her brow furrowed as she tried to remember. "Llornu? That was one of the Institute worlds, wasn't it? Set aside by the government for specialized research." It had been a long time since she'd had to review Imperial history; she struggled to remember. "That one was . . . psychic development, wasn't it?"

"Yes. That was it." Her mother sighed heavily. "Two hundred Standard years ago Llornu was the center for psychic research. It was a thing deemed important in that day, not like the rogue science it is now. There were thousands of functional psychics on that planet . . . some say millions . . .

"Then an assault of some kind destroyed the main labs. Killed so many, it's said, that it set off a chain reaction among the psychic community, feeding the agony of the dying into the brains of the survivors. They . . . well, you can imagine what happened. History says they disappeared then. In reality, that probably took a while. Borderline cases were tolerated for several decades, until . . . until it became clear just how unstable the gift was. Then the government started watching for it. Taking psychics away when they were discovered, putting them in places where they couldn't hurt anyone."

Zara tried to speak, but couldn't get the words out. Her thoughts were a maelstrom inside her. Finally she managed to force out, "Are you . . . are you telling me . . . I am one of those cases?"

Voices inside. Knowledge, where knowledge should not be. Warning, plucked from the minds of others. . . .

She stood up suddenly and walked to the window, wrapping her arms about herself tightly. Her eyes looked outward, but her vision was focused inside herself.

NO!

"You have the precursor sequence," her mother said quietly. Was that really fear in her voice, or was Zara somehow taking that directly from her mind? It was a terrifying thought. "Just that. One of several genetic markers to indicate you *might* develop the power.

"But you didn't! That's what matters. We watched you so carefully during puberty—the government watched—and the power didn't express. That's when it happens, if it does. You're safe."

Oh gods, gods, if only you knew.... What if some trauma could jar the brain into new activity? Would the latent patterns then flare to life, responding to some unknown cue that said *now, now is the time*?

That was why the government was watching her. They knew.

"What about my sister?" she whispered. Gods, was she going through the same thing right now? Were they both doomed by the same curse, suffering from a gift that would eventually destroy them? She remembered learning about the psychic syndrome in her school years, how the brain that was externally sensitive eventually turned on itself, and the sufferer went mad. Was that going to happen to her? To both of them?

"Where is she, Mom? What do you know?"

Her mother shut her eyes. There was no mystery now where the feeling of pain was coming from; it was projected from the older mind to the younger, a lifetime's grief rushing over Zara like an ocean wave. "She was kidnapped," she said quietly. "When you were both a year old. They think the intruder wanted you both, just didn't have time to manage it. You were with a nurturer at the time . . . we weren't even there . . ."

The guilt came then, a tidal wave of maternal self-hatred, crashing from her mother's brain into her own. Years and years and years of her blaming herself, of her husband blaming himself, of so much guilt and misdirected anger that in the end it couldn't be shared any more. *I should have been there!* an inner voice screamed. Zara could hear the words as clearly as if they had been spoken aloud. *I could have stopped it!*

"They think *they* took her," her mother said. "The psychics. They're out there somewhere, the few survivors, living beyond the borders of the Empire. They told us about that when you were born. How it was thought by the Empire that their gene pool must be very small, which is why they . . . stole children. How they must have had spies in the Empire, and access to genome surveys, because they seemed to know which children showed promise of the gift. How they . . . how they . . . claimed them."

Zara's voice shook as she spoke. "You're saying . . . some rogue psychic kidnapped my sister?"

Her mother nodded miserably. "That's what Azea thinks. They tried for years to find her, to get her back. There was no trail, none at all. This goes on . . . this goes on all the time. Most people don't know about it. It's kept very quiet. You and your sister were under lock and key since birth because of it . . . the government warned us . . . but in the end that wasn't enough. . . . Gods." She lowered her face to her hands again, and this time she wept. "I'm sorry, Zara. We should have told you. There was never a right time. I'm so sorry. . . ."

She had no words. The room seemed to be spinning around her, thoughts in her brain doing likewise. She was remembering Llornu now, and what she'd learned in school about the psychic community. Programs of hidden mind control and dangerous breeding practices which had gone on for centuries. Fanaticism to the point of madness. And a gift that eventually turned on itself, consuming the brain that housed it. It was just as well the psychics had fled the Empire when they did, because once all that was made public no one really wanted them around.

I'm one of them. The thought was pure terror; it took all her professional skill to keep the fear from showing in her face. *So is my . . . my sister.*

"She's out there." The words tasted strange on her lips. "My . . . twin."

Her mother nodded.

"Somewhere."

"We did everything we could, Zara."

"And if she . . . she and I . . . we've got the same potential . . ."

"But it didn't express," her mother insisted. "The time for that is past. You're safe."

You're wrong, Mom.

The Empire was watching her. It knew the signs. It had learned down through the years just how unstable psychics were, and it was taking suitable precautions. That was why she'd had to take a sensitivity test before signing on as a Mediator, to prove that her skills were rooted in kinesthetic observation rather than some weird rogue power. That's why they didn't want her working now, not until they were sure that things were all right.

And they weren't "all right." That was the simple truth. In fact, things were as far from "all right" as they could possibly be.

My sister. . . .

She knew what she would do then. Knew it in her heart before the thought ever took root in her brain. Knew that it was dangerous, but hells, at least it would get her out of the Empire. That was where she needed to be right now, somewhere far away from Azea's ceaseless surveillance, in some remote corner of the universe where she could figure out what was happening to her without anyone calling in government agents to witness it.

My twin is out there. Somewhere.

Golden eyes. Tall, lean frame. And a latent genetic sequence that might or might not have been triggered by now, launching a cascade of terrible powers—and the beginning of the degradation of her brain, that would ultimately end in insanity. A weakness Zara shared. How much time did she have left?

I'll find you, she promised her silently. *Somehow. . . .*

All men have their limits. Perhaps the truest measure of a man is how far he will go to test them.

—Zatar the Magnificent

FOUR

RIVERS OF RED, meeting a crystal ocean. How bright, how beautiful! Eddies curling about like the most fragile of feathers, bleeding crimson mist into the current. Slowly. Sensually. I savor the motion, each last precious ripple of crimson, and feel the heat of it passing into cold, brightness into dark, pain into peace. Not long now, I tell myself. Not long.

My story? It is not lengthy . . . at least, not the parts that matter. Summarize it so: I am a Braxin woman, born in the Central System, near that heartbeat of the Master Race which they call Kurat. Too near. Had I known the price of that nearness, I would have moved. I would have sold every possession I owned, I would have begged on the street for sinias, I would even have bound myself in servitude to some bizarre nonhuman life-form that desired acts it would shame me to perform, rather than remain there, where *they* might find me.

Too late.

Too late.

They say that strength is a curse in women. They say that the ability to endure pain draws pain to them, so that each is matched by Ar to that which will test her limits. If so, then the goddess was flawed in measuring mine, for I have tasted a terror no mortal soul was meant to endure.

The ocean is no longer clear, but clouded; a fine mist of crimson hangs in its drift, fluttering like a silken pennant as the currents play across its surface. Red: that is the color of terror, is it not? And passion. And . . . life.

My mother named me L'seth. It means "Gift of the Snow." Brings to mind pristine fields of whiteness, doesn't it? Yet the snow in our district was anything but white, being muddied quickly underfoot by the passage of the poor and dirty, within hours of falling.

She told me once how I had been conceived in the snow, on a cold night when she had wanted nothing more than to get inside where she could be safe and warm and could forget about the weather. Alas, fate was not obliging. Sometimes there are men who truly savor the acquiescence forced upon us by law, choosing a time and place for their sport that degrades their subjects even more. One of them found my mother that night, and since she had no pressing business, and since there was no man to claim ownership of her, he exerted his rights under Braxaná law and took here there, right in the filthy slush. Oh, he paid for the damage that did to her clothing, of course. Spilled a handful of tarnished sinias into the muck for her to dig for with frozen fingers. You can abuse a woman by Braxin law, that's part of proud Braxaná tradition, but may the absent gods descend upon you in wrath if you damage property.

Anyway, that's the name she gave me, and I guess she could have done worse.

An auspicious beginning, yes? Surely no better or worse than the lot of other women of my class. My mother valued children and so she kept me, instead of casting me out into the adoption pool. Was that good or bad? I might have wound up in some truly horrific situation, purchased by one who wanted slaves rather than family, or by some man with a perverted sense of fatherhood—yes, for there were said to be men who were so twisted they coveted girl-children to raise, and had the money or influence to get an agency to indulge them, against all custom—but then again I might have done better, and gone to some upper-class woman whose smattering of Braxaná genes had doomed her to an otherwise sterile existence, who would have treated me like a precious gift, and truly made me her own.

Other fates, other paths. Who knew where this life would lead? Women have the essence of Ar in them, the goddess of chaos, and their lives are prone to twists and turns no one can predict. Men are weak by contrast; they could never survive such uncertainty. Small comfort, isn't it?

Red. So much red. Who would have thought there would be so much of it?

Skip over the middle part of my life. That is something no woman wishes to remember, the time when growing ends and the law casts us out into the world, at the mercy of men. I beat the odds then, demographically speaking, and didn't kill myself. Is that a sign of inner strength, or of weakness? Fear of death is a powerful motivator when there is no god waiting to receive your soul on the other side of that great barrier. Our gods don't care about us; they did their job in creating the world and then went on to other amusements.

How I envy those peoples who believe in Heaven. Or even Hell. It is the thought of absolute obliteration that is truly terrifying. Who would seek out such a thing? Only one whose terror of life had come to exceed her terror of death.

Pity such a one.

I grew into the kind of woman that men desire. That was no accident, of course. The only way out of the slums of my birth was to find a wealthy protector, and I knew from my earliest days that this would not happen without my working for it. And so I spent my spare hours subjecting my body to all manners of abuse to reshape it, and I took those drugs which would stimulate growth where men liked growth to be and inhibit it elsewhere, for men are creatures of sight and touch above all else. And of course I paid the price for such alterations. In Kurat itself women might seek out doctors whose sole purpose was to pamper them, and have access to drugs that gentled the body into its intended shape. I could not afford such things. And so I vomited up my older self in a thousand bloody pools, and spent the nights curled about my pain, knowing that the only way to escape my dismal circumstances lay down such a road. And in time it was done.

Yet ironically, that thing which appealed to men most was not a thing of drugs or artifice, but the one true gift of nature I had received. My hair had that tint of red which is so in vogue now, not a thing of the cosmetician's art, but the real thing. To me it looked no different than the falsified shades, but men seemed to be able to sense the difference, and the real thing . . . excited them. No explaining it, at least not from a woman's standpoint. It spoke to them of power, of conquest, of favored blood somehow made their own as they spilled their seed at its altar. Incomprehensible, to me at least . . . but I was not above exploiting it.

In time I found a protector, and in later time traded him for another. By the night I met Satas I was skilled in assessing men at a glance, and knew this one had potential. It took little work to entrance him. Within the first zhent I had sparked his interest, and by the second I had moved my things out from my current abode to his studio, on the outskirts of Kurat itself.

He was an artist, and found in me such inspiration as brought new life to his work. Or so he told me. I don't pretend to understand it. His creations were surreal, often so abstract that I found it hard to see how my modeling had anything to do with it. Yet he would set me up naked amidst some bizarre arrangement of props, and stare at me for hours as he molded various substances to satisfy his inner vision. Weird stuff, but it paid the bills.

And then *he* came.

I had been out shopping, and was not prepared for company. In truth I didn't much feel like dealing with anyone, for the day had been long and frustrating and the manifold treasures for which I had braved the lower class open markets had eluded me for all the hours of sunlight. Nevertheless I took a deep breath upon the threshold, and prepared myself to deny all that, at least in Satas' presence. The bond between man and woman is never so strong that a few bad days cannot sever it . . . even when the woman does serve as model for such works as "Ninth Event Horizon, Repeated," and "View from the Nether Side of Pain."

Then I opened the door and I saw the Braxaná. A magnificent creature, decked out in the face paint and stifling clothing of his class. Standing there in the foyer, discussing some work of art with my patron.

B'salos!

He was. . . .

Was . . .

No. There is no adjective that suffices. The Braxaná have a language all their own, it is said, and such is needed to describe them. For that quality which they possess is more than mere physical presence, though they have that in abundance. It is more than power. What they possess is unspeakable in other languages, where words like "awe" and "reverence" are reserved for gods.

I saw him, and I knew by his dress what he was, and I found I could not pass. Let other women rave about his beauty, it was not what held me frozen. What is beauty, anyway? Flesh can be molded easily enough, if you have the money and can endure the pain. No, what held me fascinated was something more. Something intangible, that breathed across my flesh: a promise of power incarnate, wedded to a lust to wield that power. It was enough to raise hairs along my bare arms.

I did remember at some point to avert my eyes. Probably too late.

"Is this the model you spoke of?" The Braxaná's voice was liquid silver; it sent shivers down my spine to hear it.

"Yes, my Lord." It took no great insight to catch the turmoil in Satas' own voice. How dearly he wished I had not arrived just then. Never before that moment had I realized how much he truly valued me . . . or how much his male pride would suffer, if the price of losing me was not high enough.

You never know which it is, with men.

I took a few steps into the room, not quite knowing what to expect. I was loath to remain cowering at the door, but equally unwilling to test my own nerves by trying to stride past this man as if his presence didn't matter. How could it not matter? He filled the entire studio with his presence, tangibly enough that as I licked my lips nervously it seemed I could taste it. Was this some secret pheromone of the Braxaná, that had managed to seep out through his concealing costume to mark the room as his? Or was it instead something rooted deep inside my own brain, my female brain, coming from the part which instinctively understands that the true value of a man is measured in his dominance over other men?

"Stay." His voice was quiet, but it carried power, and I froze in midmotion, dreading the reason for that command. My eyes carefully averted, I nonetheless heard him as he walked over to me, and the shiver I felt as he reached out to touch me was not a thing of fear alone. A gloved hand touched my cheek, and he turned my face toward him, urging me with a touch to meet his eyes. And I did. Black eyes, black in black, eerie eyes in which the dividing line between iris and pupil could not be seen. Windows to the soul, but shadowed windows, secretive. I could not guess at what thoughts were behind them.

After a moment he turned his attention to my hair, and ran a gloved finger through it, parting it to the roots. *Yes, Great One, I do not use a cheap dye, but are you so sure drugs didn't create this color?* Apparently he was, for he nodded as his hand fell away, and I felt a catch in my throat as the bizarre inspection ended. If he had ordered me to speak then, and told me my life depended upon it, I don't think I could have managed a sound.

He turned to Satas, and in a voice devoid of any particular emotion, said, "This one would make a fine gift. What is her price?"

Satas looked as startled as I was. "Price, my Lord? She is not an . . . an. . . ." He fumbled for the word.

At last I found my own voice. "I am not property," I dared.

"Are you not?" he demanded. There was an edge of warning in his voice, but also . . . amusement. Cold amusement, the kind you see in men when they set helpless animals to fight each other to the death, to see how they die. "Have you never claimed his ownership, then?"

"I . . . ah. . . ." All words left me. Was this one of the men who had the right called Whim Death, allowing him to snuff out a human life as casually as Satas or I might squash an insect? There were no safe words for me, not anywhere.

"Do you carry proof of Ownership on you?" he persisted. "Have you used it to turn away men, who might otherwise regard you as available?"

Heart pounding wildly, I nodded. There was no other response possible.

"Well then. He owns you." He turned to Satas again. "What is her price?"

I met Satas' eyes. There was fear in them, I saw that plainly. Fear of angering this man, fear of losing his patronage . . . fear of asking for too low a price? He could not meet my gaze for long, perhaps afraid I would see his sympathy turn to greed. The bonds between man and woman are not strong in our world; it takes little to sunder them. Now this bond was about to be measured precisely.

"She is my model," he said. His voice was halting, uncertain. Could it be he really didn't want to part with me? The thought made my heart skip a beat. "I need her for my art—"

"Yes, understood, I will pay you accordingly."

For a brief moment Satas reminded me of a fish dragged out of water, mouth agape at the shock of cold, dry air in its gills. Then he managed to draw in enough breath for speech. "She has much value to me. . . ."

The Braxaná waved his hand in a short, quick motion, dismissing the thought. "You will send me the sculpture we discussed. If it pleases me, I shall have the Central Museum commission you for a work for its new gallery. Something the critics would take note of."

I could see the greed in Satas' eyes. Perhaps a bit of sorrow, also, but that was swallowed up by the greater whole, as minnows are swallowed up by bloodfish. Stupid, stupid man! Could he not hear that he had been offered nothing, that the whole bargain was conditional upon the judgement of a creature known for both manipulation and cruelty? Yet what could I say? You do not challenge a Braxaná to his face, not ever. God forbid he should get upset enough to alter his body temperature, and cripple those few precious sperm that he has. It must have been bad in the old days too, but now, with their gene pool so small that every new generation was an evolutionary feat, it had reached the point of obsession.

And so I was sold. A handful of words to enslave a human life, decades of freedom traded away for a pedestal in some central museum. A lifetime of hope and frustration traded for a critic's review, that might not even be good.

"You will come with me now," the Braxaná commanded. "I will send for your things."

I hope he betrays your trust, I thought to Satas. *I hope he receives your precious sculpture and finds it lacking, and makes of all your ambition no more than a tale to tell over drinks in some Braxaná haven, to the tune of the Pale Ones' laughter.*

But should I blame him for this, really? The blame belongs to a society that makes such creatures out of us, estranging us from one another, turning us all into objects. Not only women. Standing before the might of the Braxaná, blinded by their blazing arrogance, we are none of us truly human. Only creatures of convenience, tolerated as long as we serve their purpose. Silently, obediently. Nothing else is to be endured.

I did not look back when I left.

What words, for Zhene? An artist's masterpiece, spread out across the surface of Braxi's one small moon. Castles sculpted out of stone and glass, ancient materials that would last forever on this worldling which had no winds, no weather . . . no time. Overhead the silver webwork of the gravlock system gleamed like some vast spider's craft, the light from B'salos shimmering weirdly as the containment field distorted it. It was wonderful and terrible all at once, and as we passed through the gravlock and the sickness grabbed hold, as the body attempted to vomit up the artificial gravity which was so suddenly being applied, I knew with a sinking sensation in my heart that I would never be allowed to leave.

The adjustment didn't seem to bother him. Perhaps they are truly not human, these Braxaná. Or perhaps that which is wondrous and terrible has become so commonplace to them, they no longer notice it.

He took me to his House, where it was clear to all that I was a prisoner, property, differing from the sculptures and paintings that filled the house only in that I was harder to maintain . . . and perhaps less valuable. Truly I might have been made of stone for all the Mistress of the House noticed, and as she inspected me from all sides I half-expected her to reach out with a dusting cloth to wipe off some offending spot of dirt.

"You see things in her I don't," she said at last.

"It needs a man's eye," he said brusquely.

He used me himself, of course. Who would have expected otherwise? And I was prepared for it, knowing all the arts that please men, capable of pretending that they pleased me too. All my life had been spent working toward this end, a station in a rich house, comfort, security. Yet there was something about the Braxaná that chilled me to the core . . . or perhaps it was the passing references to my being a gift for *him*. Never a name, only that pronoun, spoken in a tone that was half reverence and half resentment. Perhaps it was all the times I would hear whispers in the hallway outside my small cubicle, whispers that ceased when I showed my face. . . .

I never asked about it. Never dared. But I couldn't help wondering: was this man testing me somehow, waiting to see if I was worthy? Or simply waiting until he tired of me himself, before passing me on to another?

The answer came soon enough. Barely two zhents after my arrival the Mistress of the House bade me pack up my few things and prepare to move. Things? They were few enough, keepsakes of a life that had little worth remembering. All my life had been lived in preparation. Now it seemed as if the thing I had been waiting for was about to happen, at last.

I wished I could feel something other than dread.

We took a shuttle to get there. That should have given me warning. As I watched the surface of Braxi turning beneath us, drawing no closer as we traveled, I should have guessed.

And then what? Run screaming out the air lock? Beg to be returned to my home district, stark naked if need be? I didn't know enough to scream. Even when I realized where we were going, and who the mysterious *him* might be . . . I didn't know enough to be afraid.

No one knows. That is his power, that secrecy. It is his protection, his comfort . . . his prison.

It wasn't long before I saw it come into view, that new third moon of the Braxin system. Not even a century old yet, its gravlocks and landing bays sparkled in the Void as the sunlight played across them. Inside, it was said, were all the amenities of a true world, including gardens and forests and even hunting preserves, transported from real planets to this place of utter privacy, to suit one man's pleasure. It was also said that there were less natural things inside, things that were only whispered about when no one from the upper class was listening: alien things, wondrous, terrifying, enticing things. Every man wanted to get a look inside the place, just once. Most of those would die of terror if actually summoned there.

I remembered the name of the satellite and spoke it aloud, feeling the sound tremble upon my lips. *H'karet. Place of the Hidden.* And as the words left my mouth, I knew in that moment with dread certainty who it was that I had been purchased for.

He must have seen the panic on my face, for he laughed coldly. "Perhaps you will do better than the others."

Pri'tiera. I tasted that word silently and felt myself tremble. Originally no more than a title for the leader of the Holding, the word has come to mean so much more: a heritage, a bloodline, a mystery. Was this what I had been preparing myself for, all these years?

I felt myself shaking as the shuttle pulled into the visitor's bay, as the vast golden shell of H'karet shut tight about us.

There were rumors about the current Pri'tiera. Crazy rumors. But he was Braxaná, wasn't he? So that meant he had to be human, no matter what anyone said about him. He wasn't more than two centuries removed from regular humans, either . . . or at least from the Braxaná ancestor who had first borne the title.

The shlesor was a genetic time bomb, someone had once told me. *The Plague of '947 was its trigger, the Pri'tiera is its fallout.*

We stepped down from the shuttle and a half-dozen guards fell in beside us. In lockstep, silent. I could hear my heart pounding in my chest.

He is only a man, I told myself.

We passed down gleaming corridors that revealed nothing of their owner. Portals to other bays, other transports, flanked both sides. No one about.

Only a man.

At last we approached a portal that was different than the others, and one of the guards had to put his gloved hand to a black plate beside it to open it.

Inside . . . inside was a vast space, a hall whose opalescent ceiling vaulted high above, whose walls were cut from Aldousan boulder opal, veins of glittering milky rock twisting through the grey stone matrix. The space was punctuated by hundreds of gleaming pillars, between which hung artifacts from ten times that many worlds. Tier upon tier of treasures, suspended from nothing visible, with a narrow walkway vaulting between them. Some were gifts that had been presented to the Holding by subject nations, images of which I had once glimpsed on newscasts. Some were less recognizable artifacts, alien pieces that seemed out of place in these Braxin surroundings, beautiful and disturbing at once. Some were clearly ancient relics, with the dust of the ages still clinging to their surface. To walk down the hallway between and beneath these things was to drink in the whole vast span of the Holding, both its present and its history. More than one could absorb in a single passage. Perhaps more than one could absorb in a lifetime.

That hall gave way to an audience chamber. Where *he* waited.

He was young, so very young. Was that an aspect of his bloodline, or of the thick cosmetics that hid his skin from sight, or was he really as he appeared, just past the age of independence? He seemed at once a monument to human beauty and a strange mockery of it, for his carefully sculpted features were almost too perfect to belong to a living creature. And cold, very cold. It was hard to imagine such a face ever betraying human emotion. One could almost imagine his features carved from alabaster, rather than human flesh . . . only alabaster was warmer than this.

It took me a moment to remember where I was, so intent was I upon studying him. When I did I could feel my face flush, and I dropped my eyes and went down on one knee, wondering if he would kill me for the effrontery.

"She has spirit." His voice was smooth, a thing of music, and something about it made the back of my neck tingle in resonance. *This is the sound of power,* I thought. It was as if I could feel his words wrapping themselves around me, and I knew that if he commanded me to move then, my flesh would obey him as if the words were my own. It was a terrifying sensation.

"Spirit and strength," my master agreed.

How much did anyone know about this man? His bloodline had disappeared from public view nearly two centuries ago. The common tribes assumed that he still walked among the Braxaná, in places like the moon where the lower classes were not there to see . . . but maybe not. Maybe he was as much a mystery to his own people as he was to the rest of us.

He came toward me then. I ached to look at him again, to study him, but I kept my eyes carefully averted. It was just beginning to sink in where I was, and who he was, and what this whole scene meant.

The potential of it.

I saw the black leather boots stop before me. I felt his presence as a palpable thing, fearful and seductive all at once. Then a gloved finger touched me beneath my chin, tilting my head up to face him. The contact was sudden, electric, and I heard myself gasp as my flesh shuddered in response.

Then I met his eyes, and the world ceased to exist. Dark eyes, Braxaná black-on-black, they seemed to spread out as I gazed at them, becoming two vast pools of inky shadow. Inside I could sense things swimming, darkling creatures that never saw the light. Shockwaves of raw emotion seemed to shiver through the blackness, and I barely had time to sense their nature before they were gone from sight. Hatred, power-hunger, lust . . . the last left me dizzied by sudden arousal, and I knew in that moment there was nothing I would not do for this man's pleasure, no act so extreme or so painful that I would not indulge him.

Then he let go of me and the black pools were merely eyes again. The alabaster mask might have betrayed a hint of a smile . . . or perhaps not.

"I accept your gift."

My master—my former master—prepared to speak again.

"She is accepted," the Pri'tiera said shortly. "You may leave."

"Magnificent One . . . about the matter of the Kardian tariffs—"

The Pri'tiera waved his hand in what was an unmistakable gesture of dismissal. "You have given me a gift. If she proves worth my time, you will have my favor. Do not ask for more now, Kaim'era." Though I did not know the complex voice modes of the Braxaná, even my untutored ears could make out the incipient anger in his voice. Apparently the Kaim'era heard it also, for he bowed once, deeply, and then without further word left us.

Alone.

The Pri'tiera walked around me, slowly, studying me as so many patrons had studied Satas' sculptures in the past. I fought not to let my fear show. The shock of discovery was over now, and I was determined to get hold of myself. I had spent my whole life preparing for this moment; I was not about to let it pass without making the most of it.

But he did not touch me again at that time, or even address me. He walked about me three times in all, then called out a woman's name. Mere seconds passed before I heard footsteps approaching. "My Lord?"

"Take this one to chambers. Mark her as mine. I will deal with her shortly."

She took me by the arm then and raised me up. I didn't dare look at him as she drew me away, but I could hear my heart pounding so loudly he must surely have heard it.

This was my fate, this. Whatever he intended . . . I would find my way. I would adapt. I would please him, as I had pleased all men. Had I not been chosen for that very purpose? Had not both men agreed the signs were right?

It struck me, as I was led into the private chambers of the satellite, that he had not even asked my name.

Mark her as mine.

The words meant branded, as criminals are branded, with a raised mark upon my forehead that burned with fresh pain at night. All of his people wore it, I saw, men and women alike. A strange and barbaric custom, once used to mark herd animals on the open range. The message was far more complex in this case, of course, not merely a warning against the theft of slaves, or a simple warning of criminal history.

I am the Pri'tiera.

That which is mine can never be another's.

Look in the mirror and know that you are my property.

No contract needed. No bill of sale. They would have been superfluous.

Pull yourself together, girl. Haven't you been working toward this all your life? You have the most powerful protector in the Holding now, bar none. Figure out how to please him and you're set for life.

I did not dare speak the implied corollary: *Fail to please him, and you have no life.*

His women attended me. Slaves to a slave. I tried to get information out of them that would enable me to assess the situation, but it was a hopeless effort. I tried to get them to voice the subtle fear that flickered deep in the backs of their eyes, that I might know its name, but to no avail. I tried to get them to talk about the Pri'tiera . . . and that was when they really shut down tight, their eyes flashing me something that might have been pity as they scurried from the room like frightened birds.

I was on my own.

It was fourteen days before he called me to him. In that time I had explored most of the wonders of the H'karet that were open to me, but I had little appetite for wonders. As each day made it more and more clear that I was not there merely to be a servant, it raised new questions. New fears. Nonetheless I put all those aside as I went to meet him, dressed in garments which his other slaves had chosen for me.

He met me in the crystal garden, a bizarre conservatory where glittering rock formations sprouted like weeds from floor, walls, and ceiling. I had to walk through half of it before I got to where he was, a pagodalike shelter whose pillars were of living Betanese coral.

I came before him and I knelt. Curiosity was burning in me like wildfire, but I kept my eyes averted. Such does the law demand.

A moment passed. Then: "You may look at me."

So I did. Looked at him, drank him in, from the surreal beauty that all Braxaná have to the more subtle signs of power. Studied his strength, his formality, his absolute confidence . . . and something more, that flickered in the back of his Void-black eyes, too quickly and too namelessly for me to define.

That something made me afraid.

I didn't know why.

He waited a long while, still as a statue, while I completed my inspection. At last, unable to hold his gaze, I dropped my eyes once more. That seemed to be the cue he was waiting for.

I heard him come toward me, then stop. A gloved hand reached out to me, and with infinite delicacy stroked my hair. Red hair. I felt myself shiver as an undefinable *something* seemed to emanate from his touch.

"Harkur's blood," he mused aloud.

"So it is said," I whispered.

"Blood once strong enough to claim an Empire. Blood once strong enough to tame my people . . . for a while."

There was nothing more to say. We both knew what had come of that Empire. The Braxaná had taken control of it within days of Harkur's death, and never let go. Ruthless barbarians at the head of an interstellar Holding. The formula had not changed, to this day. Their nature had not changed. The signs of Harkur's inheritance might have been diluted by the greater gene pool of Braxi, but those of his servants, now our masters, were pure and clear.

He drew me up to my feet, then. Not merely a physical gesture, that. His mere touch seemed to command my flesh, so that my body rose of its own accord.

My eyes met his. I could not do otherwise. It was as if someone else was inside my body, giving it commands in my stead.

"Are you strong enough for me?" he whispered.

I shivered to think of what that strength might be needed for, but said nothing. All my life I had taught myself to please men, to indulge their hungers, to win their favor. What could this one ask of me that I was not prepared to endure?

I managed to nod. I don't know if he even saw it. There was something in his gaze so fixed on me that it seemed he was searching my very soul. For a brief moment I felt an almost animal panic, primal in its tenor, that urged me to run from him, run at any cost, get out of range of his touch, his thoughts . . . it was a terrifying thing, utterly visceral in nature, doubly frightening in that it seemed to come out of nowhere. He seemed to sense it in me, for not until it had passed did he touch me again: this time a slender gloved finger to my cheek, that seemed to leave a trail of desire in its wake.

I wanted him. I wanted him as I had never wanted a man before, as I had never known one *could* want a man. It came upon me suddenly, a flush of heat spreading out from where he touched me to the whole of my body. Cells shivered, hormones flowed, blood rushed to the surface of my skin. It was all so sudden that I didn't even know how to absorb it, but just stood there, flushed with the sudden heat of my desire, embarrassed at how visible the change must be to him.

His finger dropped away from my face. A flicker of something that might have been a smile creased those sculpted lips.

"Strong," he murmured, and I thought I heard approval in his voice. "Whether strong enough . . . we shall see."

He left me then, in body at least. But it was a long time before the last of his presence faded from the room . . . or from my flesh.

I dreamed of him. Of course. Dreams are where we can express those fears and lusts that daylight forbids us from examining too closely. They rise up from the primal part of us, the animal part of us that understands everything but has no words to communicate anything.

And so I dreamed of human desire beyond all bearing, nightmares of lust and torture commingled, all the passions of all the men I had ever known in a tangled mass of memory and fear. And him. My dreams were full of him. Wanting him, fearing him. Never satisfied, not even in dreaming. It was as if something in my brain knew that it could not guess what his pleasure was, and shied away from even trying.

If only I had known the truth then. If only. . . .

Come to me

Those were the words, written on a simple card. Ink and paper: traditional, barbaric.

Come to me

With trembling hands I chose a gown myself this time, one that underscored my body's allure without overstating it. The Braxaná are all beautiful; what do such features mean to them?

I found I was afraid. Of him? Of myself? Of what I might become in this place?

Come to me, it said, and it gave directions on where I was to go.

I came.

The room he had chosen was an observation chamber on the Braxin side of the satellite. Within it a whole section of solid wall had been removed, leaving only the thinnest of force fields between viewer and Void. The time he had chosen for our meeting was daylight on the planet beneath. The vast arc of Braxi spread out across the heavens, blue and white swirling across it, continents peeking out from beneath. How still they looked from here, those clouds. Storms that swept across the planet at breakneck speed, rainstorms birthed and dying within hours . . . all motionless, from here. As if even the vibrant world of our birth paused for a moment, to seek the Pri'tiera's favor.

I heard him come up behind me. I did not turn. My heart was pounding so wildly I could feel it pulse along my skin. *He's just a man,* I told myself.

At last he spoke. "That which is mine," he said quietly, "can never return to Braxi. You understand that?"

My heart clenched up for a moment. Slowly, slowly, I drew in a deep breath, expelled it. At last I nodded.

He moved closer then. I could feel the heat of him along my spine.

So close, and yet not touching. He gave me that moment, I understand now, a last precious gift of normalcy in which I might imagine that I understood him, that he was indeed no more than a man, and that my life had prepared me properly for this moment.

All lies, all lies.

He placed his hands upon my shoulders. Bare hands. It is said the Braxaná are more loath to remove their gloves than we are to remove our most intimate apparel. Perhaps that is why the sight of his naked fingers made a shiver run through me, as though something electric had been applied to my skin. Perhaps that is why his touch made me suddenly giddy, so that as he turned me to him it seemed that I stood still and Braxi itself revolved around us.

Perhaps.

He touched my skin then, running his bare hands along the length of my neck, into my hair, along my face. And I felt . . . things there are no words for. Echoes of desire so deeply rooted that my legs grew weak beneath me . . . yet so darkly disturbing that for the first time since meeting him, I wanted to flee. It was a purely visceral reaction, coming from the part of the brain that has never been tamed by civilization. Sometimes our animal brain knows best, it is said. But where was there to flee to?

And then he turned me toward him, and he leaned down to kiss me—a foreplay the Braxaná are said to enjoy—and the goddess of chaos took full control.

It was as if the borders of my body were suddenly gone, or at least so confused that I could not define them. As if somehow I were experiencing the same scene from different viewpoints. His bare hand moved to cup my breast, and even as I felt my own flesh tense in pleasure, it was as if somehow I was inside his body, too. I could feel my own flesh warm beneath the velvet, the soft scrape of the nipple against his my palm as it moved, the stirring of heat and stiffness below in parts I neither had nor understood—

I tried to pull away from him. He didn't allow it. *Too late.* He pulled me closer—*I pulled her closer*—and with that motion the last barrier between us seemed to fall. Emotions poured into my brain that no woman should know, Braxaná emotions, violent in the extreme. Hate. Fury. A lust for sex and violence so tangled that only a true Braxaná might make sense of them. Resentment burning like a wildfire: of women, of fate, of one woman in particular, of the father who had defied Ar's curse to conceive him—

I lost track of my body then, or of his. Fragments of sexual contact wrapped disjointedly about my brain, images of flesh on flesh without body or sequence to bind them together. I knew what it was like to have the whole of my lust concentrate in one heated organ—what it was like to thrust that into another—the rush of power that came of such a moment, which no woman could ever, or *should* ever, understand. I touched his flesh and then I was inside it, and I knew at the same time that he was within *me*—and that he was sharing thoughts and sensations no man had a right to witness, that he had thrust his mind into those private places where we women nurture our wounds of the spirit, when man has raped all else.

In the end there was pleasure, greater than any I had ever known. Of course. With the full range of human sensation pouring into my head, with every touch and stroke and thrust echoing with male and female energies, how could it not be so?

He looked at me after, for a long, long while. Strange how the madness receded as soon as he ceased to touch me. Strange how cold and empty the world felt suddenly, when I was alone inside my own soul.

At last he whispered his parting words. Ominous. Seductive.

"Perhaps," he said, "you are strong enough."

Perhaps. . . .

They say that the women of other worlds pity us. They say that they hear tales of our lives, our legal standing, and most of all our treatment by men, and regard us as poor abused creatures, and pray for some god to liberate us.

They don't understand.

We who worship no living god, we understand what it is to be human. We who have no safety net of Heaven or Hell strung up to catch our soul after death, we understand what the human soul is truly worth.

For thousands of years the Braxaná have ruled us. They set no god over us to claim our spirits, for such is not their way. They enslaved our flesh with laws and violence . . . but what is flesh? Nothing more than a container for the spirit. Science can give us breasts or remove them; how can we fix our identities on such transitory attributes? Flesh is but a vehicle of communication, no more, and those abuses which give it trial soon pass . . . if one allows them to.

The soul, the spirit, that is another matter.

I pity you, my foreign sisters, on planets where science invades the mind. I pity you in those places where psychics skulk in the shadows, their secret art invading that one place which should be truly sacrosanct. For there is one privacy even the Braxaná hold sacred, and they defend it fiercely for all their subject peoples. There is one inner jewel which neither master nor invader has the right to touch.

For as soon as your soul bears the mark of another, it's not really yours any more, is it? And in this life which is so short, with nothing but darkness before and after . . . what is left, once the spirit itself has been violated?

The river of blood is exhausted now, my veins nearly empty. The shadows of death close about me, tempting and terrifying. No, my masters, you have demanded much of me in my lifetime, but this you cannot have. I have sculpted my body for you, I have lived by your rules, I have been slave to men and stranger to women, all for you . . . but you cannot have my soul. Not ever, not that.

I am Braxin.

*I do not fear my enemy when he stands in the open,
half so much as my ally when he walks in the shadows.*

—Anzha lyu Mitethe

FIVE

HANAAN ZI EKROZ did as little work as possible.

He was damned proud of it.

Sometimes people asked how he managed it. He didn't know. He could show them his files of preparatory research, he could tell them about crowd theory and human psychology and the effect of anger or love or loss on human decision-making . . . but that was just a song and dance for the masses. The truth was he worked by intuition, and because his intuition was good he was one of the best at what he did. End of story.

He wasn't psychic, of course. They'd checked that ten ways from Zeymour when he was first recruited. The last thing the Organization wanted was a psychic in their midst. Never mind the stories about what psychics really were like, about the mental links between them that could overbear other loyalties, about the instability that eventually engulfed the hypersensitive mind, awakening strange delusions and sometimes overt insanity—never mind all that. The truth was far more prosaic. There were cells of the Organization that kept an eye on the psychics. Cells that sought them out, cells that studied them, cells that tracked their actions, their strategies, their potential. And if someday Azean interests called for the wholesale obliteration of the psychic community, they needed to know there was no one in their midst who would flinch at calling the shots.

He had risen far in the Organization because of his intuition, and he had risen fast, and because he knew that those two elements were rarely combined he knew he had to prove himself constantly. So. When orders came down that the governor of Zaisa Station was an impediment to Imperial interests, he had promptly and efficiently arranged for his removal from the political scene. When orders came down that the upcoming Hanto merger would adversely affect border security, he triggered a domestic dispute that so distracted its President, the merger was forgotten. And when orders came down that Lestian trade negotiations were deadlocked and only the threat of global conflict would solve the problem, he had triggered a war without leaving his desk. Three days, that one took him. Three days. He doubted there were more than a handful of operatives who could have pulled that off.

But those were the days of simple projects. Politics, mergers and acquisitions, simple military operations . . . anything the Empire needed disrupted, he had the power to disrupt. Anger the right man, lose the right files, frustrate the right employee. Easy triggers, easily accessed. Humankind was at once chaotic and predictable, and playing upon both elements at once was an art form of which he was the undisputed master.

He had been promoted beyond such simple concerns now, into areas at once more nebulous in definition, and infinitely more crucial to Azean welfare. Often he didn't even know the whole picture he was involved in, or how other cells might play into it. That was all right. The one thing you learned as a starting operative was, no one man knew it all. Some of what they were doing was not all that pretty, and StarControl liked to keep its hands clean.

And now. . . .

He leaned back in his formchair, feeling it mold itself to his body as he did so. It must have sensed some point of tension in his shoulder region, for it answered with a soft purr of vibration in just that spot. For a moment he shut his eyes and let it do its work. He had learned long ago that the tension was a good thing, that it marked the moment when he knew he had sighted his prey, and therefore was cause for exhilaration, but the chair hadn't figured that out.

Zara Anastofal was moving. Even better, his intuition counseled: she was moving like she was supposed to move, like he had predicted she would move. Like the insect whose jagged flight helped it evade capture, like the browsing beasts who grouped together in a mass at the first sign of danger, humans had their own panic response patterns, and he had learned them. Fight, flight, evasion, denial. . . . It wasn't a simple formula, because humans weren't simple creatures, but he had stalked them for a lifetime and by now he knew all the elements that went into it. Weaving it all into a whole was the art form, of course. Try to analyze it logically and you got nowhere. Trust to instinct—*his* instinct—and the answers became as clear as codons.

His portal chimed, an unexpected distraction. The room waited until he looked up to acknowledge the sound, then informed him, "Tael er Sula. Identity confirmed by DNA scan. No unregistered weapons."

Hanaan nodded. When you had risen as high as he had in the Organization you could never be too careful.

Tael was a tall man, even by Azean standards, and lanky as well, as if the standard rationing of human flesh had been stretched vertically when he was formed. Despite what seemed an awkward frame his motions were quick and precise, minimalistic, clean. Hanaan appreciated that. He was easily distracted by kinesthetic observations, and having someone serve him whose movements were simply *efficient* was worth its weight in Soldan fused gold.

"You have something for me?"

The nod was almost imperceptible. Tael already had a data chip in his hand and he handed it over without a word. Hanaan nodded his approval as he loaded it. His readers here were completely isolated from the greater networks of the Empire; to get a look at his private data an enemy would have to make his way to this very room, this very terminal, and then convince it to work for him. Not damned likely.

The data on the chip was unveiled layer by layer: starmaps, surface probes, surveillance logs. He didn't need to look at them all closely now. It was clear from the first few displays that his plans were bearing fruit. He could feel the smile spread across his face.

"She's following the pattern you predicted," Tael told him.

"Yes." He could taste the word on his lips as he spoke it. Sweet.

He brought up the first few maps again, and the logs that went with them. Yes, Mediator Zara had left Chandra and was heading verward. Soon she would begin to alter that path, travelling from system to system in a jagged pattern that her subconscious would dictate . . . a pattern of predator avoidance. He had triggered that instinct in her deliberately. And it had taken no more than a security block on her medfiles to do it. Not quite as dramatic as staging a war in three days, but every bit as artistic. Minimum effort maximum response: that was the name of the game.

"Warn our operatives, when she decides where she's going she'll move swiftly. Possibly not under her own I.D., if she can manage it. She knows someone is watching her, she won't want them following."

Tael nodded.

"She has professional contacts who could help cover her trail, but she'll be afraid to contact anyone linked to the government. She has a few friends who might help . . ." He frowned, considering the data once more. "But I don't think she'll contact them. The fear element is strong here, I think once she commits herself she'll go it alone. Nevertheless, get her contact file out to our operatives, make sure they have all the names and faces in case they need them."

He didn't really worry about her friends getting in the way. Most humans could be scared off by some sign that the government had focused its attention upon them, and that was easy enough to do; those few who would find surveillance inspiring and help her because of it had other buttons that could be pushed.

Alone. He needed her alone, so that all the response patterns were clean. Add in another person and you added new data to the mix, data that didn't come from a split egg. No good. His analysis had been based upon the quirks of that condition, and he needed them to express freely in order to get what he wanted.

Which was nothing short of achieving the Organization's most elusive goal . . . and guaranteeing his own promotion into the ranks of its secret masters. The ones without names, who molded history from the shadows.

Someday he would sit among them.

"I am curious," Tael offered. It was a question.

Hanaan looked up with a raised eyebrow.

"Your predictions are much more precise than usual. More . . . targeted. You knew how long she'd stay on Chandra, for instance. Longer than I would have guessed, given the evasion paradigm. And now you say she doesn't know where she's going . . . but she'll wind up in the right place anyway. The place we need her to be." He spread his hands, an uncharacteristically broad gesture.

Hanaan steepled his fingers and considered how best to answer it. Finally he said, "What do you know about twins, er Sula?"

He hesitated. "That's a rather broad question."

"Then I'll narrow it down. Split-egg twins. Identicals. Two lives from a single source. Two reflections of a single soul." He paused. "Do you know how many primitive peoples used to kill one child of such a pair? Sometimes as an offering to the gods, of a thing sacred and wondrous. Sometimes in fear that if one child had the soul belonging to both . . . what did that make of the other?

"Centuries later their descendants would discover that cloning could create infinite duplicates of the same person, and they would realize that some kind of limit had to be put on the process. All technologically advanced people have done so. Are the reasons purely scientific? Or something more . . . primal?"

"Her twin's been gone for over five Azean years. Most of her life."

"Yes, and do you know what often happens when identicals are separated? When they're raised by different parents in different environments, so that the only thing they share is the pattern of their DNA?" He paused. "They often follow the same paths. Not only in ways that genetic science might anticipate, but . . . something beyond that. They might choose mates at the same age, mates who look alike, who may even have the same name. —Think about how incredible that is, Tael. Where is it written in the genes, what name a lover should have? Or that a person should change jobs at a certain age, or prefer one kind of poetry over another? Yet over and over again we find such an eerie resonance . . . as if the two were but truly one soul, divided."

He could hear the excitement rising in his own voice as he spoke, a rare display of enthusiasm. With care he modulated it. It didn't really bother him if Tael guessed how much emotion he had invested in this project—the man was bright enough to realize what was at stake here—but it was the habit of many years not to let underlings gain too much insight into his psyche, and that was a habit worth maintaining. You never knew whose brain the enemy might get hold of, or what secrets it could be forced to reveal.

Which is why the Organization was the way it was. Why most men in it would never know the name of their direct superior, much less any station beyond that. When you had an arm of the government whose mandate was to function outside the law as necessary, and which used tools and methods that were . . . unusual . . . you had to make sure that trouble would be stopped dead in its tracks.

"She will make the same choices as her sister," he told Tael. "She will flee to the same kinds of places, she will be drawn to the same kinds of people, she will be panicked by the same kinds of stimuli. Her trail may not lead us to where we want to go, but it will give us clues as to how to get there."

"She's aware of this, unconsciously at least. That's why she stayed on Chandra for a while. She needed time for introspection, before she started searching. Because the clues are all inside her. She knows that. The more she understands herself, the better she will be able to anticipate the choices her twin has made."

"Her twin is psychic, though. Won't that make a difference?"

"Is she? We don't know that." He allowed himself to smile. "She had the potential, that's why she was taken. Zara has the same potential. In her it never expressed. Odds are good that her twin will be the same. If so . . . this job will be much easier. Because once we find her twin we are going to find the people who took her . . . and then the real game begins, Tael. Taking control of the one wild card in the Endless War, learning to manipulate it . . . so that Azea can crush the might of its great enemy for once and for all."

And he, Hanaan zi Ekroz, would be there when it happened. Not at the front lines of the War, not ruling a handful of operatives from this desk, but up at the top ranks of the Organization, amidst the shadowed thrones of power. Where the goal was not one battle's success, or even the triumph of a decade, but real and permanent victory over an enemy whose offenses spanned eons.

We will find the psychics. We will learn how to use them. And we will bring the Holding to its knees at last. . . .

The man who cannot question his own preconceptions when survival is at stake will not live long enough to enjoy his prejudices.

—Zatar the Magnificent

SIX

Banished.

The word tasted vile upon the tongue. It was the kind of thing you wanted to spit out onto the streets, to watch passing feet mangle it into the dust like so much phlegm. The mere concept of it was abhorrent to Tathas, and the attendant thoughts . . . revolting.

Yet here he was. Viak'im of the proud Kesserit tribe. Banished.

He had left behind five transports, two starliners, and who knew how many planets and stations and shuttles now. It all ran together in his brain, so that he couldn't pick out the details. He remembered that when he started this trip the ships had seemed cleaner, the people more human-looking, the planets better equipped. Now it was all just a featureless drone in his brain, so many tenths of travel amidst aliens who looked strange and smelled stranger and didn't know rings about Braxin custom that he could hardly remember when it had started, and couldn't imagine the end.

He was a child of the Central System, and never had he felt it so acutely. Hospitable, familiar Braxi with its flock of tame satellites: Aldous, which was little more than a suburb of Braxi—Zhene, with its sculpted airlocks and gravlocks and the mansions of the Holding's elite—and the Citadel, shining like a small moon, even though its hordes of once-numerous Kaim'eri had passed into history like some enormous extinct beast. And the H'karet, of course, glinting in the night like a wayward star. How he had taken it all for granted! What he would not give up to go back there now!

Succeed in the Wilding and you may yet go home.

The human types which dominated the Central System were a minority in these places, and strange living things that slithered or crawled or clacked their way through life took precedence instead. Half of the languages they spoke could not even be handled by his translator, as though the weirdness of the sounds was too much even for its mechanical circuits. Half the beds he slept in were not comfortable force fields, or even sterile material constructs, but surfaces whose aromas hinted at distant evolutions, in which two arms and two legs had been rejected as a workable model for intelligent beings. Several times he slept on the floor, preferring its neutral surface to that which would cradle his body but discomfort his senses.

On the floor. Viak'im of the Kesserit, banished from the home planet, sleeping on the floor!

Easy, Tathas, easy. Did not your ancestors eschew comfort, when it suited their purpose? Was not your tribe born in the hostile wastelands, where luxuries were few? More than one of them slept on the ground, I am sure, and that was without central heating and bedfields and a host of amenities you still take for granted.

It was little comfort on those first few nights, to remember such things. True, there were still those who enjoyed the outer trappings of barbarism, but that was a *choice*. To know that the Central Computer was off-limits to him now, that the cash in his pocket and the clothes on his back were all he owned in the world, and that after a set number of days had passed—whatever number the Braxaná decided was sufficient for him to reach one of the Borders—he would be outlawed in his own homeland. . . . That was not choice, that was infamy. Yet, what was the alternative?

Only death, K'teva assured him in dreams. Offering the words instead of herself, cold comfort in the place of warm lips. He reached for her and she danced away, eyes sad, sympathetic, tempting . . . all at once. God, how he ached for her!

Where was he going, anyway? Not to the War Border; he wasn't that stupid. Though hostilities had ceased half a year ago—again—they could start up any day now, and that was nothing he wanted to be caught in the middle of. No, the Kesserit enjoyed war, but that was war waged with sword and muscle and the intoxicating rush of adrenaline . . . not this farce of a war fought in packaged space, where the only knowledge of victory came from moving lights on a starmap, and where death came too swift and clean to savor.

No, he had chosen another Border to approach. It was a more distant border, as space was measured from Braxi, and perhaps that was what appealed to him; a longer journey meant more time he could spend in the Holding, drinking in the last of his native culture. Then again, was this really his culture? This mishmash of races, where Braxi's military might was little more than a fairy tale used to scare children into proper behavior, in a place where the light of B'Salos was so distant that the naked eye could not pick it out from among the inferior stars? One night he saw a group of Braxins in a bar, half a dozen of them, surrounded on all sides by Scattered Races whose forms had been molded by alien ecologies, flanked by those few true aliens who were permitted to share such a human space. *We must all look alike to them.* Tathas thought. In that strange, disconcerting moment, they even looked alike to him.

But then, he was not part of their society any more. It might even be said that he was more alien to those Braxins than the foul-smelling green creature who hurried past him in the bar that night, a beerbag clutched in its primary mandibles—

Ikom Braxit! His soul screamed the words in indignation: I am Braxin! *Ikom Kesserit!*

Ikom Viak'im!

What now? He strode the length of the station with long, restless strides, angry at the fate which had sent him here, even angrier at himself for not having come up with some better plan than *run away*. All through his journey there had been a part of him that had never given in, never accepted this Braxaná travesty of justice. That part of him had firmly believed that he would come up with some idea that would save his own neck *and* his dignity; only now, standing on the furthermost station in the Holding, gazing out upon the unconquered Void, did he realize that wasn't going to happen. And the realization made him furious.

Ar! He turned suddenly and struck at a nearby commodities conduit, hard enough to dent its surface. Humans and nonhumans alike paused in their passage and moved to give him wide berth. He almost hoped someone would call the station guards on him. He wanted something to fight, someone to vent his anger on . . . and if it was someone who wore a Braxin uniform, all the better.

Don't be crazy, Tathas. It was as if K'teva were whispering words in his ear, gentle but firm. *Leave the Holding. Get out safely. There is always time to come back later.*

Yes, when he succeeded in his Wilding. How likely was that, really? He could bring back a thousand women for the Braxaná to breed with, each of them the pinnacle of genetic perfection, and still those god-lovers could claim they were unfit for the Master Race and sentence him to death for failure. The only hope Tathas had of winning out by their rules was to find a female whose value was so blatantly obvious that they didn't dare deny it . . . and short of kidnapping the Azean Empress or some such feat, he didn't see any way that could be managed.

No, his return would have to be managed secretly, or by some other illegal method. The Wilding was merely a death sentence delayed. For now all that mattered was that he get to somewhere safe, where he could take the time to think without having to watch over his shoulder for enemies. But how, exactly, did one do that? Hire a transport? They would expect him to have some destination in mind. Bribe his way onto a merchanter? They'd know the Outlands well enough, having plied the free planets for their own purpose, but how much could a freelance be trusted? He'd heard enough stories of the traps set for unwary travelers that he knew just how easy it would be to wind up in the Void without a force field, for the sake of the few valuables he carried. How did you determine whom to trust, on a station where everyone looked equally disreputable?

It wasn't that he felt helpless, exactly. It was that for the first time in his life he understood what helplessness was, and that if he wasn't very, very careful, he might come to that state.

Bless the Braxaná, and all their god-loving customs!

At last he took a room in a dismal inn that jutted out from the main commercial ring. It cost him twice what it should have and looked as though it hadn't been disinfected in ages, but that was just par for the course. Head cradled awkwardly on a fiber-filled pillow, he listened to the hum of a climate control system badly in need of repair and wondered just what in Ar's name he was going to do next. Return? Rebel? Or find them the perfect woman for their stupid little custom? Right now all three options seemed equally untenable, and he fell into a troubled sleep counting the tenths that were left for him to remain in the Holding, before the might of the Braxaná reached out to crush him like an insect.

He dreamed of her. Green eyes, the color of the Tor'n sea, black hair cascading over shoulders and breasts burnished olive by the sun, warm hands running slender fingers down his body.

You will make it, she said. *You will find an answer. I have faith in you.*
Flesh dissolving into mist, hair into perfume, eyes into light.

Within the Wilding or without it? He whispered the words and saw them twist and eddy into the mist, the light, the silence.

No answer.

He had been on the station nearly two days when he first realized someone was following him. He couldn't even say how he knew it. Maybe it was some primitive instinct which evolution had overlooked when it prepared humanity for the modern age, that still peered into shadowy corners and searched for predators. Or maybe it was just the normal paranoia of a man about to be hunted by the galaxy's most deadly tribe, turned up so high in volume that the very passage of air through the tunnels of the station seemed to be whispering threats to him.

The twisting corridors of the station were a bad place to get ambushed. The structure had taken shape over the years in a piecemeal manner, new sections added or altered as station politics, bribery, and occasionally the strong-armed tactics of unwelcome guests dictated. The end result was a layout no man could anticipate, filled with so many twisting tunnels that trying to go from one point to another in a straight line was a lost cause, and running away from trouble was as likely to bring you circling back to it as it was to get you safely away. He'd tried to get hold of a map of the station when he first arrived, but if such a thing existed no one seemed to have a copy. Doubtless the black market traders who plied their business on the station preferred it that way.

Was this some normal business of the station, the kind of trouble that was unavoidable in a place so far from the centers of law and order? Or were the Braxaná coming after him already? Perhaps to spill his blood for daring to stay in one place longer than a night? Ar, he would almost welcome a real fight!

He walked quickly through the station, staying with crowds, looking for some kind of space that might let him flush his trackers out into the open. If more than one person was involved they would want to get him in a place where they could surround him, preferably without bystanders to witness the act. Moving too quickly and erratically for them to enact such a plan, he did his best to memorize the area he was moving through, looking for a tunnel or system of tunnels that would suit his purpose. At last he found it, outside a darkly lit bar in the primary docking ring whose main entrances were far too public for trouble. A back hallway exiting from the main room was the perfect setting for an ambush, little used and full of twisting turns that led only to dead-end storage shafts. He took care not to remain in it long enough to give them an opening, but walked through quickly, taking stock of its turns and dead-end storage alcoves, spotting the places where enemies might take cover.

There was a ventilation shaft overhead at the midway point, with an opening he could fit through easily if the grill were not in place. Excellent. It took only a few hard blows to force the grill loose, and when he set it back in place he caught one of his own hairs behind it, barely showing. Just in case his trackers, coming through, saw its potential as well.

Heart pounding, he half expected a neural sweep to greet him as he entered the bar. But he'd been fast enough that no one following would have had time to cover him from both directions. Now that would change. He ordered a chilled glass of what seemed the most popular local brew and prepared to wait. It was faintly green and smelled of herbs that shouldn't be in food or drink, but he smiled as he pretended to sip from it. Not setting anything to his lips now that another man had handled. If his experience as Viak'im had taught him anything, it was the efficacy of drugs.

Seemingly relaxed, he waited for his hunters to arrive.

Hunters. The word should have chilled him, but it did just the opposite. *Hunters* meant there was an enemy with a name, strategies to unwind. Flesh to hurt. He understood about hurting flesh. He wondered if his tracker did, if he had the least clue what kind of destructive energy was wound up inside Tathas right now, looking for some outlet. Any outlet. Absent gods help the man who set it off.

Briefly, he wondered what the laws were on this station about killing people in a bar.

Briefly.

He had a long knife that he wore up his right sleeve, his weapon of choice. That was for the Viak'im in him, demanding blood from his enemies. He also had a neural stun he had picked up from the black market on H'serun, but that was just for backup; Ar alone knew where it came from or how reliable it would be.

In the end a man relied upon his body and his wits. If those weren't up to the job mere steel wouldn't save him.

He could feel the flush of excitement rising to his face as he scanned the patrons of the bar once, twice, and again. Not a large or particularly formidable-looking crowd. There was a group of freelancers over in the far corner, two women and a handful of men dressed in worn Void gear, gambling with piles of coins and trinkets from at least a dozen planets. A furred thing halfway across the room that might or might not be human was talking to a man Tathas assumed was a mercenary. He shifted in his seat so that he might keep a clear eye on that one. Four men at the far table were playing with holocards. One in the shadows was nursing a beer. Several more entered the room as he watched, a ragtag handful of men and women, mostly human, who scanned the room carefully before they chose a table in the darkest corner. Could it be them? He could feel his pulse race as he studied them carefully through the trickle of foam on his glass. There were six of them, and he was willing to bet that under the bits and pieces of Void gear they wore there was more than one weapon hidden. They didn't have the air of mercenaries, but every single one of them looked capable. Even the women.

He felt a sudden tightening in his groin as he considered the possibility of fighting a woman. It was rare to find a female who was skilled in combat, especially one who could counter the physical advantages of a Braxin male in his prime, but these two looked capable enough. One of them wore a sleeveless vest that left her arms bare, and the muscles that rippled beneath the surface of her skin as she called for drinks were lean, tight, ready. There were markings on her skin, regular enough that they might be tattoos, but from where he was sitting he could not make out details. She was of the Scattered Races, surely, but not so close to the human mean that the scent of alien landscapes didn't cling to her.

He had rarely fought women, and never to the death. The possibility was . . . intriguing.

The room began to fill up. No doubt some workmen's shift had just let off, and a portion of the station's personnel were now making their way to the taverns and drugdens and fleshpits that they favored. If his trackers were smart enough they'd arrive with the crowd. They'd settle in and watch him here, long enough to see that he was staying in one place, and then see that their agents were covering the back exit, with all its strategic promise. Eventually they'd decide they needed some strategy to guarantee that when he made his exit it would be in that direction . . . he needed to move before that happened. You did not win out against a better-armed enemy by playing to their tune.

He forced himself to wait half a tenth before he got up from his lone seat, scattering a few sinias on the table for the sake of the one who had served him. He paused a moment in the shadows, studying the room's other occupants with what he hoped was an appropriate air of caution. He had to seem as if the motion came from the natural caution of a man who was in the Holding's disfavor, not his certain knowledge that death was close at hand. He could taste it now, and smell it, a premonition so strong that he knew his hunters were indeed in that very room. Others might have been afraid. He was elated.

He walked to the rear exit without ever completely turning his back on the room. He doubted they would shoot him down in public, but it would be foolish to wager his life on that. He allowed himself one last sweeping glance of the room, which by now was filled almost to capacity. The casual glance of a man who thought that the dangers facing him would be simple and visible ones. It seemed to him that he heard the muffled beep of a shortcom, then. Maybe it was some other business, and not a signal to enemies waiting beyond the back corridor. Maybe his enemies weren't there at all.

We will soon know.

He passed quickly through the door itself, letting it shut behind him. As soon he was sure the patrons of the bar couldn't see him he sprinted toward the overhead conduit. The hair was still in place, telling him that the one thing he had feared most—that his trackers would stake their ambush in the same place he meant to take refuge— had not occurred. He pushed the grill to one side and hoisted himself up through the narrow opening as quickly and as quietly as he could. He could feel the pulse pounding in his palms as he pulled himself into position. Then: the grill was back in place, and the only sound or motion in the corridor was the pounding of his own heart.

Just in time.

The door to the bar hissed open, then closed. Footsteps approached, measured and wary. More than one pair, from the sound of it. He held his breath as they came to where he lay hidden, hoping they would not think to look overhead for their quarry. If they suspected that he was on to them he might.

Then he heard whispered voices—a language he didn't recognize— and shadows passed beneath the grill. Two of them. That was good. He could take two. It was a pair that he had seen in the bar, worn Void gear now parted to show the armor worn beneath. They both had neural stuns in hand, and it was clear from their stance that they intended to shoot the first thing in front of them that moved. Not military men, though. He could see that even from where he was. They lacked the stance, the readiness . . . the hardness. Amateurs: well-armed and determined, perhaps, but no more than that. They weren't wearing bodyfields either, which could mean any number of things; he suspected in this case they didn't want to be detected by station security. Good. All was good. . . .

Reflecting dryly that his standards of "good" had gone down in recent days, he waited until they were past and then quietly moved the grill aside. It was the work of moments to pull off his shoes and set them aside, then to lower himself down to the floor below. Silent. Must be silent. He listened for their whispered voices—yet another sign that this was not a trained military force—and then set off after them, keeping to shadows and dipping into side alcoves wherever possible.

They were human, which was good. He knew the human body well, knew how to slice that place in the neck where the blood ran hot on its way to the brain, so that death was almost immediate. That they were both wearing pieces of armor made the move a bit more complicated, but that kind of protection was designed to foil a frontal attack with standard weapons . . . not a man who came so close he could smell his enemy's sweat, who could twist his blade down into the reinforced collar on an impact vest, ripping open the flesh beneath.

His attack was swift and silent, and he knew with certain instinct as the hot blood gushed out of his enemy that this one would not bother him again. The man tried to cry out in alarm, but with his airway gashed open all that he could manage was a gurgling sigh. Enough to alert the other, however. Tathas dropped into a low crouch, and as the second man swung around with his stun at chest level, he came up under the man's firing arm and forced the shot to go wild. The impact sent them both slamming against the far wall, and Tathas could feel his weight knock the breath out of his opponent. His right hand grabbed at the arm that wielded the neural stun while his left slid up under the front edge of the man's gorget to grasp the throat beneath. It was a close fit, but his fingers closed around a column of muscled flesh tightly enough to feel the other man's blood pounding between his fingers.

The man drove a knee into his groin to dislodge him, but missed the target by inches; Tathas squeezed his neck hard, fingertips digging deep into pressure points as he got the grip he wanted. The man had pulled something out with his free hand, but that was all right; he wasn't going to live long enough to use it. With a sudden exhalation of breath Tathas forced the man's body one way and his head another. He could feel the vibration inside flesh as the vertebra snapped, and the hand that was holding the weapon swung down suddenly by its owner's side like a marionette whose strings had been cut.

Two down. There would be others. Tathas eased the body quickly to the ground and took the stun from its hand. No time to get identification from him, not if others had heard the conflict. He reached down to take whatever weapon the man had pulled out in his last moments . . . and saw that it was not a weapon at all, but some kind of remote locator, and its signal had been triggered. He grabbed up the first man's weapon as quickly as he could and then sprinted down the corridor to the second place he had spotted in his reconnaissance, a shadowy storage alcove angled in such a way that people coming from the other direction wouldn't see it until they were all but past it. He was barely in place when he heard footsteps coming. More than two sets, this time. Bless the absent gods, who was after him in such force? It wasn't the Braxaná, he knew that now; their men would have put up a better fight.

There were three of them in this group, and they passed him at a run. Whispering thanks to his enemies for setting themselves up so nicely, he picked off the last with the neural stun, sending him hurtling to the ground. That the others didn't notice him dropping out of the sprint only confirmed Tathas' opinion of the whole crew. He moved out into the corridor then, pausing for only a moment to cut the fallen man's throat. Time enough for prisoners later, when the odds were better; he couldn't afford the risk that a half-charged stun might allow the man to come to his senses while his fellow marauders were still standing.

He came upon them just as they saw the bodies. One of them cursed loudly, something about a god-damned *Shaka* and how much he would like to kill the whole god-damned lot of them . . . the stun silenced him in mid-curse, and even as he watched the human features distort into a grimace of agony Tathas was moving forward to take down the last one. This man had better reflexes, and swung around fast enough to get off a respectable shot as the Viak'im charged him. Tathas could feel the hot brush of pain as the beam grazed his arm; close enough to make the muscles sting, not close enough to take them out of commission. Then Tathas was upon his enemy, momentum slamming him to the ground alongside his fallen comrades, and when the man screamed out curses of his own Tathas rammed the neural stun into his mouth and pulled the trigger. The body seemed to convulse beneath him for a moment, and then went limp in a way mere unconsciousness did not provide for. Apparently taking the charge so close to the brain stem wasn't something the human body was happy about doing.

That was all of them, then. He hoped. He grabbed up what weapons he could, hoping that the noise of the brief battle hadn't alerted anyone outside the corridor that there was trouble. He wiped the blood off his left hand, onto an opponent's vest, but enough blood had soaked into his shirt that he couldn't take a chance on exiting through the bar. Surely there were police in this place who would notice. Surely, even in this place, someone would care. He turned around to go back the way the last three men had come—

And there was a woman standing in the corridor.

Maybe the fact that it was a woman was what kept him from shooting as soon as he saw her. Maybe it was the fact that her hands were on her hips, a challenging stance perhaps but not one that seemed to presage direct assault. Maybe it was something in her eyes that made him realize, with a hunter's sure instinct, she wasn't part of the pack he had just taken down.

And since it was the woman he'd been studying in the bar earlier, the one with the strange designs down both her arms . . . maybe it was just curiosity.

She looked at the bodies with cold eyes, reptilian-style lids flickering over them as she took in the details. "You've made quite a mess," she said at last. Maybe amused, maybe challenging; her voice was hard to read.

"Can't help it if they bled all over the place."

"Security's been alerted. Probably your friends. I don't think they care who takes you down, as long as someone does."

He could sense his green eyes flaring. "Then they're not very good friends, are they?"

Another man came into sight now, one of the freelancers that had been sitting with her in the bar. Tathas' finger tightened on the trigger of his stun, but he didn't raise it. Yet.

The man was somewhere in that century of mid-life when age is hard to judge. He was Braxin—or some distant ancestor had been

Braxin—but he wore the clothes of other cultures and his face bore the ritual tattoos of the Kedoushin. He looked down at the three bodies on the floor and his nostrils flared, as if tasting the sour smell of death. Tathas realized suddenly that the last man he'd stunned had emptied his bowels as he died. Not something you notice when there are still people trying to kill you.

"Not bad," he assessed. As if the bodies were a work of art whose brush-strokes he was appraising. "Kesh said you'd take all five. I bet her you'd at least lose a limb trying it." When he spoke you could see that his teeth had been dyed as well, each one capped in crimson drops. "She's a better judge of fighting men, it seems."

"Practice," the woman hissed softly.

"Who the Void are you?" Tathas demanded. He felt a drop of blood on his face and tried to wipe it away, but his blood-smeared hand only made the matter worse. "And why is it your god-blessed business who I take down, or why?"

The man's mouth twitched; his expression hardened ever so slightly. "Freelance," he said. "Always looking for new blood. Reports from Braxi hinted you might be worth watching. At least you can fight." There was a sudden high-pitched noise in the distance, which Tathas felt more than he heard. "Apparently someone signaled security. In minutes they'll be swarming all over the place. You have somewhere to hide now? Some way off this station?"

He drew in a deep breath. Who were these people anyway? They knew things he needed to know, that was clear. But there'd be no time to ask them here. That left only one alternative—and it was a risky one, in a place like this. By the Void, it was a risky one anywhere.

But what were the alternatives?

"What's your offer?" he asked them.

"Passage off the planet," the man responded. "I'll make you a recruitment speech when we're clear. You turn me down, you owe us one for the service."

"They thought you were Shaka," the woman offered. Her eyes were amber, disconcerting, and they glowed slightly in the corridor's dimness, as if waiting for him to ask the obvious question: *What in Ar's name is a Shaka?* But it wasn't the time or place for questions now. They knew that. He knew that. It was all part of their game, to tempt him with hints of their knowledge. And gods bless them both, it was working.

He thought he could hear movement now, the low hiss of station doors and the voices of others approaching. Security? He looked down at the bodies at his feet again. Station law didn't care much about motive or style; dead was dead, and those who got caught breaking the laws were generally put out the airlock while they were still protesting their innocence. What was his defense going to be, anyway? The paranoid ramblings of a Braxin who wasn't supposed to be here in the first place? He couldn't even claim that his victims had shot first, much less offer up any proof that they were *really* after him. And of course if Security checked with the Central Computer they would find out that he had overstayed the Holding's welcome already, which meant that Braxin law wouldn't so much as stretch a glove if they killed him. . . .

At least this way he would get off the station, and out of Braxin space. It wasn't a risk-free choice . . . but nothing would be.

There were sounds down the corridor. Footsteps. Voices. Time was running short.

"All right," he said. "Get me off this dump and we'll talk."

They turned wordlessly and began to move down the corridor, loping with an easy stride that spoke of other battles, other flights. Tathas followed suit. He saw the man raise his cuff to his mouth and mutter into it, "I need misdirection, station west of Aurelio's. *Now."*

A moment later a distant explosion shook the station. Probably more show that substance, Tathas mused. Only an idiot would use high explosives on a Void station, especially one as decrepit as this.

But the smoke that was carried to them by the ventilation system hinted otherwise, and it seemed to him that there were screams as well, echoing in the distance. He must have slowed down to listen, enough that the man shot at him, "Second thoughts? Want to stay behind?"

No more words. They sprinted towards one of the lesser bays, and the screams were soon left behind. Red light began to pulse in the corridors; he didn't know enough about the local security code to know if that was good or bad, but his companions didn't' seem bothered by it. Once or twice the man spoke into his cuff again, and guided them down one turn or another, away from the main halls. Once Tathas could see a contingent of uniformed humans moving past them, down the very hall they'd been in minutes before. Whoever his strange guides were, they knew how to maneuver around station security.

Their ship was a small one, and its fuel lines were already retracted and ready to go. There were three humans there already, whom Tathas recognized from the bar. They were armed, and spread out in the docking bay in such a way as to be able to cover every inch of it while not being in the line of fire themselves. No amateurs here.

The other woman in the group stared at him with raw distaste; hardly a surprise. Probably the last thing she wanted was a Central Braxin on her ship. How strange that was, he thought. Back home he had been an outsider, dreaming of freedom from the established order. Now he was one of Them.

They made room for him to board with them, and he went. No need for any words to be said. Inherent in the silence was a practiced understanding of how to exit a station swiftly and safely . . . along with the implication that such things were often necessary. If they didn't try to kill him as soon as they were away from the station, these people might be useful.

The first woman grabbed his arm as he passed into the ship, forcing him to face her. Maybe it was the ship's dim lighting that made her eyes glow like jewels. Maybe it was the knowledge that she was now on her home turf and could say what she wanted.

"One thing before we go," she warned him. "You pull any of that Braxin access-on-demand crap on one of us and I'll kick your working parts so far up into your body you'll be able to pleasure yourself without opening your mouth. That clear?"

He could feel his own eyes narrow in anger. *Not here, not now.* He forced himself so speak instead of striking her, though his Braxin soul screamed out its indignation. *Too many enemies, too much danger.* It was the first time a woman had dared to speak to him like that, but it probably wouldn't be the last. How long would he survive if he lost control every time a woman challenged him?

It's a test. You know that. He looked into her eyes, hate-filled, and thought, *She wants me to lose.*

"Very well," he said quietly. "And if you give me one direct order, even in joking, I will see to it you never give orders to anyone again."

These people might not like him threatening one of their own. Or they might respect him for standing his ground. He was betting what little he had on the latter.

Then the man who had brought them to the ship struck him on the shoulder; not an assault, but a warning. "Into the ship, now." He reached for the woman as well, but she ducked his grasp and hissed softly, moving into the vessel on her own. "Time later for ground rules, both of you. We have more important things to worry about right now."

Already alarms were flashing in the small bay, but his hosts did something to override the local control systems and they were able to launch despite that. All Tathas cared about now was getting off the ramshackle station and into the safety of the open Void. There'd be time for them to feel each other out—and ask questions—later.

Security skiffs came at them from the main ring, but not fast enough to surround them. Orders crackled over the longcom, but with no force to back them they were no more than mere words. Ignored. The few small ships in their way got out of their way quickly. Past the fifth orbit the small ship kicked into augmented drive . . . and then there was no more sign of station security, or any other official presence. Just darkness between them and the Void of Consciousness, devoid of any plan or purpose. And one small ship that hurtled toward the Border, carrying Tathas away from the Holding, and toward his destiny.

These words to the multitudes who are foolish enough to think that a smattering of Braxaná blood entitles them to enter the arena of our politics: Drink poison instead. It is simpler, faster, and will be infinitely less painful.

—Zatar the Magnificent

SEVEN

THE MUSEUM OF Erotic Art on Braxi wasn't a place women generally frequented. It was dangerous to visit a place where men would be aroused, when the law didn't protect you against the consequences of that arousal. Even those with Just Cause were wary, for in the end, could a Braxaná not simply ignore any law that displeased him? The Pale Ones rarely punished their own.

The few women who did come usually had some private agenda. Some were Braxaná in need of privacy to hatch their byzantine plots, and they hid away with fellow conspirators in private rooms under guise of physical indulgence. Some were artists braving the place to find a patron, or women of the middle classes hoping to catch the eye and the interest of a pureblood. A few were simply those who enjoyed the risk, and they wore their symbols of ownership openly, visibly, as if daring the Holding's rulers to transgress. Which was its own special kind of arousal.

K'teva walked through the Museum slowly, not meeting the eyes of the men there, even though she had the right. It was dangerous to tempt the Pale Ones, especially those who knew the color of Kesserit eyes, and who might like the thought of subjugating a woman from such a defiant tribe. This was not a good zhent to be bringing emerald eyes into a Braxaná city.

Finally she came to the hall she sought. *Shem'Ari,* the sign said. Literally translated, "Servants of the Goddess of Chaos." In more common usage it might be read as "Women Who Dare to Command Men." It was a Braxaná archetype, with sexual connotations that few outsiders understood. K'teva knew that its roots went far back, to a warrior tribe whose women had fought as fiercely as men, who were kept from power only by the application of doomsday prophecies . . . but it was hard to reconcile that with what the Braxaná had become.

The day that a woman commands men, the Goddess of Chaos will return to power and all will be lost. Or so the legend said. K'teva suspected that whoever came up with that legend hadn't looked at the Azean Star Empire recently.

She stood for a moment in the entranceway, studying the lone statue that greeted visitors to this special wing, trying to understand it. It was carved from volcanic glass and its black surface shimmered in the artificial light, seemingly liquid in its substance. It depicted a woman in some kind of military uniform, one arm upraised, her attitude that of command. Slight in stature, she was delicate of frame, yet imbued with the strength that came of inner confidence. On her upraised wrist was a heavy bracelet such as the Braxaná used to mark their slaves. Yet there was nothing of the slave in her demeanor, nor any title given to the work to hint at greater meaning. Clearly it was believed that those who knew the subject matter would not need explanation . . . and perhaps those who were ignorant could not be enlightened with a mere handful of words.

"It's said that he was obsessed with her." The voice came from behind her, silken smooth, couched in the speech mode of challenge. "The first Pri'tiera. There's no documentation for it, of course. Any such records would have been destroyed long ago. But the suggestion is . . . intriguing."

The words were a test, she knew that as she turned. She hadn't been raised to the full complexities of the Braxaná dialect but she had devoted a good part of her life to mastering it, and if she couldn't manipulate all forty-seven speech modes as well as those born to the art she was skilled enough to understand them when they were used by others.

"Obsession is weakness," she said to the speaker. Basic Mode: *Make of it what you will.*

His footstep echoed across the stone floor as he came to her, the medallion of rank gleaming on his broad chest. "Obsession," he said quietly, "can be strength." A gloved hand touched her hair, separating a thin strand, stroking it. "Obsession is passion, which is the fire in a warrior's soul."

It's been a long time since the Braxaná were warriors, she thought. She'd never say it aloud, of course. If she did, her head was sure to hit the floor before the last echo of her words had faded from the chamber. Not for nothing did these men carry the traditional sword of their forbears, the *Zhaor* . . . and not for nothing had they woven themselves a legal tapestry which allowed them to take human life at will. It was dangerous to challenge them, dangerous even to talk to them, if you were not of the Race yourself.

Lord and Kaim'era Tezal, son of Lusak and V'nista, reached out a gloved finger to touch the side of her face. When he withdrew his finger there was a film of white powder on the black leather, which he studied with dark amusement. "Dressed for the occasion, my little half-breed?"

She managed a smile. "I don't recall any regulations on cosmetics."

Apparently her use of the speech mode of light amusement had not been as successful as she'd hoped, for his eyes narrowed in what was clearly displeasure. He brushed the bit of powder off on her hair. "You walk a thin line sometimes, K'teva."

"Does it offend you?" she asked. Challenge, desire, a trace of humility. Sometimes the Braxaná dialect was useful.

He looked at the statue, then back at her. "It is not *my* obsession, K'teva." But amusement colored his own words, and she knew she had not displeased him.

He turned his back to her then, said simply "Come," and began to walk.

She let him lead her through the Museum, into parts that the Braxaná reserved for themselves. Soundproof rooms for assignations that ranged from pleasure to politics . . . or both at once. The two were never truly divided, among the Braxaná. That was part of what made their men so painfully desirable. The knowledge that not a word was spoken, not a breath was drawn, that did not somehow serve their pleasure.

He stopped before a door with a palm lock; a nod indicated that this was her destination. But as she reached up to place her hand on the sensor plate he caught her arm and held it. "That I have facilitated this meeting without demanding to know its purpose is your debt to me, K'teva. It is a large one."

She could feel her heart speed at the thought of what was behind that door. Had he come down here himself? That was surely too much to hope for. "I know," she said quietly. "I will not forget."

He kissed her before he left, a bruising kiss that was more about possession than pleasure. Even when they were being used, the Braxaná must feel as if they were the masters. Then he left her alone in the hallway, to breach the final barrier by herself.

Alone.

Her heart was pounding in her chest now, hard enough that she wondered if its beat were not visible. It took her a moment to unfreeze her limbs enough to move, and to put her gloved hand to the sensor plate of the doorway. In this Braxaná place, such mechanisms were accustomed to reading identity through leather.

ENTER, the door chimed, as it slid open soundlessly.

She walked slowly into the room beyond—a small waiting room— and then into the one beyond that. The light was set low, a twilight glow that conjured shadows everywhere. She could taste her heartbeat in her mouth as she walked, but she knew that she could not allow her tension to show. Normally she would be confident in her ability to hide her emotions, but it was said that the purebred could smell your emotions from across a room if you sweated them enough.

And then she came into the main room and she saw him. Until that moment she had not really known if he would come in person to meet with her, believing instead that the reclusive monarch might send an agent in his place. Yet there was no mistaking who he was, and what. She took one moment to drink in the details of his presence, then quickly fell to one knee in reverence. It was not a posture she was accustomed to.

He is so young! she thought. Even with the makeup you could see it. He didn't bear himself like a youth—what ruler could afford such indulgence?—but the cast of his features was that of a man barely past the age of Inheritance. *If* past it. Suddenly she wondered what would happen if the ruling line were to have nothing better than a true child to put on the throne of Braxi. Would the populace be expected to tolerate that? Would the other Braxaná support him, or would they rebel at last against the throne that had only recently been established?

If Tathas had known this . . . She banished the thought quickly. It was said that the Pri'tiera was especially skilled at reading emotions in people; if so, she needed to make sure that the only feelings he picked up from her were the ones she wanted him to know about.

The Pri'tiera of the B'Saloan Holding of Braxi/Aldous gave her a long moment to gather her thoughts before he spoke. "K'teva, daughter of Sur'ren and Xanat, who was of Braxaná blood. We meet at last in person."

"Yes." The word was whispered. Something in his presence seemed to demand her whispering.

"You are not of the lower classes. Stand."

She did so, trying to look more confident than she felt. His very

presence seemed to drain her of confidence, and all the careful sub-
terfuges which she had spent years refining suddenly seemed no more
effective than the theater games of children. "I have lived among them
for a very long time."

"I know. I have watched your . . . career. Are you done with that
game now?"

Is that all it is to you? A game? She forced her breathing to be even,
her posture to reveal nothing of her true response to his words . . . or
to his presence. By Ar, how was he affecting her so? It wasn't just his
appearance or even his rank, but something more. Something she
could not define, that tickled fear along the back of her neck. "It still
has its purpose."

"And it is dangerous to abandon, yes? For surely one of the Kesserit
horde might protest if you fled their company right after their leader
was betrayed." The words were sharp-edged, voiced in the mode of
challenge. "One of them might guess the truth, yes?"

"Do you object to what I have done?"

"No Braxaná would object," he said quietly. "The Kesserit were a
blight upon the planet."

She felt her eyes flare, and had to muster all her strength not to respond to his words with any more visible display than that. Bless him
for being able to get to her so easily. "It had to be done. The Holding
must be unified. It had—"

He waved short her explanation with a glare. "You walk among the
Braxaná now, K'teva. While we play a lot of games with each other,
this isn't one of them." The black eyes met hers, and for a brief moment they were bottomless pits of unlight that sucked in her soul; she
felt something inside him licking at her essence, an eerie sensation.
"You betrayed your mother's tribe. You betrayed a primary sexual
partner. You did it for reasons that were your own, and had nothing
to do with nationalistic concerns. Now you seek to profit from it." A
faint smile creased the whitened face. "I have no problem with this,
you understand. You are a child of the Betrayer, as are all the Braxaná." He stressed the *all* slightly as if to say, *I am acknowledging that you
belong to my Race. It could be otherwise.*

His eyes were just eyes again, but she couldn't shake the feeling that
some part of him was still inside her. Would he know if she were
lying? *Focus, focus. . . .*

"A while ago," he said, "you sent me a proposal which I found . . .
interesting. Enough so that I took a man who should be dead and al-

lowed him to flee my justice. Do you know what the ancients would say about such practices? 'If you defeat a man,' Viton wrote, 'and destroy all that he is, and all that he has possessed, be certain you kill him then, for if you do not you will have created an enemy ten times more dedicated to your destruction than that which you had before.' Yet this I have done. Viton would no doubt have declared me mad." The black eyes glittered. "Am I mad, K'teva?"

"I would not presume to judge you," she said carefully. Basic Mode.

"I spared my enemy. One of the few men in the Holding brave enough—or perhaps foolish enough—to speak against my rule."

"He invoked the law."

"Ah, K'teva." He took a few steps forward, closing the distance between them. She found herself held frozen by his gaze, as an animal might be frozen by the approach of a predator. "My dear little half-breed. Do you think that law saved him? Do you really? Are we so . . . weak in your eyes . . . that you imagine the law alone could stay our hand, if we wished to destroy someone?" His voice was soft, couched in seductive tones, but in his eyes was a black fire that warned her not to answer. "Your commonblood lover lives because several powerful men decided they had more to gain from his life than from his death. I am one of them. Now prove to me I did not err, and should not send my guards to hunt him down before B'Salos sets. Prove to me that you control this game . . . so that I may be satisfied in controlling you."

She might have spoken, but he touched her then. Just a finger to the side of her face, a fleeting possessive gesture that any man might make . . . and she suddenly felt her courage crumbling within her, the tall walls of her pride beginning to topple, and everything they guarded laid bare before him. No, she could not lie to this man, she knew that suddenly; he could *taste* her lie as if it had physical substance, he could feel it in the fibers of his being as if it coursed through his own blood . . . he would *know.*

What are you? she thought. In wonder, in horror. Willing her legs to support her, when all she really wanted to do was kneel before him so that she might have excuse to look away from those terrible burning eyes. Had she thought she would manipulate him, as she did other men? This was a creature as far beyond other men as she was beyond the herd-animals of the Blood Steppes. And he knew it. That was what shone in his eyes, that was so terrible to look upon. A confidence in power, so absolute that it burned her mind even to contemplate it.

Housed in a body that was barely past adolescence. The combination left her breathless.

"Tell me, " he pressed quietly.

"He's gone to the Narren border." She was grateful to have news to focus on so that she did not have to focus on him. "It appears he's made no contact with anyone from the tribe thus far." *His tribe, his tribe . . . not yours any longer, K'teva.* "After he crosses the border he'll have other things to focus on."

"*It appears.*" There was a silken growl in his voice, that simultaneously made her flinch and grow warm inside, as if some deadly beast had caressed her in intimate places. "I require more certainty than that, K'teva. One does not cast an explosive out into the ocean if one believes the waves may bring it ashore at one's own feet."

She looked up at him, and wondered what would happen if she challenged him. "You're watching him too," she said at last. Would he respect her for having spirit, or want to crush it?

Apparently the former, for he smiled darkly. "I have my surveillance. But I do not have eyes within your tribe, K'teva. So you will see for me. Clearly, accurately, and with no sign of wavering loyalty. Do you understand?"

Oh, she understood. If he was going out of his way to tell her that he had no spies among the Kesserit, that meant he had several. And they'd be watching her for any sign that her recent actions weren't what they seemed, or that her loyalty to the Pale Ones was anything less than absolute.

"I understand," she said quietly.

"You say you have enough contacts to steer him in the right direction, to make sure that he comes to the conclusions you wish him to draw, without him ever suspecting that you guide him. You realize how dangerous a game that is? Women have been killed for playing such games, when men are their subjects."

She lowered her eyes and couched her tone low, in the speech mode of humility and servitude. "I am my Lord's servant," she said quietly. "My actions are but an extension of his will."

"Prove it then." He spoke in the speech mode of anticipation: *I will judge you by how you respond to this.*

She felt her heart skip a beat. Then two. If he meant what she thought he did. . . .

Be honest, you always knew they might expect it someday. How could they trust you otherwise? She drew in a deep breath, trying not to let her emotions show. *It doesn't really change the game, does it? The stakes are already as high as they can get.*

Slowly, hesitantly, she extended her arms before her. Palms down, wrists bared. Resentment flared within her heart, not only for the man who would demand such a thing of her, but for the culture that had come up with such gestures in the first place. Quickly she tamped down on the emotion, hard, hoping to bury it before any sign of it showed on her face.

You are Braxaná. Behave like a Braxaná.

He stared at her for a long moment, then reached out with his own gloved hands to take hold of hers. His fingers closed tightly about her wrists, and for a moment it seemed to her that tendrils of his soul had wrapped themselves about her spirit and were squeezing, squeezing tightly. She found herself suddenly struggling for air, and not until he released her wrists could she draw a whole breath.

"I choose not to bind you," he said quietly. "But do not mistake the custom, my little half-breed; you are mine now."

She whispered something. It might have been "yes."

"Draw what you need from my House; I will see the money trail cannot be traced. I would not have this . . . experiment . . . ended prematurely for lack of resources."

"Thank you, Pri'tiera."

With a short wave he dismissed her gratitude. "The first Pri'tiera was a powerful man. It was said that there was nothing in the world which he could not obtain, if he truly desired it. Yet one thing evaded him. One thing which he wanted, which he sought for decades, but which he could never obtain." A pause. "I will have that thing, K'teva. And if you assist me in this, if you can truly manipulate your ex-consort and get him to fetch it back to the Holding for me . . . then you will be justly rewarded."

She whispered, "You know what I want."

"Ah, yes." He tipped her head back with a gloved finger, so that she gazed directly into his eyes once more. "A child of the Race. To make you one of us forever, as no mere half-breed can be. Mother to a line that will serve in the Citadel. Yes?" His mouth creased faintly with amusement . . . or was it condescension? "Very well. Prove you have the ability to guide a man across the Holding, to send him into the most dangerous place known to humankind, and to bring him back with my prize upon his hook . . . and I will regard that as proof of your own genetic worth. Thus were our people tested long before they came to this age of thrones and starships . . . thus shall they be tested again." The finger dropped away, but the black eyes did not release their hold upon her. "This is your Wilding, K'teva. A bit unusual in its form, perhaps, but then, this is an unusual age."

"I understand," she whispered.

The dark eyes narrowed; black fire played in their depths. "Do not fail me," he warned, in the speech mode of finality. *Do not seek to betray me. You will not survive it.*

"I will not," she answered, in the speech mode of affirmation. *I understand.*

He left her then, before she had time to draw another trembling breath. Left her alone in the shadows of that place, to contemplate what she had done. And who she was doing it for.

The most powerful man in the galaxy, bar none.

My master. . . .

Not until she knew he was gone did she allow herself to hate him.

Desperation has always inspired the greatest feats of strength, of endurance, and of concentration. Imagine what we might be able to achieve if we could use it as a tool to train our people, forcing them to excel beyond the normal bounds of human achievement . . .

—Anzha Iyu Mitethe

EIGHT

STARLIT THE CIRCLE waits, crowned by moonlight, stirred by breezes. Slowly the Seer moves, sacred beads glittering in her long knotted hair, soul-stripes white on her face.

Now, she whispers: call forth the ancestors, the war-fallen, the unborn.

Now, she whispers: rise the wise and the foolish, slip them free of the mantle of earth that has bound them, to come to the circle of souls.

Now, she whispers: draw them in, welcome their souls into your own, that they may taste of living flesh and you may taste of dying. . . .

Rho awoke with a groan. For a moment she couldn't even see straight, which was rare for her; even after the worst experiences she rarely bore the effects of it into the next day. So she just lay there for a few minutes, listening to the rustle of insects nearby, wondering what had moved her to sleep in a place where insects would be.

Then she rubbed her forehead and her fingers came away with flecks of dried blood on them, and she knew something was very wrong.

Focus. Focus. There were Disciplines for this kind of thing. *Focus!*

When she felt the tide of incipient panic mute to a controllable level she raised herself up on one elbow and tried to force her eyes to see again. She was outside, all right. On a real planet too, from the looks of it. Not good, not good at all. She was lying in the mouth of some kind of natural cave, such as an animal might seek for shelter. Had she dragged herself there, or had someone—or something—done it for her? Try as she might, she couldn't unlock the proper memories.

She checked her biomonitor, and cursed loudly when she found it broken. Now she not only had no way to monitor her own health and stimulate healing if needed, but the easiest way for her people to find her was now out of the picture entirely.

Looking out across an alien landscape, *Where the hells am I?*

The sun was a Zeymour-class orb in the yellow range and the foliage had evolved along traditional lines for that spectrum; the place wouldn't have seemed nearly so alarming if every plant surrounding her wasn't completely unfamiliar. Wherever she was, she was willing to bet she'd never been there before. At least the ground was damp with dew, and there were a few wispy clouds overhead in the bluish sky, which told her that the moisture parameters were likely to be within a human-compatible range. Thank the Lyu for that. All she needed was to be dumped on some desert—

Memory washed over her suddenly and was gone, too quickly for her to grasp at anything save one fleeting revelation. *Was I "dumped" here?* She searched her memory for some clue as to how she had arrived—any clue at all—but there was nothing more to be had. The past few days were a blank slate, and she had no memory of this planet save the images her bleary eyes were taking in now.

Gods, her head hurt. And she was hungry, too. She searched in her pockets and found a half-eaten snack bar, which she gladly devoured. Flavor pills in another pocket served as dessert. That wasn't going to last her very long. She looked out over the lush greenery and wondered how in a thousand hells she was supposed to figure out what was safe to eat and what wasn't. On Kysh she could have watched the native animals and taken cues from them, but in this place? It was possible the whole ecosystem was laced with substances that were poisonous to the human system. Look at Azea. You wouldn't know that kind of thing until it was too late. . . .

This is very bad.

She seemed to be partway up the side of a mountain of some kind. The earth was black and crumbly, most likely volcanic in origin. Judging from the depth of the vegetation it hadn't erupted recently, but of course that was no promise of future behavior. In the distance she could make out the blue of an unnamed sea lapping at black shores, which curved back out of her line of sight in a way that implied she was standing on a peninsula of some kind, or perhaps even an island.

That would be just great too.

With a sigh she sat down at the cave's mouth and gave the cut on her forehead a fingertip inspection. It wasn't large and it had scabbed over on its own; thank the Lyu for small favors. The rest of her ached but it didn't feel like there was any specific injury; only the normal stiffness you suffered when you'd been dumped on an alien planet, to spend the night sleeping on a chunk of unnamed rock.

With a sigh she shut her eyes, and used the Disciplines of meditation and centering to bring her mind into proper focus. It seemed to take longer than usual, but perhaps that was because her nerves were jangling over her sudden displacement. When she felt that she had her focus, and with it complete conscious control of her power, she reached out. First to the area surrounding. A thousand shadowy presences brushed against her mind, browsers and hunters and fliers and frightened little things that were just a squeak of fear down in the grasses . . . pretty much your basic oxygen-based ecosystem. She couldn't feel anything that she'd call high-sentient intelligence, but that didn't mean something wasn't out there. Her strength was in close-range, face-to-face communication, not psychic scouting.

For a brief moment she envied those telepaths who could reach out as far as stars with their senses and taste the essence of a whole world without even trying hard. Maybe if she was that strong she'd be able to make contact with her people and tell them where she was. *Nice fantasy, Rho.* As far as she knew there was only one group of telepaths capable of that, and its members weren't likely to be lost on primitive planets with nothing except a half-eaten snack bar for backup.

With a sigh she reached out again, this time to encompass the land surrounding. It was harder to focus at this distance, but she thought that this time she could sense something familiar at the very edge of her consciousness. Human? She tried to get more of an impression from it but couldn't. Finally, with a sigh, she returned her focus to her own body. Her head was pounding twice as hard as before, the inevitable price of trying to push her mind in a direction it didn't want to go.

But . . . she had found people. Maybe human. And when she got into range she'd be able to use the powers that were natural to her, and get whatever help they could give her. And then she'd be able to get back home, to whatever project she'd been working on when this planet had sidetracked her.

As she walked downhill—or climbed, rather, for the slope was fiercely canted and at times hands as well as feet were needed to maneuver down it—she tried to focus her memory enough to get some clue as to how she had arrived here. She'd been on a mission of some type, she remembered that. One of the Hasai had been with her. There had been a small ship, and they had set out into a region of space that was mostly uncharted, and then . . . and then. . . .

And then she was here. With no memory of what came between. It was as if a slice of her memory had just been cut out. But that didn't make any sense. If someone had captured their little crew and played memory games with them, wouldn't they be around here watching? Wouldn't there be some sign of their presence that a trained psychic could discern? What purpose could it possibly serve to dump her here like this, without even a clue as to what it was all about?

When she finally reached level ground her hands were so scraped and sore from gripping the abrasive lava rocks for balance that she knew they'd be swelling up on her pretty soon. It would be good if she could find civilization before then, hopefully with medicines to stave off infection.

Damn that biomonitor for cutting out on her! For a moment all she could feel was rage—rage at whoever had left her here, rage at whatever circumstances had isolated her without food or civilized medical supply—

Anger is fuel, the Hasai taught. A tenet of Braxin philosophy, adopted by the psychic community at a time when anger was all they had. Rho shut her eyes and reached out again, channeling all her rage into psychic strength. She could feel the boundaries of her power forced outward, and her head pounded as she strained her senses to the utmost, seeking any sign of high-sentient life. This time, yes, she felt the clear weight of another mind upon her consciousness. She was even reasonably sure it was human. Letting the rage subside, she allowed herself a few deep breaths before starting off after it. *What do you know. The Braxins were right.*

The yellow sun was overhead when she finally sensed her quarry nearby, though it was hard to guess just what that meant without knowing how long a local day was. When it was close enough that she could almost make out thoughts she slowed her passage, and crept up as quietly as she could to the place where she sensed them.

There were three of them. Human. One was visibly old, which told her that the planet was probably low-tech; no one with access to modern medicine suffered that kind of skin degradation any more. Two appeared to be children. All three were female, which she regarded as a good sign; low-tech societies generally regarded belligerence as man's business. Their form was not unlike her own, and but for a few streaks of natural color and slight alteration of the ears and nose they might have been from her home planet. Definitely within one or two percent of the human genetic mean.

But. Such differences might mean little to her, but to a primitive, alien people they were warning signs as vast as space itself. She was the Unknown. She was *not-one-of-us*. And whether they were going to interpret that in some weird religious context, or assign her to some natural source reputed to give birth to strange deformities—or come up with some wholly original explanation for her existence—had yet to be seen.

She watched them for a while as they cut away pieces of plants—a stem here, a handful of leaves there—and as the woman gave what seemed to be instructions to her two young charges. Dare she hope this was a healer? She'd run into enough of those on scouting missions for the Hasai to know that they were usually more curious than violent. Sometimes they had psychic power in their own right, though their society might not recognize it as such. Carefully she reached out with a slender tendril of thought and brushed against the old one's mind.

It seemed to her the woman started, and yellow-green eyes with slit pupils began to scan the underbrush in her direction. A quick warning hiss brought both of the children to her side, and gnarled hands the texture and color of aged tree bark grasped both of them by the shoulders. Yes, she was sensitive, that was clear to see. But trained? The woman's mind made no answering foray, despite its alertness. No; this one could hear the music of minds, perhaps, but she didn't know how to respond to it.

Well, it's now or never, Rho thought. And she stepped out into the clearing, so that the three might see her. Hands open: *I do not hold weapons.* Arms close to her side: *I do not claim your space.* Trying to make herself seem physically diminutive, at least enough to communicate her peaceful intent. It was hard when you didn't even have a clue what gestures meant what in the local kinesthetic vernacular, but some things were a safe guess on any Scattered Races world.

For a moment the woman stared at her in silence. She didn't run away, Rho noted. That was a good sign. She didn't pull out a weapon either, or make some superstitious gesture of protection or warding to drive away the Other. Downright hopeful. God knows Rho had been taken for a demon often enough in her duties as Hostilities Analyst. It was a bad way to start off, especially when you didn't have a clue where your shuttle was or why you were here in the first place.

After a time, when the woman seemed content that Rho wasn't going to bite her—or perhaps transform into something nasty—she came closer, to inspect her. Gnarled fingers touched Rho's arm, her breast, her hair. *Like-us but not-like-us,* the healer's mind hummed audibly. Rho couldn't tell if that was a good or a bad thing without delving deeper. Hopefully this wasn't one of those places where they killed aliens on sight. Or worse yet, tried to eat them for breakfast. She'd been to one of those planets. No fun at all.

At last the old woman grunted. It seemed to indicate approval to the children, for they came closer, and one of them gingerly touched Rho's torn jumpsuit with dirty fingers. Their thoughts weren't clear but from each there was a distinct murmur of awareness. That was unusual, in children so young. Was this whole race thought-sensitive, or had the old healer chosen her wards for that particular quality?

A psychic race, Rho thought. *Wouldn't that be something!*

What a weapon the Hasai would make of it. . . .

At last the woman grunted some order in an unknown tongue, and gestured for her to show her hands. She did so, and could feel the sharp scrutiny of a healer focusing upon her scrapes and cuts. The woman asked her something, but though Rho knew the sounds had to do with identification of the wounds, she couldn't make out more than that. Damn it, this was as bad as her psychic internship on Forrah had been . . . only back then she had known they would come and get her after a set number of days, whether she succeeded or not. And there she had known the rules.

There were rules here too, she realized suddenly. Not the taboos of this place, but outside rules. It was a fragment of memory, nameless, disjointed, arising from the confused darkness within her brain. Rules. They mattered. Her life might depend upon them.

Why couldn't she remember more?

For some reason the sight of Rho's scraped palms seemed to reassure the woman. Maybe demons didn't bleed. She took a rolled leaf out of a small sack at her side and offered it to Rho. Some kind of herbal paste, it looked like. The psychic grit her teeth and smoothed some of it onto her palms, hoping that local biochemistry was similar enough to her own that it wasn't going to kill her. If it had just been a question of healing the scratches she probably would have refrained just for caution's sake, but when strangers on an alien world offered you things to make you feel better, you took them and used them and worked hard to look grateful. She even rummaged around in her pocket for something to offer in return, in case that was expected, but the woman waved her efforts short

The salve stung, but did no worse.

Without further words the healer turned to lead her charges back the way they had come. Rho fell in behind, grateful for the older woman's slow pace through the underbrush. Her feet ached and she was thirsty, but she wasn't about to try to communicate either of those things. Enough now to listen, to taste the tenor of their thoughts, and to try to figure out where in the hells she was. Why in the hells she was here. And how in all the human hells she was going to get home.

You are sure you want this, Damaan-Rho?

Yes.

You can die down there, you know that. People have died doing this.

I know it.

We will not bring you back unless you succeed. Succeed or die. Those are the two choices.

I understand . . .

The village was a small one, as primitive as they came. Two dozen, maybe three dozen huts, a typical grouping for this level of tech. One glance at the crude thatched roofs and equally crude storage pottery told her she wasn't likely to find any means here of contacting her people, or even figuring out her current stellar position. So much for getting home quickly.

Painted faces greeted her. The natives seemed to have some natural coloration that provided markings about the face and neck, but human vanity had taken them beyond that. On the younger ones you could still see the natural markings, but the older folk had layered them under paint and tattoos—it was hard to say which—until you could hardly tell if they'd been mainstream humans to begin with, or some more exotic variety. Rho picked up enough surface thoughts to know that the tattoos were related to tribal status and the temporary paint to less weighty concerns, but there were too many colors and patterns for her to start classifying them in any more detail. Hopefully her life wasn't going to depend upon interpreting some subtle shade of ochre, or the sweep of a painted line through a plucked eyebrow.

At least they were similar to her in form. She didn't want to think about what this visit would be like if the natives weren't so close to the human genetic mean, or hadn't been Scattered Races stock at all. If the latter were the case she probably wouldn't have arrived walking, but netted or lanced or lashed to some primitive vehicle of confinement, an alien trophy to be studied and then killed. She'd been on enough hostile planets to know what that was like, and was grateful not to have to deal with it again. Of course, on *those* worlds there were back-up teams that would come in for you . . . not leave you stuck in the middle of nowhere, wondering how the hells you had gotten there. . . .

A few of the natives came and looked her over. Surprisingly few. Given how alien she must have looked to them, Rho was surprised more didn't show an interest in her. Granted, the differences between their people and hers were minor, but it was still enough to mark her as more than a simple visitor. Some of the men seemed interested, but as they looked her over it seemed that their concern was more sexual than xenophobic. That figured. Men who lived their lives as warriors, hunters, and explorers were drawn to the alien on a primal level, and their arousal had as much to do with marking territory and claiming the unknown as it did with any sexual characteristics.

She wondered if she was going to have to fend off rape to earn her place here She managed to keep a smile on her face throughout the inspection, but the cold look in her eyes was measured against the nature of each man's desire: enough to warn him that she would not be a willing conquest, not enough to make that thought exciting in its own right.

How did the deadheads get through stuff like this? They did, she knew that. The scouts of both Empire and Holding were entirely nonpsychic now, and had to rely upon purely external cues in all their diplomacy. She suspected more than a few of them had latent power, probably buried so deep by denial they'd never know it. Hells, it had to be. Last she'd heard, new recruits in the Empire were being given "tests" to make sure their insights were from a "verifiable" source. That was a nice fantasy.

Deadhead idiots. Their fear was so thick you could taste it. Sometimes when she got home from an assignment among them she wanted to scrub herself clean until she was raw, just to get off the smell of their emotional overload. Not their fault, of course. If you took boiling water and sealed it up inside a pot so that none of the pressure could escape, it would eventually blow open too.

Then, when the men were done, when the few curious children who had wandered by had finally gone away . . . *she* came.

Rho felt her before she saw her, a presence so distinct that it made the hairs on the back of her neck rise. She was dressed in layers of bleached cloth that Rho was willing to bet had not been cleaned for several planetary revolutions. Her face was painted with a chalky white in patterns that reflected the skull beneath, masking whatever natural markings there might have been. Her hair was long and tangled and likewise painted, with twigs and talismans woven into it. Her aura tasted of . . . death. Presence of death, knowledge of death, acceptance of death, defiance of death. The feeling was so powerful that Rho could taste it, and it sat upon her tongue like bitter chalk. Even the healer fell back when this one came, and Rho could understand why. Anyone with a tad of psychic sensitivity would want to get out of her way, and fast.

A long arm reached out, streaked with whitish lines to suggest the bones beneath, and painted fingers touched Rho. Her skin, her face, her hair: an inspection. The eyes were rimmed in black powder, and seemed to stare out at her as if from an abyss. Suddenly Rho found she was aware of just how much death there was in that place. Bodies of ancestors buried in nearby mounds. Stillborn children in tiny cairns by their mother's huts. Offerings on altars to the gods of hunting and killing, charms to bring death, stave off death, channel death. . . . It all rushed over her like a wave, too much to absorb. She staggered back from the woman, stunned by the power of the images. This wasn't like anything they'd taught her back home. Even the Hasai had never shown her mental images like that.

Her response seemed to please the woman, or at least fend off any potential hostility. She barked a few sounds at the healer, and Rho strained her sense to the utmost to pick up their meaning from the tangle of alien thoughts surrounding her.

Yes.

It-is-not

Here-with-you. Yes. Wait.

Wait for what? Rho wondered.

The dead whisper: Others have come.
The dead whisper: Soul-stealer, death drinker.
The dead whisper: Protect us. . . .

The healer brought her to a pool where the woman bathed, clearly expecting she would want to clean herself. Rho was loath to strip in front of others, lest the sight of her unpatterned body prove too alien for their comfort, but at least she could wash the grime and sweat from her face. They'd already seen that part of her.

She knelt by the edge of the pool and leaned forward, cupping her hands in preparation for splashing water upward. . . .

And froze.

What the hells. . . .

She reached out to the water as if touching the reflected image might somehow make it more real. Ripples spread out across a face that was remarkably un-alien. To the locals, that was. To Rho it was a face so unfamiliar it might have belonged to that of a stranger, and she raised her fingers to feel the strange flesh, searching for familiarity in texture, in sensation.

She bore the markings of this people now, in soft sweeps of color across her cheeks and brow. Her nostrils had the same funny twisted slits that the locals' did. Her eyes hadn't changed shape—the pupil was still round—but the color was a shade of yellow-green better suited to their world than hers. And her hair . . . that was still the same short length and the texture was unchanged, but the pale gold strands were brown now, and all the treatments she'd put on them to hold the style in place had clearly been removed.

For the first time since her arrival she was truly afraid. This wasn't the kind of fear you could rationalize away, or soothe with a few choice Disciplines. Sometimes there were things you really should be afraid of. Fear was a survival mechanism, after all.

With trembling hand she started to undo the front of her jumpsuit. She had to stand up to get the whole thing open. One of the women splashed her with water as she did so, a playful sign of acceptance. Why not? She was one of them, wasn't she?

Her body had been transformed. All of it. She could have been one of them in truth, for all that they could see. No wonder so few had shown an interest in her, when she arrived. She was a stranger, yes, but no more than that. Not some wondrous thing they should feel a need to explain. Or fear.

For the first time since her arrival she felt a cold knot of fear inside that no mental discipline could banish. A cold, serpentine terror, that twisted hard around her gut as she leaned over the pool and looked at herself. All of her. Alien her.

What's happening to me?

Memory Discipline. Forcing the images out, second by second, word by word. Digging them out of the dark hidden recesses where they cowered, dragging them out past whatever had driven them into hiding. Fragments. Only fragments.

—know the elements which are required, but there is no formula yet discovered for ideal combination or duration—

—artificial stimulation has proven unsuccessful. The psychic mind can see through appearances—

—Once it begins there is no turning back. Be sure you want this—

No more. The rest was buried too deeply. One of the Hasai might have been able to access it, but not Rho.

Shaking from the effort, drenched in a cold sweat, she stood up and looked around her. The storage hut she'd been allowed to sleep in seemed to be pressing in on her, suddenly. She climbed to her feet, wiping the sweat from her forehead, and then, with a shudder, she pushed her way past grain-filled urns of plaited rush, and exited the small hut. Outside she could feel the alien thoughts of the natives pressing in on her mind, and her head began to pound again. She started to walk. No destination in mind, just a need to get away from them all. Then started to run. Past wooden bowls filled with roots she had helped pound to paste. Past rolls of bark she had helped soften. Things you did in a primitive society to prove yourself useful, so that they were willing to feed you and give you shelter, until. . . .

What?

She ran and ran until she was far from the village. Far enough that she stopped at last, in a clearing atop a bleak rise. Overhead she could see three moons, nearly full now. Alien moons. Was someone watching her from that vantage point? She tried to reach out to them but it was too far away.

"WHY HAVE YOU SENT ME HERE!!!" she screamed. Willing the words into her mind, reaching out with them as far as she could into the darkness overhead. "WHAT DO YOU WANT!!!"

Succeed or die. Those are the two choices.

No answer.

It was an island.

Surrounded by islands. Not a mainland in sight.

Hells!

She stared at the map the healer had brought her and tried not to rage aloud. How could she explain to the woman that she'd hoped for some sign of advanced technology, or at least someplace to begin a search for it? Tropical island cultures were notorious for staying low-tech; the abundance of food one could find in an ocean combined with moderate temperatures meant that humans could thrive without worrying about how to make complex tools to hunt or farm, tame the elements, or travel great distances overland. Those things and war were the great technological motivators.

She could always hope the map was wrong, and there really were larger land masses out there. But. If the healer's people didn't know about them, she wasn't damned likely to find any way of getting there, was she?

She felt so frustrated she wanted to take the map and throw it against the far wall. Instead she took a deep breath and forced a smile to her face. "Thank you," she said. It was easy to pick up a language when you could sense the meaning behind each word. Soon enough she would be fluent. Soon enough . . . she would be able to speak like one of the natives, and work like them, and maybe even take a mate. She knew they were discussing that last factor. She knew now that was why they'd taken her in. A limited gene pool like this one was always looking for mates from the outside.

Something inside her was going to snap, soon. She knew that. Something nameless that had been building up inside her, seeded by rage and frustration and fear, that had become more than all those things. She had always prided herself on her self-control . . . but this monster, she sensed, was beyond her usual methods. This was a primal emotion that she didn't know how to contain. All she could do was build up the walls that guarded it high enough and strong enough to delay the inevitable explosion, while searching desperately for some way to get herself out of this situation.

Come, the healer told her. *It is time to meet the dead.*

She tried a few questions in her half-fluent best but none of them were answered. Rho didn't think it was because the woman was unwilling to answer her so much as . . . she didn't seem to understand the need for questions. Anyone who knew the language would know what *meeting the dead* meant. Surely. Questions were waved aside casually, as if to say *I have too much to do now, do not ask for answers any child could give you.*

Time to meet the dead.

Dozens of wind chimes tinkled in the cool evening air, weird constructs of stone and clay now raised on high poles to greet the night. She knew what the ritual chimes were called in the local tongue because she'd asked when she saw them in storage. *Voices of the Dead.* Here and there natives sat quietly, cross-legged, listening to the discordant notes, meditating. She could taste the change in their consciousness as she passed them, without even trying. As if the music gave their minds more power. Or perhaps it was the drugs she caught the scent of, aromatic smoke clinging to the skin of men and women alike. A drug to foster psychic awareness? Despite her growing unease, she couldn't ignore the raw potential of such a thing. She found herself pausing as she passed by those in contemplation, trying to memorize the scent. If there was a plant here that could affect psychic sensitivity in such a way, and if she could identify it, that might be worth this whole miserable journey.

That's assuming I ever get home.

They were gathering in the center of the village, in a circular arena beaten into the earth, packed hard by many generations of use. In the center was a pit edged with pale stones in which a thicket of ghostly white stakes had been erected. Each had been painstakingly stripped of its bark, and was carved in a manner that suggested human bones in some parts, though if you looked close enough you could see faces as well. Ancestors? Gods? Rho passed close enough to see drops of oil or resin glimmering on their surface, and the scent that came to her was the same as that which she'd been noticing on so many of the villagers. Some sacred substance, perhaps? The faces seemed to appear and disappear as you walked around them, and as moving shadows played across them . . . eerie constructs that set the stage well for the night's endeavor.

It is time to meet the dead.

The healer nudged her toward one of the long earthen banks that functioned as benches and took a seat beside her. There was an air of tension amidst those assembling that no psychic could miss, and despite her training Rho could feel their powerful emotions stirring things inside her. Like was calling to like, tension to tension. *Hasha,* she thought, *now is not the time to lose control.* But it was hard to tune out so many people under the best of circumstances, and these were not the best of circumstances.

Her breathing shaky, she reached inside herself for the barriers of Self that would protect her from Other. Distinction Discipline. The healer noticed her concentrating and said something to her, but Rho couldn't hear the words. Not now. This was too important, if the dead were truly coming. Or even if the natives simply believed they were.

With a sigh of relief she felt the Discipline take hold. The emotions of the others were more distant now, though still stronger than they should have been. Was that because of some strange drug in the air, or . . . maybe a consequence of something that had been done to her by the same people who left her here? Fear became a sudden knot in her gut as she realized that the same unknowns who had taken her memory away might have worked other changes as well. What would happen if she called upon some other Discipline to protect her, only to find that it no longer worked at all? If this one wasn't working completely—

Easy, Rho. You don't know that anything like that has happened. There's enough real reason to fear without your manufacturing new ones.

Hells! She wasn't a child, incapable of mastering the storm of emotions that puberty let loose. She was an awakened adult, a fully trained psychic, and a valued member of the Hostilities Project. She knew every Discipline in the book, and if they weren't working one hundred percent right now, well then, she would have to make up for the difference in sheer willpower. There was simply no other option.

The priestess had arrived now, along with a half-dozen acolytes dressed in similar white rags. As they moved in the moonlight a wispy, ghostlike light seemed to follow them. *Damned good showmen,* Rho mused, wondering what phosphorescent substance had been painted onto their rags to bring about the effect. The priestess could have been a ghost herself, or rather a living skeleton; the bones painted on her face and hands glowed like nacreous fire in the double moonlight. Ghastly. Compelling.

The priestess came to the center of the circle then, and stood still. So still. The stillness was like a wave that coursed out from her over the banks of spectators, devouring all sound, all motion. When she knew that all eyes were upon her, she raised her hand to the cold night sky and intoned, "I am Innana, child of the dead, kin to the dead, speaker for the dead. I am she who calls ancient souls to communion with the living, in the way of our people. I am she who hears their words."

A wave of whispers coursed through the crowd. Her name, voiced like a prayer.

"Are there any here whose souls are not clean enough to face the dead?" she demanded. "Is there anyone here who secretly bears such shame that those-who-came-before would not favor him?"

There was silence for a moment, then a woman rose to her feet. Across the circle a man did likewise. Then another. One by one more people rose, until there were a dozen standing. Some looked entranced. Some looked as though they clearly regretted what was to come next. Tension rippled through the crowd like a cold wind. Rho could taste it.

"Behold," the priestess said. Her words were half-chanted, half-sung, like the text of some ancient and venerated prayer. "Before the dead there is no dissembling, for they have passed beyond the need for flesh and lies. So make yourselves naked, you that would come before them. Make offering of your own flesh and your own lies, that you may be worthy of them."

The first woman to stand—one of those who seemed most entranced—said quietly, "I spoke ill against my neighbor, in order that a man might favor me more." In the utter silence of the night her words carried despite their softness. "I ask their forgiveness."

She sat, and another took her place. "I . . . stole a knife from another man's home." He looked across the circle and met the eyes of another; the victim of the theft? "I beg forgiveness," he whispered . . . and the man nodded. Then another did the same, standing and confessing his offenses against tribal law. Then another. Some were simple transgressions, small things that might be overlooked in the course of days. Others were more serious. One was a breach of marital customs, and the man confessing looked over the crowd to make sure his partner was standing too, before he spoke her name. Tears were in the eyes of both of them.

The priestess looked at Rho. For a moment their eyes locked, and Rho could taste the power behind that ancient gaze. *Go,* the priestess seemed to urge her. *Confess why you are here, what you have done. What you now plan. This is the time, the place. This is where forgiveness may be found.*

It took all of Rho's strength not to back her response with psychic power, searing it into the other woman's brain. *I have nothing to confess, unless you count vehement hatred for whoever left me in this godsforsaken place. If that's a sin in your book you'll just have to deal with it, I'm not apologizing.*

She saw in the priestess' eyes that she was not satisfied, but at last the woman turned away to address more cooperative sinners. Rho took the opportunity to draw in a long, shaky breath. What *was* it about that woman that so unnerved her? It was more than mere power, she knew that. Perhaps . . . confidence of power. Absolute certainty that no matter what happened, no matter who challenged her, all the dead might be summoned up in her defense. Who could make war with that?

Faith. It was a powerful emotion. Emotions like anger and lust paled beside it. Little wonder then that the ranks of the priesthood were so often filled with latent psychics . . . or sometimes even active ones. Rho had learned it was the first place you looked for psychics when you came to a new world.

When the confessions were done the priestess intoned something in a language Rho had not heard before. It took no psychic skill to know it was a ritual cleansing of some kind. When she was done, she raised her hands upward in benediction. "Now you are true." She spoke not to the sinners alone, but to the whole crowd. "Now you are worthy."

It seemed to Rho then that the night grew colder. Imagination, of course. Rho wrapped her arms around herself nervously as the natives began to chant their own invitations to the dead, whispering ancient poems and melodies under their breath. She could feel tendrils of their cold faith filling the arena, swirling like fog about the bases of the odd wooden sculptures. Those were the ancestors, of course. The knowledge seeped into her skin even as she studied them. Those were the spirits of the dead as their descendants had seen them, manifested here in this circle. Whitewashed bones and faces stretched thin by the night, ghostly apparitions that would . . . that would . . .

What?

Alien thoughts were in her head. Frightening thoughts. They came from the people sitting across from her, from the healer at her side, even from the children present. But most of all they came from the priestess. Yes, she was a borderline psychic, a powerful Aggressive, and her faith and training had turned this ritual into a Discipline of sorts that gave new boundaries to her power. Only . . . when the ritual was completed, there would be no boundaries any longer. Her vision of the world would flood the minds around her until the living brains drowned her in holy madness. It would be the ultimate religious communion—not with the spirits of the deceased but with the mind of one who stood on the border between life and death, drawing on the heat of living souls to balance out her internal madness.

Rho felt the priestess' eyes upon her then, and more than eyes. A dozen other sets of eyes—a hundred—that glimmered unseen in the darkness behind her. Eyes of the dead . . . or faces of delusion. What was the difference, in practical terms, when a Psychic Aggressive was placing the images directly into every brain? What did it matter where the disembodied voices came from, if they were real to her, if she could make them real to you?

Rho was suddenly very afraid.

The priestess walked about the circle, chanting ancient verses that Rho knew instinctively were invitations to all the ancestors of this primitive people. *Come, come to the circle, however you wish, in whatever guise. Appear in the air, rise up from the earth, take a body if you wish and swallow its soul for an hour, a day, a year. All that we have is yours. All that we are is yours.*

She could see the people around her changing, each in his own way. Some slumped down, as if their flesh had suddenly failed them; others stiffened where they sat, a look of fevered expectancy upon their faces. She saw pain, ecstasy, love, despair, hope . . . even fear, in some of the youngest. The fear would give way in time. The priestess would pound her reality into their heads until their own private universe gave way, and the dark things that coursed in the night would be given a home in their souls.

And in yours, a ghostly voice whispered.

She shivered. *No!*

Yes, the voice persisted. Did it come from outside her mind, or from within? *It is our way. If you mean to join our people, then you must embrace our dead.* When she did not answer it pressed on, *Have not your own dead abandoned you? Are you not here alone? Are you not afraid? Submit to them, become their conduit, and they will protect you.*

She couldn't just run. It would mean something to these people if she did, something very bad. Rejection of their dead? They would hunt her down and they would take her life and then they would curse her soul so it was bound to the earth and could never rise again—

Priestess. Her eyes. Thoughts like arrows spearing into her brain, blood seeping images ghostly cold apparitions—

GET OUT OF MY HEAD!

The priestess smiled. It was a cold expression that had nothing to do with approval and everything to do with anticipation. *See,* her eyes seemed to say, *this one is as I told you; watch her now and her true nature will become apparent.*

Rho found herself shivering violently. This was bad, very bad. How in all the human hells was she going to get herself out of this scene without offending someone's faith?

It seemed to her then there was a stirring in the air. Bits of fog congealing in the darkness near the ancestor carvings. Was it likely that the priestess could control such things, or more likely that her madness was so powerfully defined she could make everyone in this circle share it? A soft moan came from across the circle, and Rho saw one of the younger women fall to her knees, her eyes rolled upward until only the whites of her eyes were visible. Possessed . . . but by the spirits of dead, or some mental phantom loosed within her by the priestess' own power?

Wisps of fog began circling the ancestor carvings, becoming more and more defined as they did so. As much as Rho tried to shut them out, still the ghostly images remained. Was it possible they were really there? Or perhaps they were a manifestation of some other life-form that inhabited this planet, whose exudations had been interpreted as human souls? It seemed to her that there were faces hidden in some of the ghostly tendrils, and as much as she tried to shut them out, they seemed to be leering at her. *Alien,* came the whispers. Inside her head, outside her head, everywhere. *Lost one. How does your soul taste, Outsider? Soon we will know. . . .*

The priestess began to chant. It was not her own voice that she used this time, but a deeper and more compelling sound that came from the same cavity. Rho had seen enough religious rites in her life to recognize the signs of possession. Which dead spirit was the woman supposedly channeling that would choose the body of a priestess to attend these rites? There was too much madness there, too much dark religious ecstasy to wade through in search of facts. The priestess' surface thoughts were so entangled with images of death and resurrection there was no making sense of them.

And then—

And then—

The *power* seemed to arise from the earth itself, from the circle of spectators, from the very air they breathed. Rho could feel it well up before her, around her, whirling raw power that centered upon the circle of carvings and the woman who stood beside them. Power born of dozens of living minds crying out in unity, along with the thousands of dead spirits they believed to be listening. It was searing mental power, raw psychic yearning stripped of every civilized trapping, almost unbearable to contain. Rho could feel her senses shutting down in self-defense, the automatic triggers of Distinction Discipline coming into play for her protection. She fought them. Hard. Fought to remain aware of what was happening. Because even as the power flowed through her with ice-hot tendrils, even as she knew that every mind in that circle was being woven into a whole that was vast, untamed, terrifying, she knew that such power could be *used*. And she had need of it. Far more than these people did.

There was no time to wonder if it was the right thing to do. She was desperate, and this . . . this *power* . . . offered her the first real hope she'd had since being stranded here. So into the psychic maelstrom she inserted her own thoughts, feeling them swept away like leaves in a hurricane. No one seemed to notice. She tried again, fighting to keep her balance amidst the psychic winds, imprinting them with her purpose. It seemed she could actually *hear* the maelstrom now, a roaring in her head that drowned out all natural sound. No more wind chimes. No more chanting. Only her and the power, her and this raw force which could be shaped, directed, *used* . . .

Out, out, into the depths of space. She could feel the power of these people bolstering her own sensitivity, giving her the strength she needed to reach out beyond her natural limitations. Out past the heat of the sun, past the moons, past asteroids and planets and comets and blackness, reaching out screaming in need and fear and desperate hope I AM HERE I AM STRANDED COME SEE ME COME HELP ME I NEED YOU—

—and she was swatted back to earth like an insect smacked by a vast hand. Head reeling, she tried desperately to focus. The priestess was staring over her now, her eyes rimmed in red, and the thoughts from her brain were so focused and accusatory they hit Rho like a hammer.

You are alien. You are enemy. You come into our circle and call to your own dead, so that they can take what is ours. There was a strange satisfaction in the thought, as if the priestess had known all along this was how it would be. *Now we will cleanse this place.*

Rho ran. Stumbling over the first earthen bench, then vaulting the ones behind it. She seemed to move fast enough that she took the others by surprise, or maybe they were so entranced by the rites that it would take them a few seconds to respond. Either was good enough. She broke through their ranks and was at the outer edge of the circle by the time she heard people stirring behind her. By the time the priestess commanded them to follow her she had broken through the first line of trees and was chest deep in the tropical vegetation.

Where to go? There was no easy passage here except along the hunting paths that the villagers used, and it would be too easy for them to follow her there. In the darkness of forest shadows she fought her way blindly, ripping at the vines that threatened to strangle her, cursing the thorns that raked at her legs. Behind her she could hear them coming, oh, so many, she could hear them cutting at the foliage with their long curved knives, could taste their intentions along with the sweat on her lips—*knife cutting through the invader red blood on the night-soaked earth*—oh gods, what had she done, what had she done? It was the madness inside her, the screaming need to do *something*, and now look where it had led her. *Please,* she begged, *whoever left me here, if you are listening, please, let the game be over. Whatever you wanted, whyever you have done this to me, let this be enough!*

No answer.

The vines that entangled her feet gave way then, and from overhead a glimmer of moonlight broke through the canopy. A path. A hunting path. She followed it gratefully, hoping it would take her pursuers long minutes to find it. Minutes in which she might get some distance on them. So that she could get—

Where?

She stumbled as she ran, and cursed the rocks that tripped her. Where was there to go? What place would give her refuge, on this island they knew so well? Behind her she could hear shouts as they came upon the path she had taken. Voices drew rapidly closer, even as she stumbled along the narrow road. There was nowhere to go, nowhere to hide, not on this soft earth which captured her tracks so clearly that even the filtered moonlight showed them clearly. If she veered from the path they would know it, if she dove for the cover of brush they would know where to look, if she tried to find—

Something hard smashed into the back of her head. She stumbled for a moment, trying with reeling senses to stay on her feet, to keep moving. Someone had struck her. Were they that close? Or were there others who knew the way of this path, who had cut her off already?

She tried to dive for cover in the brush, but it was too late. Another impact from behind sent her reeling, and another. Then another from in front of her; they must have circled around and cut her off. She drew up her arms instinctively to protect her face, and they were hit almost immediately.

I WILL NOT DIE HERE!

A barrage of projectiles brought her to her knees; sticky warm blood began to seep out of the many wounds. Stones. They were stoning her. Of all the primitive, messy deaths to have to suffer! She struggled to get to her feet again but the barrage was too much for her: too much impact, too much pain. She swayed on her knees for a moment, knowing that once she fell the battle was lost. And then she fell. Face first into the mossy earth, as missile after missile struck at her flesh.

And then . . . and then. . . .

For a moment there was nothing. Through the ringing in her ears she could hear the sudden silence. Only one set of footsteps moving now, calm and measured. She knew who it was without looking . . . but she looked anyway, blinking the streams of blood from her eyes in order to see.

The priestess.

Her garments glowed like ghostly fragments in the darkness. Her face was a skull, all humanity extracted from it, only illusion remaining. Her mind . . . that was madness. Pure madness, pounding at Rho like the rocks had pounded at her. She intoned something in a foreign tongue, and Rho could catch the thoughts behind it. *Now the invader falls. Now her dead fall with her. Now, behold, I will bind her to the earth, so that death is a prison to her, and she may never rise again to defile our rituals—*

Knife. Silver in moonlight. Descending—

Rho reached out. It was not a move that was rational, or even one she knew she was making. It was as much a move of pure animal instinct as the dying struggles of a herdbeast, striving to tear one last bit of flesh out of the predator that had brought it down. But Rho had no teeth or claws with which to strike . . . only her mind.

The touch of the priestess' soul was like ice. Rho struggled to get inside it, to find the place were actions were initiated, the core of the reasoning soul. But she was a Receptive, not an Aggressive, and her mind was unused to such battles. Slowly the skull-woman raised her arm, moonlight glinting on the edge of her knife as her thoughts pounded *deathdeathdeath*. It seemed to Rho she moved almost in slow motion, that she had a small eternity to pit her dying strength against the icy resoluteness of the other woman's mind. Yet even so, even though it seemed to take minutes instead of seconds, the knife did descend. Rho couldn't hold it. That wasn't the kind of power she knew how to handle; it went against all her natural instincts. There were psychics who knew how to invade the mind of another and take control of it, and she wasn't one of them. Bloody tears filled her eyes, hazing everything in a mist of crimson as the gleaming blade descended. She couldn't do it. She didn't have the power. Steel sang in the moonlight, hymns of the dead accompanying it in its arc toward her flesh. Music from the mind of a priestess she could observe, but not invade. Whispers of spirits dead and gone to ease the way of steel into flesh, into blood—

I WILL NOT DIE!!!

The ice gave. Cracked. She surged forward with all her strength, even as the cold of the steel blade prickled the hairs on the back of her neck. *I will not die, damn you!* Upward and inward she thrust, into a soul whose substance was utterly without heat, mouldering shadows of thought sticky about her, like some chill web. *You will not do this to me!* Grasping the mind that grasped the hand that grasped the blade, twisting it, turning . . . steel whispered hungrily by her neck and bit into the ground. The dead screamed out in frustration. She could hear them now, echoing in the vast dark holds of the priestess' mind. Voices that were never silent, never satisfied. She thrust past them and could feel the woman fighting her now, pitting the power of her faith against Rho's innate psychic abilities. But no one had trained Rho to do this, not ever. Invading the mind of another, seeking out the place where commands were given, squeezing it until it gave . . . instinct drove Rho, hot bloody instinct, and she could taste the woman's essence boil at last, ice giving way to the fire of sheer desperation.

She stood. They stood. *It* stood, a composite life that was neither one nor the other, an envelope of flesh wrapped around silent screaming. *Do it!* Rho shouted to the priestess, and she forced her mind down the channels of muscular control, forcing the woman to stand. Forced herself into the vocal cords and the fleshy parts of the mouth, shaping them into words. Forced herself into the lungs, to send air through those passages.

"It is done," the priestess said. Generations of the dead howled in protest, but they had no power to dislodge Rho from the flesh she now posessed. She could see her own body lying still, its face dripping blood, as she forced the priestess to turn back the way she had come. Behind her were a dozen or more people—it was hard to see numbers in the forest shadows—still holding chunks of rock in case the fearsome stranger should move again. *Dead,* Rho crooned into the other woman's brain. *She is dead, dead, dead. . . .* She had to make her believe. Else this all was wasted. The minute the priestess was free of Rho's control she would just come after her again. And where was there to hide, on this small island? *You slit her throat,* Rho told her. *Remember? You saw that she no longer breathes. The stranger is dead. You know this for a fact* Could you take control of memories, as well as flesh? A day ago she would have said that either was impossible. But now . . .

She forced the possessed body to take a deep breath. Waited while the substance of her message was absorbed into the woman's brain. Then she made her speak again. "She is dead. In the care of our ancestors. They will see that she never rises to trouble our people." A brief whisper of protest surfaced in the back of the priestess's mind, was quickly strangled into silence. Rho was in control now, and she had no intention of letting loose her mental grip until the woman believed in her death. However in the Hells of the Scattered Races you did something like that.

Deep into the woman's mind she reached, past all the bleeding safeguards, into the core of her memory. The touch of her thoughts was cold, unclean, like a thing long dead and rotting. But she needed her memories to make this right. She needed the ritual that the dead were even now demanding, the words that would bind a dead soul to the earth, so that it could never roam free again.

And then she found it, and she lanced into the cold brain with her thoughts and she felt the words coming. Alien words, but she knew them now. As did all those who followed.

What we have killed in sacrifice, let no god raise. What we have bound to earth, let no prayer resurrect. What we have condemned to darkness, let no man bring into the light. . . .

She could feel the power of the incantation wrap around her like a shroud, chill and black and stifling. But its power was a meager thing, compared to some of what she had faced in the past, and it had no power to harm her. She wasn't dead, after all. And the words were not coming from a priestess of the dead, but from a psychic who had invaded her flesh and taken control, and forced out sounds without any power behind them.

Thank Hasha, she had done it.

She had no idea how.

She dared to shut her eyes for a moment, blinking out some of the blood that had trickled into them. The part of her that was inside the priestess saw the motion, and it should have registered in the woman's brain as a sign of life. But it did not. Rho was dead, the other woman knew that for a fact. The illusions cast by night's shifting shadows would not make her believe otherwise.

Satisfied at last, and utterly exhausted, Rho withdrew. Sending out one last command as she exited, words that left the priestess' lips even as the psychic's soul withdrew to its own flesh.

"Leave her here. Let the beasts have her flesh. It is the will of our dead."

And they left. Thank Hasha! They left. A ringing filled her ears as they moved away. She tried to raise her head but couldn't. Something sticky beneath her cheek. How much blood had she lost? She needed to move. *Command your own flesh, as you commanded hers.* Body not obeying. Hot warm sticky in so many places. How much blood? No strength left. *Get up, get up now or you may never do so again.* Tasting it in her mouth. Bad. Bad. Senses going, ocean roar in ears turning to whistling turning to light—

I will not die here!

Darkness.

Seeing. Shards of memory, like broken glass, edges grinding. Pain.

~GET OUT OF MY HEAD!

~Shh, shh, it is over, Shaka-Rho, relax now, let us do our work.

~SONS OF BRAXI YOU LEFT ME THERE YOU LEFT ME THERE I WILL KILL YOU—

~Normal, all normal. Rebirth is painful, Shaka-Rho. Now you must rest.

~NOOOOOOOOOOOOO

Blinking. It worked. Close your eyes, and there was darkness. Open them, and there were . . . things. Faces.

No foliage. No aliens. No blood.

Thank the Lyu.

"Are you all right?"

She blinked again, savoring the minute control that it gave her. A face swam into focus above her. Familiar. Hasai. "Thera?"

The face bobbed up and down. It was attached to a head now, beneath which a body slowly came into focus. Still no plants or insects. This was good.

"I need you to do some tests now. Standard response inventory. If you can."

Rho drew in a deep breath and nodded. Her head was pounding, but it was the pain of trials come and gone. Other faces were coming into focus now. All Hasai. Shards of memory began to surface, things that had happened the last time she had seen those faces—

"Focus, Rho. Focus."

She drew in a deep breath and did as asked. Moving her muscles one by one, then group by group, to test the responsiveness of each. It was hard, and her head hurt, but in the end each one did what it was supposed to do. Mind and body were well connected.

"Very good." Thera smiled. She was an older woman; you could see it in her eyes, the accumulated wisdom and patience of more than a century's life. "Now I will return your memories to you. Shut your eyes and try to relax. This will not hurt, but it will be . . . disconcerting."

She tried to obey, but a stray thought erupted: *You know what happened the last time they did this.* Bits of memory, almost within grasp. . . .

"No, Rho. Do not fight. We will give it all back to you now; you must trust us to do it."

She sighed heavily, and tried to relax. It was hard, when so much information was missing. But she trusted the Hasai. She trusted Thera.

~All right, she thought to them. *~Do your job.*

—and memories came crashing back into her like a tidal wave, slamming into her mind with a force that left her gasping—Damned Braxin scout dirty stinking muscles like steel LEAVE ME ALONE who thought they'd in this part of the galaxy NOOOOO invasion of body and mind damned Braxin arrogance

pounding into her WILL NOT LET THIS HAPPEN tears tears tears WILL NOT BE HELPLESS no defenses against sheer physical might WILL NEVER BE HELPLESS AGAIN—

When it was all gone, when the tsunami of remembered fear and shame had washed over her, she lay gasping upon the bed, unable to speak or even think aloud. Oh, Hasha. What he had done to her. What she had done to herself, in order to see that such things could never happen again.

"Rho?"

She steadied herself with a deep breath.—*It's all right. I'm all right.*

~You remember what happened?

She shut her eyes. A tear trickled out from one lid, though whether from pain or fear or hate or just exhaustion, she could not have said. *~Yes. I asked you to make me Shaka. I asked you to help me find the power that was in me . . . or let me die, if I couldn't have it.*

~And?

Her body felt strangely sore, as if the Braxin scout who found her on Xylas had just finished using her. She banished the memories with effort, knowing they would surface again in her dreams. *~I am . . . Shaka?*

The wordless affirmation bathed her brain in warmth. *~Yes. Shaka. One of the few. . . . I'm sorry there was no other way to awaken the power in you. Desperation, sustained despair, fear of assault, all these things are components of awakening. But in the end we don't really understand enough to of the process to control it artificially. We have to rely upon catalyst cultures, such as the one you visited, to trigger the proper sequence of emotions. For some it is enough, and they find the power within themselves. For others. . . .*

The mental voice trailed off, a whisper of mourning in its wake.

~They are real, then? The natives?

~Oh yes. Quite real. We've used this planet often; it has a number of host cultures that suit our purpose. Their legends are such that we can use them repeatedly, and each time they will interpret the experience in such a way as to remain a useful tool. Very rare, that. Usually we have to send down operatives to remove portions of memory in key individuals, in order to use the same group of people again.

~The legends . . . are of your making.

~(Gently) Of course. (Pause.) We have many such worlds. (Pause.) Did you think that your people were the only ones to alter local cultures, in service to the Lyu? The Hasai have many such . . . laboratories.

It was all too much to take in. For a moment Rho just lay still, feeling the veil lift slowly, painfully, from so many memories. Terror, despair, rage . . . enough emotion, it seemed, to awaken a power in her which few had mastered. The ability to move into the body of another and command it. To break a human mind with simple thought. Powers coveted and feared by the people who served the Lyu, which few ever dared to court. She knew in that moment that it was the pain inside her which had made this awakening possible. That all the desire for power in the galaxy would not have opened her mind to such things, had pain not already carved a path in that direction.

Now she was a weapon of the Lyu that few could equal. Now she was ready to fight the War in truth.

~*Shaka-Rho?*

The title felt strange. Tasted strange. The colors of it had not yet mixed with her own.

~*Yes?*

~*(Hesitation) There is another matter of concern. . . .*

She sighed deeply. Too much, too much. Couldn't some of this wait?

She must have broadcast the thought unconsciously, for a whispering inner voice responded: ~*It cannot wait.*

~*Very well. What is it, Thera?*

The woman hesitated, then spoke. Only spoke. It was rare for the Hasai to use words like that, devoid of all psychic trappings. "I am sorry," she said softy, "We should have foreseen this. We didn't know it would happen while you were being Tested. It would have been against protocol to interrupt."

Rho looked at the older woman. And sat up in the bed, that she might meet her eyes on their own level. Nothing in them but human gaze. Nothing behind them that any outsider would be allowed to see.

"Thera?" She could feel her own eyes narrow. A tendril of thought began to reach out to the Hasai, to pick up her surface thoughts. Instinct. It was blocked. "What is it?"

The Hasai put a hand over hers. The touch was strangely sterile; not a conduit for emotions, but a substitute for them.

"Your sister," she said quietly. "She has left the Empire. She is looking for you."

A leader of men has two choices, and only two. He can bear himself with flawless strength every waking moment, so that no man ever has the opportunity to see weakness in him . . . or he can divorce himself from the company of common men entirely, so that others know only rumors of his strength, and cannot gain enough information to threaten him with less obliging judgement.

—Zatar the Magnificent

NINE

THE DELEGATION OF Kaim'eri left the H'karet as soon as their business was concluded. Of course. No one ever stayed in the Pri'tiera's domain a moment longer than they had to. The only exceptions were his staff, of course, who were not permitted to leave.

The Pri'tiera watched them leave from the guest dock, each one in his own little transport. Afraid of sharing the same air, no doubt. He could still taste their paranoia on his tongue.

It was always a bad moment, when they left.

For a brief moment emotion threatened to well up inside him. What was it today, hatred or fear or simply envy? Probably the last. He didn't deal well with seeing men of his own kind, with being reminded that he could never taste the freedom even the lowliest Braxin took for granted.

You could, you know. Walk among them. Your father did, occasionally. His father did often.

Too afraid, too afraid. All his world was fear, built on fear, maintained by fear, devouring fear for energy. A few brave Kaim'eri had once told his father that there were whispers in the Citadel of strange powers possessed by his family, and that a few had even dared to voice suspicions as to what those powers might be. His father never told him what he'd done about that. He didn't know if the Pri'tiera had hunted the men down openly, arranged their deaths more quietly, or set loose so many rumors of his own that theirs were lost in a tempest of speculation. Any of those actions would have been within the purview of a Pri'tiera, and no one would have questioned their use. But they didn't talk much in those days, he and his father. The family curse hadn't claimed his soul yet, and he was too busy sowing his seed on the planet's surface to sit still for lessons.

They'd always assumed they had time. Even with the notoriously shortened life span of the Priti'era's line, there was no reason to assume they wouldn't have their fair share. The Plague wasn't due for decades. The diseases of the soul that typically felled those of his line rarely struck before midlife. The Pri'tiera was still in his first century, robust and strong, and there was no reason to think that time would be denied them.

Then there was the shuttle malfunction. And the safeguards weren't enough. And the most powerful man in the Holding was suddenly a scattering of sparks in Braxi's night sky, that soared down to the earth like the expiration of fireworks.

He wondered if the Kaim'eri knew how young he really was. He wondered if it would make a difference if they did. Certainly he'd aged a century in that day, when his father had died. Fencing for power with men he'd only known from stories before that. Struggling to hold onto a throne that was so new, compared to the length of Braxin history, that the metaphorical paint on its surface was barely dry. Having to convince dozens of hostile Kaim'eri that he was capable of ruling them, without ever being able to argue the point . . . because once you were reduced to the point of arguing, you had already ceded the battle.

And yet. Here he was. Was it because they respected him now, or because they had learned to fear him? Or was it because they feared the power his family had, that supernatural aura which exceeded even the legendary Braxaná presence?

He could see it in their eyes today, while they'd talked. *You are not like us.*

If only they knew.

With a sigh he walked through the public portion of the H'karet. He knew enough of its history to be able to pick out the parts that various Pri'tieri had added to it. There were only four, after all. Zatar the Magnificent had lived a full lifetime, but the rest had all fallen short. There was never a specific disease to blame, or a condition that scientists could attempt to control or cure. The cause was a mystery to outsiders, which they no doubt ascribed to the ubiquitous Braxaná demon, inbreeding. The price of power.

He knew what it really was. His father had, too. Knew it like a primitive gear, knew the mortality of the motor that contained it, feeling metal surfaces wear down over the years, knowing there would come a day when a bit of slippage *here* and *there* would add up to a skipped beat, and then to two . . . and then to nonfunction. It wasn't happening to him yet, but he had watched it happen to his father. And he knew the day that the power had begun to unfold in him just what had caused it, and knew that it would claim him too, in time.

He found that his footsteps had taken him to one of the observatory chambers. Such places had to substitute for the real thing when you no longer trusted yourself to walk freely among the common folk. For a moment he balled his hands into fists, feeling a wave of frustration well up inside him; then it settled back down into the black recesses of his soul where such emotions normally simmered. Deep within the shadows of *self* where no one else could ever see.

It had taken him years to learn to control the curse. Frightening years. The family rings in his father's library had said that was the usual way of it, that it rode the mad tides of puberty when it first appeared. Until that day, he'd hoped he might be normal. Even a dominant trait skipped a child now and then. Pri'tiera Semir had sired three children, of whom only one was affected. His own older brother had been perfectly normal . . . though the Pri'tiera suspected he would been happy to trade that normalcy for the kind of power the curse brought.

He didn't know exactly what the curse was about in those days—no unaffected child would ever know the whole truth—but he knew enough to hope that it wouldn't get him.

Futile hope.

Through the observatory window he could see Braxi, and beyond it the tiny glimmer of Aldous rising. If he quieted his soul, if he reached outward with all his capacity, sometimes he imagined he could actually feel the people on those worlds. As if they were inside his head, whispering their little hopes and despairs and unfulfilled dreams just too softly for him to make out the words. Sometimes he thought that if he closed his eyes and just listened to the voices they would carry him away, and he would forget who and what he was and just become one of the whispers.

He never did, of course. Not while he was awake. Sleeping . . . that was another matter. The power he so carefully disciplined in his waking hours was uncontrolled while he slept. Most of the dreams he barely remembered, save for fleeting snatches that whirled through his brain as he awoke, sweat-drenched and shaking. Fragments sometimes remained, terrifying. Bits and pieces of alien lives melded to his own. Thoughts and sensations he couldn't hope to understand, pouring into his brain like a flood tide, drowning out the Braxaná normalcy. Sometimes when he first awakened he had to lie there in the darkness and remind himself who he was, over and over, until his identity took root again. Sometimes he lay in the dark and could not remember who he was. Those nights were the most frightening of all.

That too, was part of the curse.

There was a time when he could have sent agents to Azea to kidnap someone to help him. A minor psychic, perhaps, who knew all the appropriate Disciplines but lacked the power to be a threat to him. Or maybe a scientist from the mysterious psychic community, who knew their practices well enough to provide him with answers. Two centuries ago he could have done that. Not now. Now the psychics had fled the Empire, and if there were scientists who knew their ways they didn't advertise their existence. The madness of the psychics had made them unpopular.

The Pri'tiera stands alone, his father had taught him.

It was rumored that the fugitive psychics had gathered somewhere in unclaimed space, beyond the reach of Braxin and Azean law. What they were doing out there, or what they intended, no man knew. What kind of society did you have when nearly all its members knew they would go mad in time, that the seed of power they harbored would eventually turn upon itself and devour all rational thought? He remembered stories he had heard in his childhood, of what the psychics had done in the Empire when they were still living there. Terrible stories. Only the might of Llornu had kept the madness in check, and when Llornu was gone . . . no place would have them now.

That was why the Pri'tieri died young, his father had told him. Because some men would rather die than be reduced to madness.

He ordered the force field to give him a reflective surface and gazed at the image of himself which it provided. Purebred Braxaná—ten times, a hundred times, a thousand times over. The purity was a weakness, he knew that. If the small Braxaná gene pool was so in need of fresh blood that they were mating with outsiders, then the even smaller gene pool of the Pri'tiera's line had blessed well better join the game. But where did you look for someone with the requisite traits who could also deal with the unique intimacy that the curse engendered? The only ones thus far who had proven capable of that were women so weak in spirit that being invaded by his mind was merely another facet of their subservience. Good for pleasure perhaps, but not what you looked for to breed a possible Pri'tiera.

He'd thought the little Kesserit traitor had potential. If not for politics he might have tried her out himself. But he didn't think a soul with that many divided loyalties could survive the experience of being laid bare before her master.

Do you know what you are doing, my little one? Or are you swimming in waters too deep for any outsider to fathom?

She was an interesting one. Playing her ex-consort like a puppet across the length of the Holding, while seemingly unaware that the very contacts she used to do it were playing her as well. A true Braxaná would have understood that. A true Braxaná knew that there was no word spoken, no action taken, that did not serve some greater political purpose. Did she think that all she was doing was setting up her Kesserit puppet to fetch some genetic material the Pri'tiera wanted, to win the favor of his line? That was no more than the glove of the matter, its outer skin.

She said that she knew her princeling well, and if the right hints were set before him she could guess at the conclusions he would draw. Yes, but what would he do then? Retrieve a packet of DNA for the Pri'tiera, hoping for a favorable end to his Wilding? Or would he do what a true Braxaná would do and seek a living descendant of the crucial bloodline? Would he bring *her* back to the Mistress Planet? Would he give her over for breeding?

The Kaim'eri would have told him that it made little difference. They had long since passed the point when they would turn up their noses at a viable bloodline just because it was delivered in a bottle. The shadow of racial extinction was a harsh teacher.

But. To him! A woman of *that* lineage, stolen from among the psychics. She would be most likely be psychic herself, yes? And trained. She would know the ways of the curse, and would know how to discipline it. The value of such a creature to him was a thousand times greater even than Harkur's blood. He would have sent men after such a prize long ago if not for the questions they would ask. Now there was Tathas, who was so wrapped up in his own personal melodrama that he wouldn't think to ask those questions. Tathas, who probably would die en route and fail utterly at his task . . . but if he didn't . . . if he brought home such a woman . . .

He gazed up at the portraits of his predecessors, which flanked the entrance to the Pri'tiera's chambers.

Then. Things will change. You will see.

You ask me, how is it I can say that all psychics are strong?

I answer . . . because those that are not strong do not survive their Awakening.

—Anzha lyu Mitethe

TEN

*R*AGE. *ALL ABOUT her. Rage in the air so thick she can choke on it. Rage like fire in her heart, searing the blood that shoots through her veins. Rage clashing and reverberating throughout the house, until the screeching discordancy is near to deafening her.*

One chance. That's all she'll give him. One last chance.

She waits at the door with patience. Of course. Always patience, that's her hallmark. He's used to her being calm, always calm . . . no matter what he does. No matter what her rage screams inside for her to do. This time the calm is false, a mask meant to hide other things, but she doubts he will notice that. Or care.

The portal finally fades, triggered from within.

He looks up from a holo he's been playing with, some ridiculous mock-military game that gets more attention than his family these days. Gritting her teeth, she waits to see how he will greet her. One last chance, she tells herself. The rage is hot inside her, battering at the gates of her spirit, but she wields the words like a mantra, fighting to keep it controlled. One final chance.

His eyes narrow, his ear tips flaring in an expression she knows too well. He stands, his expression dark, and the rage in his voice stokes the fire in her soul to even greater heights.

"Where in the human hells have you been?" he demands.

"Out," she says curtly. Giving no ground.

The rage is building in him, she can feel it. Fire calling to fire, stoking her own hidden furnace.

"I don't like not knowing where you are."

She shrugs. The motion feels surreal, as if her body isn't really her own. A stranger talking to her mate. A stranger who will be struck by him. She starts to walk past him, toward the bedroom. He rounds the couch quickly and gets in her way.

Just touch me, she thinks. Touch me now, go ahead, I am ready for you—

"Not good enough," he growls.

She shrugs again, her heart pounding. The secret which is hidden up her left sleeve is hot, sharp, ready to explode into motion.

"Did you hear me?" He grabs her by the arm, pressing hard enough to leave bruises. "I said, not good enough—"

And the hand which belongs to somebody else moves forward, slow motion like in an entertainment holo, so that she can savor every moment. Left arm moving forward, spilling the knife out of her sleeve. Right arm moving forward, catching it, turning it, twisting it upward oh so slowly, painfully slowly. Rage like a bonfire devouring her flesh as she thrusts the knife into him, under the rib cage, tearing upward toward the heart. She can feel the tissue parting, hear the muscle screaming in protest as it is ripped asunder. Somewhere in the distance he yells, but she's not listening any more. The music of his death is so much more meaningful, red droplets pattering percussion on her skin as the rage plays its tune upon his heart—

Zara sat up in her bed, trembling. For a moment the room seemed to swim around her and it was hard to bring it into focus. She drew a few deep breaths and fixed her eyes on one piece of furniture, trying to make it stand still. After a few moments, it did. The rest of the room eventually stopped moving as well, though the edges of it still shimmered in time to the pounding of her heart.

By all the gods of humanity, what's happening to me?

Her hand still shook from the force of twisting the knife blade into a man's flesh; the sweet smell of human blood was thick in her nostrils. If she shut her eyes the fires of that terrible hatred might come roaring to life again inside her . . . and so she kept her eyes open, and turned on the light, and sat upright in bed, fearing the very thought of sleep.

Zara was used to bad dreams. When your job required that you take center stage in major cultural conflicts, and sometimes you were the only hope that alien entities had for peace and prosperity, bad dreams were normal. It was the price of success, a teacher had once told her. He'd had some convoluted theory about how the nightmares were a manifestation of the secret inner guilt all Mediators bore for having the kind of insight which could lay bare the secrets of their clients. Zara thought it was just stress. Stress, and the utterly reasonable fear that a single wrong word might prove a catalyst of the wrong sort, and trigger a cascade of mistakes that would end in some horrible disaster.

It even said it in her school files: *All the great Mediators have night-mares.*

But the dreams she'd had back then, in the comfortable regularity of her former life, were as different from her current dreams as fire and ice. Back then she had dreamed about the minutiae of her job gone horribly wrong. Failure to interpret an alien language properly, leading to disaster. Failure to anticipate a burst of hostility, leading to violence. The simple burden of having a job with so little margin for error, upon which so many people depended, and then failing to do it properly. Textbook fears. Intellectual terrors.

Now . . . now the dreams were different. Darker. Not about her own life, any more, but bits and pieces of alien experience. As if in her sleep she became someone else, a creature of alien motivation and passionate, terrifying emotions. Once or twice, when she awakened, she wasn't even sure who she was anymore. Just for a moment. But those moments terrified her.

Was she going insane? Was this what insanity felt like? She didn't know. There was no one to turn to and ask. She'd started to call her mother once, but had stopped before the augmented connection could be established. What was she going to say to her? What could her mother possibly say that would help? She hadn't even had the courage to tell her own daughter her history; what was there to indicate she'd be any more communicative now, if told that her daughter was slowly going mad?

She had the Kevesi sequence in her genes. That was a psychic thing. Didn't the psychics normally go insane, as they got older? What if she'd inherited that tendency, and the accident had somehow triggered it, so that it was finally expressing? How much time did she have left, if that was the case?

Her sister would know. Her sister had been kidnapped by the psychics, had probably lived with them for years now. She'd know the rules.

But how to find her?

It's a large galaxy, she thought as she wended her way from planet to planet, from station to station. Always heading outward, away from civilization's core, into the unknown reaches where it was said the psychics were hidden. *And I don't even know where to start.*

One thing was certain. She would not find the answer in the Star Empire, or in any space that Azea controlled. And so . . . beyond the borders she went, past the point where Azean law held sway, into the

political maelstrom that lay beyond. Hoping against hope that there
would be a sign of her sister somewhere out there, or of the people
who had abducted her. Praying she did not go insane before finding it.

Kevesi Sequence, the library file said. *Among humans, a series of codons believed to be linked to the development of psychic sensitivity. While the Kevesi Sequence has proven a useful predictor of psychic potential in most Scattered
Races, by itself it does not guarantee the actual expression of such power. As of
yet the genetic and environmental factors which trigger the so-called Awakening are not fully understood. Exploration of this question was the primary mission of Llornu's Institute for the Acceleration of Human Psychic Evolution,
whose charter set forth the primary goal of isolating the necessary codes and
then introducing them into the Azean race as a whole. With the destruction of
the Institute's homeworld the project was abandoned, and it is believed that
most of the original research was lost. The Kevesi Sequence is known to be
linked to several genes which control the chemical development of the brain, for
which reason genetic alteration of the Sequence is considered a high-risk procedure and is not advised for either inwomb or early-life genetic manipulation.
No direct link to mental instability has been proven; however, given the known
tie between psychic sensitivity and insanity there are many scientists who believe that such a link exists, and that only the lack of opportunity for experimentation since the fall of Llornu has kept it from being discovered to date. See
also: Imperial Guidelines for Prenatal/Postnatal Genetic Manipulation.*

Emotions. Crashing into her like waves on an ocean shore, dragging
her out into an undertow of hunger and pain. *Fear/running/shame. Lone-
liness/lust/despair. Loss/anger/searching/failure.* Emotions that didn't seem
to have anything to do with her current experience . . . as if the flood-
gates within her mind had just been ripped open, and random emotions were pouring through. No longer contained within dreams, but
slipping into her waking world. First a word, then a thought . . . then a
tidal wave washing over her. *Terror/loss/screaming/screaming/screaming!*
Emotions cresting in her brain and then withdrawing for a time, but
only long enough for the next wave to take shape. Faster and faster,
they came now. More of them each day, until she barely had time to
settle her mind between them. No place, no time was safe.

What if there was a medical problem at the root of all of it? Chemical imbalances could skew the mind, as could various diseases and deformities. Hasha alone knew what the accident might have done to her; some microscopic brain damage that had gone undiscovered, perhaps, but which now was blossoming into a major threat to her sanity. But she was afraid to get a medscan to find out. Any physician she consulted would surely discover the government block on her records, and then . . . who could say what would come of that, here in independent space? *Every man for himself*—wasn't that the credo of the so-called Outlands? What if her physician decided the information was worth something to someone, more than she could pay him?

The paranoia was real, at least. Her own emotions. A life raft of familiarity to cling to, in a vast ocean where all else was unknown.

She could no longer read people as she used to. All the gestures and expressions and fine shadings of vocal tone that had once been so clear to her were drowned in that alien ocean, as was her ability to focus on . . . well, anything. It was getting hard to think clearly at all, much less focus upon anyone else. Everything she had been in her life was gone, every skill she had taken for granted was lost to her, drowned out in that relentless tide. Had they known this would happen to her? Is this what had been on her secret medfile, the parts that were sealed away from public view? Is this why they had wanted her to leave her job . . . so she could fall to pieces in private?

In all of her years doing Mediation in war zones, in all of her work between hate-filled rivals, political adversaries, even trigger-happy terrorists . . . she had never been as afraid as this. Never been afraid of something inside herself, rather than a threat from without.

Never been as afraid to give it a name.

You know what it is, an inner voice whispered. You don't want to know, but you do.

NO!

Turn to face me—yes that's it—turn to face me and see who I am—yes there's the light—see my face—see the hate—such hate twisting me I can feel it twisting my soul until it screams for your death—there's the blade, remember it? Ritual knife scored symbols etched in blade and handle running red with blood your blood—hate dances hot in my brain stupid fool did you think I didn't know? Ikna god of destruction drinks your blood and I laugh and I dance and

the ostra bellows and I dance in its blood too all the world is filled with hate and joy—

A bar on Orknea. Somewhere. Maybe not Orknea. The planets and stations were all running together now, details lost as her mind overloaded.

Newscasts were running overhead, volume low. Sometimes a waiter passed through them and they played on his skin momentarily, a mobile tattoo. News from the Empire. News from the Outlands. Sensationalistic reports, mostly, meant to entertain rather than inform. Outlanders seemed to have a taste for violence.

The graphic content of such reports might have upset her, once. Now . . . mere pictures meant nothing. She had far worse images running in her brain day and night. Even the laughter of drunken locals that accompanied any image of disaster from inside the Empire didn't bother her much any more. The Empire was hated here. All megalithic governments were hated here. The Outlanders valued their freedom to speak their mind, raise genetically inferior children, and laugh at the misfortune of others. *Braxi, Azea, they're all the same.* A barkeeper had said that, while offering her a drink laced with drugs that would have been illegal in either territory. *Governments gotten out of hand, using the law like a choke leash. To hells with them.* To the violence raging on the newscast he simply would have shrugged and said, *Freedom has its price.*

She watched with a shiver as the newscast moved from tragedy to tragedy, its voyeuristic scan savoring each sensationalistic detail. To her it seemed surreal, almost comforting, images without emotion. If only the pictures in her head were like that. Maybe in time she would learn to distance herself from them, so that she could watch them unfold with a stranger's detachment. *Not my emotion. Not my problem.* But wasn't that itself a kind of insanity?

Then the image before her changed, and she stiffened in her seat.

MURDER IN BETA STATION RING NINE, the holo announced. Pictures flashed one after the other in the air before her, bodies and blood and—

A knife.

MOTIVE UNKNOWN, it continued.

Closeup on the blade. Crusted blood seeping into finely etched lines, a delicate scrimshaw of horror.

ARTIFACT STOLEN FROM NUMASNI'S MUSEUM FIVE LOCAL DAYS AGO . . .

Hasha. She knew that design. She had seen it when it the blood was fresh, had watched as tendrils of crimson dripped down the handle. Her dream.

Was it a dream?

. . . BELIEVED TO BE DEDICATED TO THE IKNA GOD OF DE-STRUCTION. ITS SIGNIFICANCE IN THIS CRIME IS UNKOWN BUT INVESTIGATORS SUSPECT—

She fell back, as the picture changed again, stumbling against the slender table until it toppled, spilling its drinks across the floor. "Hey!" An Artuzi sitting near her moved out of the way as she nearly fell into him . . . her eyes seeing nothing but the holocast, which even now was widening to include the whole of the crime scene: bloodied imprint of a body, investigator's tag where the knife had been laying, and the gutted corpse of what must once have been a favored pet—

An ostra. By all of the human hells, an ostra. She remembered it bellowing in fear and rage as its master died, remembered the feel of its flesh against the knife blade and fear pouring out with the blood—

No! I wasn't there! It didn't happen!

The room was crowded and her flight sent her stumbling into one patron after another. As she touched each one, emotion stabbed into her with stunning force. Fragments of other lives, shrapnel of human suffering.

not going to take one more day of it
damned if I'll back down
who does she think she is anyway
ought to show him what I think
if he leaves I'll die
(hatred!)
(despair!)
(longing!)
(loneliness!)
(fury!)

Out into the corridor. Someone yelling something about a bill she had to pay but she couldn't stop. What if the police came? What if someone official grabbed hold of her and she drowned in his emotion, all the repressed violence that went with such a job—

Other people's emotions, an inner voice whispered.

No!

Tears poured down her face as she ran through the visitor's ring. Several people reached toward her but something in her expression must have scared the hells out of them. Blood on her hands. Ostra trumpeting in terror. Someone else's hate in her brain. *No no no no no!*

At last she got to the room she had rented and she sealed the portal with trembling hands once, twice, three times over, stabbing at the mechanism until her fingers were raw. Then she leaned against the door, sobbing, and slid down slowly to the floor, all the strength leached from her limbs.

You know what it is, the inner voice whispered. It sounded like her mother's. *You know what's going on.*

"No," she sobbed.

Other people's emotions. Other people's memories. Other people's pain.

She had no more strength for denial. Head bowed, she drew her knees up to her chest and wrapped her arms about them, trembling. "No," she whispered hoarsely. "I'm not psychic. I can't be. It doesn't happen to adults."

How much do they really know about how it happens? Or why?

In the distance a couple was fighting. Their anger overlaid a wave of sexual hunger from the floor beneath. Sorrow pressed down on her from overhead, stifling, suffocating. And loneliness—so much loneliness!—loneliness from all sides of her, that universal essence of humanity which comes of being trapped in a shell of flesh, unable to reach out to others with more than words or simple touch—

Only she could. Without trying. She could touch them all.

This is why they go crazy, she thought.

The couple below her was having sex. The waves of selfish hunger were rhythmic, penetrating.

How do I stop it? she begged. To her mother, her gods, the unknown, long-lost sister—anyone or anything that might know the answer.

You can't stop it, the inner voice whispered. *Not once it's started.*

Pounding below. Madness within.

She wept.

Think as the enemy thinks, and you will be able to anticipate him.

Want what he wants, and you will learn how to entrap him.

Feel what he feels, and you will know how to seduce him.

—Anzha lyu Mitethe

ELEVEN

THE FREELANCE SHIP looked like a ramshackle construct, all the best and worst pieces of spacer technology welded together with a crude and careless hand. The outside was scarred and pitted from close scrapes with station debris, which spoke of a force field array that was less than adequate on its best days. The outer seal on the airlock had been badly repaired several times and each attempt had left deep scorchmarks in the surrounding frame. There was a lingering smell about the hull that hinted at some vital mechanism about to overheat, and other scents Tathas didn't want to guess at.

But.

She moved with a swiftness that belied her appearance, and maneuvered with a grace that would have done the finest transport proud. So did her crew, taking up their accustomed positions with silent efficiency, dodging the best that station security had to offer with seemingly no effort. So. The ramshackle façade was just that, Tathas assessed. Protective coloring, in a world where the majority of freelancers held their ships together with little more than spit and a curse.

He was glad to have the time to observe them. It gave him time to appraise their competence, and to make a few decisions about his own fate.

There were five of them in all. The woman with the lizard eyes and tattoos seemed to be in a position of some authority, which made his skin crawl . . . but he wasn't going to last long in the Outlands if he expected every crew to conform to Braxin ideals, was he? The man who had ordered them aboard was human in appearance but not in movement; beneath the loose-fitting jumpsuit he wore, Tathas was willing to bet there were joints and muscles that were far removed from the human norm. The woman who had confronted him on the ramp was perhaps the most human of them all, at least to his eyes, though he noticed that once when she reached for a com, long claws flexed forth from her fingertips. From where he was standing he couldn't tell if they were natural, or some high-tech somatic alteration, but from his standpoint both were equally distasteful.

The other two men disappeared into the bowels of the ship before he could get a good look at them, but both seemed human enough. Tathas had dealt with a few nonhumans in his time and he was grateful his current circumstances would not be testing his diplomatic skills. Although he understood on an intellectual level that creatures with eight legs and eye stalks might well be intelligent beings capable of civilized discourse, it didn't mean he felt comfortable discussing the weather with them.

He watched the viewscreen as the small ship accelerated, but if there was a particular moment when the view of real stars gave way to a computer-generated simulacrum, he couldn't make it out. It was said that the human mind could not look upon the true essence of the superluminal Void without going mad. As Tathas looked over the crew, one by one, he wondered if any of them had ever tried it.

Only if there was a profit in it, he decided at last.

Finally the work of seeing to their immediate safety was done. The commander—he assumed the man was that—ushered him into a small chamber just back of the bridge, and the two women followed. Moments later the two men who had gone below joined them. They were human enough, though one was so scarred about the face with deep, jagged furrows that it was hard to read his expression. They must have been wounds of honor, Tathas thought, like the ones a Kesserit might bear from tribal contests. There was no other reason to look like that, in a world where science could replace damaged tissue at will.

The leader called up a round of drinks in small matching glasses while the others took seats about a well-worn table, laughing about the station security they'd just left behind. Apparently it hadn't impressed them much. The glasses were passed out, and two of the crew downed their contents with the kind of brusque efficiency which implied that the point of the drink was not how it tasted, but how quickly it got into your bloodstream. Tathas sniffed his own drink, caught the tang of alcohol, and decided to take a chance. If they meant him any harm there was probably blessed little he could do about it anyway.

It burned his throat like fire but it felt good going down. A few seconds later he could feel the knot of tension at the back of his neck ease just a bit. He forced his hands to a casual position on the table, to keep from looking like he was ready to go for his weapon at any minute. There was blood crusted under one fingernail.

"My name is Raija." The one who spoke appeared to be their leader, so Tathas' nod acknowledged him as one. "These are Kesh and Tali'l"— he indicated the lizard-eyed woman first, then the one who had challenged Tathas on the ramp. "Fatu and Homani." The two men nodded, curtly, coldly. "We use no family names here, no subnames, no honorifics . . . no ancestral recitals."

"I understand," he responded. "I'm called Tathas."

"Yes," Kesh said with a grin. Her teeth were all filed to sharp points. "We know."

"I'm sure you've guessed we're freelance," Raija said. "You know what that means?"

Tathas nodded. The word could mean nearly anything, but from the way it was voiced he was willing to bet the man wasn't talking about itinerant laborers. Much as he wanted to ask for a fuller explanation, he sensed that in this company it would be a dire mistake to admit the extent of his ignorance. "Of course."

Tali'l snorted. "Not the same as in the Central System, *Braxin*. Not the same as anywhere within the Holding. Rules are different here."

He felt his hackles rising at her tone but refused to let it show. Instead he said, with a carefully measured disdain, "I'm sorry, did you not catch my name?"

She started to spit out some response but Raija hissed a warning and waved her to silence. It was good to see that a man was really in charge of things; you wouldn't guess it from her attitude.

"We take jobs where we find them. There are very few easy ones in the Outlands. Finding someone whose wit is sharp, who can handle himself in a fight, and who has the freedom to go where business calls . . . those things are rare in combination."

"And you think I fit the bill."

Raija's eyes sparkled, as if at some private amusement. "Maybe."

Tali'l snorted. "He's still a Braxin."

"A warrior of the Central System, caught in the very act of death-dueling. Banished now, homeless, seeking allies in a world not of his making. Very promising, I think."

"You seem to know a lot about me."

"You made the news when you were arrested. Outlanders like

nothing more than a good scandal from the inside, be it Holding or Empire. The more trouble there is back home, the less likely anyone is to bother us out here."

"And you think, based on that alone, that I could and would help you." He leaned back in his chair; the springy material buzzed in protest and then adjusted to his new posture. "You can understand that a man in my position might consider such confidence . . . questionable."

Raija's eyes narrowed . . . but he was not displeased, Tathas thought. He expected to be challenged. Good.

"I know what you were. I know what your options are now. I'm willing to bet that a lifetime on Braxi hasn't prepared you for what's out here."

Tathas drained the last drops of liquid from his glass before answering. "Maybe I'm more adaptable than you give me credit for."

"How much do you know about the Outlands?" Homani asked him.

"Enough," he told him.

"Perhaps." Raija's faint smile implied that he saw right through Tathas' subterfuge . . . but that was all right, as long as they both played the same game. "But no doubt the reports from inside the Holding are . . . let us say, biased. Yes?"

Tathas nodded ever so slightly. "Perhaps."

"You'd have heard, for instance, that this stretch of space is lawless. Not true. Each planet, each station, each ship here has its own code of law. Cross the wrong one and you'll wind up on a short flight to a sun."

Tathas smiled faintly. "So I gather."

"Dangerous place for someone who doesn't know the rules," Kesh offered.

Raija poured himself another glass of the alcoholic liquid. "You'd have heard that the Empire and Holding hold no sway here. Again, not true." He took a quick swig from the glass, draining half its contents. "They take territory and they lose it. They expand when the War is going well, claim planets and rape them into submission . . . and then withdraw again when their resources are needed elsewhere. Sometimes the Braxaná Lords come out here to earn their moment of glory . . . and they don't much care what rubble they leave behind when they finally go home to claim their laurels. In shattered planets or shattered lives."

Homani cursed softly under his breath. Tathas couldn't make out his words but the tone of it was that of pure venom.

"The War Border's right next door, of course. What's Braxi's territory one day there is Azea's the next. Refugees from both sides pour into Outland space, drunk with rage at everyone and everything around them. Into this territory, which is as unstable as anything you'll find in human space. A wild and rocky shore, where the energies of two imperial oceans crash into one another, over and over again."

His eyes were fixed on Tathas. Dark eyes, with highlights of burnished pewter. Hard to read.

"Many a man has drowned in that double riptide, Tathas." He said it quietly. "I think you are one of the sort that can swim."

"I think you are making a lot of assumptions."

"Am I?" Raija chuckled. "I'm a good judge of people, Tathas. I've seen all forms of human hate and desperation and I know what they drive men to do. You might say . . . it's my business."

"And is that how you view me? Hate-filled and desperate?"

"Aren't you?" The words were a challenge.

"No," Tathas said. Smiling now. "Not desperate."

"Hate-filled?"

He forced a shrug. "This isn't Braxi. When I'm ready to act on my hate I'll go home."

Kesh grinned; he seemed to have her approval in this bluffing game, anyway.

"So now." Tathas settled himself more comfortably in his chair. "You've made it clear why you think I could be useful to you. Maybe you're right. Time will tell. Now I'd like to hear what you're offering, besides transportation off that . . ." He fumbled for a word that would capture the vile essence of the place, but could find nothing that didn't require some obscure Speech Mode. At last had to settle for ". . . station."

"What's in it for you," Homani muttered.

Tathas spread his hands wide, waiting.

Raija nodded. "Profit, first and foremost. We take big risks, we win big prizes. You share the risk, you share the reward." The sharp eyes studied Tathas as he spoke. "I know you came out here with nothing. That's part of the Wilding custom, isn't it? Well, money's the ticket to freedom in the Outlands. With it you can go where you want, do what you want . . . impose your own law on some station, if that's what appeals to you. Without it, you're likely to be snapped up by the first station that sees some profit in detaining you."

Fatu snorted. "Love of bribes is the one thing all the Outland stations have in common."

Tathas nodded, his eyes fixed on Raija. Giving them nothing yet. "Go on."

"Information. You've got your own agenda, I assume. Very well. Help us with ours, and you can access what we've got." The pewter gaze was fixed on him, piercing through to his soul. "I know there's more you want than just a safe place to hide, Tathas. Isn't there?"

"Women," Tali'l said sharply. "He needs to abduct a woman in order to go home. Remember?"

"Ah yes. That . . ." Raija waved casually toward his female crewmates; his expression was anything but casual. "These are off limits, of course."

"Of course." Tathas glanced at Tali'l, noting the cold fire in her eyes, and couldn't resist baiting her. "They're your property, after all."

Tali'l cursed and began to rise. Fatu grabbed her wrist to hold her in place, and muttered some warning in a foreign language. Tathas was going to add *I could do better elsewhere*, just to savor her reaction, but after a moment he decided the moment was perfect as it was.

The lizard-eyed girl just seemed . . . amused.

Tathas glanced down at his empty glass, tapped it on the table. "Is there more of this?"

With a whispered warning Fatu let go of Tali'l and poured another round for all of them. Tathas downed his as quickly as they did theirs, as if he, too, had interest only in its effect, not its flavor.

"Information," he said at last. It was a question. *Show me what you're worth.*

Raija smiled. "Do you know why those men came after you on the station?"

He shrugged. "Someone on the home planet wants me dead. They're too scared shitless to try to do the job themselves, so they hired . . . freelance."

"No, I mean the men themselves. The ones who actually attacked you. Not the ones who set them up."

"Money, I assume. Or some kind of favor that has local relevance."

Tali'l smiled darkly. "Wrong answer, Braxin."

"No payment," Raija agreed. "No bribery. They attacked you because of what they thought you were."

"What they thought I was—" He tried to remember back. What was it they had said? *Damned Shaka, they should all be killed.* "Shaka? Is that it? I don't know the word."

Fatu mumbled something under his breath. It had the flavor of the kind of thing primitive people might mutter to ward off evil.

"It's a kind of psychic, " Kesh told him.

"Psychic? They thought I . . . was a psychic?" He knew the astonishment showed on his face this time, but he couldn't manage to mask it; the revelation was simply too insane to absorb. "That's crazy."

"Is it?" Raija asked.

"Of course. I'm . . ." Again he floundered for the proper word, one that would sum up the complete idiocy of such a belief. But in the end there was nothing suitable in any dialect this crew would understand, so he finished up simply ". . . I'm *Braxin*."

"Yes. From the one culture that has made war on psychics throughout all of human history. Killing any child that showed the least promise of developing such a talent. Seems unlikely, doesn't it?" The gray eyes glittered. "So you have no idea who might spread such a rumor? Or why?"

Not here. Not now. Not with his head still reeling from the revelation. "No."

"How much do you know about the psychics?" Kesh asked him.

He was grateful for the opportunity to turn his attention to a more concrete question. "An Azean phenomenon, mostly, nurtured within the Empire, with scattered examples on backward . . . on planets outside the Holding." A faint smile. "There they're killed on sight. I can't answer for other places."

The crew looked at one another. It took all the self-control Tathas could muster not to ask them what was going on.

"They left Azea several centuries ago," Raija agreed. "It's rumored that their society fell apart at that point, and only scattered individuals remain, in hiding. They needed Azean science to keep them sane, and now, and now, divorced from the Empire, they're hard-pressed to survive, much less establish any kind of meaningful society. At least, that's the *official* story."

"Yeah," Fatu muttered. "Right."

Raija leaned on the table, drawing close. "They're out there, Tathas. Out there somewhere in the vast empty reaches where neither Holding nor Empire have staked a claim. Where not even the petty little landlords of the Outland stations dare to go. We see signs of them now and then. Sometimes bands of them will come to the Outlands, do one thing or another, and then disappear again. People either try to kill them or get the hells out of their way. No one knows what their real agenda is, or even how many of them there are. Some say they regard the rest of us as subhuman, life-forms only to be tolerated for as long as they don't get in the way."

"And the Shaka?"

"Is a kind of psychic. A new kind, or so it's said, born of the madness inherent in all of them. A creature with the power to invade other human minds and twist them to its purpose." He leaned back in his chair. "Back in the days of Llornu, when the psychics were an accepted part of Azean society, they claimed no such creature existed. Now . . . people in the Outlands believe it does. They talk about things they've seen happen, which nothing else would explain. And they hate the Shaka with the kind of hate that's born of pure terror."

"And they thought I was one of them?" Tathas' eyes narrowed as he tried to make sense of it. "Our people have killed psychics throughout all of recorded history. One would think we'd be the least likely race in the galaxy to have these . . . Shaka."

"One would think," Raija said quietly.

It was all too much to sort out. Especially with this crew watching his every expression. Finally he said, "*You* seem sure enough I'm not one of them."

Tali'l snorted again. Raija grinned. "As you say, you're Braxin. If you had powers like that, the Holding would have dealt with you long ago."

Homani smiled darkly. "But we're taking bets the story will be interesting, when someone finds out why your attackers thought you were one."

"You can research that story out here," Raija told him. "Trace it back to its roots, and find out who wants to do what with you. Make your plans. Finance your revenge . . ."

The words faded out into silence. The five of them looked at him.

You have nowhere else to go, he told himself. *And you do need money, transportation . . . allies. Any road you choose for the future will require those things.*

Do you have any better prospects?

"You said I would owe you help for one job, if I came aboard. Tell me about it."

It was Kesh who answered. "Abduction of a young girl from Horras Station and delivery to one of her father's political rivals. Spoiled rich kid, she'll have a handful of bodyguards to deal with and they'll all be well-equipped. Payment is in precious metals, if it comes off clean, good in any civilized system. A million and a half in Braxin sinias."

"And if it doesn't?"

Fatu's scarred face cracked into something that might be called a smile. "Do we really have to answer that?"

He looked them over, one after the other. They weren't the companions he would have chosen on Braxi . . . but that was another life. Another Tathas. In the current context, in his current need . . . yes, they would do. All except the one woman; she was bound to be trouble. But he would deal with that glove when it came off.

"All right," he said at last. "I'm in."

He drained the last drops of liquid from his glass and held it out for a refill.

That night he dreamed of K'teva.

He was walking through Kurat searching for her on a street filled with Pale Ones, when suddenly he saw her in the crowd. Unwilling to call out her name, he quickened his pace, and tried to catch her attention with some small gesture that others would not notice. He wanted to tell her that he had found safety, at least for the moment, and now would have time to plan his eventual return to Braxi. But the Braxaná surrounding were like statues, immovable, and they blocked his way. The more he struggled to find a way to reach her, the further away she seemed to get. At last, frustrated and infuriated, he began to push his way through them. Hands grabbed him from all sides and he could no longer move. He screamed out her name then, and as the pain of a neural stun ripped through his flesh he saw her turn to him, looking at him—not with green eyes, oh no, not Kesserit emerald green eyes and not lenses but true black-on-black, midnight eyes, Braxaná eyes! And she smiled at him and turned back to the crowd, and then there were only Braxaná on all sides, an implacable tide of grey and black hatred—

K'teva!

The ship's library was probably impressive by Outlander standards, but to Tathas it was sorely lacking. There was a limit to how much material you could store on a single vessel, and keeping it updated constantly was a chore that would have required more electronic effort than it was worth out here. To someone accustomed to the Central Computer System, with its nearly infinite database and continuous stream of updates, such a collection seemed sparse, almost primitive.

But . . . this was all there would be, out this far in the galaxy. He had left the Central System behind along with all its amenities. Time to get used to that.

The cabin they assigned him was small and had no starmap display, so he followed Homani's instructions and found the small room set aside for research, such as it was. He tested its starmap capacity and found it adequate, if not inspiring, and the ship's computer was Braxin enough in its command logic that he had little difficulty giving it orders.

Then he called up the library access. And sat for a moment, staring at the screen before him.

Where to start?

Finally he told the system, "Shaka."

A lengthy menu of choices filled the screen. That was the price you paid for an overpopulated galaxy, he thought; every possible combination of sounds was a word in some human language, somewhere. He gave the computer a few additional phrases to narrow the search, and soon had what he wanted.

The file was immense. The references went back in history nearly two thousand years, with cross-references to folk legends before that. For as long as mankind had walked upright, it seemed, there had been legends of men who could force others to obey their will by some supernatural vehicle. Tathas thought of the Pri'tiera and their brief but dramatic meeting. It would be easy to explain away the presence of such a man with legends like this, and fear him for more than he was. Tathas refused to give him that victory. Whatever the Braxaná might want to be viewed as, they were men, plain and simple. Allow them to be more than that, and you allowed them . . . well . . . the right to rule.

He grit his teeth against the thought and read onward.

The Shaka of Outland lore were more than charismatic leaders. They were fully trained psychics of the highest order. According to some sources, they had the ability to do more than simply overwhelm other humans with the force of their will, but to actually place its thoughts in the heads of other people, to alter their emotions . . . even, it was rumored, to manipulate the bodies of others as if they were their own.

All legends, of course. In the years of the Institute, Llornu had steadfastly denied that such powers existed. Of course. The psychics would have been run out of the Empire centuries ago, if such things were known to exist.

Thus is the wisdom of Braxin tradition demonstrated at last, he thought.

Tathas read the files through, but found little helpful information. Least of all any clue as to why his assailants might have thought he was one of these Shaka creatures. But he certainly understood why they would want him dead, if he was one. Oh, yes. The Braxins in their wisdom had been killing psychics for centuries; it was the one custom all the tribes agreed on. The rest of the human worlds had chosen to look the other way while the secret laboratories of Llornu had turned out more and more deadly breeds of telepath . . . and now they all played at being shocked that such terrible things could exist. It was their own blessed fault, he thought. Who knew how many of these Shaka had been nurtured in secret, in the days when the psychic Institute had the wealth of an Empire to call upon for its protection? What the Outlands were seeing now was probably only the tip of the glove.

He called up some information from the time of the psychic diaspora—

—and froze, as a graphic image took shape before him. A woman's image. *Functional Telepath,* the caption proclaimed. It took him a moment to realize who she was. It took him a moment more to realize *what* she was. When he did at last, his heart skipped a beat in his chest.

By the gods who abandoned us. . . .

Years ago, when he was but a child, his father had taken him to an exhibit at the Central Museum in Kurat. Something about *Glorious Braxin Heritage;* he no longer remembered the exact title. But he remembered standing before an antique painting, a work so ancient that the Museum computer said it was actually done by hand—pigments layered on a blank surface bit by bit without the aid of electronic imaging—so old, so fragile, that forcefields had been woven into its substance to protect it, and the light in the chamber passed through special filters to remove from its spectrum all wavelengths that might damage the precious object.

He remembered that painting. He remembered what the Museum computer had said about it. He remembered being fascinated by it later, and reading all he could about Harkur the Great, and the first Pri'tiera's obsession with finding his long-lost bloodline.

There were those who believed the bloodline had surfaced once, from seeds spread throughout the galaxy long ago. A genetic inheritance that had flared to life when recessive traits met and commingled, in a time and place no Braxin ever would have anticipated.

Anzha lyu Mitethe.

Telepath. Azean Starcommander. Traitor. Loved and reviled by the Empire that gave birth to her, raised her up to power, and then ultimately drove her away.

He put his hand to the image. His fingertips tingled as they touched its surface, tracing the line of its hair. Red hair, of that odd shade that so many Braxin women imitated now, because she had brought it to prominence. Pure crimson, blood-rich in color, so unlike the hue of natural hair that only on her did it look like anything other than a cosmetician's trick. On her . . . and on Harkur the Great. Her ancestor?

She was lost now. No one knew where she had gone, he read, though some pundits had made a nice living coming up with creative theories about it. She had disappeared when the psychics fled the Empire, and the best information the library could offer him about her subsequent fate was a hint of rumors that she had gone to take control of them, to bring them . . . where?

He stared for a long time at that image, trying to see past the muddled bits and pieces of history that were now swirling inside his brain, to make some sense of it all.

Had she fled to the wild places out there, past the Outlands, beyond the reach of human-dominated space? If so, she was surely dead by now; human flesh had its limits. Had she procreated while she was still alive? There would have been no reason not to, in a world where she was among her own kind.

Zatar the Magnificent had wanted to claim Harkur's bloodline for his own purposes. He had spent the second half of his life seeking some way to do so. And failed. The ancient bloodline had been lost long ago on Braxi, drowned out in the relentless interbreeding which the Braxaná had deliberately encouraged. You couldn't work to obliterate tribal identity for so many thousands of years and then expect one man's genetic trail to show up clearly. There was only one place where that bloodline was believed to have surfaced . . . and even that was untested, unproven.

He stood up, and in a whispered voice called for a starmap. *Outlands,* he told the computer. *Yerren sector.* Suns swirled around him. Nebulae curled through the still air.

Are you really thinking you can use her bloodline for your Wilding, Tathas? Do you know the danger involved?

Yes, he knew it. That's why the blood was rushing hot through his veins now. That's why his senses suddenly felt so acute, so . . . alive.

He drew in a deep breath, savoring the sensation. Part fear, part elation, part . . . hunger. A hunger so primal it was almost sexual in its
urgency, and as he gazed upon the portrait of Harkur's most famous
descendant, as he thought about what her bloodline must be worth to
the Braxaná—to the Pri'tiera himself!—he could feel his groin tightening in anticipation. Fear and elation could do that, when they were
properly combined. He knew that from his death-duels among the
Kesserit. Only when the stakes were sky-high and death was the price
of failure did a man ever feel this alive.

*They will be psychic. All her descendants. You must assume that. Psychics
one and all, and guarded by a nation of psychics. Hidden away in some corner
of the galaxy where no man has found them yet, defended by creatures whose
very name makes the Outlanders quail in terror—*

The door hissed open suddenly. Someone began to step into the
darkened room . . . and then saw him, and stopped.

It took him a moment to focus on her. "Tali'l?"

"I didn't know you were here." Her tone made it clear she sensed
the strangeness of his mood, and was wary of it. That was as it should
be; women could sense it when a man was in such a primitive state,
and those who were not adept enough to deal with it were best off
keeping their distance. "I just needed to check the map." She didn't
move any further into the room, but stood in the narrow door frame,
watching him. Dark eyes studying him from top to bottom, wary as a
shersa who had caught the hunter's scent. Was that observation accu-
rate, he wondered, or some fantasy born of this strange moment? "It
can wait."

"No need. I'm done here." With a short command he banished the
starmap. *There'll be time enough later.* He drew in a deep breath and
counted to ten silently, fighting to still the pounding of his heart.
Thoughts raced through his mind, hot and red and violent. *Later,* he
promised himself. *Later.*

He was going to have to squeeze by her to exit the room. She saw
it too, but did nothing to move out of his way. Challenging him? This
was a bad time for it.

He came up near to her and put his hand against the wall behind
her head, leaning close. Testing her. A Braxin woman would have
known from his expression just how far she could push him, and what
the consequences would be if she exceeded that measure, but he was
willing to bet Tali'l had no such insight. A shame. The game might
even be fun if she did.

"You need something from me?" His voice was soft, a thing for the two of them alone. "I owe you all so very much, I would be glad to . . . accommodate."

Her eyes narrowed. Her lips tightened. Her anger was a perfume that wrapped itself around him, mixed with other scents, other emotions. Hardly surprising, Tathas mused. Hatred could be a powerful aphrodisiac. "Your laws don't hold here, Braxin. I *suggest* you don't forget it."

"Why do I bring out such anger in you, Tali'l?" His tone was a whispered challenge, "What inner secret disguises itself as hate, so that you can voice it safely?"

He saw her nostrils flare ever so slightly. "You think a lot of yourself, Braxin."

"And you as well," he countered easily. "What is it you fear, Tali'l? Rape? You imagine that since I could have any woman I wanted back home, I would just take any woman I wanted here?" He made a *tsk-tsk* noise and shook his head, but his eyes never left hers. "Rape's no sport on Braxi, Tali'l. What point is there in it, when the law makes victims of all? But here in the Outlands, where a woman doesn't have to submit . . . where one might even . . . struggle . . . now *that* has potential."

"You're a sick bastard."

"No," he said, savoring the scent of her. The rich, complex, promising scent of her. "Just Braxin. As you keep reminding me."

He left her then, passing so close that he could feel her body's heat as he squeezed through the doorway. Did she feel threatened? Good. It seemed to be the game she wanted, and it was certainly more natural to him than the empty-headed chatter which passed for social repartee in these parts. Maybe they would get along after all.

Laughing softly to himself, he returned to his cabin.

Maps. They ran through his head when he lay down, images racing through his brain as he tried to go to sleep. And later, in dreams when he did sleep, they returned. He stood in the middle of a starmap so vast that he could see individual planets in scale, and the borders of the display were beyond the limits of any one room. And later awakened to create imaginary maps in his mind, studying them star after star, and wondering.

The psychics had gone . . . where? Somewhere no freelance scout could find them, that was the one sure thing. There were people who would pay a small fortune for such information, and therefore little doubt that scouts, being what they were, had tried to find it. All in vain. He'd read of scouts sent out by the Empire for two years' journey past the borders of civilized space, in search of some clue to where the psychics had gone. Those who had come back had returned empty handed. No, the pundits said, they must be even further out, or in some place where space was so sparsely populated that scouts would not go there, for how else could they evade such efforts consistently?

And yet.

It didn't fit what the freelancers had told him. Or what he was reading between the lines in the Azeaside library files. Because the psychics did show up in civilized space now and then, that was clear. *No one knows what their real agenda is,* Raija had told him. Could you maintain an agenda of any kind with a four-year round-trip journey attending each task? What about these rumors from the Empire that the psychics were stealing children for some god-blessed unknown purpose? Was there a reason one would do that, only to seal the child up in a starship for two years before getting home?

He stared at the maps his mind provided in frustration, knowing the answer was right in front of him, unable to capture it in words.

There was too much regular contact. They had to be closer to the center of things than most people believed. But if they *were* closer, near to the borders of civilized space, then scouts could easily find them. And also then there would be the added risk for them of the Empire or Holding expanding, and the shell of the Outlands expanding with it, until their secretive psychic territory was engulfed by that of "normals." So much for privacy.

No. No. It just didn't add up. He was missing some vital piece of the puzzle.

Lying still in the darkness of his tiny cabin, he struggled to think things through without falling into the mental traps that had already defeated so many. Tried not to take for granted the same assumptions. That way lay failure. No, he needed a new understanding, one that was compatible with all the stories he'd been told. . . .

And then it came to him. So suddenly that for a moment his heart seemed to stop beating.

There is no planet so far away that scouts will not find it, eventually. Secrecy can't depend upon such a distance alone.

Stars. Swarmed in his vision. Clusters of stars so tightly packed that you could practically use a surface pod to go from world to world, thinner regions where lone stars shone dimly, the glistening belt of the Greater Galactic Plane cutting though the Void—

Whatever planet you chose to hide out on, no matter how far away it might be, scouts would run across it eventually. Or some technological genius working in a basement laboratory would locate a signal of Azean type coming from a hundred thousand light-years' distance and trace it to its source. Or some mathematician with too much time on his hands would work out the optimum course vector for a group of humans seeking privacy among the stars. . . .

All of that had been tried, many times over. None of it had worked. Which meant, in plain Braxin, the psychics weren't out there.

No, he thought. *They're right here.*

It was the only answer that made any sense. The only one that explained their frequent visits to Outland space, and their alleged excursions inside the Empire. They were here, within reasonable traveling distance of both territories. Protecting themselves by other means, while scouts scoured the distant borders of human space for their mysterious missing empire.

Like hiding a grain of sand on a beach.

But that meant there would be good chance of discovery, didn't it? No human-inhabitable planet was going to remain unexploited in the Outlands; no complex station would go unnoticed. No, they would have to deal with the men who discovered their secret, deal with them individually and in a clandestine manner, so the pattern of it was never noticed. . . .

His heart was beating again. Hard. He could feel the energy surging again, hot blood feeding the thoughts to him in spurts of insight.

If he went seeking the psychics, if he was aggressive enough—and smart enough—to find the right clues . . . then they would have to send someone to deal with him. Perhaps to kill him; what is the death of one stranger in the Outlands? Or perhaps to wipe his mind clear of all relevant memories—as these Shaka were said to be able to do—so that as he gazed at his "to do" list of suspect planets, he would remember already having explored that one, and found nothing. Oh, they would be skilled, and well-practiced, and they would have many means to work their will upon those who threatened their privacy . . . but they must do *something*. That was the key. You can only hide a grain of sand on a beach if no living man knows exactly which grain of sand it is. Once someone figures it out . . . he must be dealt with.

Warrior though he was, he knew he couldn't stand up to powers like that directly, nor to the psychics' two centuries of experience in dealing with potential invaders. If, on the other hand, he found another who was searching, and made sure those efforts were known . . . then he could watch and wait. Eventually, if his "bait" searched in the right direction, the psychics would come to him. Would they notice a lone Braxin standing in the shadows, marking their trail home? Would they even be aware of a man who had made no obvious effort to find them, other than to watch those who were engaged in their own search?

He shut his eyes for a minute, his blood pounding through his head with such force that sparks of crimson played inside his eyelids. Did such a plan guarantee he could get to their homeworld safely? Did it give him any way to find out if the progeny of Anzha lyu Mitethe existed, or even—folly of follies—steal one away from them? No. Of course not. But it was a start.

They would lead him along the beach themselves, and show him where the grain of sand was hidden. And then—

Exhausted, elated, he thought, *It will all fall into place.*

The door hissed open suddenly. He sat upright and pushed off the blanket, a warrior's reflexes. Who was invading his privacy here, in a room he'd been told was his? A figure approached, barely visible in the near-darkness. He tensed one arm behind him, against the bed, ready to launch himself at the intruder—

—and then he caught the scent. And recognized it.

Tali'l.

She came to him in silence, her footstep too soft to hear above the pounding of his heart. He began to whisper her name—a question—but she raised a finger and placed it to his lips, ordering him to silence. He caught her slender wrist in his own hand and pulled it away angrily. *Do not dare to command me,* he thought, *not even by gesture.*

"Security override," she whispered. "Voiceprint, Tali'l."

It took him a minute to realize that there must have been some sort of surveillance in the room, or perhaps the potential for it . . . and that she had just shut it down. Wordlessly, she leaned down close to him. Hands stroking his chest, down towards his thighs, alien claws bared just enough to leave scratch marks behind, not drawing blood.

He grabbed her hands before they got down too far and pulled them away from his body. He'd be blessed if he was letting a potentially hostile female down in that region with claws drawn.

She laughed softly.

"Ah, my dear Braxin. Afraid?"

"Just careful," he whispered. "Always, with an enemy."

Did the accusation anger or excite her? It was impossible to tell in the darkness. The faint blue gleam of the portal control backlit her as she drew her hands from his grasp, providing an icy halo that accented her slow, easy motions. Hand rising to the closures of her tight jumpsuit. Claw-tips snapping them open. Lithe, slender body revealed as the fabric parted . . . if there were alien markings on her skin he couldn't see them in the darkness. Then: the scent of her, concentrated by the closeness of the jumpsuit, alien in its exotic muskiness but human enough for him to taste its meaning. Oh yes. The Azeans liked to believe that love and love alone inspired human intimacy, but Tathas' people knew better. Hate, fear, rage, frustration . . . each of these things could set the blood to stirring. Primitive emotions, demanding a primitive response.

She drew close to him, close enough for him to feel the warmth of her body against his skin, and her claws traced lines along the edge of his hair and down the side of his face. Stinging but not cutting deep. Was she inviting him to some mutual indulgence, or trying to bait him to make an aggressive move so that she could then slash out at him, claiming self-defense? He kept himself still as a hunting animal, fixed upon her with all his senses. There was light enough for her to see that she had aroused him . . . but no way for her to know that the heat of his blood had begun even before she entered the room. No way for her to know that it had as much to do with his desire to pit himself against hidden empires and return home in triumph than the brief pleasure of an alien coupling.

It would be good to douse all that energy in a woman's heat, he thought.

Assuming one didn't get killed for trying it.

He reached out to her, running one hand along her skin, over her breast, down the muscled flat of her stomach. Human skin, with human flesh beneath. A relief, that. He hadn't had many non-Braxins in his life, but he knew that finding alien features where you didn't expect them was one sure cure for arousal. Her breasts were high and firm, testament to a life lived under the lesser gravity of ships and stations, and taut beneath his touch. She gave no sign that his touch pleased her, but then, he didn't expect her to. It didn't suit the game she seemed to have come to play.

She slid a sharp-talonned hand down to his thigh, stroking the blanket that half-concealed him, pulling it out of the way. He caught her slender neck in both his hands, cradling her chin in what might have been an endearment with a different woman, at a different time. *Feel my strength,* he thought to her. *Be aware, I could break your neck in an instant if I chose. As I will, if claws stray where they should not.*

In the darkness she moved, lithe as a dancer, sliding a leg up and over his, shifting her weight upon onto the bed, until she came to straddle him. Stirred by the urgency of the moment he reached down for her hips and pulled her onto him, hard. The pleasure of the sudden immersion was blinding, and for a moment he had to send his mind elsewhere, unwilling to give in so soon. Starmaps swam before his eyes as he forced himself to remember them, to count the tiny glowing spots, to send his mind *elsewhere* . . . anything rather than give her the triumph of controlling him so easily. At last the need passed and his mind surfaced in the present moment, and the heady scent of a woman who cursed him under her breath even as she rode him for her own pleasure. Using him, and making blessed sure he knew it.

He grabbed her suddenly. Lost in the moment—drunk on the illusion of dominance, perhaps—she offered no resistance. He pulled her down beside him and then shifted his weight until he was on top of her, forcing her legs apart with his own. Did she attempt to throw him off, to take control again? It was hard to tell; the fevered motions which might have been struggling were much the same as those which passion might inspire. Her claws flexed as she cried out, but that might have been pleasure as well, rather than the desire to rend him to bloody bits. No way to tell the difference now, and it didn't matter. He held her hands over her head where all they could tear were the bedclothes, and then drove himself into her, over and over again, until all sense of past and present were gone, all fears of the future drowned out in pure physical heat. She cried out beneath him. In pleasure, frustration, or fury? Whatever its cause, the effect was electric. The fire in his loins gathered into one blazing spearpoint, pleasure so intense it bordered on agony . . . and then past, present and future all exploded as the single moment claimed him. Spasms of fire surged through his body, again and again, squeezing his flesh like a vise, forcing out the last drops of hunger and need in him from him, into her. And she received them. Oh yes. Powerfully at first, with equal urgency . . . and then with sudden stillness, and a shuddering of the flesh that told him that however much she might hate him in her heart, the heat of her flesh had been sated.

For a moment he lay there, reveling in the sensations of the aftermath. Only for a moment. Then he withdrew, releasing her arms. A clawed hand swept down by his face as soon as she was free, but he shifted his weight and rolled off to the side, not wanting to know whether she intended a caress or some sharper blow. It was a more enjoyable moment without that knowledge.

There were a thousand things he might have whispered to her, then, and taken pleasure in. A thousand ways to bait her still, this Shem'Ar who had come to take him in her own way, at her own pace. But the moment was perfect. There was no need.

Everything had been said.

After a few moment she rose up from the bed. He watched the blue light glimmer on sweat-filmed skin as she dressed easily.

She turned then and looked at him. He couldn't see her expression in the darkness. Was she smiling, perhaps? Or cursing him silently?

Does it matter which? he thought.

She left then, without a word. The door swept shut behind her. He lay back in the darkness, eyes shut, savoring the fading scent of mixed sweat, as the ventilator labored to clear the room of it.

For the first time since leaving Braxi, he slept peacefully.

There are two Awakenings that all psychics must endure. One comes at puberty, when the mind is suddenly open to all the thoughts and emotions surrounding. It is a brutal assault, which weeds out the weak, and it can drive undisciplined minds to insanity and even death.

The second comes later, when the psychic realizes what manner of world he now belongs to, and what price he has paid for his power.

It is hard to say which is the more disturbing experience.

—Reflections: The Later Writings of Anzha lyu Mitethe

TWELVE

THE RECEIVING CHAMBER of the reigning Lyu was large, too large. You wouldn't think the leader of the Community would need a chamber so large. After all, it wasn't like diplomatic teams from the Holding and the Empire were going to come here to visit. The day that either government found out where the Community was the entirety of it would be moved somewhere else, with no delay. The Tsikari had no love for outsiders. Yet the receiving room of the Lyu was large enough to hold diplomatic teams from both Empires, with enough room between them for a neutral zone to be declared. Grand plans for the future, perhaps? Or just a reflection of the ego of the ruler who called this space her own? Probably a bit of both, Rho mused. After all, they were not supposed to remain a fugitive people forever.

The place was golden, all golden. Golden pillars arched upward to meet a ceiling of glittering pyrite crystal. Burnished bronze walkways with golden highlights were inlaid with mosaic patterns of Ikna citrine, suggesting the blazing rays of a golden sun. Shadows and highlights were all in the same shades, dust-streams and reflections, all golden. Rho knew that the designer of the Palace had intended it to be a homage to the yellow sun of Llornu, in this place where no star shone. But for generations raised without a sun such things no longer had meaning, and such decoration became merely . . . exotic.

She took in a deep breath as she entered, using her Disciplines to quiet the storm of emotion inside her . . . or at least to hide it away well enough that others wouldn't sense it. She wasn't yet accustomed to what the changing had done to her mind, or how easy it was for others to pick up on her emotions now. Was that a problem unique to the Shaka, or was it simply the price of developing Aggressive skills so late in life? Most de-

fensive mental patterns were learned at puberty, when they first became necessary. Did those with natural Aggressive skills have to tiptoe
through their teenage years, choking back on every emotion before it
was broadcast to the world at large? Or was this simply what came of
an adult Awakening?

Shaka. The thought brought back memories . . . and anger.

Hide it. Hide it away.

Dressed in the traditional garments of her rank, the Lyu appeared at
first glance to be part of the room itself, a golden presence that filled
the space with light and energy. Rho had time to study her as she approached, aware that every step she took down the long audience
chamber reinforced the woman's status as Autarch, and her own as
Petitioner. Perhaps that was the purpose of the place, she mused. Certainly the mosaic pattern of the walkway, in which solar flares of glittering crystal blazed forth from the base of the woman's throne, would
seem to suggest it.

The woman who wore the Lyu's crown was part Azean, part . . .
something else. She was a kind of hybrid that would never have existed
on the home planet, but here, where selective breeding was the name
of the game, such mixtures abounded. Even pairbonded Azean couples
might choose to mix their DNA with that of some other Scattered Race,
in the hopes of creating a child of unusual telepathic potential. So it had
been with this woman. The golden skin of the Star Empire bore the stri-
ated markings of some other race; the features were more angled, more
deeply sculpted than Azean features would have been; the eyes were
swept outward and upward with an alien cant. It was impossible to see
her hair, for the formal headdress of the Lyu covered that over with a
cascade of crimson feathers, but Rho was willing to bet it wasn't the
gleaming white of the Empire's ruling race. That brilliant white hair
was the first thing to go when you started mixing DNA.

The Lyu had chosen formal attire for this meeting, with a broad
golden collar and matching headdress that reflected the lights of the
chamber in a thousand points of fire. From the top of the headdress
cascaded a waterfall of slender blood-red feathers; it almost looked like
hair from a distance but it didn't move like hair, and as the Lyu nodded her acknowledgement of Rho's approach the air currents in the
room rippled through the fine wisps like a breeze across a bird's tail.

That was all just for show, of course. The only piece of adornment
that really mattered was the one affixed to the front of her collar, just
above her heart. From a distance Rho could not see the details of it,

but as she approached she could make out a slender crystal vial with tiny serpentine wisps of fog moving through it. Inside the fog, she knew, would be a thin sliver of cryogenic casing, and within that, invisible, the delicate twisted strands of human DNA. More precious than gold, or even human life . . . at least in the view of those who still served the vision of the first Lyu, and who ruled the stars in her name.

Rho came to within what she thought was a polite distance and forced herself to bow her head in proper greeting. Minimal. She didn't feel very respectful right now, and while she'd give the woman her due, she wasn't going to part with one ounce more than that.

"Shaka-Rho." The Lyu spoke with the measured tones of formality; the psychic echo behind them was minimal, unconscious. "You requested an audience."

"Yes." By responding in spoken words she indicated her own preference for such formality. Now that she was Shaka, of course, she could have done otherwise. The words would flow from her as easily as they did from the Lyu, or any other telepath.

But. Then there would be emotions involved. The telepath hadn't yet been bred who could communicate mind-to-mind without some emotion seeping through. Only by using more primitive means of communication could one maintain true mental privacy.

And she needed that privacy now. Oh yes. If the Lyu saw what was in her head right now, she'd probably be shoved out the nearest airlock. Or worse.

"I congratulate you upon your recent trials," the golden figure said. Even her lipstick shone metallic, a deep bronze that matched the paint above her eyes. "Hasai-Thera said you came through with flying colors. That's good. We have need of more Shaka, to safeguard the Community."

Rho took a deep breath and forced herself to be calm. One needed time to take the measure of a speaker, to taste the emotions that hung about each living mind like a haze. The Lyu would be tasting hers now . . . and gods help her if any of her true feelings were evident. Rho didn't even know what would happen then. No one in recorded history had ever defied the Lyu, not since their exit from the Star Empire so very long ago.

"Thera said she was pleased to have a Hostilities Adjustor qualify," Rho offered.

"Yes. That is a valuable skill also. To have the two in one will serve us well."

She bowed her head slightly. "I am honored to serve my people."

The Lyu settled back into her golden throne and regarded her with half-lidded eyes. Rho stiffened, sensing from the scrutiny that her cursory examination was done. Could they move on to business now?

"Shaka-Rho." She said the words as if tasting them as they passed her lips. "You asked to see me." She paused; the golden gaze was piercing, a blade thrust right into Rho's soul. "This is not a surprise, I think."

She said nothing.

"You have questions. I will hear them."

Rho drew in a deep breath, preparing herself. She didn't know what would happen if she antagonized the Lyu . . . but part of her didn't care. A dangerous part. Finally she said, in a tone as devoid of emotion as she could possibly make it, "I have a sister." The tone was not that of a question, but the psychic tenor could surely not be mistaken.

The Lyu regarded her for a long moment, silent. Rho had to fight back the tendrils of her own thoughts from reaching out to taste her emotions, so that she could guess at what she was thinking. A telepath as skilled as the Lyu would surely detect such an effort. An autarch as powerful as the Lyu would surely find it offensive.

At last the Lyu nodded. Crimson feathers fluttered in the golden air. "You have a sister."

"A twin."

The head nodded slightly. "Yes."

She swallowed hard, trying not to let the anger sound in her voice. She knew she couldn't keep it out of her mind. "Why wasn't I told?"

"It did not serve the Community for you to be told."

"But now it does." The edge in her voice was unmistakable, even to her.

"Now it does."

Anger was a lump in her throat. "And why is that, all of a sudden?"

The golden figure stirred slightly. If she was surprised or offended by Rho's tone there was no other sign of it. "Because now she seeks you."

It was not a surprise. Thera had told her the same. But hearing it from such a source gave the words new weight.

"Why now?"

"Because she has learned of her heritage, perhaps. Because she feels the first stirring of powers she does not understand. Because she knows what it is to be a psychic in the Star Empire, and she is afraid."

"But if she is—" She stopped suddenly, the words sinking in. ~*The first stirring of powers. But that would mean . . . she wasn't psychic before now?*

~Exactly so.

~(incredulousness) That isn't possible.

~(utter calm) Apparently it is.

~She's my twin, yes? Identical.

~(confirmation)

~Then the power should be the same.

~ Yes, Shaka-Rho. By all the rules as we understand them, it should be the same.

It took her a moment to understand that. To weigh the implications of it. Even to one who wasn't a Hasai, some things were clear.

"Is that why you left her there?" She had to switch to speech again, not trusting her own emotions. "To be raised among the Azeans?" She practically spit out the last word.

"We didn't choose to 'leave her there.' " If the Lyu caught any hint of the anger behind her words she gave no sign of it. Calm, the leader was unshakably calm, golden and confident; no mere words could make her otherwise. "It was an accident. Unfortunate timing. We meant to claim you both."

Images swirled about Rho, prodding at the edges of her mind. She opened up enough to let them in . . . and saw the Community's agent caught in the midst of kidnapping two children, hurrying away with one while the other was left behind . . . she could feel the frustration attendant upon the images, long days of hot debate in the halls of the psychic community. *Go back, go back and get the other one, she is one of ours!* Emotion answered with logic, so cold a logic it hardly felt human. *No. Leave her there. This too will have purpose. . . .*

She felt herself tremble as the understanding came. "It was an experiment." She whispered the words, struggling to absorb their implications. "You left her behind as an *experiment.*"

"We 'left her behind' because we failed in Acquisition. You know the risk that would have been involved in a second effort. All the Azean authorities had been warned by the first attempt that we wanted the second child; getting through them again would have been all but impossible—"

"But a skilled Shaka could have done it."

Silence. Cold, thick silence. "Perhaps."

"You chose not to try."

"It is not so simple, Shaka-Rho."

"No? Then explain it to me."

A delicate telepathic ping warned her that she was near to crossing the line as far as acceptable behavior was concerned. She bit down hard on her frustration, forced calmer emotions to her foremind, and nodded. *Control is the key to all things,* the first Lyu had written. *Without control we are nothing.*

"You were a promising child," the golden figure said at last. "But only that, and no more. Do you know how many promising children there are, that we watch for years, only to see them come to nothing? Do you know how many humans carry the genetic sequences that are in your flesh, without them ever being triggered? Do you know how many come *here,* and dedicate their adolescence to our cause . . . only to learn when they mature that whatever quirk of fate divides psychic from nonpsychic has left them on the wrong side of the divide?"

The golden eyes narrowed as the woman leaned forward in her seat. Slowly the volume of her thoughts rose, until each word was accompanied by a shimmering wave of emotion, impossible to shut out or ignore. "Do you hear them at night?" she whispered. "I do. All the cries of those who have been brought to the gates of our world in vain. Who now live among us as lesser creatures, knowing we would never call them that in words, but suffocated by their own inferiority nonetheless. I hear them screaming out their frustration with their crippled, inadequate minds. All about me. So very many. . . ."

She leaned back once more. The pounding waves of emotion ceased, becoming mere ripples in the golden air, passing into streams of dust. "When we brought you here, it was in the hopes that you would become one of us. We also knew that you might not. Which is a harsher fate, Shaka-Rho? Never seeing heaven, or being brought to its gate and denied entrance?"

"And that was why you never told me she existed? You wanted to see if I would Awaken first?" Rho could hear the edge of anger coming into her voice, and she let it stay there. This, she deserved. "Well I did. That was years ago. So when did you mean to tell me about this?"

The golden eyes fixed on her. Amazing, how anything so warm in color could be so utterly cold in substance. "In time, Shaka-Rho. All things in their time."

"When?" she demanded. The woman's utter calm was infuriating. "When she died, maybe? 'By the way, Rho, you had a sister once. I'm so sorry, we left her in a barbaric empire where they fear the crazy psychics and sometimes they do terrible things to them, and she's gone now—' "

"It wasn't like that."

"Then what *was* it like? Or don't you think I have a right to know?"

The golden eyes narrowed in anger. "Must I spell things out for you as one would for a child? You are no infant, you know. You serve our mission, yes? That sometimes entails . . . sacrifice.

"She didn't have your power, Shaka-Rho. Or *any* power, to the best of our knowledge. The same genes, but no Awakening." She leaned forward on her throne. "Do you understand now? Do you grasp the value of such a thing, the unique opportunity she provided? We didn't plan to use her that way, we would have preferred to claim her when we claimed you, to raise her among us . . . but since we failed in that, and since you both had identical genetic potential . . . what a perfect test case for the effect of environment on latent genetic sequences! Worth any price.

"And look what it has gained us! Certain proof of what our scientists have always postulated: that genomes alone are not enough. The Awakening can neither be programmed nor predicted. Our scholars will spend centuries analyzing every moment of her life to this point—and yours—until we know which elements caused one of you to Awaken and the other to remain . . . what Azeans would call 'normal.' Perhaps, if we learn enough, we can Awaken those hordes who cry out their frustration at night . . . that would be a good thing, yes?"

Softly she said, "And I couldn't be told this at the time?"

The golden eyes were unblinking, emotionless. "Of course not. That would have changed the parameters of the experiment."

"Why? I'm already Awakened, right? My part is done. So what, did you think I would interfere with hers? Skew your precious experiment?"

Quietly: "Isn't that your intention now?"

She could feel a flush of anger rise to her face.

"We had to make sure she wasn't interfered with."

"And I couldn't be trusted."

"You're human, Shaka-Rho. The bond between identical twins is legendary. The attraction between split-egg twins who are raised apart, equally so." ~*We did not wish to have to argue with you. As I am doing now.*

"And you aren't human, I suppose?"

For the first time since her arrival Rho could see a flicker of emotion cross the Lyu's face. "I am the Guardian of the Community of Mind. I am the Commander of our eternal mission. If I were weak enough that human emotions could have interfered with my duties, I would have passed those duties on to another long ago." Her hand fluttered up to the vial she wore over her heart. "Do you doubt my dedication?"

Rho bit her lip. "No."

"Do you doubt my judgement?"

"No." She said the word because it had to be said, but she knew that insincerity hung about the word like a cloud, which any psychic could read. Nor did she try to make it otherwise.

"We are more than a people, Shaka-Rho. More than a nation. We are the guardians of humankind's most precious dream. We are its soldiers, commanded to protect a priceless genetic inheritance, and to wage war against those who would obliterate it. These goals are more important than one person, or any single family's happiness. Our Founder understood that. The Hasai understand it as well. Now you have been raised up to those ranks wherein human destiny is crafted, and such understanding is necessary. One person means nothing, in the face of such a campaign. —Ah, that disturbs you. Tell me, are you more bothered because I feel such a thing, or because I admit to feeling it?"

She said nothing. There were no safe words to say.

"You will learn, Shaka-Rho. It will take time, but understanding will come. Not all of our people are aware of the full scope of our mission, but as Shaka, now, you will be initiated into those secrets. You will see . . . the battle is worth fighting. At any cost."

"Perhaps." She whispered it, while an inner voice stirred to accuse her. *And you, Rho? You have manipulated people as well. You have twisted whole worlds, to suit the Community's agenda. Is that so different?*

I did it to protect them, she told herself. *To prepare them for battles to come, so that they might protect themselves.*

Yes, yes, the mantra of Hostilities Adjustment, the inner voice chided. *Excuses for playing God, Rho. You're no better than the rest of them.*

Distinction Discipline. She visualized the patterns in her mind and bit down hard, concentrating on them. Shutting down the conduits that shunted thought to the outside world, turning off the parts of the mind that accepted thoughts from others . . . was the voice that chided her coming from within her, or from the outside? If the latter, now it would be gone.

Mere seconds passed before she felt in control of herself again; in the stillness of the golden air it seemed like an eternity.

"Are your questions all answered now?" the Lyu asked quietly.

She considered for a moment, then nodded stiffly. No, not all answered by any means—a thousand questions still battered at the edges of her consciousness, demanding to be heard, answered, perhaps evaded—but as for what might be said here, and now . . . yes. That much was finished.

What have you made of us? she thought. Not daring to let the words out beyond the borders of her own brain. *What have we made of ourselves?*

She bowed. Formally. Remembering the words from one of her Adjustment texts: *Formality is the last refuge of the uncertain.* So be it. A thousand thoughts were buzzing in her head, but this was a place in which that noise would be heard by others. Better to put distance between herself and the Lyu—between herself and all the psychics—before she stopped to scrutinize them. "I thank you for seeing me."

The bronzed lips broke into a faint smile, cold, a ritual expression without any real warmth. "It is good that you come to ask such things. Our Adjustors must be sure of what they do."

She wasn't sure any more, that was the problem. All her certainty, all her pride, had been built upon the bedrock of identity. Now . . . she was a different creature than she had been. What did that make of her purpose?

She needed space. She needed time to think.

"Have I your permission to . . . to seek her?"

"It was assumed you would do such, when you knew."

Rho drew in a deep breath, exhaled it slowly. "That's not an answer."

"No. It is not."

She waited, unflinching. *I'm not a mindless puppet, you know.* She made no effort to transmit her thoughts, but was pretty certain the Lyu could hear them anyway. *You want my cooperation in your pet projects, you answer my questions instead of dodging them.*

It seemed to her that a hint of a genuine smile creased the woman's lips then. Nearly imperceptible, but undeniably genuine.

"Go where you wish," the Lyu told her. "Do as you will. Know you are watched, and make your choices appropriately."

~Everything you do, everywhere you go, every choice you make from now until the moment of your death, will teach us things about you. About our power. About ourselves.

Rho tried not to respond to that mentally, as she left the chamber.

In the end the leadership of our tribe will not be determined by who is strongest, or the most intelligent, or even the most determined. It will be won by men who wage war against allies as well as enemies, using means that are never direct, gathering intelligence where others do not even think to look for it, and above all else, perpetually preparing to face the unexpected.

—Zatar the Magnificent

THIRTEEN

LORD AND KAIM'ERA Tezal, son of Luzak and V'nista, sat at his desk in silence, contemplating the latest bill to come before the Kaim'erate. It was a complex creation, with hands that were thrust into the economic gloves of nearly a hundred planets, but he thought at last he had managed to isolate the parts that mattered most, and (more importantly) to whom they mattered. In that deadly arena of personal rivalries which lesser men called *the government,* such information could be priceless.

He called up his files on the Kaim'eri Sulas and Zosar, noted other points of confluence in their agendas, and decided that they were probably cooperating behind the scenes, even as they waged bitter war in public. Yet another facet of the ever-changing game which was Braxaná politics. He added a few notes to each man's file, recorded elsewhere that the pair seemed to be focusing their financial interests on the War Border of late, and then shut the file down.

He had property near the War Border as well. He rarely used it as more than a stopping-point for journeys that were for . . . well, for things that he wished to keep private . . . but if those two were building strength in the sector, perhaps he would be wise to do so as well.

It would certainly make his mission easier, if he was able to watch them closely.

The door chimed.

"Yes?"

B'SETH, the House announced.

He raised an eyebrow. "Let her in."

The heavy panels parted and his Mistress came into the room. She didn't ask why he had locked the door; she had lived with him long enough to know that there was some business he kept secret from everyone, even her. Maybe she sensed, on that primal intuitional level that Mistresses seemed to have, that knowledge of some things could prove fatal to her.

In this case it might not be an overstatement.

She waited until he looked up to acknowledge her entrance, then told him, "I have the information you wanted."

He raised an eyebrow. "On K'teva?"

She nodded.

He tapped up a screen from his desktop and gestured for her to come toward him. In a black-gloved hand she held out a slender gold ring. In a black-gloved hand he received it, and dropped it onto his private reader. The one that was connected to nothing outside the room, not even the Central Computer System.

Most of importantly of all, not the Central Computer System.

The machine whirred for almost a tenth of a second as it wended its way through encryption as complex and byzantine as Braxaná politics. Then the information began to appear before him: frequencies, planets, people. And last of all the text of a communication, itself painstakingly decrypted, which had been sent from the Central System itself.

"This was sent by K'teva's people?" he said quietly. "You are sure?"

"As sure as one can ever be, with her."

He nodded. K'teva might be half Braxaná in blood, and therefore entitled to organize a Great House of her own, but thus far she had not done so. Which meant that those who wished to spy upon her had to wend their way through a tangled maze of information conduits, nothing like the ordered and precise intelligence empire that a true Braxaná would have established. In theory such disorganization made her moves more vulnerable to outside scrutiny, but in fact . . . in fact it was like playing a board game with someone who knew the rules but not the strategy, and therefore was prone to do things so unexpected that it might give them an advantage.

Sometimes, if the element of surprise worked in their favor, such players could defeat their betters in a match. More often, they controlled the board for a very short while and then were soundly trounced.

"It's confirmed, then," he mused, reading meaning and motive into B'Seth's research. "She's tracking Tathas."

"So it would seem."

She was doing it indirectly, and her efforts were not unskilled, but to a man who was accustomed to uncovering the secrets of the Kaim'eri themselves, the trail was clearly marked. The little half-breed was watching Tathas. That meant she knew where he was. She might even know where he was going. For a woman of mixed blood with no House to back her, it was an impressive effort.

But what's the purpose in it? he thought. *That's the question that still needs to be answered.*

"It has to be more than affection," he mused aloud.

"Are you sure?"

"Oh yes." A faint expression, almost a smile, flitted across the painted face. "Her heart is cold, B'Seth, as cold as winter nights on the Blood Steppes. Ambition burns much hotter in her than the gentler emotions ever will." He steepled his black-gloved fingers on the desk in front of him. "In that, she is very Braxaná."

"You say she met with the Pri'tiera."

Still studying the screen, he nodded. "She seeks his favor, no doubt. And why not? He could give her the breeding rights she hungers for, without even consulting the rest of us." Not for the first time, he felt a hard knot of anger rise in his gut, at the reminder of the Pri'tiera's power. *We weren't meant to be ruled by one man. Not even one of ours. It isn't our way.*

The Pri'tiera was young, shamefully young, they all knew that. Inexperienced. Thus far he had shown himself to have respectable potential—as well he should, given the bloodline he came from—but at his age it might be no more than just that, *potential.* Was K'teva trying to manipulate him? That was a dangerous game, even with so young a Braxaná. It would raise interesting questions if she could pull it off. About both of them.

Such questions might be useful, in the hands of the right men.

"One of our informants reported in," B'Seth told him. "He was able to tell us exactly what information she's sending out there. It's at the end." She smiled slightly. "I think you'll find it . . . interesting."

He scanned to the end of the file. And frowned, as he read what was there.

"You are sure about this?"

She shrugged lightly. "The man's a good contact. He's been reliable in the past. Even more important . . . what purpose would he have to make up something like this?"

He read again the testimony of a mercenary of the Narren frontier. The man had indeed been a reliable informant in the past, and was well paid for it. He was one of the lynchpins of Tezal's own Outlands intelligence network.

That's right, he had written. *It was a courier who told me, one out of the Central System. Said there was evidence this Kesserit fugitive was a Shaka. (Pause.) That kind of information's worth money to the right people, you know. Anyway, he seemed to be spreading it around . . .*

Shaka. The file said it was some kind of psychic. How curious. "And you're sure this information came from K'teva."

"You have all the data there, my Lord."

Yes. Well organized too, and presented with the clarity and brevity that was B'Seth's hallmark. The trail led back through half a dozen informants, but it clearly had begun with K'teva. So. The little Kesserit half-breed had sent out word that Tathas was some kind of psychic, to the very people who would want to kill him for that. Did she want to get rid of him, perhaps? No, he decided. It was too convoluted an effort for that. The man was in such disfavor that a simple assassin could cross his path one tenth after he left the Holding and no one would think twice about it. K'teva had the money and the contacts to pay for that ten times over. No, she had something else in mind. Something far more devious and complicated, he was willing to bet.

Something worthy of the Braxaná blood in her, he thought.

It was too bad she had not been raised by his people. She would have made a worthy adversary if she had been. Now . . . he was not quite sure what she was. Sometimes he wondered if she knew herself.

"Shall I continue to monitor her?" B'Seth asked.

"Yes." He tapped the ring. "She's up to something, and I want to know what it is. Use whatever resources you need for the project."

His other mission demanded that he have a network of informants second to none. B'Seth didn't know about half of them, but even half was more than most Braxaná could muster. A man could do no less, when the very fate of the human-explored galaxy rested on his shoulders.

And what part will K'teva play in all this? he wondered. *That of an ambitious spectator, who dreams of wielding power but lacks the skill to claim it? Or will she prove to be more than that, perhaps one of those rare women who can set the Braxin system to stirring, a catalyst whom none can predict?*

Those women often met with rather violent ends, he recalled. Which was, in itself, a tribute to their accomplishments.

It has yet to be seen where this one's road will end. . . .

Envision a child, newborn, cradled in its mother's arms. Light assails its newly opened eyes from all directions, too much data to absorb. Overwhelming. The face of its mother, the form of its own hand, sunlight pouring in the window . . . all these things are but visual chaos, input without interpretation, that its tiny brain cannot yet sort out. A cacophony of data, frightening and fascinating, without meaning or form. How will it learn how to distinguish near from far, large from small, soft from sharp? Its brain lacks even the language to frame such concepts now. All it can do is stare at the light and absorb the chaos, and slowly struggle to sort out which images matter and which ones do not, so that the latter can be ignored . . . while its brain works desperately to create the neural pathways necessary to make sense of it all.

This is Awakening.

—Anzha lyu Mitethe

FOURTEEN

OUT PAST THE Border, in the Outlands, few things were *large*.

The planets, such few as were populated, were governed in small bits: continents and islands, plateaus and plains, each with its own master, each with its own laws. The moons which were pressed into service had rarely been zeymoformed, being more often than not barren spheres sprinkled with tiny stations, each paying regular bribes to some pirate band or local chieftain in order to safeguard its existence. The ships which plied the trade lanes were mostly private transports from the Empire, reoutfitted for a variety of duties. Even the stations that dotted the stellar reaches were small, bits and pieces of hardware cobbled together as time and necessity dictated, in a region where sophisticated building supplies were scarce and the machines required for interstellar construction even scarcer.

After all, if the Empire chose to expand into this region of space tomorrow, those who valued their independence would have to move out quickly. And it was far easier to move small things.

Yet in the depths of the Azeaside darkness there was one exception to this rule. Varozha Station represented the closest thing to a cooperative effort that existed at the frontier. Or so all the locals said. Approaching it on public transport—a sad little vessel that had once been some rich Azean's star yacht, now pressed into dirtier service where Azeans did not deign to travel—Zara tried to be impressed. Certainly by Outland standards it was grand enough, a sprawling station with several public docks and a host of private ones. Never mind that the parts of the station didn't quite match up, in scale or in style . . . as if someone had tried to assemble a picture from pieces of all different puzzles, Zara thought. Never mind that the identicodes near the docks had gone unpainted for so long that passing stellar dust had all but scoured them clean. Never mind that its nodes and rings had been assembled in seemingly random array, and the cost to maintain proper gravity in each must have been astronomical. For the Outlands it was impressive.

After all . . . it was *large* .

Zara watched the approach through the tiny window of her tiny cabin. Even from here she could feel the minds of her fellow passengers pressing in on her. Yes, she knew now, that's what they were. All the thoughts and emotions crowding her brain that seemed to come from nowhere . . . that's what they were. Other people's thoughts. The pressure never stopped. Other people's hates and fears, punctuated by random sparks of gentler emotions, which burned her brain like warm compresses burned frostbite. Sometimes when she had physical distance from other people it would quiet down a bit—like now—but that only worked so long as no one was experiencing any intense emotion. As soon as someone did it would come stabbing through her, ripping through all the safeguards she was trying so desperately to erect.

Day by day she struggled against the onslaught, believing in her soul that there must be some way to shut out the terrible flow. But if there was, she didn't know how to do it. Night after night she trembled in the grips of other people's nightmares. She was gaunt from the stress of the constant battle, and the image which gazed back at her from the mirror field, when she dared to look at it, seemed to be that of a stranger. Could so much of her have changed, in so short a time? It seemed like decades since she had left the Star Empire, and yet in that small part of her brain which was still functioning, she knew it was only days. Many days, to be sure, and each one an eternity in its own right, but not yet enough of them to add up to any sum which others would recognize as meaningful.

How much longer can I last like this?

Now there was hope. Such a small hope. One name, whispered in the shadows of a bar by someone who seemed to know what he was talking about. "Go find the Shamisi," he'd told her. Glancing both ways as he did so, as if afraid someone would overhear. "Start looking there."

At first she thought he had meant some other race that had connections with the psychics. Or maybe some political organization. Then she'd seen the concert ad. *Sweetest Voice in a Thousand Systems*, it had cajoled. *Performing for Five Vesuvian Days Only.* And above that all, in big block letters: *THE SHAMISI AT VAROZHA STATION.*

So now she was here. Coming to see some Scattered Races singer whose professional name was never voiced without an article. Bone tired, brain weary, Zara was dreading the mere concept of arriving in a public place, much less a crowded one . . . but she was determined to follow up the one solid clue she'd been given. So many people just gave her a blank stare when she asked about the psychics, or worse yet, turned on her as if the very question had been an offense. This man had at least seemed to know something. Whether or not that *something* would be of any use to her had yet to be seen. But at least she had somewhere to go now. Some clue to follow. Maybe this one would send her in the right direction, toward people who could help her protect herself from the continual alien onslaught. Toward her sister, who had been claimed by them so long ago.

If not . . . what then?

Don't think about that, she told herself stubbornly. Reminding herself of what her mother had told her, so long ago. *Live day by day. Face your problems one by one. You'll get through them, if you don't let them get to you first.*

She wished she could believe that.

The concert station itself was impressive even by Imperial standards. A display by the entrance explained that a consortium of traders had built the place originally, in order to serve as a cultural center for Outlands society. If Zara had any questions about why, they were dispelled when she passed over her final Imperial Credits for conversion and payment. Whatever the Shamisi was, she exacted a price that performers in the Star Empire would envy. *Five performances only,* declared glowing words that hung above the portal.

The machine at the main portal processed her money and gave her a small chip. She looked at it curiously, not grasping what its purpose was until, two doors down, she had to insert it to gain entrance to the main promenade. How bizarre. In the Empire they would just have taken a surface scan of her DNA and used that to verify the purchase later. But of course that meant that the local computers would know who she was, and when she had arrived. Outlanders were notoriously hostile toward the concept of anyone tracking them.

The "promenade" turned out to be a series of elevated walkways that twisted and crossed through a vast open space, filled with fake plants and floating sculptures. She could hardly negotiate it with a thousand alien thoughts pounding in her head, and for a moment thought she wasn't going to make it. *Move it, Chandran, or we'll all be late!* Somewhere a child was screaming because it was hungry, and its cries reverberated in her brain. Someone else was cursing a fellow traveler for having caused them to have poor seats for the concert . . . or maybe only thinking that loudly. Zara could hardly tell any more; the inner voices had become so loud it was impossible to distinguish mental voices from real ones.

Please, she prayed, please let this Shamisi have the answer. Some kind of answer, some kind of hope, anything. If she doesn't, if this is just another dead end . . . I don't know how much longer I can go on like this.

The concert hall itself was quieter, a minor blessing. Minds were settling down in expectation, their normal buzz muted as they prepared themselves to receive the performance. Thank the gods. She eased down into her formseat with a weary sigh, feeling it adjust itself to her countours. The mechanism was overworn and didn't quite get the shape right, but it was better than nothing. Zara shut her eyes and pretended she was out in the black reaches of space alone, with not another human mind nearby. Which was very likely where she would have to go, if she couldn't find some help soon.

A sudden hush alerted her to the start of the performance, and she opened her eyes.

There was a human girl on the stage, who waited silently until all eyes were upon her, without moving. She was small and young and not prepossessing in either her person or her dress. A tiny girl with plain, straight hair that hung down to her waist, and almond eyes that were not nearly as large or appealing as they might have been. Her dress was a simple sheath of blue-gray shimmersilk that changed color slightly as she finally moved, shifting her weight, but never did anything dramatic. Plain and lovely, suitable for a nightshift on the town . . . but decidedly underdressed for the Outland's preeminent diva. Was this the Shamisi? Was her talent so great that showmanship was not an issue? Zara found herself fascinated by the girl's almost hesitant presence, so utterly unsuitable for the grand stage of . . . well, anything. She reminded Zara of the gentler browsing beasts of her home planet, that would startle at the sound of anyone approaching and bound for cover. If one of them had been molded into human form and given a nice dress, it might have looked like this.

The girl approached center stage and then simply began to sing, without preamble or introduction. Like her physical presence the music was unimpressive, almost mundane. Her voice was pleasant, a liquid soprano, but it was hardly in a class to justify the usurious price of attendance. Were the Outlands so starved for entertainment that they had fantasized her greatness? Zara looked about the audience, mystified. The man sitting next to her caught her eye and grinned. "First time?" he whispered. "Give it a few, you'll see."

So she sat back, and she did. Trying to shut out the murmur of the minds surrounding her, which seemed at least to be focused on something other than her now. A welcome relief.

The first song was a simple ballad in the Ikna style, something about lost love. It was hard to make out the words at first—the girl sang it in a strange dialect that Zara had never heard before, probably some Outland construct—but as she relaxed, as she let the soft voice sink into her skin, the words became clearer. Or perhaps not the words themselves, but at least the story behind them. Something about a pair of lovers who took jobs on distant planets for a while, trying to save up the resources to be together forever. Their hunger to be together, the joyful certainty that separation was but a temporary necessity, rang clear through the music, and Zara found herself remembering relationships she had treasured and lost, remembering how precious each had seemed in its heyday. The words were simple and the voice that sang them was quiet, but somehow in combination they stirred her memories.

It wasn't until the end of the first piece that she realized she had been so drawn into the music that for the first time in many days she had not been aware of the minds surrounding her. That for a brief time there had been *only* music—no pain, no fear, no gut-wrenching despair. Nothing but the girl's soft voice, the music that cradled it, and the stories she wove.

Zara drew in a breath softly, slowly, trying to understand what had happened. The man who had talked to her before glanced over, saw her expression, and grinned. "Ah . . . y'see." She couldn't even nod. Now that the music had faded the cacophony of a concert hall full of human minds was starting to press in on her again, twice as painful for her brief respite. If the girl sang again, would it quiet those alien voices? Every cell of her body was on edge, straining to know. *Please tell me it wasn't my imagination,* she begged silently.

It wasn't.

The next song was a haunting poem of love and loss, its minor refrain well suited to the Shamisi's young voice. After a moment Zara just shut her eyes and let the music seep into her brain without interference from other sensory input. It was like a warm ocean tide, gentle but insistent, bearing away all the sands of consciousness and leaving clear pools of serenity in their wake. Now there was no sense of Other surrounding her, none at all, only ripples of emotion that spread out from each note, lapping against the walls of her consciousness. Yes, love was like that. Yet, loss was exactly that, velvet and bittersweet pain. Bits and pieces of verse floated through her awareness, not truly connected to the music, so much as borne upon its tide.

> *Let my devotion give you wings*
> *So that, in memory, you fly. . . .*

When that song faded Zara held onto the final note as long as she could. A lifeline to sanity. What was this girl, that she could have such an effect on her? Even when the minds surrounding her began their invasive murmuring once more, it seemed to her it was softer than before. Less distracting. Was that something real, or her own desperate imagination? Did this girl really have some power that could alter her mind, healing the internal wounds enough that random thoughts no longer stung her in passing—

Power.

Her eyes shot open.

By the Golden . . .

The next song began before she could process the thought any further. This was a ballad of ancient adventure, set in a time and place when bloodshed was a personal matter, swords against flesh as opposed to energies against starships. The Shamisi drew her audience into it slowly, beginning the performance with little more than a whisper as she described the verdant meadows of the first scene. Then a forest's shady sway, silently ominous, surrounding. If she sat back and relaxed Zara could feel the presence of rain-dampened foliage around her, and could sense the tragedy in the making. Were all the others feeling these things so acutely, she wondered? Or were her own fledgling psychic senses colluding with the girl's innate power to draw her further into the music than most could go? There was no way to know for sure, and as the song progressed she cared less and less about trying. There was the heroine, her beauty a crystal waterfall in the soul. There was the hero, whose strength set human nerves to humming.

There was the enemy, a monster, a dark minor chord that reverberated in one's very soul, like a fear rising out of the hindbrain, threatening to swallow all hope—

The end of the song left her gasping. After a while she raised a shaking hand to her face and realized that tears had been running down her cheeks. Her soul felt like a sponge that had been wrung dry of water, now thirsting for the next precious drop. All about her she could see people stirring, but she no longer needed to look at them to know what they were feeling. Yes, the music had moved them, but not as powerfully as it had done for her. Not so powerfully that they would look at the girl and call her talent by its proper name. For them there would still be the euphemisms polite society used to hold at bay that which was alien, frightening. *Emotive brilliance. Powerful phrasing. Fusion of alien vocal styles. . . .*

Except it wasn't really about any of that, was it? You didn't know that if you were merely human, because you couldn't sense the full range of what that music was carrying. But Zara knew. Zara's mind was an open wound, and the girl's emotions had poured into it, and even as she trembled in fear and wonder she knew what the proper label for that was.

The singer was psychic. Her music, her voice, it was all just a vehicle for that forbidden talent. Disguising it so that the common public would not know. Diluting it into doses they could absorb without trauma. Controlling them, without their knowing they were being controlled.

As Zara watched the girl take a drink of water and prepare herself for the next song, she shivered in a mixture of fear and elation. *She knows where the other psychics are,* she told herself. *Or they know of her, at the very least.*

She can lead me to them.

When the final number ended the concert hall was silent for a small eternity. And then the applause began, and the cries of adulation, and with them a wave of emotion from all the minds surrounding Zara. Following upon the peace she had tasted so fleetingly, the volume of it was enough to make her physically ill. She stood up and managed somehow to convey to the people nearest her that she wanted to leave before the crowd was done showing its appreciation. They let her go by. She caught their thoughts as she pressed past them, spearpoints of emotion that stabbed into her soul. *Ungrateful chit . . . utterly rude . . . insult to a great performer . . .* At last she was free and she stumbled into the promenade, swallowing back on the hot bile that had risen in her throat. That's how it would be again, when the Shamisi was gone. That's how it would be for her whole life, if she couldn't make contact with her, or if the girl wouldn't help her.

She can. She must!

The applause began to die down, and with it the mental focus of the audience began to disperse. In moments the rest of the crowd would be emerging and she would be overwhelmed again. Desperately she looked for some exit that would lead to a back corridor, some place the common public was not meant to go. She had to find her way backstage to where the Shamisi would be, but she couldn't take the same route all the fans would be taking. Their minds would swallow her whole.

She chose the only door that did not fade automatically as she approached, and opened it manually. It closed behind her even as people began to emerge from the concert hall, shutting out the sound of them with a force field's certain soundproofing. The corridor she had entered was clearly meant for workers, and lacked all the embellishments of the public spaces. Good enough.

She followed her instincts, trusting to the gods of all the human worlds that somehow she could sense where the Shamisi was, and instinct would lead her there. Several turns and several portals brought her around to the back of the stage; the few workmen who passed her raised eyebrows or curled antennae to see her there, but no one bothered to stop her. That was the Mediator's art, always looking like you belonged where you were, so that no one questioned your presemce. Even in her current state it didn't fail her.

At last she came to a busier area. Her heart racing, she followed the sound of mental chatter to join the people who were already gathered there. Stagehands, mostly, muttering technical jargon as they shut down the systems that had been used during the performance. There didn't seem to be any members of the common public about, or any open space where they might attend upon the object of their adoration. Zara took a quick breath and then squeezed her way past the technicians, ignoring random thoughts that strayed in her direction. Right now she was focused on one thing only, and the opinion of a stagehand about her right to be here—or even her breast size—was of little concern.

At last she came to a security portal guarded by a human sentinel. She didn't need insight into his thoughts to know what was beyond that door; his posture said it all. Mustering all the courage she could, she walked up to his post as though it were the most natural place in the world for her to be, and said to him in a voice that was utterly, professionally calm, "I'm here to see the Shamisi."

Black eyes looked looked her over, disarmingly Braxin. Did the races mix much, in the Outlands? She hadn't thought about the possibility before.

"I'm sorry," he said. "No visitors after performance."

She drew in a deep breath. "I have important business with her."

He shrugged. "Those are the rules. I'm sorry, no exceptions."

She felt the Mediator's mask slip from her face for a moment, letting a glimpse of her real emotions show. It took effort to choke out the words with any semblance of dignity. "Please. I have to talk to her." If she told him the truth, would it matter? If she told him that her sanity was frayed to the breaking point, and this young girl was the first sign of hope she'd had since her spiral downwards into madness had begun—that if she couldn't talk to her she didn't know where to turn next, or if she even had the strength to leave this place—would that matter? She choked back on the words and the tears that would surely follow them, not yet willing to sink to those depths. "Gaston sent me," she said at last, citing the name of the one who had told her to seek the performer. It didn't look like the name meant anything to him. Nor did the trembling in her voice seem to affect him at all. For one brief, mad moment she wondered if she could move him out of her way by force. Surely it was better to attempt such folly and fail than to simply give up, when hope was so close she could taste it.

"She doesn't see anyone after performances," the guard told her. His voice was neither harsh nor sympathetic, simply the bland communicative tool of someone doing his job. "No fans, no reporters, no nothing. I'm sorry. Those are the rules, she doesn't break them for anyone."

Zara said nothing. She couldn't get words out past the lump in her throat. So close, so close. The tears were coming again now and she didn't know how to stop them.

"You don't understand," she whispered at last. "I *have* to talk to her. It doesn't have to be here. Some other time. Some other place." She drew in a deep breath, trembling. "Please. Tell me how."

The black eyes fixed on her. For a moment there was a strange sense of vertigo, a sense of something indefinable sweeping past her. A shadow, a ghost. She grasped at it with all her mental strength, willing it to taste the full extent of her fear, her desperation. *Please help me,* she begged. *I have nowhere else to go.*

With a short grunt the man reached into his jacket and drew out a wafer-thin data chip. "Five Standard Days," he said shortly. "When the concert's all over, that's when she handles business. You come here"—he tapped the chip against an open palm, then offered it to her—"She'll talk to you."

Taking the chip from him, she tried to compose herself. "Thank you."

"It's a one-shot," he warned her. Surprised, she looked into his eyes as if for some kind of explanation, but he offered none, and his expression was unreadable. One-shot chips were commonly used in handling illicit information, where you didn't want any trace of it hanging around as evidence. They played one time and then erased themselves. If you tried to copy them they would fry any equipment they were running on. She'd had that happen to her once as Mediator, and had never forgotten it.

"I'll be there," she promised. Cradling the translucent sliver in her hand.

Five days. She could make it five days, surely.

She turned to go back the way she had come, but a grunt from the guard drew her attention back to him. He was pointing another way, across the backstage area and up a flight of stairs. "You'll beat most of the crowd that way." A dry smile twisted his lips. "It's where the rich ones exit."

She nodded gratitude for the tip and headed in that direction. Even from this distance she could sense the murmur of the concert crowd, caught in the inevitable bottleneck of the exit. The thought of diving into that mass of humanity and nonhumanity, with all its mental exudations, made her feel faint inside. Hopefully upstairs the situation wouldn't be as bad.

Did he know that was a concern for her? she wondered. No way to know now. But in five days' time she would be able to ask that . . . and many things. Her hand closed about the chip as if it was the most precious thing in civilized space to her. And wasn't it? Was there anything in her world that mattered more, right now?

The stairs led up to a sweeping veranda, floored in copper faux-marble veined in grey and black. Most of the patrons had left already, and it was a relief to come a place where there were few people about. She paused by the head of a golden balustrade to draw in a deep breath, trying to shut the distant clamor of strangers' thoughts out of her mind. *Five days. You can make it that long. One at a time, girl.* Once she got off Verozha Station she could hire transport to some hovel of a hotel that was off by itself in the starlanes, and buy herself five days of solitude. It wasn't a luxury she'd been able to allow herself during her search, but now that she knew there was an end to searching . . . or at least a signpost to help plan the next phase of it . . . she could spare a few days to be alone, and to nurse her wounded soul.

Feeling more hope than she had in days, she followed a series of discreet signs pointing to the visitors' docks. A few people passed her, murmuring affluent knots of humanity, gathered like herdbeasts about their most vulnerable members. Glittering women in shimmersilk gowns and men in robes of sleek silverskin, flanked by husky bodyguards from some hi-gravity world who scanned the entire area before letting their precious charges emerge. Wealth was a risky thing in the Outlands, and few men or women of substance would travel without a contingent of bodyguards.

The main walkway took her to an exit portal that shimmered prettily as she passed through it, wasting energy in a last display to please the patrons. From this direction she'd be passing the private bays first, a luxury the wealthy paid dearly for, but eventually she should come out near public transportation. A sharp turn revealed the first of the small docks, each rented for the shift by a particular family or charter group. Most of the patrons had already left, and viewscreens overhead showed dozens of ships already in transit, weaving their way through a crowded periphery to the open blackness of space beyond. A few of the portals were still unsealed, allowing her to peek in as she passed. Bodyguards hustled their charges into tiny vessels as the pilots made a final check of astrogation and force field control. Their thoughts were so focused she was hardly aware of them. Families gathered at entrances, smoothing glittering clothes as the solid hull doors opened for them—

And then she stopped, as an all too familiar sensation lurched in her gut.

The portal before her was open. Inside the dock she could see a few figures moving toward a small vessel, whose pristine, gleaming hull proclaimed wealth in quantity, as well as the desire to show it off. Ostentation was rare in the Outlands, which spoke volumes for the owner's importance . . . or perhaps for his foolishness.

Wrong. Something's wrong.

The feeling was sudden, a hot wave of dread that washed over her body and was gone before she even knew its name. It was like what she had felt in the Mediation chamber, right before the bomb had gone off. And yet . . . no. Not a bomb. She knew that somehow. Knew that the thoughts which had just reached out and stabbed her in the gut had nothing to do with explosions and killing. But something bad. She knew that.

Go on. Move on. Ignore it. Get out of here.

But she couldn't. Curiosity warred with fear inside her, the desperate need to understand what she was feeling balanced against the gut certainty that it heralded trouble. In the end, by a fraction, the former emotion won out. She felt her legs move, bringing her through the portal and into the dock itself. A guard looked up with a warning hiss and pulled some kind of weapon on her; she didn't even recognize its type. Two guards, she noticed. One small teenage girl. Daughter of somebody important, no doubt. Or at least somebody rich.

The *wrongness* throbbed inside her head. She knew she should turn and run, that it was the only safe thing to do . . . but she couldn't. She had to know.

"Who are you?" The guard had a slurred Outland accent which normally might be unclear, but these words he spat out had enough professional venom to make their meaning clear. "What are you doing here?"

"Something's wrong," she whispered. Her head throbbed as she looked around the small dock. Clean, it was clean, nothing but a few transport cubes by the lift. Where was the feeling coming from?

Something focused on this place. That's what you felt last time. Bombs don't have thoughts, even psychics can't sense them. But the people who set them up do.

"Look, I don't know who you are, but you need to move out now." The other guard waved with a military-grade stun towards the portal behind her. "Don't make any trouble, please, we don't want that."

Don't want to shoot an unarmed woman, the thought came, clearly as if he spoke it aloud. *But if I have to I will.*

Then the teenage girl put a hand on his arm. She opened her mouth to speak, to say something to maybe calm the moment—

And then Zara knew.

She *knew.*

"It's you," she whispered to the girl. "They're coming for *you.*"

The first guard's eye narrowed. "Who the—"

And then the door of a transport cube split open, hissing protest at being forced so suddenly. A dark figure lunged for the small ship and was between it and the guards before any of them could come about. He held some weapon Zara had never seen before and he fired one, two, three, four shots, even as the guards turned toward him—

And more cubes broke open and there were other figures, swathed in black, bolting across the space to take the guards as they turned—

The girl screamed. Her fear broke over Zara with the force of a tidal wave, leaving her reeling. She tried to put one foot in front of the other and stumbled, just in time for some sort of projectile to whiz over her head. *Portal, portal, find the portal* . . . But something hit the control panel and sparks flew as the portal sealed itself, closing off the only possible escape.

I'm going to die. The thought wasn't her own, but a terrified teenage keening, the sudden panicked recognition of *mortality* as a human state. *Oh Hasha I'm sorry dad I shouldn't have come you were right you were right you were right—*

Guards. Pain. Blinding impact. A terrible weight on Zara's chest that kept her from breathing, but was it her pain or someone else's? Coughing blood, but nothing came up; it wasn't hers. Dark figures moving toward her, away. Borders between minds blurred as they caught up the girl, whose shrieks filled the echoing space to capacity, whose mental screams filled Zara's head to bursting. *Oh Gods, whatever you came here for, I don't know anything about it, please let me go.* Maybe in another time and place Zara would have tried to be heroic, but right now it was all she could do not to vomit up all those alien thoughts onto the floor of the dock while they watched.

They'd kill her if she vomited. She knew that. They'd kill her if she did anything that delayed them, or even distracted them. She could taste that knowledge, as hot and as bitter as the bile in the back of her throat.

The girl stopped screaming suddenly. Dead, or just unconscious? Zara felt sickness well up inside her with numbing force and she forced herself to swallow back on it, hard. She wanted to try to stand again, but a red-hot thought from someone else's brain warned her that if they thought she could fight back they'd kill her on the spot, so she stayed as she was, crouching, trembling.

"Her!" a voice barked out suddenly. "Take her!" An alarm began to sound in the distance; one of them cursed. "No time for questions now, just do it!"

She didn't even realize they meant her until two of the black-clad figures grabbed her and jerked her to her feet. *I have nothing to do with these people!* The scream was trapped behind a lump in her throat; she couldn't get it out. The hands of the men burned as they grabbed her, their flesh a conduit for thoughts as violent and dark as a beast's. *No! No! You don't understand!* Terror flooded her soul in hot, bile-driven waves. Not fear of death, or even of pain . . . fear of suddenly losing the only hope she had left. The sudden terror of being trapped in space with murderers' thoughts pounding in her brain, while the Shamisi left this place and disappeared into the darkness beyond, never to be found again. *I can't leave here!* Terror of being no more than a conduit for other people's emotions forever—

She struggled. Desperately. But the strong arms held her and dragged her toward the ship, and when at last she annoyed them enough with her struggles they struck her across the back of the head, twice. Professional blows, just enough to drive her down into darkness . . . and into a pit of blissful silence where finally, mercifully, even the fear was extinguished.

Information, intelligence, that is the heart's blood of any war. By the time guns move into position and men begin to fight the greatest battles have already been won or lost, and violence alone cannot alter their course.

—Anzha lyu Mithethe

FIFTEEN

GOOD DATA, HANAAN thought, was better than good sex.

He looked at the spread of details before him, ordered the computer to rearrange a few things, and then sat back with a sigh that was as eloquent in its satisfaction as the first leisured breath after lovemaking.

The report from Orknea was . . . priceless. Not that his contacts had understood that; if so, they'd have charged him more for it than they did. After all, they thought they just were reporting on a woman who had gotten drunk enough to act erratically in a bar. Hanaan knew the woman's drinking habits, however—as he knew everything about her—and that didn't explain what had happened on Orknea. Only one thing did.

Zara's powers were awakening.

It was a heady concept. Most operatives in the Organization would have cursed it happening, because it inserted a new and unknown factor into their pursuit paradigm. But for Hanaan it was confirmation of all his work, and the first sign that this risky campaign was going to pay off.

Zara the Mediator was psychic; he knew it now for a fact. That meant her twin almost certainly was . . . and probably had been for most of her life, given that she'd been raised in a place where there was no reason to suppress such a power.

The pieces were all falling into place.

He alerted a few more of his Outland contacts to his need for information and then put Zara's case away for the day. Much as he would like to focus all his time on this one assignment, there were other things to do. Fortunately most of the actual work could be handled by subordinates; he was little more than a conductor in such cases, telling his instruments when to create their music and when to be silent.

It was the conductor who was praised most when the orchestra played well.

The next item was an odd one. It was a request for audience from one of his field operatives, a Tashi named Duroka who ordinarily never set foot within the Empire itself. His assignment was the Outland frontier, and he was good enough at passing for a freelancer that dealing with humans within the Empire could be . . . awkward. Hanaan remembered the man's last visit, and the trouble he'd had to bail him out of after he had wrecked half a bar on Sota over some disparity in his tab. Apparently in the Outlands that was not only acceptable but typical behavior. Hanaan had had a good talk with him then, about long-term plans and future assignments and how decidedly unpleasant it would be for both of them if Duroka made enough mistakes within the Empire to get himself killed before any of that bore fruit. The man had stayed in the Outlands ever since . . . until now.

"Send him in," he ordered the room's computer.

The agent who entered was dressed in an unimpressive manner, neither festooned with holsters (his weapons would have been taken from him upon arrival in the Organization's complex, of course) nor partaking of the sensationalistic colors and forms that so many freelancers preferred. That was good, Hanaan noted; he was learning how to dress for the Empire. He didn't fear the man or he wouldn't have allowed him in his presence, but he was wary enough to keep the desk between them, and offered him a nod of welcome rather than the clasp of a hand, which would have brought him closer. There was enough hidden weaponry between them to ameliorate any problems which might arise, provided there was a second to use them, and he preferred to keep it that way.

"I'm surprised by your visit," Hanaan began, "but honored by your long travels to reach me."

Duroka made some complicated hand signal of greeting, a Tashi custom. He was a mongrel through and through, both in genes and behavior, but in Hanaan's presence he liked to pretend otherwise. "May the suns of all the human worlds shine favorably upon you and yours," he responded.

It was a sweet sentiment, if a bit bizarre under the circumstances. He doubted either he or Duroka had stood beneath the light of a natural sun for some time.

"Is there food or drink you would like, Duroka? My facilities are at your service."

"I thank you, but your people have seen to my needs." He did not take the chair that Hanaan indicated, but remained standing, an odd restlessness evident in his manner.

"So what brings you here?" Hanaan asked. "Your past service has earned you the right to audience, you know that. Though I must admit I'm surprised you've come so far just to talk face to face."

The Tashi's eyes glittered. A pair of crystalline inner lids swept down over them once and then tucked themselves again into the recesses of his orbital fossi. "Some news can't be trusted to normal channels."

Normal channels. That would mean passed along through his superiors. Hanaan nodded slowly as the picture came together. Either Duroka feared his superiors would garble the message . . . or if not, that they would claim full credit for it. Either possibility was intriguing.

Hanaan leaned forward on his desk. "Go on."

"There's a Braxin in the Outlands."

"There are many Braxins in the Outlands."

"Not like this one. He's on a mission, as sure as I can smell it. And . . . he's being tracked."

Hanaan raised an eyebrow. "By whom?"

"Don't know. Covered their ass well, whoever it is. But I found a link in the chain that was willing to talk, for the right price, that is." He paused expectantly.

"Yes, yes, all your expenses will be covered. As usual." Hanaan waved a hand to urge him on.

"I got hold of one of the messages," Duroka said. "It cost an arm and a leg." A calloused and fight-scarred hand pulled a hardcopy out of his pocket. It was an old thing, worn from its travels and stained with faded brown spots of Hasha knew what. Hanaan took it from him.

At least three agents paying for information on the Braxin, the note said. It was handwritten, in an oddly twisted scrawl which hinted at someone trying to disguise his handwriting. *Confirmed source, Central System. Outbound this from one: Subject is shaka.*

"You know what a shaka is?" Duroka asked.

"Oh yes." He licked his lips, reading the note again. Anyone who hunted the psychics knew what a shaka was. The legendary warrior-psychic, who could fell men with no more than a thought. When the Institute had existed it had denied that such creatures existed. Now, in the wake of the Institute's destruction, there were enough reports of such creatures in the Outlands that most who lived there believed in them.

Hanaan did as well. It was one of the reasons that finding and getting control of the psychic community was so important to the War effort.

Now he understood why Duroka had come in person. The man understood the value of this intelligence, and didn't want it included in some report that might or might not include his name in the final draft. Oh, Hanaan understood.

He briefly considered downplaying the message's importance, but the Tashi had been a good agent and he deserved better than that. He fingered the dirty hardcopy as if testing the feel of it while he said quietly, "You know this has great worth, Duroka."

The Tashi grinned. One tooth had been capped in turquoise, an Outland custom. "I figured."

"I will see it acknowledged appropriately."

Duroka bowed, accepting the promise.

"Do you seek promotion?" He tried to keep his voice from betraying his true emotions as he asked it. The Tashi was ill-suited for any position other than the one he currently held, that of free-roving informant, but if he dreamed of more and had come here himself to make it happen . . . that was something to know now.

But Duroka simply smiled his twisted smile. "Not my place, you know that. I'm happiest where I am. But the price of living has gone up quite a bit . . . if you catch my drift."

Hanaan nodded. "I understand. I will see it . . . compensated for."

"And I thank you."

"The Organization takes care of its own."

"Well it does, well it does."

"You'll get me more information on who sent this?"

"Oh yes." Again the crystalline inner lids fluttered. "May I send it directly?"

For a nanosecond Hanaan considered. It was against regulations, and for good reason. If every operative who scoured the galaxy for information were to ignore the chain of command and just send things wherever they wanted, to whoever they wanted, the Organization would be an unholy mess.

But this . . . this was different.

"Yes." He said it quietly. "This matter only. You understand?"

The alien eyes gleamed, lizardlike. "I understand."

Hanaan was only half watching as the Tashi made some complicated gesture of leavetaking, and his nod of acknowledgement was automatic. His attention was fixed upon the small piece of writing in his hand, and the vast universe of potential that it was key to.

Braxins active in the Outlands. Seeking psychics? Hunting them? He tapped the hardcopy thoughtfully as the portal sealed behind Duroka. Part of Hanaan wished it said more. Part of him welcomed the challenge of its terse, noncommittal message. His operatives would trace this to its source and then he would have more to think about. All things in their time. Puzzles were not solved overnight.

First the Chandran going psychic. Now Braxins in the Outlands, and a race to find the ones with power. The very thought of it was intoxicating.

All in all, not a bad day.

A closed mind is a deadly weakness.

—Zatar the Magnificent

SIXTEEN

"**W**ELL," RAIJA SAID darkly. "That was certainly not our cleanest work."

The viewscreen showed open space, finally. Not station rings, not security skimmers, not even the piecemeal rigs of the free-lance bounty hunters who usually flocked around Outlands crime scenes like carrion birds on rotting meat. Yet the crew didn't seem very happy, Tathas noted. Just bitter, that they'd had to waste time dodging security and leaving a path of blood behind them that half the galaxy would want to follow.

"So what the hells happened back there?"

Homani looked up from the very stiff drink he'd been nursing since the last pursuit had fallen behind them. Tathas could smell the alcohol from across the room. "She knew we were coming, we had to move before she could warn anyone else—"

"Yes, yes, I didn't mean that part, you all did what you had to." Raija's expression was dark. "I mean the *girl*. How did she know we were there? We never trust outsiders with real information. How in all the human hells did she get such precise details of our plan?"

"Something could have slipped through our employer's end," Fatu muttered.

Tali'l snorted. "Not damned likely. Then we'd have had a good deal more trouble than one Chandran muttering half-assed warnings to the guards." She looked up as Kesh came in. "Get anything out of her?"

"Not me. She's barely coherent. You can try if you like."

"And the kid?"

"Scared herself wet, but she'll survive." She glared at Fatu. "No one hit *her* on the head."

He glared back. "She didn't start having seizures on the damned dock."

"A blow to the head only scrambles so much," Kesh pointed out. "Sooner or later we'll have the truth out of her."

"So do we have more trouble coming?" Tali'l asked, changing the subject. "You think?"

Raija shook his head. "Hard to say. We need to go over the kid's ship and make sure there's nothing on it that's going to bring trouble to us. Ten to one there is right now."

"I'm on it," Homani said. In one smooth motion he stood up, chuted the remains of his drink, and headed out to the lock.

"We should have taken the damn guards with us," Fatu muttered. "Or killed them. We should have had time. We *should* have been half a galaxy away from that god-damned station before anyone knew something was wrong."

Hoping to dispel a mood that was going nowhere constructive, Tathas asked quietly, "What can I do to help?"

Raija held up his hand. The palm was tattooed with a cross-and-circle symbol, something about an ancient Vorastrian god of luck. "Nothing for now. Homani will check the girl's ship for tracking programs. We've got two Standard Days to make rendezvous with our employer and I'm going to keep us out of traffic until then. Not all that sure we're clear of trouble, yet." He glanced toward the passenger section, his eyes narrowing. "Talk to the woman, if you like. See if you can find out where the hells she got her information from."

"I'm hardly a psyche counselor," Tathas pointed out.

"Yeah, well that makes six of us." He snorted. "Maybe a Braxin will scare her enough to bring her back to her senses." He glanced toward the viewscreen; it showed nothing but stars. "Tell her we'll let her live if she just tells us where she came from, how the hells she knew what we were doing. She's not what we came here for, she hasn't seen our faces, we can let her go."

"Is it true?"

"Does it matter?"

Silence.

"No," he said at last. "Not really."

You signed on for this, Tathas. You knew there'd be killing. What difference is there really, between the guards who got in your way and this woman? You didn't hesitate where the guards were concerned.

He'd killed a number of people in his life. Some had been friends, some enemies. One was his own father. It was the way of the Kesserit, that kept them strong down through the ages. But every one of those men, without exception, had known the risk and accepted it. Every one had faced him with a sword in his hand, ready to fight. Even the guards in the dock had signed on for a killing game, knowing that sooner or later someone would be pointing weapons at their heads.

Not the woman. He had seen that in her eyes. She hadn't chosen this game, she had been thrust into it unwilling . . . and unprepared.

Does that matter? his conscience chided him. *With the stakes that are being played for, does one woman really matter?*

He left the room without further words.

The chamber they had put Zara in was barely larger than a closet, but that was all right. When the whole of your consciousness was wound up in a tiny black ball, and the darkness beyond was a vast unknown space teeming with hostile emanations, the smaller the better.

Zara wasn't afraid. She had gone beyond *afraid*, into realms where normal human emotions no longer had sway. Words like *afraid* were for mundane threats, finite fears that had clear boundaries. You were *afraid* something would happen. Then it did or it didn't. Then it was over with.

This . . . this was infinite.

If she could still her nerves enough to concentrate she could hear them talking. Not in words, which didn't get through the walls of the ship, but in thoughts. Red-hot spearpoints of thought, stabbing into her skull. *I say just kill her. Safer that way.* Ice-cold frozen-blood thoughts, twisting in her gut. *What about torture? That'll get answers!* And sometimes, if she listened closely enough, keening terror-thoughts from the ship's other captive. Those were the worst of all, flooding her brain with someone else's pain, someone else's hopelessness, until she could barely breathe. When the other girl finally fell asleep she felt it resonate throughout her entire body, and slumped against the wall in relief, wondering if she would ever know such peace herself.

The crew came in to question her, sometimes. They wore the same masks they had in the assault, which she was grateful for. As long as she didn't see their faces they might think it was safe to release her. She wasn't about to tell them how much a trained Mediator could learn about them just from their voices, their gestures, their word choices. Of course, she was hardly in shape to be making objective observations right now. It was hard enough to focus on human speech when all the hates and fears of your interrogator were pounding in your head. No wonder psychics went insane at an early age. Imagine a whole lifetime like this!

Ah, my poor sister, are you still alive? Or did this happen to you, and did it overwhelm you, until you lost your hold on sanity and let the thoughts of others sweep you away forever?

The portal opened. Again. This time the light in the room wasn't turned on, but the portal was left open slightly, allowing a dim band of illumination from the outside corridor to fall across the floor. She blinked as her eyes adjusted, taking stock of her newest tormentor. He was male, strongly built, and he moved with an almost animal grace. Oddly, she wasn't assaulted by his mental hostility the way she had been with the others, which sparked her interest immediately. Could it be there was someone on this ship who didn't regard her mere existence as a personal affront?

He studied her for a moment, silent in the near-darkness, and she used that moment to try to gather up the bleeding shards of her spirit, so that she might be coherent when she spoke. It hadn't mattered with the others—giving them answers only brought her that much closer to death—but she sensed that with this one it might.

At last he spoke, and the quiet cadence of his voice sent a shiver up her spine. "So you're the one who gave the warning."

Braxin. He was Braxin. She'd never met one before but she was trained to recognize them, and his accent had all the signs. The pitch of his word endings. The twist of a sibilant. By all the human gods, were there Braxins involved in this? Were they taking her to the Holding? A new panic welled up inside her, and for an instant it choked off all coherent thought.

He crouched down before her, his shadow coalescing into a compact mass at her level. There he waited, watching her in the near-darkness, poised with a readiness she could taste like salt on her tongue . . . but not overtly threatening. Not *immediately* threatening.

The others hadn't been like that. The others had wanted her scared, and they had loomed over her as part of the game. They had done other things too, as if those things would get them answers. It had just driven her deeper into her shell.

"You know you have to talk to us eventually, don't you?" His voice was calm, conversational, all the more powerful for being understated. "They're going to keep trying until they get what they want, one way or the other. You know that, don't you?"

They. They. He wasn't one of them. She clung to the strand of knowledge like a lifeline. "I'm trying," she breathed. That was already more than she had given some of the others. Was he aware of how much each lucid sentence cost her, in this state?

He nodded. Darkness moved against darkness, haloed by light from the corridor behind him. He wasn't wearing a mask, she realized suddenly. That's why he had left the lights off. The sudden thought of his being there with his face naked, rather than hidden behind swaths of cloth like the others, was disconcerting . . . and strangely intimate. Shaken, she looked down at her hands. Anywhere but at him.

"Tell me about what happened in the dock, Zara."

With a ragged sigh she nodded, knowing even as she did so that the words she had to offer weren't what he wanted to hear. "I was passing by on my way to public transportation. That's all. I don't know why I stopped to look inside. I really don't." Tears started flowing from her eyes, more from frustration than fear this time. How she wanted real information to give him, that would end this nightmare! But she didn't dare tell him the truth of the matter, which she had come to realize . . . that the thoughts of the kidnappers had drawn her in from the corridor, had telecast their intentions to her, and she had picked them up without realizing . . . "I really don't know." The explanation wasn't good enough, she knew that. The others had made that clear. They wanted someone to blame, someone to punish, to kill . . . and all she had to offer was herself.

Would the Braxin strike her? One of the others had, when she'd told him her story. He'd cursed her for a fool for expecting anyone to believe such a simple-minded tale and hit her across the face hard enough to draw blood in her mouth. And in fact this one did reach out toward her, and in the semidarkness the move was twice as frightening. She huddled back as far as she could get against the wall and trembled. But the touch came without violence, one finger on her cheek, then two, then his hand gently touching her face. His palm was warm and thrummed with living energy. Yes, his essence was dark and violent and frightening in the way that any alien energy was frightening, but there was also strength and stability and a sense of controlled masculinity that stroked and soothed her on a hundred different levels, so that she found herself sighing softly when the touch was finally withdrawn.

"You knew we were coming for the girl," he said at last.

She caught the faint aspiration at the end of the verb, which in his own native language would have indicated a question. "No," she said haltingly. Never mind that he was Braxin. She was glad for someone to listen to her without threatening her or hurting her, and afraid that the wrong word would shatter the spell. "I really didn't have any idea about that. I didn't even know she was there at first. I just felt . . . as if something was wrong. I came inside to see what it was."

It was closer than she had come to the truth with any of the others, and she trembled as she heard the words leave her mouth. She could sense his eyes narrow with sudden interest, and the intensity of his mental scrutiny lanced into her brain like fire. She cried out sharply and pulled away from him, trying to will herself to fade into the wall, to be anywhere but here.

"I'm not going to hurt you," he said quietly.

"I know." There were tears in her eyes now. "I know, it's not you, it's not anything you're doing. It just . . . hurts."

"What does?"

She shook her head, unable to explain. What was she going to say to a Braxin that would make this any better? They killed psychics on sight, didn't they?

Again the heat of his scrutiny touched her, but this time she was ready for it. *Focus,* she thought with wonder. That's what she was feeling, his *focus.* When emotions were focused directly on her she sensed them more acutely. That's what had happened in the Mediation chamber right before the explosion, she realized suddenly—someone nearby had been focusing his thoughts on her, wondering whether she knew about the plot, whether she would break up the meeting before the bomb went off, and that had made the vital connection—

"Tell me about it, Zara."

I wish I really could read minds, she despaired. *I wish I could know what you were thinking, what it was you wanted from me that the others don't, how to play to that desire without getting myself killed, so that you'd work to keep me alive.*

She whispered it. "What?"

"What you're feeling now. Tell me."

Fear raised the hackles on her neck. "What does it matter?"

"Maybe it doesn't," he said quietly. Strong, soothing; his voice had a hypnotic quality her exhausted soul could not resist. If she just closed her eyes perhaps it would carry her away, far from the pain and the fear. "Maybe I'm just curious."

Oh, it mattered to him. It mattered so much to him she could taste it. But he wasn't going to say why it mattered. And she wasn't going to tell him why she couldn't talk about it. Around and around they would go, a dance of words, until he got angry and hurt her, like the others had, or simply went away.

Which was worse?

"I'm tired," she whispered. Her tone was a plea—for solace, for safety, for understanding. "I'm hungry. I've been afraid for my life since we left the station. Now, under the strain, I'm starting to see and hear things that aren't real. Is that such a surprise?" She wished she could see his face. She needed the cues of facial expression to know how to maneuver with this man, which words were safe and which would get her killed. He had his own agenda, clearly, and if she could just figure out what it was and play to it she might gain an advocate in this nightmarish situation. Perhaps even a protector. But the darkness offered her no information. "It doesn't mean anything."

He mulled over that half-truth in silence. She shut her eyes and hesitantly, tentatively, let herself *feel* him. Exploring the presence that pressed against her soul with all her newfound senses, like a blind sculptor might caress a model to learn its curves. It was the first time she'd tried to use the power consciously and it surprised her how little pain there was, when she accepted it rather than fighting it.

Anger. That was the strongest impression. Boundless rage over something, somewhere. A hot tide of hunger for killing—no, for a vengeance that went beyond killing, for a destruction of enemies so total that death would seem merciful by comparison. *Frustration.* Plans dead-ended, aspirations cut short, a lifetime of promise ripped loose from its moorings and cast adrift on a wild and unpredictable sea. *Determination.* A spirit that would not, could not be conquered. *Pride.* A sense of identity that reached back through the centuries, to something greater than a single man. A searing strength of self-image that fed the hatred, highlighted the frustration, fueled the determination.

She was tied to all that, somehow. Maybe. He wasn't sure about that yet. It was in something she had said . . . or not said. Something he was searching for. What? She struggled to sort out what she was getting from him, to understand.

"Tell me about yourself," he said quietly. "Who you are, where you came from."

She drew in a deep breath, grateful to be offered a safer line of questioning. "I'm Chandran. From Chandra itself, originally."

"Inside Azea." He said the name as if the taste of it was strange on his tongue, an alien sound he had to roll around in his mouth and explore before he could expel it.

"Inside the Empire, yes."

"Go on."

"I was a Mediator."

"That is . . . some kind of diplomat?"

The question took her aback. It was hard for her to imagine that someone might not know what a Mediator was. That would be like . . . like . . . like not knowing what an Astrogator was. Or a Starcommander. "Yes. We . . . mediate disputes. Analyze the points of intransigent hostility on each side and develop communication channels to allow both parties to work past them."

"Is that what you were doing in the dock? Mediating?"

She shook her head. "No. I'm not working any more, I . . . I quit. More or less." She shut her eyes for a moment, stilling the flow of words. She had to be careful what she said to him. Even normally mundane phrases like *I quit my job* could lead to things like *the government is looking for me,* or even—in time—*I sense other people's thoughts now.*

"On vacation," he offered, with only a faint touch of irony.

"On vacation," she agreed, in the same tone.

"And you happened past the dock by accident, and stepped inside because of some generally ominous feeling—"

"Yes," she said. Almost defiantly. Somehow he brought it out in her. With the others she'd tried to be as submissive as she could, just to stay alive. He . . . he didn't seem to need her to play that game. Or want it. "Yes, it was an accident, unplanned, unintended, all of that. So I wound up in the wrong place at the wrong time and I'm very sorry about that—gods, you don't know how sorry I am—so just tell me what it is I have to do—"

A sense of wrongness stabbed into her brain suddenly, awareness of anger suddenly taking spark within him . . . desperately she tried to remember the exact words she had just spoken, to remember what little she had learned about Braxin culture and figure out what she had done so wrong—

"I mean, if you tell me what it is I have to do, then I'll try to cooperate. Please."

Breathless, she waited for the storm to break. But it didn't. The spark she had sensed in him dissipated as rapidly as it had formed. She'd guessed right then. Women didn't address Braxin men in the imperative, at least not in Central culture. Which was easy enough when you had a language where imperative verbs didn't look or sound like anything else, but in what passed for a common tongue in the Outlands it was anything but clear.

So many traps here, she thought despairingly. She'd never wend her way through them all.

"I'm . . . sorry," she offered.

"Nothing to apologize for," he said stiffly. "This isn't the Holding."

"I mean, that I don't have more information to give you."

For a long time he looked at her. She could feel his scrutiny like hot fingers going over her face.

"You've told me enough," he said quietly. "For now."

The shadow before her stretched upward as he stood. She realized he was about to leave. The thought filled her with sudden panic. What if he never came back to her? What if she never had another chance to figure out his agenda, and was left to the mercy of the others, who didn't give a damn about whether she lived or died? "Please—"

"I'll be back," he told her. As if he could sense the cause of her panic. "You're safe for now."

Safe. She laughed bitterly inside as he went to the portal and stood there for a moment, still watching her. *Safe* was a concept she'd left behind in the Empire. *Safe* was a life full of family and friends, and a head full of thoughts that were only your own. *Safe* was a thing of freedom and open spaces, and above all else, hope.

He turned to leave then, but not before someone in the hallway behind him scurried out of sight. A woman, maybe? Zara thought it looked like the one with the claws, but in the shadows it was hard to be sure.

He left her then, and the last light was gone, and she huddled in the tiny cell and tried to remember what safety felt like.

"Raij?"

The mercenary leader looked up, saw Tali'l in the doorway, and nodded a welcome. The starmap that had been projected before him was banished with a touch.

"Busy?" she asked.

"Making sure we have alternate paths to safety. Haven't made it this long trusting to luck, have we? What's up?"

She took a few steps into the room and then sealed the portal behind her. It seemed to Raija she made a point of doing so, as if she wanted him to notice that she was shutting all the others out. "Got a concern, is all. Wanted to talk to you away from the others."

"All right" He pushed a chair her way and turned his own to face her. "Go ahead."

She sat down and steepled her fingers before her. For a few long seconds she said nothing, but contemplated her fingers—and the thoughts beyond—in silence. Finally she said, "I've been thinking about the woman."

"The one who gave the warning in the dock? Yes. . . . She still isn't telling us anything useful. We may have to resort to other means."

". . . and what you said about how that whole incident shouldn't have happened, because we never trust outsiders."

Raija's eyes narrowed. "Go on," he said quietly.

She looked up at him. In the dim room's lighting it was hard to make out her expression, but it seemed to him there was a glint of fierceness in them, such as he normally saw in her only during operations.

"We did trust one outsider, Raij."

It took him a moment to realize who she meant. When he did, his indrawn breath was a soft hiss. "Tathas."

She nodded.

"Why, Tal? What's the benefit for him?"

"I don't know that. Maybe some deal he cut with the locals. Or with the girl's father. Maybe something bigger is going on, that has to do with Braxin politics none of us know about."

"He's been isolated on this ship since we picked him up. How would he have passed on such information?"

"Messages can be sent from anywhere, Raij."

"Homani would have picked that up on his scans."

"Are you so sure of that?" she challenged him. "Enough to bet our lives on it? Do you know all the ins and outs of Braxin technology, enough to say he doesn't have something on him that Homani can't detect?"

He licked his lips as he gazed at her, as if tasting the edge of anger in her voice. Finally he said, in a quiet and steady tone, "Your distaste for his people is hardly a secret."

Her eyes narrowed in fury. "And I dealt with that, didn't I? You said he was one of us, at least for this venture, and I accepted it. Now I'm

just looking at facts the way they are. Take this one. There's no dis-
cernable leak in our information network. Save one. An outsider.
Fact." She leaned forward; her voice was low and intense. "Has this
ever happened to us before? *He's* the only element that's different
now. Fact."

"And you'd like him off the ship. Fact."

She shrugged. "I'd like a lot of things, Raij. But when's the last time
you knew that to get in the way of business?"

He leaned back in his formchair, steepling his fingers as he watched
her. "True enough."

"How much do we know about him? *Really* know about him? How
much do we know about what drove him here, where he's going, what
he really wants? I'll tell you what we know." Her expression darkened.
"Rumors. Speculation. Snippets of news broadcasts from the Holding,
designed for public consumption. And then guesses you made, based
on all that." She drew in a deep breath. "I trust your guesses, Raij. Always have. You're the best judge of people from here to the human
hells, especially when it comes to picking crew. All I'm saying is . . .
maybe this time there are factors at play you don't know about. Maybe
this is our first warning that something bigger is going on."

He said nothing. Just sat there, watching her.

"Damn it, Raij!" Unable to sit still anymore, she got up and began
to pace. "You wanted him because he's strong and fast and ruthless,
and you thought you knew his price so you could buy his loyalty. Well
he *is* all those things, all right, and you knew enough of his price to
sign him on. So what now? Do we stop asking questions? Do we just
sit back and figure nobody's ever going to bid higher than we did?"
When he still didn't speak she demanded, "Am I wrong, Raij? Tell me
I'm full of shit on this and he's incapable of selling us out, and I'll go
away and never ask questions about him again. He'll just be another
happy, well-adjusted member of our crew and nothing will be wrong."

He said it quietly. "You're not wrong."

"He's Braxin. You know that." She saw his eyes narrow as he prepared to cut her short and she said quickly, "Forget that I hate them!
That's personal shit, I wouldn't come here and bring that to you. But remember their culture. They *pride* themselves on treachery, Raij. It's part
of their social code. Sell out an ally to get ahead in the world, and all
your fellow Braxins applaud you. Even the ones you screwed over. Shit,
their own gods played that game, and they worshipped them for it."

Silence.

"You know I'm right, Raij."

"Yes," he said quietly. "You are. I'm sorry to say it, but you are."

She exhaled noisily, relief and exasperation all in one sound. "And?"

He sighed. "Homani will check the obvious, first. And we'll watch him. Nothing more we can do at this point, is there? He doesn't know where our rendezvous point is so he can't make things worse . . . even if he is the traitor. And I'm not so sure he is."

"You'll need to—"

"I know what needs to be done, Tal." His tone was stern. "Meanwhile, he's *not to know*. You understand? It may be he isn't guilty of anything—my gut instinct still says that's the case, no matter what you think—and I don't want him driven away if you're wrong. We wait. We watch. No one says a word to him. You got that? I'll do what's necessary to see if he's an enemy, and you don't make him one in the meantime. Is that clear, Tali'l?"

Her dark eyes sparkled. "Quite."

"I'll talk to the others. You don't. All they'll see in you is race hatred, you know that."

She nodded.

He got up from his chair and turned away from her. The viewscreen behind him showed open space with a sparse scattering of stars; no ships, no stations. "I'll be glad when this one is over," he muttered. "Damn job, cursed from the beginning. Last time I ever deal with kids . . ." He snorted. "Or Braxins."

With his back turned, he couldn't see her smiling.

The woman was psychic.

No. Tathas corrected himself. The woman was psychic . . . or else, some force that was psychic had used her as a pawn.

There was no other viable explanation.

She could just be lying, he told himself. *Covering up important information with an act designed to mislead you. Is it possible you want to find the psychics so badly you're seeing third gloves in the darkness?*

But he shook his head, dismissing the thought. If all his years as Viak'im had taught him anything, it was how to read people . . . and this one was broken. The truth was trickling out of her like water from a cracked urn, only no one else saw it because they were all too busy trying to make new and bigger cracks. Maybe it was from some past abuse, maybe it was just the cost of having that kind of power—or being used by that kind of power—but at any rate, the kidnapping by Raija and his crew wasn't the cause of her upset, merely the second glove. He had seen that clearly.

How easily the truth had flowed out of her, in response to the simplest kindness. Thank the darkness for that, he thought. If she knew that he was Braxin he was sure the interview would have gone quite differently.

As it was. . . .

I just felt as if something was wrong, she had said. *I came inside to look.*

Had she sensed something about to happen inside the room? Or been sent an impulse from elsewhere, to warn her? Either would explain her movements. Nothing else would.

Or else you just have psychics on the brain, Tathas.

With a sigh he rubbed his forehead. Yes. He had psychics on his brain. He'd probably see them in his breakfast rations if he let himself go. But in this case no other explanation worked. Raija's crew was all missing it because they were so fixated on the concept of having been sold out by someone that they couldn't see the Void for the stars, but he could.

She was a psychic, or a tool of psychics. Battered enough that she was currently no threat to him, mentally. It didn't really matter whether she had the power herself, or was known to those that did. Either would suit his purpose. She was the perfect bait, ready to be cast out into the Outlands to reel in the contacts he required. The only problem was that he didn't have control of her . . . yet.

Rendezvous with the agents of Raija's client would be in a little more than three Braxin Days. Two and a half Standard? The Outland time conversions were making his head spin. Standard chronometry had been established by Azea, hence the Braxins would rather die than adopt it. But it wasn't all that bad an idea, was it? Get everyone on the same calendar, the same time divisions, the same cycle of shifts, even if there wasn't a planet attached to it? Yes, every now and then Azea actually had a good idea. Maybe his beloved people should learn to steal good things rather than just spit on them for their origins.

Three days. After that they'd probably do things to the woman that no mere kindness was going to heal, and she'd wind up worthless to him. He had to have a plan before then.

Not only for her, but for himself.

Starbright spaceships skimming novadust, engines roaring silently, searching . . . for what? Their scrutiny is a twisting in her gut as she hides behind a small sun, dodging their mechanical gaze. But the sun flares out a vivid corona to mark her location and all is blinding heat—

Lean and hungry predators combing the forest, flesh-eating plants uncurling their hunting tendrils, as something very small and very frightened skitters past—

Eyes everywhere, eyes everywhere, they watch in darkness, they hear in silence, ships cloaked in darkness, waiting

As the corona explodes and she screams as a thousand more ships appear—

Nowhere to turn, nowhere to go, every path has been anticipated—

"No!"

Drenched in sweat, Zara sat up in the darkness and hugged herself, willing the terrible dreams to go away. They did so only slowly, as if reluctant to depart before they had finished their work.

Which was what?

More than just nightmares, she thought with a shiver. She knew it instinctively . . . just like she knew that the inspiration for them lay not within the confines of her own brain, but in images she had snatched from someone else's. The Braxin, maybe? The lizard-eyed woman?

She shut her eyes and shuddered, trying to make some sense of the images. Among Mediators it was believed that dreams were an impor-

tant facet of human perception, allowing the inner mind to communicate intuitions it had no words for, insights the conscious mind might
otherwise reject. When you add to that a wild psychic power that
spasmed each time a stray thought tripped across it, you got . . . what?

Trouble coming, she thought. *Enemies, powerful enemies. Watching, planning . . . hunting. Disaster in the making, death and destruction on the horizon. But for whom? Am I in danger, or the whole ship and crew? Or the girl,
perhaps, whose terror keeps invading my mind, whose dreams could conceivably do the same?*

Probably all three, she decided. Some of the images definitely resonated with personal fear. Some hinted at something grander in scope.

Should she warn someone? She laughed shortly, bitterly, at the
thought. Who? Who would even take her seriously, much less help her?

She had no great desire to see her kidnappers prosper, but if their
ship went down she'd be going down with it. Their fates and hers were
intertwined right now. But who would believe her if she told them
where she had gotten her information from, or credit her crazy
visions?

What if they just took this as one more sign of unknown conspiracies and killed her on the spot? Or felt she wasn't telling them enough,
and tortured her for more details? Shivering in remembered pain, she
drew her knees up to her chest and clasped them tightly, like an animal protecting its most vulnerable organs. Her life as a Mediator hadn't
taught her to endure pain. Those fleeting lessons in physical suffering
which the ship's captain had already provided were already more than
she could handle. What happened if it got worse?

They're out there. Enemies. Predators. I can feel it. Waiting for . . . what?

She had to tell someone. But who?

She leaned back against the wall, shutting her eyes, trying to concentrate. Going over all of the crew in her mind, shadowy figures she
distinguished from one another by voice, by manner, by their interrogation methods.

Except for one. One alone, who had not gone masked, even though
darkness had guarded his features. One who had spoken to her without causing pain, without the need to intimidate her, and even more
important . . . he had seemed to believe her.

He's Braxin.

The thought brought a strange thrill to her flesh, like a fingernail
running up her spine.

They can't be trusted.

Was trust even an issue here? All she needed was someone to listen to her. To credit her visions. And then to do whatever needed to be done, to save them all from certain annihilation.

He'd kill you on the spot if he knew what you were.

But maybe he would wait, and not do that. Maybe he would want to be sure, and somehow in that time she could reach out to him. Even Braxins were human, weren't they? Subject to the same Scattered Races template that had produced her own people. Strip away the racial prejudices, the violent culture, the obsessive misogyny, and you had . . .

What? What was left? What *was* a Braxin, when all those things were gone?

Shivering, her arms wrapped tightly about her knees, she remembered that at one time in her life such a question would have fascinated her. She would have risked anything to explore it, for the sheer intellectual exercise. Now . . . now only one thing mattered.

He'll listen to me. He must.

Afraid to sleep again—afraid to dream—Zara waited in the darkness, hoping that by the time he came to see her again it wouldn't already be too late.

Something had changed.

Tathas could *smell* it.

A faint whiff of challenge when the men passed him in the hall. Smugness as an intangible aroma which wafted in Tali'l's wake as she passed.

A lifetime spent preparing for combat made a man aware of such things. Not on the conscious level, where observations were processed intellectually, but deep within the hindbrain, where the most ancient of the five senses fed its input right into man's primitive response system. *Danger* was the scent of a predator upwind. *Threat* was a smell that made the muscles tense in preparation for desperate action . . . *fight* or *flee*.

He was smelling those things now.

Yet nothing around him had changed. And certainly the tension in the air was appropriate for a vessel now one Standard Day away from a rendezvous with a client who might or might not have betrayed them.

He trusted his senses. He always had.

So what was wrong?

He had planned to talk to the girl again, but put it off for a shift or two. No telling what they would make of his interest in her, when thus far his interrogation had produced nothing.

. . . Nothing he would tell them about, anyway.

Was the sense of unease coming from her, perhaps? Broadcast somehow through the substance of the ship, so that her own fears might take root in the brains of her captors? No, if that were the fact then he would see a change in the others, as they responded to the same mental intrusion. And there was nothing. Nothing he could put his glove on, nothing he could identify, only . . . the smell of danger.

The rendezvous point was growing steadily closer, the crew making preparations to transfer its precious cargo. After that piece of business was done and there were no more distractions Raija would address himself to the woman in earnest, ready to peel away her brain layer by bloody layer if that would lay bare her secrets. After that . . . there would be nothing much left for Tathas to use for his own purposes.

She didn't sign on for this, he thought.

He waited as long as he dared before returning to her, hoping to identify the source of his disquiet first. But it eluded him, and the sense of danger increased hourly, and by the time he finally slipped away from the others to visit the captive again, the stink of danger was so pungent in the air he could taste it.

One Standard Day left. Not much at all.

The portal opened to any outside touch. He left it open just a crack, enough to see her frightened eyes looking up at him, not enough to illuminate his own.

She looked like Ar herself, he thought. Tangled hair, sweat-matted, spoke eloquently of restless hours spent trying to sleep in the cramped quarters. Dust had gotten caught up in her tears and now streaked her face in ragged lines of gray. Hunger and fear had hollowed her eyes and cheeks, and in the dim lighting from the hallway the resulting face looked almost skeletal.

Chaos and terror: it filled the small room to bursting, he could taste it on his tongue as he looked at her. A thrilling, fearsome thing, to taste someone else's emotion like that. Almost more than a human soul could bear. She wasn't going to last much longer.

Slowly he crouched down before her, the way you would with a wary animal. She hadn't looked nearly this bad the last time he'd seen her. Had they done something to her that they hadn't told him about? Was she already too far gone to be of use to him?

She looked up at him, and the bloodshot eyes widened. Before he could get his first words out she whispered hoarsely, "They're coming."

His own words died in his throat. He forced himself to take a long, slow breath, and to release it with equally measured care before he dared to speak.

"Who?" he said quietly.

"I don't know." Her whole body was shaking. "I really don't know, you've got to believe me. But they're out there." The hollow eyes fixed on him, something wild and terrified in their depths. "Do you understand? They're there . . . coming closer."

He forced himself not to respond to the imperative in her speech, as his Braxin soul would normally like to. This wasn't the time or place to be arguing semantics. "How do you know?" he whispered.

"Behind the sun. Behind the sun. They're coming from behind the sun." She lowered her head to her knees and began to rock. "So many of them. Taking no chances. Hungry, they're so hungry . . ."

He reached out and took her face in his hands. She started like a frightened animal, but did not draw away. A dirty hand crept up over his and touched it gingerly, then grasped it; he had the odd impression she was somehow grounding herself with the solidity of his flesh. He raised her head up until she faced him, and waited until she was looking in his direction.

"How do you know?" he said firmly.

"I dream it," she whispered. "Every time I close my eyes. More violent each time, and closer . . ." She drew in a ragged breath. "Tell me they're only dreams, please. Tell me I'm just going crazy."

He considered all the answers he could give. Where each one might lead. Finally he said quietly, "I don't think they're just dreams, Zara."

She closed her eyes. "I know," she whispered. "I know."

"You don't know anything more."

"No. I've tried. I've tried. I can't control it . . ."

Can't control it. A wild talent? Tathas had heard rumor of such things when he was young, right alongside tales of the monsters who waited under the bed at night and the minions of Ar who would make you impotent if you ever allowed a girl to tell you what to do. Silently he cursed his people for their willful ignorance of all matters psychic. He suspected the most ignorant commoner on Azea knew ten times more than he did, just for having lived in a world where discussion of such things wasn't taboo.

Softly he said, "Have you told anyone?"

She shook her head, eyes wide and frightened. Her voice was a cracked whisper. "They won't believe me."

"No." She was right. They wouldn't.

"They'll think I have some other source of knowledge. They . . . they'll hurt me to get at it."

Yes. Yes, they would do that.

"You understand." she whispered. "You can help. Please."

What could he do? The ship wasn't his. Its crew hardly knew him. It was doubtful they'd trust him, least of all if he came to them with tales of wild psychic power inside their ship. They'd probably ask why he hadn't just killed her, since Braxins were notorious for doing that with anything psychic.

But there were reasons for that, he told himself. The Great War had almost been lost once, in the years when Anzha lyu Mitethe commanded the Border forces of the enemy. She had shown them just how dangerous psychic power was . . . and she might have turned that lesson into the ultimate victory if her own people had not driven her so mad with rage that she left the Empire altogether.

If not, she would have destroyed us all, he thought somberly. No, the Braxin Holding never admitted such things, not in so many words. But any schoolchild knew it. And she had never been found after that, he recalled, though legends of her presence abounded in any place where strange things happened. Which meant that her seed might well be out there somewhere, infecting the human gene pool like a plague. Waiting for the right day to surface again on one side of the Border or another, and bring them to the edge of disaster once more.

Was it any wonder that his people killed that seed, anywhere it surfaced?

But this woman . . . he gazed down at her sweat-streaked face in wonder. How could a creature of such vast power be so helpless?

And so valuable, he reminded himself.

"I'll take care of it," he promised. Not having a clue how he would do that . . . but the promise had to be voiced. He could see it take hold of her as she nodded, a lifeline of comfort in a universe gone mad. That was good. If he could manage to save her from all this she would feel indebted to him, and do what he needed her to do without resistance. That was important. Escape from this ship might be the end of her troubles as far as she was concerned, but for him it was only the beginning of a greater campaign. She had to be willing to serve him when he needed her to . . . and the more grateful she was to him when they got to that point, the easier it would be.

In the darkness of the control room, Raija sat alone. Listening to the ship's recorder as it played back words spoken in darkness, elsewhere.

They're out there.

The woman's voice resonated in the stillness, eerie, hollow.

Behind the sun. Behind the sun. They're coming from behind the sun.

So many of them. Taking no chances.

So . . .

She knew there was an attack coming.

She trusted Tathas enough to warn him.

He digested those two thoughts as the rest of the recording played out. Thank the gods he'd told the ship to keep recording what happened in her room, even between interrogations. No. Thank Tali'l. She had alerted him to the Braxin's possible treachery, and now here it was, laid out before him.

The Braxin and the woman knew each other. That much was obvious even from this tape. The manner in which she spoke to him was worlds apart from how she dealt with the others.

She'd never have warned Fatu, that was certain.

Or Kesh.

Only the Braxin.

Only the strange, mysterious Braxin, whose true origins were unknown, whose motives were guessed at from news vids and whispered rumors, launched from planets light-years away. . . .

With a sudden curse he hurled his drink across the chamber. Sticky Sallongian liquor splashed across a starchart.

He had trusted.

Trusted his intincts.

Wrong this time. Wrong!

What was the connection between the two of them? What agenda did they serve?

I dream these things, the woman had said.

Memories of something she'd been programmed to forget? Whispers overheard, and not understood? Or a warning deliberately implanted, meant to be triggered in the freedom of open space, not here in the storage closet of a freelancer ship?

Didn't much matter, did it? Any way you looked at it, the warning was a real one. Trouble was coming. *From behind the sun*, the woman had said. That implied an assault in normal space, where suns could be seen. Probably inside a planetary system, with heavenly bodies close enough to make a difference.

The rendezvous.

His blood ran cold in an instant; a soft hiss escaped his lips. Of course. That had to be it. A trap was planned at the rendezvous point, where his client was supposed to receive the stolen goods. Maybe the client had betrayed him . . . maybe another had overheard something said in carelessness, and made the arrangements independently. It didn't matter. They'd sent the woman to foil him in the kidnapping, and now that she'd failed in that, the instructions originally implanted in her were starting to leak out. That's why his crew hadn't been able to force the knowledge out of her, no matter how hard they tried; she didn't have access to it consciously. Doubtless she was intended as a courier to some other conspirator, who would know the keys to unlocking the information she carried.

Information she had offered to Tathas.

With a growl of profound irritation, he shut off the speaker. So much for an easy transfer of the goods. He should have known things wouldn't go that smoothly.

They were going to have to deal with the Braxin. Soon. Otherwise he'd be tipping off their enemies as soon as they changed course. And the woman had to be incapacitated, that went without saying. He wasn't going to take the chance that she had some way of sending messages out into normal space. If she did, any stellar system they docked in might be their last.

Only a fool would leave the two of them free and able with so much going down.

He wasn't a fool.

Cursing the Braxin under his breath, he told the ship to bring Tali'l to him.

Tathas was resting when Tali'l came to him. Well, he looked like he was resting, anyway. In fact his brain was churning away at a fevered pace, trying to take disparate fragments of plans and weave them into an ordered whole. Outside . . . he might have been asleep, for all Tali'l would see. In the same way that a resting predator might seem to be asleep, when in fact all its senses were on full alert.

"It's the woman," she said. "They want to move her."

He opened his half-lidded eyes and regarded her. How like a predatory animal she was herself, he thought. She never lost that aspect. Even now, in this casual conversation, he could almost imagine her taking his measure, deciding what kind of stride or blow would bring him down. An interesting fantasy.

"Which one?" he asked.

"The messy one." Her tone was derisive. The kidnapped girl had kept up some minimal hygiene once they'd given her tools for it, so "messy" meant his psychic. "C'mon, Raija wants your help."

"He needs help to move a girl?" He swung his feet over the edge of the bed and began to rise . . . then he realized he didn't have his weapon on him. With the mood in the ship the way it had been of late, that was bad. But reaching for it in front of her might make things even worse, if she thought to ask why he wanted it. After all, he was among allies. They wouldn't hurt him, so he shouldn't need a weapon in their presence. Right?

Cursing himself silently for ever taking it off, he left the neural stun on the bedstand.

The ship was quiet, preternaturally so. Only the hum of engines could be heard as they walked the narrow corridors to where the psychic woman was being held. At the end of it, near the portal to the storage closet they were using as a prison, Fatu and Homani waited. Tathas nodded to them. "You need me for this?"

Fatu snorted. "Raija wants her to stay calm. She goes hysterical with all of *us* . . . so he said call you . . ." His tone was mildly resentful; it seemed that he thought Tathas' presence was unnecessary, perhaps even an affront to his own competence.

"What are we doing?"

"Moving her to forward quarters," Homani told him. "Raija wants vid on her, and there's no outlet for that in this closet."

Tali'l reached forward and opened the portal. In the darkness beyond Tathas saw familiar, frightened eyes. He steeled himself against betraying any sign of compassion and nodded. "All right."

Slowly he knelt before her, letting her accustom herself to the triple threat in the doorway. He didn't dare soften his expression lest she respond to it and give him away. "Come on," he said quietly. "We're moving you to a better place."

There was more terror in her eyes than usual, if that was possible. Boundless, bottomless terror, that made the hair on the back of his neck rise. He forced himself to meet her gaze steadily, willing her to draw strength from him, then pointedly looked away. It wouldn't be good if the others saw any connection between them.

She was quiet as he gathered her up from the floor, one arm behind her back, another beneath her knees. Trembling as he touched her. He started to rise up, lifting her—

—when suddenly she twisted in his arms, her face pressing close to his cheek as her hands grasped his head—

And she whispered in his ear, "They're going to kill you. Now!"

There was no time to think, only to act. His hands were full, his balance wrong, and three of them were behind him. If he took time to question her words or their source he'd be dead. So instead he rose to his feet in a fluid motion, the woman still in his arms, and turned to face them.

Tali'l's talons were bared. Her eyes were fierce. Her expression said it all.

With a silent apology he threw the woman towards Homani. Surprised, he caught her; the glitter of black from his weapon was visible for a moment beneath her tangled hair before he growled in anger at the tactic and simply let her fall. But his instinctive response bought Tathas a precious second in which to close distance with Tali'l, grabbing at her wrists to control those deadly talonned hands. He got one and missed the other, and she nearly gutted him as he jerked her forward, ripping the side of his tunic as she fought to stay on her feet. But that was okay. He'd pulled her between him and the two men now, so they had no clear line of fire. Hopefully they'd care enough about her for it to matter.

Talons raked for his face. There was a black glistening substance on their tips now which, he noted grimly, was not likely to be nail polish. He ducked the blow and threw the full weight of his body against her, still holding her other hand fast. Good but not good enough; he felt the sharp nails rake down his back as he lifted her off her feet and heaved her with all his might over the psychic's limp body, into whatever man was standing closest. Homani cursed and Fatu fired, but the shot went wild. In the close confines of the ship's corridor, Tali'l's body had slammed into them both.

All right. He had survived the first second of an ambush, that was good. He spared a second to get his bearings, dodging a second shot, this one less wild than the first. Tali'l had fallen, cursing, the wind driven out of her by his assault, and Homani had stumbled beneath her weight. Fatu had been knocked against the far wall but was re-gaining his balance now, and his expression was grim and determined as he pointed his neural stun at Tathas' chest—

—And the psychic kicked out, hard. She hit him on the side of one knee, right by the kneecap, and his shot pulled off wild to the side as the leg folded beneath him. He was close enough to Homani that the shot grazed the man's shoulder, and Tathas heard a cry of pain and frustration as that man's arm went limp.

He didn't dare stop to think about how bad the odds were, or that there was nowhere to run, or what might happen if the others came. He just dove at Homani, driving his shoulder into the man's chest with all his Braxin strength, honed by a lifetime of combat. He could hear bone snap in the man's chest as he brought down the butt of his stun upon Tathas's head, then the sharp retort of bone against wall as the force of the assault snapped his head back into the wall. Tathas lunged for the weapon and grabbed it, twisting it and firing into Homani's side before it was even loose of his hand. The man's body convulsed too violently for Tathas to grab it up as a shield, so he sim-ply grabbed the stun and turned quickly to see what was coming at him. Just in time. Claws raked towards his groin—Tali'l had decided not to waste time getting to her feet, but simply to lunge at him from the ground—and Fatu's own weapon was swinging around to take aim at his head. He fired first and saw the man's face tighten and then go limp as pain shot through every muscle in his body. Two down. He looked into Tali'l's eyes—so alien, and yet so comprehensible in their hatred—and then saw a faint smile flicker over her lips as she reached down towards the psychic who was half-pinned beneath her, talons closing about the slender, dirty neck even as she moved her body lithely to the far side of her. Too close and too uncertain to risk a shot; he could see in her eyes that she knew it, too. So he kicked out at her, meaning to catch her underneath her chin but striking instead just beneath her nose; he could feel the force of the blow shattering the bones of her face, sending her reeling against the far wall, to collapse on Fatu's inert form. Probably dead, with that kind of blow. He didn't stop to check.

He grabbed up Fatu's weapon, glanced down the hallway to see if others were coming, then looked towards the psychic. She was bruised pretty badly and seemed half-dazed, but at least her neck wasn't bloody. The wounds across Tathas' back already felt hot and feverish, which was a bad sign. What had Tali'l put on her claws?

"We have to get out of here," he told her. "Can you stand?"

The woman struggled to her feet. She seemed to have a reserve of strength that had survived her longs days of confinement and torture, which was a good thing. Tathas' whole back was beginning to stiffen up and he wasn't sure he could carry her.

"I think so," she gasped.

Out of here. Out to where, in the middle of the Void? There were only two answers, and one of them involved facing Raija. Tathas had had the benefit of surprise in fighting Tali'l and company, since they didn't know he'd been warned of their intentions, but there'd be no such luck the second time. Just seeing him alive would tell Raija that something was seriously wrong, and he'd be ready for trouble.

He grabbed the woman by the arm and pulled her behind him. She was limping, but she didn't fall. His back burned in stripes where Tali'l had clawed it, and he was beginning to feel light-headed. Poison? A numbing agent? Running would probably only make it course through his veins even faster, but there was no alternative. He ran. Pulling the woman up now and then when she stumbled, her own strength barely up to the sprint. Once she jerked back and whispered harshly "Not there!" and he moved without question down a side corridor instead, trusting her talent.

Into the receiving bay. He looked around quickly and wished he had something more destructive to use than a neural stun, so that he might shoot out the vids that were pointed at them. One could only hope Raija wasn't watching the vids yet. It had all been so fast, mere minutes passing since Tali'l's claws had first been bared. If Raija had been waiting for them to report to him after Tathas' death, it might take him a while to realize his plans had gone wrong.

One could hope.

"There." He pointed to the lock at the far end of the bay and tried to shove her toward it, but his left arm would no longer do what he told it to. The whole of his back was on fire now and his head was pounding as if someone was kicking at it from the inside. He blinked and forced himself to focus and grabbed up the stun in his right hand, feeling a hot knot of fear forming in his gut. You dealt with poison by lying down and keeping still, right? Until help came. The calmer you were, the more time you had.

Yeah, right.

The lock was sealed. He cursed as he tried to open it, then cursed again as he realized he couldn't even blast the mechanism; the stun only worked on living tissue. He imagined he could hear Tali'l laughing at him as he fed in the only security code he had, willing it to work. The pain inside his head was blinding. The lock stayed shut. Had they not trusted him from the beginning, or was Raija one step ahead of him now, reprogramming locks and seals before he could get to them?

Something touched him on the arm. He whipped about and had his stun in the woman's face before he realized it was her. She was offering him something she'd found, a long bar of some lightweight synthetic substance. He tried it against the faceplate of the lock mechanism, fighting the dizziness that now accompanied every movement. Blessed faceplate was too well seated to pry loose. In a rage of frustration he battered at the edge of it with all his strength, feeling his poisoned blood course through his veins like acid. The wall wasn't quite as tough as his tool and dented just enough to give him a crack to wedge it into, but suddenly his hands were too numb to do the work. It was the woman who finally took the tool from his hands and used it to pry the control panel loose, until its innards spilled out like the intestines of a gutted animal.

"You know how to do this?" she whispered.

Pain pounded behind his eyes. "Maybe," he muttered. "Assuming I'm conscious long enough."

She cursed, a remarkably colorful expression that combined speculation about the ship's origins with some interesting scatological imagery.

He pushed himself away from the wall and grasped at the edge of the opening for balance. Colored cables swam in his field of vision like snakes. "Air lock," he muttered. "Default will be *sealed,* so we can't just rip it all out . . ." One questionable benefit of belonging to a tribe that regularly flouted Braxaná law was that sometimes you had to take shelter in unexpected places. No, he had never messed with the insides of a starship, but he'd broken into enough buildings in his life to be able to make some intelligent guesses about basic portal security. "Here," he muttered, pointing with a numb hand while two, three, four copies of the same cable swam in his vision. "Break that connection. Now here." Her fingers were shaking, she was that afraid—or maybe simply that weak—but she managed to do what he told her. "Connect those." The portal slid open suddenly . . . halfway. Good enough. He tried to get through it but suddenly the floor was overhead and the walls were spinning, and he felt her shove him through the opening just as the shriek of an alarm filled the bay—

—her hands pushing him from behind and the floor rushed towards his face—

Fight it, man. Fight it. If the poison takes you out now you're not going to live, you know it.—and he caught himself before it hit him, and drew in a deep breath, and forced the world to be steady once more.

"You all right?" she asked him

He gestured back towards the gutted panel. "Rip it out."

She hesitated only an instant—then the lights went out and he heard her move. Sparks filled the darkened bay as she ripped the connections loose. The ship's portal began to close suddenly and she managed to get inside just before it shut, losing her balance and falling half on top of him. Dank hair, tangled about his face, breath chill with dread. His body was so numb it could barely feel her weight.

Outside there was a clanking noise. Tractors trying to reattach, no doubt. Let them try. Their controls had been gutted, and it would take a complicated manual override to make them work now.

We have to get out of here.

She tried to help him up but he wouldn't let her. Braxin pride. The ship they were in was small and dark at first, but as he took his first steps into the main chamber the emergency lights came on. It was a small ship but nicely outfitted, with plush seats done up in some sleek animal skin. He used them for support as he staggered toward the control room.

More clanging. Then the floor shook beneath his feet, dropping him to his knees. He could barely feel them hit the floor. *Not now, not now, you can't lose consciousness now* . . . He heard Zara come up behind him as the hull began to vibrate. Ten to one Raija was trying to break into it manually.

"Get her moving," he gasped. "Fast."

He heard Zara brush past him without feeling it. She trembled as she did so, and not from weakness. *She's feeling my pain,* he realized. *Like the poison is in her own flesh.* He tried to concentrate on something else so that it wouldn't affect her as much . . . but would that help? How did this strange power work, that now threatened to make her share the pain of his dying? His legs no longer had any feeling in them at all, and his left hand was a dead weight by his side. He pulled himself up into a chair with his one good arm as the lights came on, and a moment later the engines rumbled to life. *Don't do a safety check,* he thought, *just get her moving, we're dead if we stay here.* Apparently Zara thought so too, for the small ship jerked forward with a burst of acceleration that nearly threw him from his seat. He could hear metal tearing off the side of the hull, and that was a good sign, because it meant that the various mechanisms holding the pleasure craft captive weren't strong enough to keep hold of her.

Then they were free, and there was no more shrieking of metal and synthetic. Black space surrounded them, the starless superluminal night splayed across a dozen viewscreens. Illusion, he knew that. There were stars out there all right, just no way to see them. Yet it was said that this illusory darkness could drive a man mad . . .

Suddenly the viewscreens filled with blinding light and the ship shook to its very core. For a moment, it seemed to him, the engines faltered.

Raija had armaments. Of course Raija had armaments. And of course this ship didn't.

Not good.

He forced himself to his feet and managed to get into the tiny bridge. There was one seat next to hers and he dropped down into it. "They're going to blow us to pieces, you know."

"Better than what they were doing to me before," she answered grimly.

"You can't tell when they're going to fire at us?"

She shut her eyes for a moment. "I don't know," she whispered. "Probably not well enough to help."

"Then we have to lose them. Yes?" He looked at the controls, trying to focus on them clearly enough to make out their configuration. "Or die trying."

Fuel tanks twice the normal size. Gravitic compensation impressive. Someone had outfitted this little craft for racing.

They were struck again. A red light blinked on the control panel, warning of an atmospheric breach in storage. Mechanized systems moved quickly, automatically, to seal it off.

"Strap in," he muttered. "This is going to hurt."

She looked at him, and seemed to realize what he had in mind. "The ship has no starcharts for this part of space."

"Then we fly blind." *Compensation,* the readout beckoned. He set it as high as he could. *Emergency deceleration* blinked on a panel and he confirmed it. *Subluminal?* Yes.

"We don't know what's out there—"

"—And we know what's *here.*" Another assault shook the small ship. This time four warning lights came on. "You have a better idea?"

She met his eyes. If he could see straight he might have read more into her expression. As it was her face was just a hazy blur.

"No," she said.

Another blast came toward them from Raija's ship as they pulled away from it, trailing tractor cables—

—and the emergency deceleration force field grabbed them and held them in place, as the tiny ship began evasive maneuvers—

—and a burst of something nasty passed barely a hands' breath in front of the nose of their ship, and shot out into the starless Void beyond them.

Stay awake, he told himself. *Just stay awake.* Poison flowed molten in his veins, the only real sensation in his world. Too real. He could feel it eating into his flesh like acid, even while his outer senses blurred and dissipated. *Stay awake!* Then the emergency deceleration kicked in and it was one too many trials for his poisoned flesh. Crushed between the awesome forces of natural momentum and artificial gravitics, bruised along the entire surface of his body by the force field that held him in place, he felt his consciousness fading, and no longer had strength to fight it.

Take her out of here, he whispered silently. *Anywhere. A ship that big can't match our deceleration, they'll lose us . . .* Then even the silent words took too much effort, and there was only pain. Hopefully the woman wasn't absorbing all of it. Hopefully she'd be able to cling to consciousness, and bring them to safety.

The last thing he saw as they went subluminal was a blazing sun right in front of them.

The greater the danger men face together, the greater their propensity toward alliance.

—Anzha lyu Mitethe

SEVENTEEN

IF KLATH HAD been female it would never have seen the shooting star. The females were all gathered in the birthing hut to do some secret female thing which involved incantations and offerings, and that probably would have seemed more important than staring at the night sky.

If Klath had been male it would never have seen the shooting star. The males were involved in some pre-Festival testing of strength that involved fire and spears, and no one without fully developed male genitals was permitted to watch. If Klath had been male it would have been doing that, in the hopes of winning a prime place in the Festival and thus having a shot at the best mates, hunting grounds, and wealth-songs.

If Klath had even been a child still—a child!—there would have been duties to see to, for Festival time had duties for every age group, even the youngest.

But for the *istali*—the Uncommitted—nothing.

And so Klath spent the night beneath the night stars, and searched for craters on the two moons that were visible that night, and saw the great star fall from the sky.

What a *whoosh* it made as it came through the atmosphere— a whisper at first, the kind that you know is much louder at its point of origin, a distant roar muted by miles of darkness. It blazed across the sky brighter than anything Klath had ever seen, and as it fell to earth the *istal* imagined it could feel the ground beneath it tremble. Not that the males would notice, for all their drums and fires. Not that the females would notice, for all their incantation and dancing.

Only the lone *istal* lying on its back on the mountain top, staring out across distant valleys.

After the star struck the earth there was a faint glowing in the distance for a while, and Klath wondered if some sort of fire was going to start. But they were in the middle of the rainy season and things were wet enough that a real wildfire would be hard pressed to get going. After a while the glow died down and there was no more visible evidence that anything unusual had happened.

The wise ones said such stars were gifts of the gods, sent to earth for people to find. Klath could use a gift. Something to shock its mind and body into commitment, perhaps, so that it would no longer be stuck in this genderless limbo: neither male nor female nor child proper, neither sexed nor unsexed, simply . . . waiting. That was what the ancient word meant, *istal*—Waiting.

Waiting could drive you crazy.

Klath stood up, wiping the clinging wet leaves from off its tunic as it did so. It hadn't been able to see the exact spot where the star landed, but it had a pretty good idea of roughly where it had gone. Right over the next mountain ridge . . . out of sight of the village. Which meant that if any of Klath's people *had* seen it coming down, they would have no idea where it went. And in Festival time everyone had better things to do than to search out curiosities in the brush, for gods must be satisfied and births arranged and matings celebrated and children taught . . . yes, everyone had something to do in this time, better and more important than heading out to the next ridge to see what had fallen from the sky in the middle of the night.

Everyone except *istali,* that was.

Istali had no better purpose than anything.

The grass was wet around Klath's ankles as it started walking. Not back toward the village, with its bonfires and godsongs. Away. Down the mountain ridge, into the valley, across to places where there were no villages. In the wet season there would be enough things to eat on the way that it wouldn't starve, and the warm days and temperate nights were perfect for travelling. What more did an *istali* need? Surely nothing from the pantries of its household, whose keeper would demand to know why it was packing supplies. And then when it answered her, telling her about the star, someone else would be sent to accompany Klath across the valley, or perhaps even take its place entirely. After all, when your body couldn't even decide what gender it wanted to be, why should people trust you to do anything right?

A day's journey, Klath estimated. There and back. Maybe there'd be some fabulous mystery at the other end, or a discovery that could inspire *istali* flesh to sex itself at last. Wasn't it said that the gods used such stars for transport? Or maybe it was a piece of the heavens that had fallen, jostled loose by the passing of the moons. Or maybe just . . . something mundane, that burned the trees and shook the earth and was gone before any of the sexed ones would notice.

Did it matter? It wasn't like Klath was needed here. It wasn't like a single lonely *istal* would be missed.

As it began to hike down the mountain ridge, picking its way with care, it wondered how long it would be before anyone would even notice it was gone.

Zara could feel it when the Braxin woke up.

The first warning was a shooting pain across her back, three stripes of it. Sharper than the day before, when the poisoned claws had first scored him; infected perhaps, despite the best of her efforts. Then there was a hazy disorientation, strong enough that she had to grab hold of a rock to keep from losing her balance in the swift-running stream. Then: Surprise. Recognition. Memory, returning in battered fragments from a battle fought eons ago.

No fear, she noted. Many things in him, many dark and terrible emotions, but no fear.

She could sense him pulling himself to his feet, cursing his injured flesh, and she struggled to return awareness to her own body. Never had another soul drawn her in like that before. Was her power so much greater now than it had been when last she had tested it? Had fear and deprivation stripped down her last inner defenses, so that she could no longer shut out any stranger? Or had their strange relationship, born in an atmosphere of terror and violence, provided a bond that increased her sensitivity?

A bond with a Braxin. Gods forbid.

Hurredly she left the stream where she had been bathing and went to put her outer clothing back on. She'd never taken the underwear off. That wasn't something you did on an alien world where you didn't know who or what might come along . . . and where the threat you had brought with you was more frightening than half the possibilities Nature might provide. Her clothes weren't dry yet, either, though most of the bloodstains had washed out of them. The result was wet layers of permacloth sloshing against each other, making it almost impossible to get everything in place by the time he wandered downhill in search of her.

She could feel the sunlight wash over his skin as he broke through the tree line and came into the clearing, and shook her head to get rid of the feeling. He looked . . . he looked . . . damn, he looked good. It was the first time she'd seen him in good light, at least standing up, and even bruised across his face and back, limping lightly, and stained with the dirt and sweat of their travels, he was an impressive figure. The animal intensity she had sensed in him when they met on the ship was ten times stronger when she could see him moving. Hypnotic. Disconcerting. She tried to focus on his face, and the details that weren't Braxin. Dark hair allowed to grow, wild now in its disarray. Strong jawline, marked with stubble where a precisely edged beard had once been cultivated, then removed, now was reasserting its ancient rights. Piercing eyes that made her feel weak inside, confused as to whether she should be feeling fear, or . . . something else.

He blinked as he looked around the clearing, taking it all in with a kind of dazed curiosity, as if he hadn't put it all together yet. Then he looked at her, and a finger rose to the band of cloth wrapped around his chest. "You did this?"

It was easier when they talked; his feelings faded from her head when she could focus on spoken words. "Med kit was lost in the crash. It was the only thing I knew how to do without it."

"Crash." He said the word as if tasting it. Then he looked around at the surrounding trees, the water . . . and her. "Well," he said at last, "it's not a sun."

She remembered the main screen blazing with solar fire and shuddered. That had been a close call, for sure. The ship had managed a course correction, but barely, and now there wasn't much of it left. Enough to get them to the only planet in the system with signs of life and then smash itself into debris trying to land. If not for the personal fields they'd had on for the deceleration they'd have been scattered across the landscape along with the smoking remnants of the small ship and its contents.

Long steps, couched in pain, brought the Braxin to the edge of the stream; she kept a wary distance. He turned to her then, to take her measure. He had green eyes, deep green, the color of forests and evening shadows, a startling color. "You're all right?"

It was such a mundane question that for a moment she didn't know how to respond. "I'm alive," she said at last. "Nothing's hurt that won't heal. You?"

He nodded. A dry smile played across his lips as he did so, that set off his features to such advantage it made something female inside her tighten up. "Anything left?"

It took her a minute to realize he meant the ship. "Not worth saving. It was a pretty rough trip." She nodded back the way he had come. "Right over the ridge, if you want to take a look. Still smoldering, last I looked."

"You carried me here?"

"Ah." She turned away. The green gaze was far too penetrating. "Kind of . . . dragged you, actually. It was still burning at the time, I thought it best to get some distance . . ."

Silence fell, at least of the human sort. Animals chirruped in the shadows.

"I'm sorry," he said at last.

"What? For the crash? Ship was on automatic, it did the best it could—"

"That I threw you at them."

A flush rose to her face as she remembered. "Oh. That. It's . . . it's . . . I understand."

"Three to one. No other option."

Yes, an inner voice chided. *Be grateful for small favors. Here you are, alone on this unknown planet with a Braxin, for who knows how long . . . but he didn't throw you into the arms of enemies to hurt you. That's a good thing, isn't it?*

"I know," she said softly. She shrugged. A spear of pain shot through her shoulder, reminding her just how hard she'd hit the floor back then. "So we're alive, right? That's a start."

"Yes," he said quietly. "A start." His voice was steady but the lie of it blazed about him, a blinding corona of rage. Whoever he was, whatever he wanted, he needed to be somewhere else, and soon. Even death would have been preferable to being marooned indefinitely on a benign planet. Being alive was not enough.

We could be here for the rest of our lives, she thought. It was a frightening enough concept in its own right; she shook to think of what this Braxin would be like when it became clear that was their only option. Didn't they have some ritual of rage in which they killed whoever had sparked their anger?

He looked at her again. The gaze was as steady and even as before, but the emotion behind it was so strong this time it hit her full in the face. Powerful feelings, all fused together, sheathed in a shell of red-hot rage. She cried out and staggered back, raising her hand up instinctively to shield her face.

"Zara—"

"Not your fault," she gasped. Tears of pain squeezed out of her eyes as she struggled to concentrate on something else. When had she given him her name? Hearing him speak it gave the onslaught mental focus, gave it power. "It just . . . comes on like that sometimes . . ."

He said nothing. There was an animal quality to his stillness, a preternatural alertness that was both predatory and cautious. Minutes passed. The assault eased . . . or maybe she just figured out how to absorb it. Slowly his emotions slid into the dark places of her mind, allowing her own thoughts to surface again.

Oh, gods. She'd never survive this. The day he understood what she really was he'd surely kill her. How long could she wait for that moment, that time bomb to explode?

The green eyes were watching her. Unreadable.

Waiting will only make the fear worse.

At last she said, in a whisper, "Your kind kills psychics."

His eyes narrowed briefly. She feared a new onslaught of emotion, but none came.

"Your kind kills Braxins," he said quietly.

He took a step down toward the stream. She could see the back of his shirt now, scored and bloody, the homemade bandage peeking out from parallel slashes in the fabric. Grateful to be free from his penetrating gaze at last, she wrapped her arms around herself and shivered.

"So. The ship is gone." He muttered something under his breath in his native tongue, probably a curse. No, that wasn't right. The Braxins considered the active involvement of gods a bad thing and regarded a blessing as ill fortune, didn't they? He was probably blessing their luck, with the same ill will. "No communications equipment either, I take it."

"Burned to a crisp."

"Supplies?"

She said nothing.

"So . . . alive in the middle of nowhere, with nothing except the clothes on our back and . . . whatever's on this planet." His face tightened, and again she could feel the waves of incipient rage battering at her psyche, a flood tide about to be loosed. "Any sentient life?"

"Your guess is as good as mine."

His eyes narrowed. "Can't you . . ." The words trailed off.

She bit her lip. "What? Scout them out?"

"You sense things, don't you? From other minds?"

The green eyes were fixed on her. Forest eyes, shadow eyes. If she wasn't so afraid of what might be behind them she could lose herself in their depths completely. Just swallowed up and obliterated by all his Braxin energy, and then she would never have to hurt again.

"I sense emotions," she said quietly, looking away. Anywhere else but his eyes. "Sometimes." She laughed dryly, a sound that turned into coughing as it left her throat. "Seems to have just gotten me into trouble, so far."

He managed a dry smile. It was for her benefit, she sensed; he didn't feel like smiling.

"Can't control it, then?"

She could taste the edge in the question. "No." Would that set off the anger inside him? She might lie, if she knew what lies were safe with him. "I can't control it. Or even make much sense of it, sometimes. It just . . . it just comes."

"I would have thought they'd have ways to control it . . ."

"They?"

"Psychics."

She shrugged stiffly. "Maybe *they* do. I don't."

She could taste how much he wanted to ask more questions. *Go ahead,* she thought, *I've got damned little to tell you about. No lifetime spent studying strange powers, no shadowy empire behind me with secrets for you to learn, nothing but a mentally battered Mediator who just wishes she knew how this damned mental floodgate was opened in the first place, so she could shut it tight again.*

Exhaustion and fear had been warring within her for too many days now and she was near the breaking point. Maybe he could sense it. Maybe that's why he turned away instead of asking her more questions—or maybe he simply guessed that she had no answers for him yet. He walked down to the edge of the water. "Safe?" he asked, indicating the placid surface.

"As much as anything ever is, on an unknown planet."

With a slight wince of pain he loosened his shirt and let the bloody tatters slide from his shoulders. "Then at least one thing can be dealt with." Before she even realized what he was doing he was out of his nether garments as well, sliding free of them like an animal might slip free of a discarded skin. Her face flushed as she turned away, but not before the sunlit silhouette of his body etched itself into her mind. Lean, hard muscle, skin so pale it could have been carved from marble, sinews that flexed not like human sinews at all, but like the toughened cords of a predator . . . she hadn't seen all that in the half-darkness when she had bound the bandages around him . . . or perhaps she hadn't wanted to see. Now, as he walked down into the water, she could not help but be drawn back to gaze at him, grateful that at least now the water covered the more sensitive parts of his anatomy. What happened to the much-vaunted sartorial conservatism for which the Braxins were famous? The lords of the Void who wouldn't even take off their gloves in public, much less their pants? *That's the Braxaná,* she corrected herself. *I guess not the others.* What was this creature, so like and unlike all the stories she'd been told? She gazed in wonder as he splashed water over his torso, noting the long red bruises that marked his flesh here and there, souvenirs of their desperate landing. Probably most of them were her fault, dragging him through the brush.

Then she realized he was looking back at her. Her face flushed even hotter as she suddenly focused on the ground by her feet.

"I took a few blows in the fight on the ship," he told her. His amusement washed over her, as if he could sense her thoughts, her inappropriate guilt. Warm amusement, sweet and inviting, that promised respite from uncertainty and fear. *Come to me,* his essence beckoned. *Drink me in. Drown in my presence.* It was more terrifying than his anger. Physical trials she could deal with, but this . . . this was a whole new class of danger.

Wordlessly she did the only thing she could, and left the clearing. Letting the cool shadows of the forest beyond veil his presence in deep green shadow . . . which even like his eyes, continued to watch her.

She could hear him chuckling softly as she left.

Tathas waited until she was asleep before he let the rage come and take him.

You are Viak'im. You have a destiny. You will NOT live out your life marooned on some backVoid planet while the Kaim'eri mock your failure before all the Kesserit.

In fury he struck at the ground beside him, hard enough to make a small crater. His knuckles hit rock and bled. Hot blood, warrior's blood. Wasted here on this vile planet.

But what could he do?

Think, Tathas, think. Either there is a ship on this planet or there isn't. If there is, you must find it. If there isn't, then there must be a way to contact the interstellar community. Freelancers are always looking for signs of life on these backVoid planets; send out a signal one of them can trace and someone will come looking. Right?

And if the inhabitants of the planet didn't have the technology to send out such a signal?

Then I will do what I must. And if that means dragging some primitive culture into the modern age, until they learn the technology I need them to have, so be it.

And if there were no sentients at all to work with? What, would he build a transmitter from rocks and tree branches, and power it with wind?

With a snort of rage he curled his fists into the alien dirt, driving it under his fingernails.

I will NOT be stranded here!

He looked at the sleeping woman. So peaceful now. She was almost a different person when she slept, the fears and tensions of her waking life peeling back from her like the coarse skin of some armored fruit. For a moment, in reflex, he almost reached out to her, driven by a need to vent his tension in purely physical relief . . . but no, she wouldn't understand that for what it was. Azean culture had gotten sex all tangled up with weak emotions somewhere in its history, and lost sight of the fact that the act was one of primal tension and release in its own right. No matter what he did, no matter how he approached her, she'd be reading all sorts of things into the effort that he hadn't intended, and if those imaginings were upsetting enough it could push her over the edge. And he needed her sane too much to risk pushing her over the edge right now.

She would sense my hunger, he thought. *She would know.*

It was a strangely erotic thought. And a disturbing one. Was the psychic bond stronger when the bounds of physical intimacy had been breached? Might the power flow back into him, if that happened, so that his mind was violated by her emotions, the way hers seemed to be invaded by his?

A cold chill ran up his spine. *No wonder my people fear this thing.*

Sleep was long in coming, beneath a sky of unnamed stars, and brought with it dreams better not remembered.

The gods came from the stars, Klath knew that much. The *istal* even knew a few words in the Divine Speech because the priests taught all the younglings that much as soon as they could speak. Klath knew what the gods were called and it knew how to greet them, and most important it knew how to tell false gods from true. For the world was full of demons and devils that masqueraded as gods, and unless you knew the right names and applied them correctly they would devour your soul and steal your children away to be slaves in a place so terrible that no starlight shone there, ever. *Ratuarr* they called it—the Great Emptiness.

Thus far its journey had not been difficult. The valley floor was lush and damp and there were colored mosses the *istal* remembered from its childhood, fragrant and edible. It followed a stream for a while and drank deeply before leaving its banks behind, knowing the thick dew of morning would provide it with refreshment again come sunrise. The night was comfortably chill and it found an embankment of reeds so thick that, mashed beneath its body, they felt like bedding.

No one came looking for it. No alarm trumpets sounded in the distance. No voices carried on the wind, crying out its name in hope and fear. There was no sign that anyone noticed it was gone.

Had it expected anything different?

On the second day it began to climb again. The ridge was steep and rocky, with few handholds, but its agile fingers wrapped themselves around tree stumps and it pulled itself upward. Soon it reached the crest of the ridge, and it stretched itself in the early morning sun, looking for signs of whatever had fallen from the sky. It was not hard to find. The land was scored as if by some black knife, beginning just behind the crest of the ridge and continuing down into the next valley. Black rocks could be seen scattered along the path, with some dark mass at the head of it.

Fear caught in its throat for the first time since it had left home. If this truly was a thing of the heavens, who could say what power might lay close about it? It had heard tales of strange rocks which fell from the sky, that drew other rocks toward them like lovers. But after a moment Klath swallowed hard and continued its journey toward the strange gash in the land. If this was a thing of the gods, then clearly it had been sent here for people to find it. Maybe just for him!

The noonday sun was warm as it reached the black streak, and the mists withdrew obligingly. Klath spread its shalorri to drink in the sunlight as it stepped warily along the trail of the fallen star. The black streak was earth and moss seared as if by heat, with small half-melted bits of . . . *things* . . . along it. Klath picked one of them up warily, not so certain it wasn't going to harm it. It looked like a piece of parchment folded and then half-melted, and it crumbled in its hand as it touched it. Some of the pieces looked like they too had been burned, or at least melted. Some were of such odd shape and substance that it was afraid to touch them. If the gods sent down their magic to earth, and it arrived like this, how did you know which pieces you were supposed to collect? It chose a handful of the most interesting and put them in its pack. Maybe one would prove of value enough that the village would praise it for collecting it. Maybe the priests would read meaning into these odd pieces and the gods would look with favor upon the poor *istal* who had collected them. Maybe their magic would inspire *istali* flesh to commit itself at last, so that it might join the Rain Festival dancers in their celebration of the village's newest genderlings. . . .

It was then it saw the trail.

Its heart almost stopped as it recognized footprints. They were not like those of any animal it knew, pressed into the charred moss. One creature, on two feet, dragging something heavy . . . larger than its own people, judging from the size, but also bipedal. Not an animal then, but a Person.

Tales of angels and demons raced through its head. All the names and warnings and incantations it was supposed to remember were suddenly gone. There was no doubt about it now, it was tracking some creature that might well embody ancient legends . . . and equally ancient threats.

Shalorri quivering, Klath edged its way along the sides of the alien trail. Its ear-hoods were pricked to catch even the slightest sound, and the hairs on its skin noted every miniscule shifting of the breeze. It knew that it should go back to the village and get one of the wise ones, a priest perhaps . . . but then this would become a priestly matter, and the males and females would aid them, and a lone *istal* would be of no interest or use to anyone.

Teeth gritted in determination, it moved on.

The trail led down into the valley, to the side of a stream. Now it could hear sounds. Strange sounds, like and unlike speech. The voices of angels? Or demons? Its shalorri trembled, but it forged ahead. Wary now, like a prey-animal, pressing its way through brush and trees slowly, hoping its motion would pass for that of some beast's casual passage, or perhaps the wind.

And then it saw. In a clearing.

People. And not People. Something else, that walked on two legs like People, and had eyes and mouths like People, but were not creatures of this world. Something so terrible that for a moment Klath was frozen in fear, recognizing in an instant just what it was that had fallen to its planet. And in that moment, while it was frozen, they saw it. Small, dark eyes in a stony face fixed on Klath; the *istal* could feel their power. The mouth of one shaped some kind of sound, but did not voice it. The shorter one knelt a bit, and seemed to grow smaller. That would be the slave race of the demons, Klath guessed. The other . . . the other had skin as pale as the petals of the *frondaa,* with dark fur along the head like a beast, marking its face in dark stripes. Klath knew the pattern of those markings from its childhood lessons.

They did not move, for a moment. The clearing was so still Klath could have heard the breeze in the leaves, if not for the pounding of its heart. Finally, its courage girdled in desperation, Klath voiced the Challenge of Demons, in the ancient tongue which the priests had preserved. There was power in such words, he knew, and a true demon would be forced to answer him, and to identify itself.

Do you come from the Stars or from the Fires? he demanded.

Both creatures seemed startled by its words. Perhaps they did not expect a mere *istali* to know the Words of Power.

Then: *From the Fires,* the pale one answered, in that same tongue.

Fear gripped its heart. Klath turned and ran. Tearing through the shrubbery as if it was made of spider-knitting, not caring if there were thorns to tear its skin or stones to cut its feet. Not daring to look back, to see if the demons were following it. Probably they weren't. Probably they thought a mere *istal* was no threat to them, and would let it go.

Klath had to get to its people. It had to tell them the truth . . . that the demons had come at last, and if all the people of this world did not rise up to destroy them utterly, then the whole world would be given over to demons, and the precious light of the gods extinguished forever.

"Something's out there."

Tathas watched her as she leaned into the breeze, senses strained to the utmost. "Human?"

She hesitated, then shook her head. "Not sure." A pause. "Coming this way. Quickly."

The Kesserit drew himself up, loosening the knife in its sheath. It was the only thing left from the crash that still worked as a weapon and it wasn't balanced for throwing. He doubted the woman could fight, so right now that was all he had. He glanced about for cover but there was no time, for just then the thing that she had sensed approaching broke through the brush at the far end of the clearing and stared at them.

It was Scattered Races, he judged instantly, body true to the symmetrical, bipedal blueprint of the type. But there the similarity ended. Skin hung in lizardlike folds over an awkward, skeletal frame; large eyes set in ball sockets moved independently of one another, taking in all corners of the clearing.

For a moment none of them moved. Some of the folds along the creature's back stirred, fanning out slightly as if testing the wind. Zara moved slightly, shifting her position, but said nothing, and made no move forward.

Then it spoke. Garbled words, filtered through a speech apparatus not well suited to the language it was struggling to pronounce. Tathas could hear the psychic's gasp of surprise as she made out the words, and his own knife suddenly seemed a million miles away.

"Are you of the ones they call Braxin?" the creature asked Tathas.

In his own language. His own dialect. The creature spoke his native tongue!

"Yes," he told it. "I am Braxin."

Without warning, then, the creature bolted. Tathas might have taken off in pursuit had not the woman fallen at the same moment, letting out a scream of pain. Torn between the two, he lost those precious seconds he might have needed to overtake the alien.

"What is it?" he asked, kneeling by her side. "What is it?"

"Danger," she whispered. "Danger danger DANGER . . ." A fit of trembling overtook her, and her eyes seemed to roll upward in her head as she whispered fiercely, "Not that name, not demon-names, no, no, tell the priests! Kill the Fireborn . . ."

He wanted to chase the creature down, but he knew he couldn't leave the woman alone. Especially not now that they knew there was a threat out there in the woods. She was hardly in a state to defend herself with alien thoughts pounding through her head, tears of pain pouring down her face as she struggled to absorb them. What if there were others like that, who came for her while he was gone?

But as soon as she was capable of moving they needed to move. Quickly now. That thing would be back, maybe with other things like it. And based on Zara's fevered mutterings he was willing to bet the reception would not be a good one.

He spoke Braxin. . . . ?

At least that meant someone had made contact with this blessed backVoid planet. Contact meant communications. Communications meant starships.

So why didn't he find that comforting?

Klath crashed through the woods, sliding down the hills of rubble in its rush, nearly twisting its ankle as it stumbled down to the valley floor. Its incantations would hold the demons at bay, but not for long. It had to get back to its people, it had to warn them!

For generations now tales had been told of the first great Invasion, when the Pale Ones had risen up from the fires of Hell and swarmed across the surface of the planet. The stories were horrific, of atrocities performed upon living flesh and living souls both, so terrible that Klath had only heard whispers of them, for they were deemed too terrible for children or weakling *istali*. But it knew the prayers which the village voiced every turning of the moon, begging the gods for help in fighting the demons the next time they arose.

And now here they were, the demons arisen again. And it, Klath, was the only one who knew!

Klath ran. Its weak *istal* frame wasn't made for running—it lacked the hardened muscle and fortified joints of fully sexed males and females—but it ran anyway. Across the valley floor, its heels spewing up wads of moss as it pounded across the earth. Until its breath wheezed through its small lungs in pain, and all the world began to spin before it. It ran. To do otherwise was to fail its people, to grant the demons victory. And it knew from the tales of its people just what that would mean.

Night was falling by the time it stumbled over his home ridge. Scattering the stones from the campsite where it had watched the star fall—so long ago!—it tried to catch its breath as it sighted the lights of its village, at last. Grasping a nearby tree it doubled over, coughing up phlegm that was speckled with blood. Its feet burned like fire and red-stained footprints led back in a trail from the place in the valley where it had cut them open on a bed of sharp rock. Its shalorri fluttered helplessly in the growing darkness, unable to dull the pain. But. It had made it this far. And from here the journey was all downhill, and surely this close to the village the gods would be watching over it.

Stumbling through the woods, then across cleared earth, at last through the neatly manicured farmlands with their rows of spiked bushes bearing armored fruits, Klath muttered prayers under its breath as it approached the great meeting hut. It was Festival time now and both males and females would be inside, dancing and laughing and sharing the feast. Almost too far away to reach. Klath wanted nothing more than to lay down for a moment and catch its breath. It seemed its whole body was on fire now—even his shalorri felt like red-hot knives were playing along it—and its limbs felt like they were about to explode. But. The *istal* kept going. Stumbling now, not running. He had no more strength for running. Muttering the prayers that would protect him in a voice that grew steadily weaker—

—And then it threw open the door to the meeting hut. At first no one noticed it, but then, one by one, all eyes turned its way. Music stopped, eating stopped, and all grew silent. What a sight the *istal* was, standing in the doorway, covered in the blood and debris of its desperate journey! A few younglings began to chatter but their mothers shushed them quickly.

Klath tried to speak, but found its voice had left it. With one last effort of sheer will it forced its body to make the sounds, its mouth to shape them.

"The demons have come!" The name of the dreaded creatures hung heavy in the smoky air. When no one responded Klath coughed and cried out, "I have seen them!"

The room was still, utterly still. Did no one hear it? Or was it simply that no one believed it? It was only *istal*, after all. With a cry of despair Klath fell to its knees. *You must understand! You must believe me!*

At last one of the priests came forward. An ancient, withered hand took hold of Klath's own. "How do you know this?"

Pain ran in hot flashes along Klath's shalorri as it tried to force out more words, to make them understand. "I saw . . . a star fell . . . on the far ridge. I went to find it. They were there. Two of them, one demon, one slave . . . just like the priests describe them. I spoke the Greeting to him and he answered me. He answered me!"

And it repeated the demon-greeting then and there, so that the priest might know it had gotten the words right.

The grip on its arm tightened.

"You are sure? He said that?"

Klath nodded weakly. Couldn't they see that the room was spinning? Couldn't they feel the heat that was searing its skin? Its throat was burning, it could hardly draw in breath. "Yes. He gave the Answer. They're here, do you understand? He was only the first . . ."

The priest stood. His shalorri spread out about him, a glorious hood of crimson and gold that proclaimed masculinity and power. Klath felt envy lodge in his throat like a red-hot coal.

"My people . . ." the priest began. He waited until all eyes were upon him, all whispering silenced, before speaking the next words. The words they all feared the most. "As it is said . . . *they shall come to you in your time of joy and in your time of forgetfulness, when you have no thought for history. They shall come to you when you celebrate life and loving, and have no thought for darkness. They shall come to you when you believe they shall come no more, and have set your weapons aside. They shall come to you when children run free in the night, no longer fearing those who might feast upon their souls . . .*"

He looked out over the assembled. His shalorri quivered, bright with authority.

"Festival is over," he said quietly. "Arm yourselves. We begin the Hunt come dawn."

Night. Darkness. The primal dishonesty of an evening's quiet, right before a storm.

"What is it?"

Zara shook her head, and drew her arms closer about her huddled form, legs folded into them. "I don't know. Something new . . . something . . . violent, very violent. Hungry."

"Headed this way?"

She nodded miserably. "That seems to be when the feelings are the strongest, when something is focused on me. Or in this case, on us." She looked up at the Braxin, then quickly away. "I'm sorry I can't do better," she whispered.

It had been a day since the alien had fled their company. Tathas had tried to track it, but his Central skills were hardly suited to such terrain, and he'd soon lost all sign of it. It was travelling in a straight line, though, which seemed to imply it was running toward something, blindly enough that it wasn't taking time to complicate its trail. Ten to one any trouble which came would come from that direction.

And yes, trouble was coming. The woman was sure of it. Now that she was less terrified of him than of the dangers surrounding, she was more willing to speak of her visions.

It was a good thing he hadn't used her that night, he mused. She might not be as cooperative if he had. Now . . . there were two of them alone here, and an unknown planet, and the woman sensed that trouble was coming. Human political differences had suddenly become a very small issue.

"Can't focus more?"

She bit her lip. "It's directed at us, or I probably wouldn't be picking it up at all. Someone's intentions, violent, bloody . . . isn't that enough?"

He paced off the dimensions of the small clearing, drawing mental clarity from the motion.

"Shouldn't we be getting out of here?" she whispered.

"Run away?"

"Well . . . yes."

He shook his head, studying the terrain.

"Seems kind of rational to me," she offered

"Azeans run," he snapped.

"Not Braxins?"

"Not Kesserit." He dropped into a crouch and picked up a handful of earth, testing its consistency with his fingers. "Not when there's something they want here, that they are not going to leave behind."

"What can you want here that's worth the risk of facing . . . that?" She gestured weakly toward the east, where the worst premonitions seemed to be coming from. Right now she wanted nothing more than to be headed in a different direction.

The green eyes met hers. There was hatred in those eyes, and anger, and a storm that swirled in the depths of his soul, threatening to engulf anyone who so much as looked at him wrong. If any of that was directed at her she would have been blinded by the force of it . . . but it wasn't. She was pretty sure of that by now. Whatever rage burned inside him, she was only peripherally connected to it.

He said it quietly. "They spoke Braxin."

"And so . . ."

"My people have been here."

"You sound surprised."

"This far out? We've waged no war here, sent no explorers, no traders, not even scouts. Braxi isn't due to come into this region until—"

He stopped suddenly.

"Until?"

"It's very far away from the Holding," he muttered. "And there's an arm of the Star Empire between home and here, which would stress supply lines beyond tolerance. There would be no point to it now—not even to sending scouts out to explore the place. Braxi doesn't invest exploration teams in planets that are this inaccessible."

What a strange, incomprehensible creature he was. Did he think she didn't know about the Schedule of Conquest? Didn't know that eons ago Braxi had crafted a master plan for domination of the entire galaxy, with a timetable for every region?

Your people weren't due out here yet, she thought. *Yet someone came.* "There are independents, aren't there? Mercenaries, scouts . . . people who might take off on their own, looking for . . . something of profit?"

"Sure there are. They come in, make maps, get samples, maybe grab up a few natives to show off back home . . . and leave." He hissed softly; the spear of his frustration lanced into her battered brain like a red-hot brand. "They don't stay around long enough to teach the natives their language. They certainly don't set up a blessed reception committee for the next round of visitors."

"So what do you think happened here?"

"Don't know." He drew in a deep breath and shut his eyes for a moment; she could taste in her mouth how hard he was working to keep his emotions under control. For her sake? "But they were here. Come and gone. Whatever vessel brought them here may still be on this planet. If not . . . they may have had some communications equipment that's still around. Or the makings of such. Can we afford to leave that behind?"

"Are you so sure they're gone?" she said softly.

"The ship picked up no interstellar-level communication on the way in. Braxins would still be using their gear, if they were present. Aliens . . . aliens might not know what it was. They certainly wouldn't have anyone out there in the interstellar community to talk to." He shook his head in frustration. "If only we knew more about them."

"The natives?"

He nodded.

She smiled weakly. "Well, to start with, I'm not sure I agree with you that they're human in origin. The Scattered Races are primarily predatory in their somatotype, while the creature we saw had sensory apparatus associated with prey as well. My guess would be an adaptable, omnivorous creature, that at one time in its evolution was hunted by life-forms as large and as dangerous as it was. That said, it is tool-using, social, and probably organized into reasonably complex communities. Visual display is extremely important and probably plays a part in social hierarchy." She paused, going over the memory of that telling moment in her mind, when the alien had first appeared. "I could be wrong, but I don't think this one ranks very high. None of the physical appendages that might have been used to establish rank seemed very well-developed. Size matters to it, of course, but that's not a big surprise. It may have spoken to you instead of me because you were larger. If so, then by observing more of them we might get a good sense of rank." Again she paused. "Not a very muscular creature, given its structural potential. If it's a typical specimen, then I would guess we're dealing with a food-production culture, rather than hunter-gatherer. Of course it could be very young, and that would explain a lot also. Not yet fully developed."

He stared at her for a moment, before finding his voice. "All that from that one brief appearance? Your abilities are . . . impressive."

She laughed shortly; it was a strange sound to be making, after so many days of living in fear. "Not my 'abilities,' Tathas. Just a Mediator's training. Anyone can do it, if they learn the signs."

"Others would not have their training bolstered by psychic sensitivity."

She shook her head emphatically. "That's not relevant here—"

Or was it? She had spent her whole lifetime training to "read" alien cultures. Who was to say that some latent psychic ability hadn't played its part in that process, feeding her knowledge on a level she wasn't consciously aware of?

Even the Mediators hadn't known what she truly was, she thought. *I have never known what I am.*

As if he sensed her thoughts—and didn't want her lost in them—he prompted, "Anything else?"

She shook her head and tried to focus. "It wasn't carrying weapons. That means no major predators in the vicinity, and no hostile or unpredictable neighbors."

"Or some natural means of defense."

"Possibly. But even alien species who have such tend to arm themselves in dangerous territory. It's one of the key differences between full-sentient species and mere animals. Animals are happy to have fangs and claws. Humans want a rock to throw before anyone gets close enough to test such things."

"They are arming now," he said quietly. A question.

She shut her eyes. "I don't know, Tathas." A weary hand lifted up to rub the space between her eyes, as if that could shut out all the errant thoughts that were assailing her. "I feel the hostility out there, somewhere . . . I'm guessing it's focused on us, if it's that strong . . . whether it's natives with guns or a thousand field mice who are irked because we're sitting on top of their warrens . . . that's beyond me. This is all too new, too unknown. . . . I'm guessing in the dark." She sighed deeply, then looked up at him again. "I'm sorry. I really am."

"And here I thought all psychics were omnipotent," he said. There was a dry humor to the remark that startled her. Not a tone she would have expected from one of *them*. His mouth even curled a bit when he said it, into something that was almost a smile . . . such a jarring change from the angry shadows of his usual expression that her breath caught in her throat for a moment.

"This one's not," she said, looking quickly away. It scared the hells out of her, those rare moments when she was attracted to him. What kind of fool felt sexual desire for a Braxin?

It's just the circumstances, she told herself. *Perfectly understandable. He saved your life, now you depend upon him . . . purely human instinct, to feel a bond . . . survival mechanism. Nothing more.*

Was it?

They set up camp in a place he said would be defensible. She wasn't a warrior, but she trusted his instincts. More and more she had the sense that whatever was focused on them was way beyond such defenses in scope, but when she suggested that he just shrugged it off. She wasn't yet sure if she should admire him for his self-confidence or curse him for his foolishness. Ditto that for when he went off trekking through the woods alone, promising her that his actions had purpose and would pay off in the morning.

All she knew was that as the night wore on and the hostile thoughts in the distance grew more and more intense, the distant mountains were looking very good to her.

Dawn: a searing white glare over misted mountains, beneath a harsh blue sky bereft of clouds.

The High Priest cast five white birds into the sky and watched the pattern of their flight for a few moments, shading his eyes against the rising sun, while the people of the village gathered around him. Males, females, younglings, even *istali;* no one was going to miss this occasion for so mundane a thing as sleep.

"All is well," he announced at last. "The gods favor our enterprise."

The sixth bird was sacrificed and its blood used to adorn the warriors. So would the favor of the gods be carried into battle.

They had never fought full-sentient creatures before, of their own species or any other. But they knew the ways of fighting. Their ancestors had decreed that each generation must be ready and able to repel the armies of demons that would surely come, and they had been faithful to that teaching. Fire-hardened spears were at hand, unblooded but sharp. Young males practiced kick-blows in the muddy street. Shalorri rippled like the wind, fans of colored skin that increased the visible mass of the small army tenfold. The incense of War filled the muddy streets with its noxious but stimulating fumes.

And the drums beat. How they pounded! Warrior fists on taut skin surfaces, beating out the rhythm of Holy War with all the force of thunder. Soon the sound would reach neighboring valleys, where other villages stood. Soon the wild drumbeats would wake up the males in distant places and alert them to the threat that now stood upon their world in the form of a two-legged creature, like and unlike themselves. *Demons!* the drumbeats cried out. *Wartime! Arm yourselves and prepare!*

Runners had been sent out the night before to mobilize neighboring villages, but there was no way to know yet if they had reached them or not. How many demons were there out there in the woods, how many traps had been set against just such a contingency? The warriors paused in their beating and waited; the morning was so silent one could hear the wings of the sacred birds fanning softly, in their wicker cages. Then . . .

War! A distant beat resounded, echoing over valley and vale, mirroring their own. *We hear! We come!*

From the sidelines, where it huddled alongside the younglings, Klath watched the warriors gather. It ached to be standing among them, or even among the females who were seeing them off. And it ached with physical pain besides. The heat that had taken root in its flesh last night had not been banished by the dawn, but spread; now it was like a fire itching at the insides of Klath's skin, that no motion or ointment seemed to quell.

No good alerting the nurse-females. They had other things to do now, besides scratch an *istal*'s back.

No use complaining aloud at all. *Istal* problems? No time for them.

Dawn. He'd already erased all signs of their camp, but not well. Her protests had gone unheard.

"They'll know we were here. It'll give them a starting point for tracking us."

"That's fine."

Was this some quirk of Braxin logic, or was he simply insane? She stared at him in amazement as he studied the campsite one last time, then put his hands to his mouth, turned to the east . . . and yelled. Whooped, really. It was a loud sound, inarticulate, that carried over the woods in the crisp morning air and must have been audible for miles.

He listened for a moment, then did it again. A different sound this time, ululating. Then a third one. Finally, satisfied, he lowered his hands and just listened for a moment.

"What in the human hells was that?" she asked. "Braxin war cry?"

"Unexplained noise," he said. A faint smile that was either self-confidence or utter lunacy creased his lips. "Come on, time to move."

"They'll come here, they'll find this site in no time, they'll be on our trail. . . ."

"Of course they will," he said evenly. "That was the point."

She blinked. Utter lunacy. She was stranded with a madman.

"You coming, or you going to sit here and wait for them?"

Shaking her head, she got to her feet and followed him into the underbrush, along a trail he'd broken sometime during the night. They moved quickly, quietly, but she was sure it wasn't quiet enough, not for life-forms raised in this environment.

The trail brought them to a stream, quick-running and deep. "This," Tathas said, "is where it gets interesting." He glanced behind him. "Not much time. I suggest we move quickly."

She followed him into the icy water, flinching as it rose about her thighs. Followed him as he turned into the direction of the current and bade her to follow, slipping and sliding along the rocky bottom. They moved quickly, but not without effort, and when they stopped at last some distance upstream to catch their breaths it was a good minute before she could speak.

"That *was* a Braxin war cry, wasn't it?"

The green eyes met hers. Something that was not quite a smile flitted across his face.

"Far to go still," he said quietly. "Let's get moving."

The howl resounded across the mountains, over the valley, into the village. A horrific unnatural screech, that seemed to have demons laughing in its wake.

The warriors froze, their shalorri stiffening instinctively into combat-posture.

Another cry answered. Not from the same source. A weird, high-pitched cry that made Klath's skin crawl.

"Those are the two," the priest said. He didn't sound very sure of himself.

Then came the third.

Silence reigned after that. The whole village straining for another strange cry from the throat of a fourth creature . . . but there were none.

"There are more than two," someone muttered.

"Maybe," said Yaltah. He was the one who was leading the warriors. "Who knows the way of demons?"

"An army perhaps," another muttered.

Both his eyes turned toward the speaker, narrowing to slits as their hoods darkened ominously. "You are afraid? Stay home with the younglings."

"I'm not afraid!" a youngling cried. "I'll go fight the demons!"

A female reached past Klath to cuff the child into silence. It was a soft blow, affectionate, bespeaking her pride in the youngling's spirit even as it admonished him. Klath felt an ache inside its soul, for the days when such affection might have been directed at it.

I would go if you would let me. Just to prove myself useful. Maybe I would even die in battle and then you would know I was worth something, even without a gender.

There were so many warriors he could hardly count them. Youths and fathers and grandfathers and even a few priests . . . all had turned out for the hunt. The females would stay behind and pray with the younglings, offering birds to the gods while their mates and sons braved danger on behalf of the village.

No. On behalf of the *world*.

"We know where they are now," a warrior offered, pointing in the direction of the strange cries. He was a young male who normally helped clean up after the sacred birds. "Their mistake, yes?"

"Or a trap," a more seasoned elder cautioned.

"Their cries are to strike fear into our hearts," a priest pronounced. "Therefore resist that fear, and the gods will protect you."

Drums beat in the distance, resounding across the valley. Warriors were being sent to aid them from another village, the drums said, but would not arrive until nightfall.

"All right," Yaltah said. "Trackers first. Let's move out."

He turned in Klath's direction, and for one giddy moment Klath thought they were going to invite it to come along. After all, the *istal* had seen the demons, and no one else had. But he merely waved to someone past Klath and then turned back to his troops, barked a few rough orders, and led them into the fields, toward the distant woods.

Sick with envy, Klath watched them go.

"Something's coming," she whispered. "So sharp, so sharp, it hurts . . ."

"New direction? New intent?"

She was huddled on the ground, arms wrapped about her knees, shaking. "I don't know. It's . . . different. Not like what I've been getting up until now." How could she describe it to him? The hostility of the locals had been painful, discordant, unnerving . . . but not like this. This was cold, precise, a sleek blade to their crude bludgeon. One single mind, she guessed, focusing on her with such intensity that she could taste it. "I don't think it's the locals, Tathas. It doesn't feel like them."

His eyes narrowed. "Another life-form?"

"No. Maybe. I don't know." Tears squeezed out of the corners of her eyes as she tried to concentrate.

"Hostile?"

Was it? No dark images accompanied this one, like it did with the other natives. No sense of intent at all. "I don't know," she whispered at last. "But it's hunting us. I can feel it."

"Then we'd best get moving," he said quietly.

She nodded weakly and let him help her up to her feet. She could feel his Braxin essence thrumming just beneath his skin, restless and angry as always. Compared to what was assaulting her brain it was almost familiar, oddly comforting. She resisted the instinct to lean against him for a moment, to draw strength from his closeness. Not something you did with one of *them* . . . but gods, how tempting it was.

"Come on."

I know where you are, she heard whispering in her brain. Voice without words, intent without identity. *I will find you!*

Shivering, she followed the Braxin back into the brush, and toward the village beyond.

"Ayyyyah!"

The triumphant cry of Yaltah shattered the midday air. Even before they could see what he was yelling about, his troops knew that something of importance had been discovered.

Quickly, anxiously, the column of warriors spilled into the clearing. It was wide enough to contain them all, and in the center of it was a mound of dirt surrounded by scuff-marks, which the trackers were studying.

"They were here," one said. "Many hours."

"Until dawn," the other offered.

Down on all fours, they sniffed the ground. Wrinkled noses told what they thought of the demons' smell. One of them huffed about the edges of the clearing and then snorted. "Piss," he said.

"You sure?" Yaltah asked.

The other tracker came to the spot, sniffed it, and nodded. "Piss."

Yaltah looked at the priest, who nodded his understanding. Bodily functions meant that the flesh the demons wore was real, not merely some kind of metaphysical shell that looked like flesh. Creatures that pissed had to eat and drink. They could be wounded. They could die.

"All right," he said, gripping his spear tightly. "Let's find them."

There was a trail; the trackers had no trouble finding it. Whoever these demons were, they hadn't taken the time to obscure their passage. Following them through the brush was painfully easy, not even as challenging as hunting. Animals had instincts, and knew how to walk without disturbing the earth. These demons appeared to have none.

After a short while the trail led to a stream, deep and swift-running. Yaltah ordered his trackers to search both sides, and soon they picked up the trail again on the far side of the water, almost directly across. A narrower trail this time, as if the demons were being more careful. Maybe at this point they had sensed someone was coming after them.

Fleeing. That was good. That meant they were afraid.

The brush gave way to open ground. The trail was harder to follow now, and sometimes they lost it along a rocky stretch, but it always picked up again.

Once more they smelled the creature's odd urine.

Once, on the branches of a thorny bush, they found a few threads of fiber. The color and texture matched up with the story the *istal* had told, of how the demon was dressed. There was a small spot of red on one of the fragments. Blood? The priest said it was a sign from the gods.

And then they came to the end of the trail. The end of the part they could follow, anyway. Footsteps scuffed along a granite ridge led to the edge of a precipice. There was nothing beyond that, save a nearly sheer drop down to the valley floor below. Jagged granite spars and crevices stood out in sharp relief in the midday sun, promising a treacherous descent.

"Search," Yaltah said quietly.

The trackers searched. There were no other trails, they reported. Nothing leading away from the granite flats, save the one trail which had brought them there.

One of them crouched down on all fours and gingerly, warily, leaned over the edge. He had to wait a few seconds until the breeze shifted, before he could pick up currents from the valley floor; when he did he breathed in deeply, his nasal flaps shivering wetly.

"Down there," he confirmed. "I can smell them."

His companion, following a more immediate scent, discovered other signs. A few drops of blood on the edge of a sharp outcropping. A shred of fabric torn and lost when something wearing fabric had let itself down over the edge.

So. They had gone down to the valley floor. Scaling the jagged rock face with care, hoping no one would follow them. Yaltah studied the land to both sides of the area with a practiced eye. There was an easier descent possible to the north, a long hike from where they were. Nothing better to the south.

You are crafty, Demons, but not crafty enough. You do not count upon our dedication to track you down and destroy you at any cost, or our understanding that if we do not, the very world we live in is at risk.

"We have ropes?" he asked quietly.

The one in charge of supplies huffed and nodded.

"Then we follow. Quickly."

He looked out over the valley—ostensibly so peaceful, but now made a haven for fearful things—and added, "I want their heads by nightfall."

WE KNOW WHERE YOU ARE, the alien voice screamed in Zara's head. *WE WILL FIND YOU.*

The source of it was closer, now. She was sure of that. Even as the natives moved farther away, following the false trail Tathas had laid in the middle of the night, this other . . . *thing* . . . was closing in on them.

In the distance she could see the village. It was a small thing, housing maybe four dozen families at most. There were a handful of larger buildings, no doubt meant for public gatherings—perhaps ritual use of some kind—but the smaller living huts were indistinguishable from one another, with no signs of wealth, armament, or magical significance lending any one or another greater importance than their fellows.

"Tribal," she whispered. "Rule by consensus, most likely. Religion probably nature-linked."

"Shh."

In the silence of the hot afternoon, hiding prone in a bed of high grass, beneath the white alien sun, they studied the village. A faint sound came and went with the breeze: alien voices chanting in unison, singsong, just loud enough to hear. It seemed to be coming from one of the larger huts.

"Remind me why we want to be here?" she whispered.

"Aside from the fact that it is the last place they will come looking for us . . . because I want to see what's here." He shifted position, parting a clump of seeded grass to get a better view of the largest hut. "If there are any relics or records of interstellar visitation, they will be here. Somewhere."

Relics. That meant communications equipment. A means of getting off this planet, before all the hostile minds that were searching for them caught up to them. That sounded good.

A native shuffled in the doorway of one of the smaller huts, dragging one foot as though it had been injured. It was hard to see it in the shadows, but Zara thought its eye-hoods had been painted. She stored that tidbit along with all the other data she had observed as the creature disappeared again, fitting it into the cultural whole like a piece into a jigsaw puzzle. Gods willing she wouldn't be on this planet long enough to finish the job.

WE ARE COMING FOR YOU!

Tathas was close enough to feel her flinch. The green eyes fixed on her with concern . . . both for her and for their mission. "Zara?"

"That same one. The new one. It's so strong. Almost like words in my head."

"You think it's coming from the village?"

Startled, she considered that thought. She was so used to thinking of herself as being pursued, it hadn't even occurred to her she might be heading *toward* the mysterious presence.

"I don't know," she said at last. Her whispered voice was shaking. "But it's aware of us, and the others aren't . . . that scares the hells out of me."

He nodded grimly. "Humans have evolved psychic ability. There's no reason to assume aliens can't as well." She could see the tension along the line of his jaw as he said it, could *feel* the rush of fear along his skin. Zara was one thing; he had gotten used to her. But alien psychics, with unknown powers, linked to a group that was already flooding the air with hostile intentions . . . that was bad even if you weren't Braxin, and hadn't been taught from childhood to fear all things psychic.

And he was, and had been.

Which meant that whatever confrontation they were heading toward, she might be the only one able to confront it.

He hasn't failed you yet, she reminded herself.

Sleek, silent, he shouldered his way forward along the ground, randomizing his motion so that the grasses which parted for him seemed to be shifting in the wind, no more. She tried to do the same. Where his pale skin showed through his shirt there were now bands of sunburned flesh, crusted with the last remnants of protective mud he had applied to it hours ago. Where recent wounds crossed those bands they were livid red, bloody in appearance.

Whatever environment his ancestors had evolved in, she thought, it sure as all hells wasn't tropical.

The chanting was clearer now, if that's what it was: many voices in unison, a strange harmony of efforts. They steered clear of the hut it seemed to be coming from and made their way to one of the other communal buildings. If there was any sign of interstellar contact, Tathas whispered, it would probably be there, in a place where tribal possessions were stored.

She admired his courage, even if his optimism was downright insane.

The source of the strange voice inside her was close now, very close. More than once she whipped about suddenly, as if to surprise something that was creeping up behind her . . . but there was nothing there.

Yet.

They managed to get to the nearest communal building unseen. Outside of the one injured native in his hut, there seemed to be no one moving about. Tathas took in the hut's decorative support poles, topped with bird-shaped finials and hung with talismans that probably had magical significance, and then slipped inside. She glanced about one last time to make sure no one was watching, then joined him.

WE ARE HERE, the voice proclaimed.

The inside of the hut was shadowy, cool. The walls were lined with animal skins painted in complex, mostly abstract designs. Her Mediator's mind started automatically classifying them according to accepted categories: form, materials, possible purpose. Richly woven mats on the ground at one end implied an audience chamber of some kind, perhaps for a priest or seer. The building smelled of strange herbs and distant smoke, perhaps some narcotic mixture.

Tathas was studying the designs on the walls intently. "Anything useful?" she asked.

He shook his head; his expression was grim. "Nothing." By the base of each support post was a sizable carving, mostly of birds; he crouched down and studied the talismans strung around their necks. "Blood sacrifice," he said quietly, fingering a crusted brown blade that hung on a beaded cord.

But nothing Braxin. Nothing interstellar. Nothing of even moderate technological complexity, or any sign that such had existed, in their history or elsewhere. She could taste his frustration.

She was about to say something encouraging when a sound at the entrance of the hut made her whirl about. Tathas rose to his feet with

a warrior's fluid grace and had his knife in hand before she had finished the turn.

It was an alien.

The alien.

Zara had only seen it for a moment the last time, but she was sure
it was the same one which had come to their camp. In this light it
seemed to have more color to its skin, but the shape and proportion
were the same, as well as the wary way its eyes came about, each one
independently, to fix upon them with bifocal intensity.

There was a moment of silence. It seemed as if the entire world had
ceased to move, as the three of them stared at one another.

Then it screamed.

It was a horrible piercing sound that made Tathas' "war cries" seem
like whispers by comparison. It rang through the hut and the village
and the fields and mountains beyond, probably as far as the distant
armies that were searching for them. Certainly as far as the next hut
away, where the chanting suddenly ceased.

Oh, shit, she thought. *This is not good.*

Tathas was the first to move. With almost preternatural speed he
launched himself across the hut toward the alien. For a moment she
thought he was going to kill it, but then she saw that he hadn't pulled
his knife. Instead he had swept up one of the bird carvings, and with
a jingle of talismans he swung it into the side of the alien's head. The
creature went limp almost immediately, his eyes drooping in opposite
directions as he fell.

Tathas threw the bird aside, grabbed her by the arm, and ran.

They could hear others coming now, from whatever communal hut
or hiding place they had been chanting in. There was no telling how
many were in the village, but judging from the ruckus they were making it was not going to be good. Zara stumbled as he pulled her beside
him, trying to match his pace; if not for his grip on her wrist she would
surely have been left behind.

Then they saw them. A dozen of the aliens—no, more—all larger
than the first one they had seen, with giant hoods of flesh about their
shoulders and heads that added to their bulk twice over. Blood-red
markings ran down their sides in streaks and across their faces, a fearsome display. Natural coloring, or the marks of some sacrifice? The
Mediator in Zara struggled to make sense of it even as the frightened
animal she had become gave all its strength to running.

They were larger than Zara, larger even than Tathas. Their limbs were longer. They were sure to be faster than the humans . . . and they were sure to be angry.

I told you this was a bad idea!

Across the cultivated fields they ran, vaulting over spiney fruit-bushes in a desperate attempt to reach the higher brush beyond. If they got that far there might be hope. Zara didn't look back; she didn't need to. Her mind could *feel* the presence of their pursuers, and gage their progress with oddly clinical precision. Two rows behind them were the leaders of the group, with slower members fanning out behind. Now one row behind. She could feel the sharp leaves scraping against alien flesh even as it scored her own legs in bloody stripes. Hands were reaching out to her, alien hands, meaning to rend her limb from limb in their rage that their sacred places had been invaded. She cried out and Tathas understood; he sprinted faster as the trees grew ever nearer, almost pulling her off her feet to force her to keep pace.

And then—

And then—

The world shook. The ground trembled. The heavens spun dizzily above them, and though Zara struggled to stay on her feet—though she knew that her very life depended upon staying on her feet—she fell.

I HAVE FOUND YOU.

Force-waves of numbing power pounded in her head. Not internal this time, but something being applied to her from the outside. With effort she managed to focus her vision enough to look about her . . . and saw a field strewn with fallen aliens. Their hoods were crumpled now, and they lay between the cultivated rows, twitching helplessly in the grips of that numbing power.

She looked over to Tathas. He seemed to be in the same shape she was, disoriented but conscious, and in much more control of himself than the natives. Once she was sure he was all right she looked up, struggling to focus upon whatever might be the source of the terrible assault.

And she saw it.

Her.

She saw *herself.*

The figure was tall, lean and dressed in tight black garments made out of some kind of leather. Her skin was paler than Zara's own, but of the same Chandran hue. Her hair was cut short, in a crown of short spikes, but of the same color. Her features were as familiar to her as the image in a mirror.

—eyes staring at her, like and unlike her own—

Zara felt the world grow dizzy about her as the stranger came toward her. A strong hand closed about her shoulder.

"Sister."

She looked up into that face. So familiar, yet so alien. She tried to speak, but whatever weapon had brought her down had robbed her of the capacity to make coherent sounds . . . or so it seemed.

"Come," the twin said. Her accent was strange, a thing not of cities and empires but of open reaches and illegal spaces, where dialects mingled in their own unique patterns. "The effect will wear off them soon; I need to get you out of here."

And in her brain she heard, as clear as day, and marked with wonder, *I have found you at last.*

She let the strange mirror-image draw her to her feet. She was dimly aware of other humans standing nearby, similarly dressed. ~*It's all right,* one of them said. The words appeared in her brain as clearly and as precisely as spoken language. ~*You're with us now.*

They started to move away, clearly meaning for her to follow . . . but they had not moved toward Tathas. She stopped where she was and tried to reach back to the Braxin, to help him to his feet so he could escape this place as well.

Hatred was a red-hot spike in her brain. A strong hand fell on her arm, preventing the motion. "No."

"He's with me," she managed

"*No.*"

She looked at the mirror-image (*your sister, call her your sister!*) and stared at her without comprehension.

"He's *Braxin.*" The name was spat out, like some noxious venom. "Let him go."

"He saved my life!"

"Then he wanted you for something. Do you think he'd care otherwise?"

She could see Tathas struggling to his feet on his own, defying the lingering power of the field stun. Not far away, the aliens were also struggling to recover.

"I don't care why he did it." She tried to make her voice as strong and as determined as she could, to match the other's unspoken challenge. "And I don't care what he is. I'm not leaving him here."

A brief pause. Silence, but not silence. She could sense thoughts flitting back and forth between the newcomers like angry insects.

At last one said to her, *~You see what we are. He can't come with us.*

She answered in equal silence, not knowing if they would hear her words, *That's his choice to make. Not yours.*

The first of the aliens rose to its feet. The flaps of skin on its back flexed, stretched, and began to take on solid mass once more.

"We have no time for this," her sister growled. She turned to Tathas, a weapon in her hand.

Zara stiffened. "You kill him, *sister,* and you'll have more trouble on your hands than one wounded Braxin, I promise you." The weapon did not waver. "Don't start us out this way, please."

A finger flicked across the controls of the stun. One setting exchanged for another. "Very well," she growled. "We'll argue about this on the ship." Zara could sense the hatred inside her, a veritable firestorm. The tenor of it reminded her of Tathas. "So sorry, *Braxin,* but I won't have you disturbing the myths here."

And she fired. The Braxin's innate strength was evident for the one second in which he resisted the force of the blow; then the stun shut down his muscular responses and he fell to the ground in a heap. Two of the newcomers grabbed him up quickly, carelessly, like one might haul a bag of garbage, and one of them threw him over his shoulder. Zara bit back her instinct to argue with them about it; this was not the place or time. The aliens were on their feet now, though they were no longer moving forward. Gods alone knew how long their fear of the seemingly magical weapon would hold them at bay. They needed to get out of there.

"Come," her sister said, in a tone that said this time there would be no delay. That was fine with Zara. Glancing back one last time to make sure the aliens were still motionless—and they were, as if the weapon had stunned them too—she matched the quick gait of her rescuers, following them into the shadows of the forest, and toward whatever vehicle had brought them here . . . and safety.

Tales are told of the night the star fell, the night the demons came to earth. They are told in the female song-tongue, for it was the females who saw the final battle, when the slaves of the demons rose up against their masters and struck the Pale One down. It was the females who whispered prayers as the slaves withdrew, carrying the demon's body away in triumph. It is they who sing the tales today.

Tales are told of the istal *Klath, who braved the demon's wrath to protect the sacred relics of the tribe, and for that was granted the one thing it desired most. Brave it was then, the* istal *Klath, whose voice gave warning of the coming of demons. Brave he is now, the warrior Klath, who leads bands of males in patrols along the ridges. For when the demons come again—as they surely will—he and his comrades will be ready.*

Thus they have sworn to the gods, who watch over all things.

Thus it shall be.

Deception is not merely a tool to a Kaim'era. It is an art form.

Understand that, and you will have taken your first step toward understanding our government.

—Zatar the Magnificent

EIGHTEEN

IT WAS TIME.

The Pri'tiera of the B'Saloan Holding of Braxi Aldous took a deep breath, drew the persona of *absolute power* about him like a suit of ancient armor, and commanded the portal, "Let him in."

The mental essence of Tezal, son of Luzak and V'nista, preceded its owner into the room. It was an intense presence, that struck the Pri'tiera with almost physical force as the elder Kaim'era entered. One part utter confidence, one part focused intent, and one part the knife-edged wariness of an armed warrior. Impressive, as always. Not all of the Kaim'eri were so impressive. Some were more blunt in their mental emanations, more brutal, lacking the subtlety and self-discipline that could have made them truly dangerous men. In a more competitive age such men would never have been able to gain a Kaim'era's rank, much less defend it against rivals . . . but these days, with the Master Race winnowed down to nearly nothing, sometimes the second best could hold on by their glove tips for a while. At least until they were noticed by more ambitious parties.

Not for the first time, the Pri'tiera wondered what sort of emanations he himself gave off to others. Not for the first time, he suspected that the force of his own presence was as much the result of the family curse as any expression of personal strength. If he hadn't inherited that forbidden power, how would he measure up? The question both frightened and fascinated him. There was a part of him that hungered to be truly tested, so that he might prove himself the equal of men such as Kaim'era Tezal once and for all . . . and an equally strong part that dreaded what such a test might reveal.

He was surprised that some of the more perceptive Kaim'eri hadn't figured out his secret by now. If they had, then they kept silent for reasons of their own, and not as a service to him. The Kaim'eri cared no more for concepts like "greater good" and "political loyalty" than did a Kuratti shark in blood-filled waters. Weakness was the scent of blood in their nostrils, drawing them in for the kill like bestial predators were drawn to injured prey. If one of them had figured out that the power of the Pri'tiera's presence depended upon a condition that was taboo in the Holding he would keep that secret only for so long as he had something to gain from it. The sacrifice of a leader was nothing to these men in their pursuit of personal rivalries, and treachery was an art form much admired. To bring down the bloodline of Zatar the Magnificent with a mere handful of words would win a Kaim'era the admiration of all his peers, and certain advantage in the shark pool of Braxaná politics.

There are no creatures more deadly in all the Holding, his father had once told him. *You must learn their game, or you can never rule over them.*

His father had intended for him to serve as Kaim'era himself, as part of his training. Maybe if he had been able to do that he would feel like less of a stranger among them now. But the elder Pri'tiera's untimely death had robbed him of that option, and thus he was continually forced to fake an understanding he did not have, among men who were born and bred to detect the faintest hint of dissembling. If at any moment he failed, if at any time they sensed the least bit of weakness in him, he would go down so fast the ghosts of his ancestors would barely notice his passing.

"Pri'tiera." The elder Kaim'era's bow was deep and formal; if he felt less respect for the youthful Pri'tiera than he had for his impressive father, he was too skilled to ever let it show. "You wished to see me."

"Kaim'era Tezal." He pitched his voice in the speech mode of Challenge. "I am told by some you are among the most loyal of my servants."

He sensed rather than saw the man stiffen. "Not by Braxaná, surely."

"No. Of course not." No Kaim'era would ever call another "loyal," much less refer to a fellow purebred Braxaná as a "servant" of anyone. Those words were considered insults in such company. "But by those who watch the Braxaná."

The tension he had sensed in Tezal eased a bit. "I see."

"I have need of one who is loyal," he said. "Not to me alone, you understand, but to the Holding."

"We are all loyal to the Holding," Tezal answered quietly. Basic Mode. *Interpret that statement as you wish.*

"Perhaps." Again he chose the speech mode of Challenge: *Prove yourself to me.*

He took out a small object from his pocket. It was slender, and might have been mistaken for a needle had its substance been of simpler stuff. But its surface gleamed like oily silver, reflecting the room's light in ephemeral ripples of color as it moved, and it responded to the heat of his fingers by pulsing slightly, like a living thing.

He held the item out so that the Kaim'era could see what it was. Tezal's face was impassive, but the Pri'tiera could taste the flash of recognition in his brain. Of course. No Kaim'era existed who had not used such a thing at one time or another, though few would admit to it.

"A courier capsule." Tezal's use of the Inquisitive Mode revealed a question behind the words: *Why are you showing this to me?*

"Just so," he answered. His use of the Basic Mode left the question unanswered. *I'll let you worry about that for a while.* He let the item slide down into the black leather cup of his palm, watching as it pulsed slowly, going nowhere. "Biologically neutral, and thus undetectable by any but the most sophisticated security equipment."

"I'm familiar with the type." A wave of guarded tension rippled through the man's mind, too swiftly and too subtly for the Pri'tiera to identify it. Curiosity? Nervousness? Anticipation? The Pri'tiera wished that his power gave him more insight into this man's psyche than it did. But Tezal's thoughts were as controlled as his expression, and equally difficult to read. It was part of what made him so dangerous . . . and so useful.

Win him to your side and your throne will be that much more secure.

He dropped into a language complex that implied Hidden Significance and said, "There was a shuttle accident on Leykat Five. Terrible accident, mangled bodies. Medics were looking to ID the corpses when they found this inside one of them."

"I assume there was a message inside?"

"One word. Or one name, rather. *Tal'kreet.*"

Recognition flared brightly in Tezal's mind for a moment. "That is . . . in the War Border. A trade planet. Yes?"

"Yes. A trade planet. One in which some of the Kaim'eri have invested funds, of late."

Tezal shrugged. It was a studied and deliberate gesture, patently false. "The War Border is always ripe for speculation, my Lord. Fortunes are gained and lost there with each new military campaign. Not a game to my liking . . . but some consider it good sport."

"And you would imagine that such a capsule would be part of that picture, would you not? A means of transporting secrets between . . . shall we say . . . investors?" The use of the language complex that hinted at both challenge and personal focus wove subtle threat into the words, implying that he knew more about this matter than he was revealing . . . and that the end result might not be good for Tezal.

Keep them on the defensive and you will have them off balance, his father had said. *As long as they are wondering about what manner of web you are spinning, they will not be able to catch you in their own.*

But Tezal gave no sign of being shaken. "Use of couriers is no crime," he said evenly. "They've long been popular among those who distrust the security of interstellar transmissions. Insert an encrypted message into a courier, let him make the journey at a human pace . . . delivery's delayed a bit, but no one can pick your words out of the Void and use them against you."

"Yes. You would think that's all this was, wouldn't you?"

Tezal's face was impassive, his mind a closed book. The Pri'tiera cursed his inability to read him better.

He held up his hand, allowing Tezal to observe the biomechanism as it pulsed blindly, purposelessly. Inside a courier it would mimic the living rhythms of human tissue, and become all but transparent to standard security scans. "The skin isn't of Braxin manufacture, you see."

Tezal raised an eyebrow.

"It's Azean. Or so my experts tell me. Bioengineered using techniques outlawed in the Holding . . . but common in the Empire." He glanced down at the capsule, then met Tezal's eyes directly. "You see now the cause of my concern, Kaim'era. A courier was sent from somewhere inside the Empire, carrying the name of a planet currently under military contention to someone within the Holding . . . alas, dead men can't be interrogated, so we can only guess where it was headed . . . but I am sure the intentions were not, how shall I say, *loyal.*"

Tezal's expression was grim. "Indeed. And do you have thoughts on who the intended recipient might have been?"

"I know he's on Braxi, in Kurat proper; the courier was headed there," the Pri'tiera said. "Most likely one of the Braxaná; perhaps even a Kaim'era." He paused. "And I believe I have a man who will find him for me."

Surprise flickered in the back of the Kaim'era's eyes . . . not at his words, but at the Imperative Mode he had chosen, and what it implied.

"Your network is second to none, Tezal. And you are one of very few Kaim'era with no major investments in the War Border. You see . . . I have checked."

"Indeed," he said quietly.

"No real estate, no businesses, no political ties to that region . . . nothing in your portfolio that would be impacted by affairs on Tal'kreet. You are one of only a handful of men for whom that is true, Kaim'era. All others must be considered suspect in this."

Did a smile flicker briefly in Tezal's eyes, or was that only in his mind? "I am surprised your own House does not investigate this," he said in the Inquisitive Mode.

"My House's efforts are focused elsewhere at the moment. I need one who can focus on this problem here and now." He paused. "I'm asking you to serve me in this, Kaim'era Tezal."

"To uncover the name of the one for whom this message was intended?"

"Yes. Only, there may be more than one man involved. That's why I need someone with no . . . shall we say, conflict of interest? No way to know now who will be implicated."

The Kaim'era's mind flared with sudden intensity at those words. Of course. Any Braxaná worth his gloves would recognize what he had just been offered: free rein to take down his rivals in the Pri'tiera's name. All he need do was track down one real traitor for the Pri'tiera, and he could condemn as many men as he liked along with him. He would have to put on a good show, of course—any manufactured evidence would have to be of the highest quality—but that was the kind of game that men like Tezal excelled at. Now the Pri'tiera had offered him the backing of his office, which meant that the Kaim'eri themselves could be his targets. What Braxaná would turn down such an offer?

Serve me, Tezal. I will pay you well for it, in the only coin you truly value. Power.

What was it to the Pri'tiera whether a handful of Kaim'eri lived or died for this? They all hated him, he could sense that every time they came into his presence. What he needed was one or two that would have reason to be loyal to him. In Braxaná terms, that meant convincing them that they would benefit more from being in his favor than from conspiring against him. More from his life than from his death.

Tezal's dark eyes were fixed on him. The man's mental emanations were intense, but far too complex for an untrained psychic like the Pri'tiera to decipher. That was to be expected. Rumor had it that Tezal's House was one of the largest and most influential in the Holding; he must be sure that any new variable could be factored into the whole without upsetting the overall balance. Financial holdings and speculations, bribes and political conspiracies . . . all must be weighed. Along with the pros and cons of committing himself to serve the youthful Pri'tiera, instead of seeking his downfall.

That was the real issue, of course. No Braxaná Lord would ever state such a thing openly . . . but only because no Braxaná Lord would ever have to.

Finally, slowly, Tezal held out his hand. Palm upward, gloved fingers cupped about it.

"I will need the capsule," he said quietly.

The Pri'tiera dropped it into his hand, and watched as his fingers closed over it. A knot that he had not known was in his chest loosened a bit.

"I will need good evidence," he responded.

"Of course, my Lord. Only the best." Tezal bowed slowly, deeply, respectfully. "It is an honor to serve the Holding in this matter."

It seemed to the Pri'tiera that this time the gesture of respect was genuine. It pleased him to imagine that it was. It pleased him to forget for a moment that this man, too, hated him, and would only be loyal to him for as long as the price was right.

But that was good enough for now.

You see, my father? I did learn something from you.

But it was not until Tezal had left his presence that the knot in his chest went away completely.

To fear the unknown, is to give the unknown power over our soul.

We do not surrender to our enemies thus; why should we do so for a mystery?

—Zatar the Magnificent

NINETEEN

Mirror images . . . and not. Twin portraits painted with the same living pigments, in the same proportion, but by differing hands, in differing styles. One sharp-edged, sketched in lightly with a stiff brush, slim and spike-haired and ready for anything. One softer and more delicately blended, bruises brushed on lightly in a crimson wash, longer hair tangled about shoulders bowed with exhaustion, tired of everything.

"Sister," Rho said. Testing the word on her tongue.

"Sister," Zara answered.

Rho put out a hand. Zara touched it, palm to palm. Through the contact Rho could feel discordant emotions coursing, a chaos of psychic output. Is this what happened to psychics when they had no training? She clasped her fingers between Zara's own and then—with but a moment of hesitation—pulled her into an embrace. Flesh to flesh, gene to gene, a circuit closed once more that had been open since Rho's abduction.

"I've been looking for you," the Shaka said, and she held her sister tightly.

The Mediator wept.

They stood like that for a long, long time. At one point Rho had to invoke Distinction Discipline to close down the mental channel between them; Zara's thoughts were that strong, that wild, that intrusive. Clearly she'd never found a means of disciplining her talent. All that would change with time, Rho told herself. A few years of good training and her sister would be able to control her output just like the rest of them did. As for input . . . that was a harder battle. Psychic-Receptives were programmed by their genetic code to absorb every stray thought in the neighborhood. The trick was not shutting them out—you really couldn't—but learning how to ignore the ones that weren't important.

It was a long and hard lesson, that Rho remembered well. Receptives who failed at it generally didn't last long.

"You're home now, sister." She whispered the words rather than sharing them mentally; Hasha alone knew what was in the other's head right now, that might drown out gentler contact. "I can sense what you're going through, but soon that will all be over. We can teach you how to control the power, even how to shut it out of your mind. There are ways."

In her arms Zara trembled. A faint thought came flitting through the bond between them, not launched by conscious effort, but psychic in tenor nonetheless. ~*Thank you. . . .*

With effort Rho forced herself to end the embrace, so that she might stand back and study her sister. *How different we are,* she thought. *And yet . . . not at all. The mental resonance is the same, even I can feel it. How many more similarities lurk beneath the surface, waiting to be explored?*

We have a lifetime now to do that, she thought with wonder.

Zara met her steady gaze and then looked down. "I'm sorry," she said quietly.

"For what?"

"To be such a . . . mess." She laughed softly, a sound without humor. "But this is all so new to me, you have to understand that. Little more than a Standard Month ago I was living a 'normal' life in the Empire, with not even a clue that you existed . . . or that my mind was capable of . . . of what's happened."

"What do you mean?"

"The . . . power, the sensitivity, the . . . whatever you want to call it. The feeling like every thought in my vicinity is screaming in my head. Picking up other people's dreams. All that."

"Is . . . new?"

She nodded.

Rho was stunned. For a minute she could find no voice. "But . . . this is a thing of childhood. The change comes with puberty. The hormonic triggers are . . . are known."

Zara looked at her blankly. Of course she wouldn't know all that, Rho thought. The databanks of the Institute had been destroyed when the psychics left, two hundred years ago. The fact that all of them had fled the Empire after that meant there was no one left for the Empire to experiment with. Add to that a secret campaign in which the psychics had deliberately spread misinformation about themselves—the ridiculous notion that all psychics went insane being the centerpiece of that effort—and how could one expect a mere citizen of the Empire to know about the Awakening? Or any other truth of psychic existence, for that matter?

So she stated it calmly, in words that could not be mistaken. "There must have been some sign of this before."

Zara shook her head. Her thoughts were a tangle of doubt and confusion; Rho wished she had the talent herself to sort them out and soothe them, the way a Hasai would be able to. "Sister." Zara's voice was soft and even, and very, very certain. "I worked for the government. They screen for psychic sensitivity, on a regular basis. Especially in a job like mine, where subtle issues of sensitivity are so important. So I can tell you outright that whatever the 'signs' of it are believed to be, they didn't show in me when I started my job, not that any expert could find."

Rho was speechless.

"What's wrong?" Fear flickered at the edges of Zara's awareness. "Tell me."

Rho took her hand. And just held it for a moment. "It doesn't happen that way," she said at last. "Not in all our recorded history. That it did . . . that you are my twin. . . ." She shook her head as if that would clear her head, but not all the Disciplines could do that at this point. "You share my potential, the same genetic programming, the same exact set of biochemical parameters . . . and yet . . . the power came to me, and not to you. . . ."

"It did in the end," Zara reminded her.

"So you are . . . Awakening *now*?"

Zara nodded miserably.

How could Rho explain to her sister what that fact implied? How could she capture in a mere handful of words the Great Work of the psychic community . . . seeking to isolate those factors, biological and environmental, which would release or inhibit psychic Awakening? It was the project the Institute had been founded to explore, centuries ago, and even now it was the centerpiece of their research efforts. Find those factors, learn to isolate and then reproduce them . . . and any child with the Kevesi sequence in his genes might become a functional psychic. Which meant, by extension, that *any* child could join their ranks . . . because in an era of genetic manipulation, having or lacking a particular genetic sequence was not a measure of fate, but simply of medical expense.

"Sister?"

She and Zara were the key. Together. That random fate which had separated them soon after birth had provided an experimental laboratory equal to none, and had done the seeming impossible . . . proven for once and for all that the genetic sequences which controlled psychic potential were not the whole picture. Something more was required. Rho's history contained that element. Zara's did not. Somewhere in their backgrounds, in the things they had done, the people they had known—maybe even the foods they had eaten—was the key to that great puzzle.

That it should be so close at hand, after all these years, was . . . staggering.

That she should be a part of it was simply more than she could absorb.

"Is everything all right?"

She forced herself to look at Zara again, and pitched her voice to soothe the lines of worry which had appeared on her sister's brow. "Everything's fine. I was just . . . surprised. Your development hasn't followed the normal patterns . . . but that doesn't mean anything is 'wrong'."

"Ah. Good to know." The Mediator sat in a formchair and sighed as it molded itself around her. "It sure feels 'wrong' from my end."

With a faint smile of sympathy Rho walked over to the commissary outlet and called up two drinks, one clear, one a cloudy amber. She swirled the latter around in its cup before offering it to Zara.

"Here. Drink this. It will help."

Zara hesitated. "What is it?"

Do you trust me so little, my sister? "A compound that will quiet your mind for a while. We use it in training, especially with Receptives."

Zara sipped gingerly from the cup, and then, when it did no obvious harm, drank down the contents. Barely a moment passed before Rho could feel the effects of it take hold of her. It wasn't a drug they used often, for its effect on trained psychics was less than pleasant; as one student had put it, "it's the mental equivalent of having your eyes gouged out." But Zara wasn't a trained psychic, and maybe a few hours without all the thoughts of the world crowding into her head might be good for her.

An indefinable tension seemed to bleed from the Mediator's shoulders as the constant barrage of outside thoughts quieted, then went silent. For her own part Rho couldn't imagine an existence without the thoughts of others as a constant background hum. But then, she had been raised to it. Raised to expect it and to control it, so that it didn't distract her from her work or skew her own thoughts. When Zara had proper training she would know how to do the same thing. And then she probably would react with equal horror to the concept of a drug that would dull her senses to the point where she could no longer hear the thoughts of others.

The Mediator sat back with a sigh and closed her eyes. "Silence," she whispered. "Blessed silence. I never thought I would have that again."

"It won't last," Rho warned. "And the body builds up a tolerance to the compound, so it's not something you can use often. But for now, for your peace of mind . . . know that it's available."

The Mediator opened her eyes. How soft she looked, Rho thought. Soft hair, soft eyes, soft everything. Not the kind of person you would send down onto an alien planet to deliberately warp their religion. Not the kind of person who would devote her life to the ultimate war, and preparing for a campaign that might not be concluded for eons.

Yet we are the same person, in raw potential. Anything I have become, she might become.

"At first it was . . . beyond bearing." Zara raised a hand to rub between her eyes, as if that might massage away the intrusive thoughts. "All the images pouring in, the emotions. After a while I got better at ignoring it . . . but it never really went away."

"It never will," Rho said gently.

She smiled weakly. "I was afraid you were going to say that."

"There are people who would kill for your gift."

"Then they can have it. Yank out whatever part of the brain is responsible for this and give it to them, please . . . then I can go back to my normal life."

"This *is* your normal life now, Zara." She said it softly, willing compassion into her voice and mind. "I'm sorry. You'll get used to it in time, I promise." She took a sip from her own drink, watching her sister closely. "That the power took so long to express in you . . . I can't begin to guess why that is. It's something the Hasai will want to study, I'm sure."

"The Hasai?"

"Call them . . . the most talented among us. The ones who can deal with thought in its purest form, without the need for verbalization. They direct most of our research."

"Ah, yes. The Institute was originally a research organization, wasn't it?"

Rho snorted sharply. "Yeah. You could call it that."

Zara raised an eyebrow.

Rho shrugged stiffly. "The early data on their true purpose was lost when Llornu was destroyed. Most of those who survived went insane in the aftermath, or at least developed a healthy aversion to remembering what came before. Rumors speak of shadowy political agendas, an attempt to manipulate the War for secret purposes . . . but who can say where the rumors started? The bulk of the psychic community never heard the details. They lived, they learned, they served as needed—"

"Conditioned to serve."

Rho's face darkened. "Yes. *Conditioned*. Each psychic a tool, primed to contain the instructions of the Institute's elite and carry them out blindly, no matter what the cost. Never mind if it involved the destruction of a planet or a people, or the betrayal of one's own kin. All that mattered was that the nebulous plans of the leadership be advanced one step more." She raised her own cup as if in a toast. "And that, my dear sister, is why the Institute no longer exists. May its founders tour the human hells for all eternity." She sipped from the cup. "Speaking of human hells." Her expression darkened. "Your Braxin."

"He's not *mine*."

"Then have done with him."

Zara shook her head. Her expression was grim.

Rho leaned forward, her gaze intense as she studied her sister with all her senses. "He's an enemy, Zara."

"He saved my life. Does that mean nothing to you?"

"It means he had some personal motive to do so. Nothing more. Or have they ceased to teach Braxin culture in the schools of the Empire, these days?"

"They teach it. To children. And when you grow up, they teach you that individuals should be judged in their own right, according to their actions."

Rho's eyes narrowed, and she tossed down the rest of her drink. "And *that's* why the Empire will never beat the Braxins. It's too busy dissecting its own motivations to act."

"You know that isn't true."

"I know that two hundred years ago the War might have been won. But the hands of our Founder were tied by political necessity, so that she couldn't act. It could have all been ended then. *That's* your precious Empire, Zara. Snatching defeat from the jaws of victory."

Zara's eye shone with a strange light. "Are you sure you hate only the Braxins?" she asked quietly.

"Azea failed us."

"So you hate them too?"

"They failed us." Her voice was fierce, and she knew that if not for the potion Zara had been drinking her sister's brain would be seared by the fire of her rising emotions. "Us, Zara. You and me. Those with the capacity to serve them better than any other, those with the power needed to win the War and establish the Star Empire as the ultimate authority from one end of the galaxy to the other. So what did they do? Left us in the hands of madmen, to be experimented upon like laboratory animals for centuries. What did they do when those madmen died? Collected us into camps where we could be *watched and evaluated,* because Hasha knows anyone with a power like ours is either insane or an enemy.

"You know it's true, Zara. Look at your own history. Tested when you joined the Mediators, you said, just to make sure you had no psychic potential. What if they'd discovered the truth? You think they would have let you go free, with maybe a polite request that you choose some other job?

"No, sister. *They fear us.* And out of fear comes hate."

"Yes." Zara met her eyes without flinching. "Out of fear comes hate." An odd strength was in her gaze, that pierced through the layers of softness. "I agree, sister."

There was a long silence.

"Damn your stubbornness," Rho growled at last. "He's got no place in our world, can't you understand that? He'll probably go insane the moment we dock at the homeworld."

"That's his choice then," she said quietly. "I owe him that much, don't you think?"

"*I* owe him nothing."

"Then do it for me. Or aren't you glad to have me alive?"

For a moment Rho said nothing. Then, slowly, a shadow of a smile crept across her face. "I am," she said. "Though if you're half as stubborn as I am, I may come to regret it."

Zara smiled faintly as well. "I think that comes with the territory . . . sister."

Rho snorted. "So I won't kill him. Or order anyone else to do it. No other promises."

"That's all I ask."

"What he does to himself . . . once he knows who we are, and where we are taking him . . ." A faint smile crept across her face, an expression utterly without warmth or humor. "That's his affair, agreed? His own *choice*."

"Agreed." The Mediator's voice was steady but her eyes glimmered with uncertainty. Her eyes searched deep into Rho's own for some hint of what secret intentions might be masked by those harmless words. Good for them both she had taken that potion, Rho reflected, or she might actually sense them. And it was better for both of them—and for their nascent relationship—that not be the case.

The walls were thin. Tathas could probably break through one of them if he wanted to. Clearly whatever manner of ship he was on, it hadn't been outfitted for holding prisoners. They'd had to improvise.

Like Raija had done with Zara.

At least they hadn't put him in a storage closet.

He paced the small cabin one more time, measuring its parameters in his brain. Noting the forcebed control panel (now without power), the commissary outlet (now without power), the pale circular place on the floor where a formchair might have sat once. Now gone. They had emptied the room before he was put inside and shut down every device that might give him access to . . . what? Food that he would throw at the door? Some piddling knife, that would make or break his fighting skill? He could kill most humans with his bare hands if he had to. So forcing him to sit and/or sleep on the floor accomplished . . . what?

That's good. Focus on anger, on indignation. Look at how they're treating you! Don't think about what's out there, beyond that wall you could so easily break down.

Psychics.

A *ship* full of them.

In that dim, insubstantial moment on the planet, between when the field stun had begun wearing off and the neural stun had taken him down, he had seen them communicating without words, those foreign troops. Seen them looking at one another, seen the comprehension in their eyes as information was exchanged, soundlessly. Seen them . . . and feared.

It was a new kind of fear, that had nothing to do with swords slicing into flesh or power being wrested from his control. It was well beyond the fear even of being forced to bow before the hated Braxaná.

Psychics. They were the demons of Braxin mythology, so monstrous in the minds of his people that for as long as Braxins had existed they had killed them without question. It was one of the few traditions which all the tribes had agreed upon, long before the planet was unified, and the utter intolerance of the ruling Braxaná for any manifestation of the power, no matter how slight, had only increased their fervor. Braxi's own gene pool had been scrubbed clean of the taint long ago, and any foreign gene pool that showed promise of providing infection was cleansed with equal enthusiasm.

Except for the Azean Empire, where the Braxins could not reach.

Except for the Azean Empire, where a planet full of fools had encouraged the maverick gift, had bred humans like animals for it, had sought the genetic key that would enable them to spread the taint to all those of Scattered Races ancestry.

Thank the absent gods they had failed in that last quest. Their own greatest creation, the mad Starcommander Anzha lyu Mitethe, had turned on them in the end, destroying their laboratories and their leadership in one glorious blast of pyrotechnic cleansing. Then she had fled the Empire for the Outlands, or perhaps somewhere beyond, with a ragtag following of half-mad psychics, mentally crippled from the horror of absorbing the death of so many others.

They were out there. Everyone knew it. Braxin parents used tales of them to frighten their children into obedience. Braxin Fleet Commanders used hints of them to keep their recruits in line.

And now . . . here was a ship full of the half-mad creatures.

And he was their prisoner.

He paced quickly across the room, three steps across the room and three back. The movement was a rhythm that helped control his fear.

It's not like you weren't looking for them in the first place, you know.

Four paces to where the chair had once been. And back.

I didn't expect to meet them like this.

Across the room again.

What did you expect then? he demanded of himself. *That you would control your first meeting?*

He grit his teeth as he thought, *I should have had time to approach them carefully. On my terms. It would have been on my terms.*

The door slid open. It was the woman who looked like Zara, the one who had called her sister. The utter self-confidence of her manner reminded him of K'teva, and for one brief moment he ached for the loss of his half-breed consort. But this woman bore such hatred for him that he didn't need to be psychic to sense it; you could cut the sensation with a knife. She looked capable, in the way that the best Kesserit warriors were capable; not only fit but alert, and utterly without fear.

Amazingly, she and Zara were twins. He could see it clearly now that his vision wasn't made hazy by assault weapons. Multiple births were rare among Braxins, split-egg multiples even more so. A queasy sensation that was both primitive and undefinable stirred in his brain. Fear?

And then he realized she had put it there. He grit his teeth and struggled to ignore the alien sensation, hating her for having a power he could neither understand nor overcome.

She grinned. The expression was coldly triumphant and contained nothing of amusement. "So, Braxin. Here we are."

He watched her warily, like a feral beast might regard a human handler. "So it seems."

"You're a long way from home."

Prodding, prodding, he could feel her thoughts prodding like cold fingers around the edges of his brain, seeking answers to unspoken questions. How did you stop such a creature? How did you keep such a woman from invading the very privacy of your soul and laying it bare?

He managed to shrug. "I like to travel."

The cold gaze hardened. "You chose strange travelling companions, for a Braxin."

"She was going my way."

"Tell me then, where did you intend to travel with her?"

"Hadn't decided yet."

With a soft hiss she moved closer to him. She wasn't armed, he noticed. That was a bad sign. It meant she felt she didn't need weapons to overpower him.

"Don't lie to me, Braxin."

"Don't give me orders," he responded.

Rage flashed in her eyes but she made no move against him. Yet.

He could feel his heart pounding in his chest as his body prepared itself to do contest with the unknown. What weapon did she have in her person, that made her so confident? Or did she just think that being psychic would be enough, that his fear would unman him? If so that was to his advantage, at least for the moment.

Fear can be a source of strength to the warrior, Viton had once written.

It is a conduit of raw emotion that allows him access to his most primitive re-flexes, which lie buried beneath the confines of human reason.

And then he felt it. A thing that had no words, slithering like a cold snake inside his brain. The utter foulness of it was so repulsive it made vomit rise in the back of his throat.

"No!" He spat the word out, hoping that she absorbed his hatred and defiance and choked on it.

"Your people are weak." Her eyes were shining strangely, glinting in the room's dim light as her inner focus went elsewhere. "Bred to be weak, raised to be weak, in mind if not in body. Barbarians all of them, counting on brute force to rule the weaker races, abusing their own women to convince themselves of their worth. But strength of body means nothing here, Braxin."

"Get out of my brain!"

"Or what? Or you'll force me out? Or your racially superior self will somehow overwhelm me?" She spat on the floor by his feet. "You have no armies here, Braxin, no slaves, no starships . . . nothing but yourself. How is your strength measured now, when there's no one listening to take your orders?

He felt his pride gather into a hard knot in his chest. Another handful of the wrong words and it might explode. Which is just what she intended, of course. The Braxin propensity toward rage was no secret; all he had to do was lose control and attack her and the whole god-blessed ship full of psychics would come down on his head.

That she wanted that to happen was painfully clear.

Of course he might be able to kill her before they got to him, which made it a tempting thought. But not a timely one.

"I am Kesserit." He muttered the words through gritted teeth. "Not Braxaná. My people have not relied upon armies or starships or *slaves*—" he spat the word "—since before the Coronation."

"Ah yes . . . Kesserit." She grinned. "I recall how much of a mark your tribe has left on Braxin history."

He could feel the rage swell up inside him. But the minute he gave in to it he was ceding control of the meeting to her. To a woman. That thought held the fury in check for a moment . . . but he knew it would not last much longer.

And then she was in his mind again. He could feel her presence there, an alien and unclean thing. The sensation of someone else inside his own flesh made bile well up from his gut in pure revulsion. He tried to force her out, but he had no more control of such maneuvers than a newborn had control of its flailing limbs.

"Now, *Braxin.*" Her voice was pitched low and strangely without its normal cadence; the focus of her mind was clearly elsewhere. "It's said that your kind fears being controlled by a woman more than anything else. Very well. Zara seems to feel you aren't typical of your race. Let's see if she's right."

And the alien consciousness that was inside him became a fireball of pain, that shot down his limbs through the network of his veins, searing every inch of his flesh. He had borne many wounds in his life but never one that invaded every cell of his body at once like this, and never one applied from inside his own person. It took all his strength—and stubbornness—not to cry out in his rage and agony at the invasion. But he would not give her that pleasure.

~*Now you know what it is to be violated,* the thought came.

His fingers flexed as if of their own accord; he knew it was *her* power doing it, but despite his rage he was helpless to stop her. Raw strength wasn't enough; he lacked any understanding of how her power worked, so he could not counter her assault. Tendrils of foreign thought slid into his brain, stroking memories to life with a cold touch as they passed by. Images from his life flashed before his eyes. Sulos. K'teva. His father. *"The bi'ti of the male must not submit to the female,"* the elder Kesserit told him, *"else its very nature is compromised."* He screamed out his rage but his voice was no longer his own to command. He was trapped inside it like an animal in a cage, prisoner in his own body as its keeper poked and prodded the most sensitive parts of his psyche, searching for the core of his weakness.

And then, deep within him, his reason struggled to the surface.

You can't fight her on her own terms. You will lose.

Cold tendrils of hostility wrapped themselves around a handful of cells in his brain and squeezed; ice shot through his groin as his flesh responded, the nerves in his nether parts twisting and knotting in agony. For a moment his consciousness wavered; he fought not to lose control. If he lost consciousness, even for a moment, she'd see to it he never woke up again.

Fight her on your terms!

Twins. They were twins. True split-egg siblings, stamped out of the same genetic mold. Early Braxins had killed such as soon as they were born. The bi'ti, the warrior spirit, was an unwholesome thing when divided. Each half would feed upon the other. Weaknesses were shared, compounded. Kill them when they're born. Don't weaken the tribe.

Weaknesses shared.

He tried to think clearly. The most he could manage was scattered thoughts, held together by a fraying thread of agonized consciousness.

Weaknesses shared. Did Zara have a weakness? They had talked enough on the planet that she might have dropped hints of one, if so. Desperately he tried to summon up those memories for review, but the effort was beyond him in his current state. Fragments swam hazily in his vision as his enemy took hold of the fabric of his soul and twisted—

And then he remembered.

And he knew.

From somewhere deep inside his soul a last spark of strength came howling to the surface. Rage was its fuel, hatred its focus. The emotions didn't manifest in his body but he let them fill his soul to the breaking point, until it seemed he was nothing but a fulcrum for them, a screaming maelstrom of emotion rooted in pure desperation.

He shut his eyes—

Tried to shut out the pain—

And envisioned the woman before him without her power. The same room, the same prelude, but now the battle was different. Now he had the upper hand.

In his mind's eye he slammed her back against the wall. She struggled as he pinned her against the flimsy structure, but though she was strong in her own right she was no match for Kesserit battle-strength. He smelled her own fear as she tried to break away from him, but the weight of his body pinned her against the wall. And now there was something other than pain in his groin. Hot fury, throbbing in his veins along with his blood. He grabbed the upper edge of her black leather pants and pulled back on them violently, holding her against the wall with his other arm across her throat; the seams gave way with a tearing sound, the scent of fresh blood rising to his nostrils from where his nails had raked her flesh. She struck at him, and she was good, and maybe in another time and place she would have been able to win her freedom . . . but he was a Kesserit warrior who had taken down men twice his size, with better training, and her best blows gained her nothing.

In the distance—in another world—her grip on him faltered. In this one she never had a chance. Of course. She was a receptacle for other people's thoughts, and the more focused they were the stronger they'd hit her. That was her genetic inheritance, and whatever tricks she might have learned for taking control of Tathas' body clearly had not made up for that weakness.

Zara's weakness. He knew it well. And in the world of his imagination, where Rho had no power over him, he focused the full force of his spirit upon her. All those black and terrible emotions that had possessed him since the Wilding began; he let them fill his body until the foreign pain was driven out and then he forced himself into her and pounded the message home. *Who is in control now?* Each thrust a new expression of his hatred, not only of her, but of the circumstances that had brought him to this place. This foul place where women ruled, and must be put in their place in that way which nature had provided for, the ultimate act of domination—

Hands. Pulling him off her. Away from her? He blinked, dazed, as the images he had conjured faded.

She stood before him. Dressed, still, if clearly shaken. There were crewpeople beside her and some beside him—two of them had hold of his arms—and they all looked very confused.

"Forgive me, Shaka-Rho." It was one of the men holding on to Tathas. "We thought—we thought—"

Tathas laughed. Long laughter, hearty laughter; by the absent gods, it felt good pouring through him! Poor foolish psychics, he thought, that for all their power couldn't tell false emotions from true. The violence of his images had reached them and they had thought he was really raping their precious leader. And they'd come running to save her. A whole blessed ship full of psychics, dropping everything they were doing because *he* had voiced a threat in a language they understood.

"I'm all right," Rho said. It was clear the contest had shaken her . . . but equally clear she was not going to give him the satisfaction of admitting it. "He's done nothing to merit your concern."

The two men flanking Tathas released his arms. The Braxin spared no glance for the others, even as one of them asked, "So what do you want us to do with him?" Tathas' attention was on her and her alone as he tried to analyze the strange glint in her eyes, that might be hatred or respect . . . or both.

"Leave him be," she said quietly. "He wants to tempt fate and come with us, submit himself to all the power of the homeworld and see if he can survive it . . . test himself against a nation of psychics . . . let him."

A faint smile flickered about her cold, cold lips, and was as quickly gone. "He's earned his ticket."

An alliance exists when the goals of two individuals coincide and they choose to pool their efforts for mutual benefit. But humans are complex creatures, each serving a thousand secret agendas, and that which has priority one day may not the next. Woe betide the man who does not acknowledge this fact, nor recognize the moment when a road shared becomes a road divided.

—Zatar the Magnificent

TWENTY

Hᴀɴᴀᴀɴ FIRST KNEW for a fact that something was wrong after the Zukriti job.

Not that anything had been wrong with his plans. Flawless as always, they had focused upon manipulating the emotional weakness of a Tucharan administrator, to destabilize a treaty he was in charge of. The preparatory work had been perfect. One hint, whispered in his ear, that his third wife had cheated on him . . . one clue, left in the proper place, that another wife had let slip a precious secret to a rival . . . one suggestion that his rivals were discreetly deriding his twelfth marriage, and wondering if his sixteenth under-heir was really his own child . . . it stood to reason with such a man that his self-control might snap, and that any plan put in motion by one of his wives might become suspect. How unfortunate for peace that his primary wife had served as key counselor in his troubles with the Holding. How unfortunate that her advice had been a key factor in establishing the temporary truce under which his planet was now prospering. . . .

No, that had all gone off perfectly. Hanaan's operatives had observed the man's increasing agitation as his nascent paranoia was unleashed (that facet of his persona having been the jewel of Hanaan's reconnaissance), and it took little work to direct the emotion where he wanted it to go. A truce with the Braxins was never a sure thing anyway, since they regularly broke treaties, and once his paranoia was triggered the administrator was likely to make ready for war, "just in case." Which of course the Braxins would notice. Which of course would inspire them to move first, preemptively. . . .

At least that had been the plan. Hanaan didn't know why the Organization wanted this particular treaty broken, but that didn't matter. Maybe they had secretly moved some monstrous vehicle of war into position and were ready to take out the Braxins, provided the enemy attacked first. Perhaps it was something more subtle, in keeping with the twisted politics that ruled Zukriti's segment of the War Border. It made little difference to Hanaan. His orders came—in this case simply, *Braxin must break the truce with Zukriti*—and they were fulfilled. That simple

Except this time it hadn't been.

Hanaan looked over the last report yet again. Usually in a project as neatly managed as this one mistakes would jump off the page at him, but not this time. Oh, all his reconnaissance had been perfect, he'd confirmed that. His psyche files on the administrator were second to none. And the initial reaction vectors had unerringly pointed to success. He'd all but filed this one away in advance, so sure was he of the results.

But there was no war.

The Tucharan administrator had fumed, as predicted. His wives had reacted to his mood exactly as anticipated, helping to push him further over the edge. Every piece was in place, every psychological adjustment perfect . . . but the whole of it failed to result in what was required.

Hanaan had failed.

It had been years since he had failed in anything.

He couldn't accept it.

Was it possible that there was some reason Braxi hadn't responded as anticipated? He checked the data again and shook his head in frustration. No. Braxin habits were too well known, and this played right into them. Hanaan checked for the hundredth time to make sure the local Braxin commander had been aware of Zukriti's covert preparations (damn well should, since Hanaan's own operatives had leaked the information) and when that came up positive again he sat back in his formchair and let it whir in frustration as its best efforts failed to massage any tension out of his body.

It had all been planned perfectly. Executed perfectly. It should have gone off perfectly, in the end.

But it didn't.

Failure didn't bode well for him, at the position he was now in. Every cell he was in charge of consisted of half a dozen operatives who would happily tear him to bits to get his job. Just like he had done on the way up. If they caught wind of this they'd have a field day.

What would his superiors think, when word of this failure reached them? Would they wonder if they had done the right thing in his last promotion? Would they consider giving another man his desk?

Questions would be asked. He'd better have the answers.

With a growl of frustration he set the database to search for similar cases. Anything dealing with the Braxins, where they had not responded as anticipated. It was a long shot, but maybe somewhere in that data he'd find some clue as to what had gone wrong.

He left the office, triple-sealing it behind him, and went to get a fresh cup of chas. Thank Hasha no one had access to his computer by any other means. It was a rare luxury in this modern world to lock a portal and have it actually mean something.

He returned a few minutes later, expecting to find at best a case or two which had been rooted out for his perusal. Certainly no more than that.

But there were more. Many more.

He sealed the portal from the inside, stood before the database display, and gazed at it in amazement. A full docket of cases had been listed for him, subcategorized under several headings. Had there been that many project failures? He'd seen the annual efficiency report and didn't remember that many being noted.

He sat down and began to read. The files were long, of course; one could not manipulate the affairs of empires without recording every minute detail. But Hanaan had always functioned best on an intuitive level and so he skimmed the reports without attempting to analyze them, just pouring the raw data into his brain in the certainty that somehow his mind would find a pattern in it all.

And it did. Though it took many hours, and several stiff drinks before he could bring himself to believe it . . . it did.

All the major failures the Organization had suffered had been linked to Braxi somehow. It was the "somehow" which was the most unnerving. For only a few of the cases were *obviously* linked to Braxi. Some dealt with politics in regions where Braxi would not move in until a year later. Some dealt with economic issues that would only indirectly impact Braxin interests. Some had connections so tenuous, so utterly ephemeral, that not until time had passed and the full course of history was known would anyone have realized that Braxi would benefit.

But enough time had passed now, and the pattern was clear to him. In cases where Braxi was involved, the Organization was failing at ten times the rate of any other project category. Hanaan was sure he had never seen mention of that in any report. Was such a thing only discussed at higher levels, or was it possible no one had yet noticed the pattern?

As he gazed at the reports, letting his vision unfocus as his intuitive senses took over, he realized suddenly there was more to it. The annual statistical summary he'd seen recently should have listed all these project failures . . . but it hadn't, he was sure of that. With a chill heart he brought up the summary again. He couldn't access all underlying data for it—internal security didn't allow that—but even within his own sector of authority he could see that the statistics had been altered. No one analyzing the annual report would catch hint of the bizarre pattern of failure he had just identified . . . the information had been neatly, efficiently removed.

He leaned back in his formchair and took in a deep breath.

No one of a lesser rank would be able to get whole cases exempted from that database. Even at his own rank such a thing would be difficult.

Which meant . . . this was *big*.

He shut down the display and for a moment just stared into the distance, struggling to absorb all the implications of his discovery. Was it possible a fellow officer had sabotaged the Organization's efforts from within? It wouldn't take much. In the case of Zukriti, a simple word of warning to the local Braxin forces would have been enough. So it would have been in all the cases where Braxins were directly involved. The others . . . they would have required a different kind of channel, but little more effort.

We have a leak.

The thought was chilling.

Whoever was responsible had a Security rating at least as high as Hanaan's own. To go any further in this investigation he would need an ally in high places.

Clearly, he had to tell someone about this.

But who?

He knew the name of his own direct superior and how to contact him, but that was it. The others of that rank were nameless, faceless presences to him. The rank beyond that was something he inferred from reports but had never dealt with directly, a level at which every officer's security clearance was said to be approved by the Emperor himself. Only in such company would he be safe revealing what he had discovered. But how did one determine which channels were safe to use and which were not, in reaching out to such an authority?

He could submit a report on the matter in the prescribed manner . . . but that would only work if his direct superior wasn't involved in the sabotage. And even if the man wasn't involved in this himself . . . if he passed on the information just as Hanaan had given it to him . . . then it would be *his* name on the report, and *his* reputation garnering credit for uncovering what well might be not only a threat to the Organization, but to the Empire it served.

This kind of discovery could get a man promoted. Maybe even into those shadowy ranks where the Emperor's whim determined the fate of nations.

Or it could get a man killed.

Alone in his office, Hanaan asked himself, *What matters more to you? Getting this information out and saving the Organization, or reaping the rewards that will come to the one responsible?*

It wasn't really a question that really needed asking, was it?

He dreamed:

The figure is misty, a form comprised of shadows and secrets, as befits one at the highest levels of Azea's covert authority. It is a man's form, dressed neatly but in nondescript garb, as befits one who needs no medals to indicate his rank. Through the mists one can see that his skin is the deep and perfect golden color the Azeans have claimed as their own, and his long white hair is caught back in a neat queue at the base of his neck. Authority glows about him in a dull aura, combined with all the natural qualities of his race: a moderate temperament, unquestioned intelligence, and a loyalty to the people that made him what he is.

He sits at his desk and calls up the day's workload. Skimming through some documents, reading carefully through others, he comes at last to one that seems to shimmer in the air before him as the computer manifests it. He reads. He reads more. The white brow furrows in concern as he orders the computer to magnify a particular portion. Then he calls up another copy of the report, from another department.

The two do not match.

He sits back in his formchair, contemplating the disparity and its meaning. That there is an error in the report sent to him is unusual enough; the Organization is fanatical in its perfectionism at all levels. That it is a large error, easily noticed, seems meaningful. That it is not present at all in the second copy is . . . intriguing.

He checks the routing of each copy. The first had been sent directly to him, an unusual move. The second had gone through the normal chain of command.

It is a message meant for him, he muses. Which he was meant to discover. The routing is part of it.

A secret, even in this place of secrets.

Who sent this thing? Some headstrong young upstart who meant to test his limits? Or a trusted operative who might have reason, if only in his own mind, for circumventing protocol?

He looks at the document's origins and notes the name of zi Ekroz. Yes. A capable officer. Not one to stir the waters lightly.

The message of the routing is clear. Ranks between us are not to be trusted. *Such a man would know the magnitude of such an implication. He would not make that statement without good cause.*

He leaned over the desk and dictated orders to those who waited, beyond the shadows, to serve him.

"Bring zi Ekroz to me."

Hanaan would have said he could work through anything. That was before he had sent out the doubled report with its imbedded secrets to the pinnacle of authority, in defiance of all protocol. Now it was hard to think about anything else.

The dream which had inspired him had been so neat, so simple. Life was rarely that perfect. Would the unnamed officer who received his report pay enough attention to note the error he had chosen? Would he put in the analysis required to decipher its meaning? Would he respect the request that was being made, or simply note a black mark against Hanaan's record for 1) writing sloppy reports, and 2) bothering him with them?

It was hard to work on anything with such thoughts running through his head. Even the latest report on the fleeing twin gained little more than half his attention. She was lost now, but his intelligence suggested that was because she had found what she was searching for. Good. When Hanaan could concentrate fully again he would be able to define a target sector for search, and would extend his influence into the space surrounding it. If she had found the hidden psychic community, the Organization would soon know where to look for it. If not . . . then he would wait until she surfaced again, as any traveler must, and pick up the trail anew.

Patience. That was the key to any successful mission. Patience and attention to detail.

Pacing helped also, sometimes.

He was rounding the corner of his desk with a nervous stride when the portal chimed. He waited the second it took for his security apparatus to verify the identity of the visitor and then commanded it, "Open."

It was a man he did not know. In uniform.

"Hanaan zi Ekroz?"

He stood with his hands behind his back, hoping that as he squeezed all the blood from his fists it was enough to leave the rest of him looking calm. "Yes?"

"Communication with you is required, regarding errors of data that have come from your office." The man nodded toward his desk. "You will please bring with you all records regarding such."

He bit his tongue, wanting to ask questions, knowing they would not be answered. If his direct superior had found out about Hanaan's breaching protocol he was not going to give fair warning of his intentions. Even if the message had gone where intended, there was no telling from this man's demeanor if Hanaan was to be granted the audience he sought, or taken to task for fouling up a report.

He had prepared a data chip for just such a moment. He had also prepared duplicates, and in the event of his disappearance they would be delivered to higher offices. He had not worked in the Organization as long as he had to be careless now, not when the security of the Empire might be at stake.

They took the tube a long way, to a section of the station Hanaan was not familiar with. From there they passed through numerous checkpoints, some automated, some manned. There were no signs or landmarks anywhere to indicate how far he had come, or where he was. Hanaan prided himself on his sense of direction, and his ability to retrace his steps anywhere, anytime; the realization that he could not do so in this case was unnerving.

As it was meant to be.

At last they came to the portal of what appeared to be a conference room. The guard—for surely the man was that—offered up his own DNA for identification, and the portal shimmered and faded. Then he stepped aside. "Please enter."

Hanaan did so.

The room was dark, shadowy, not unlike his dream. There was a conference table at one end and a formal desk at the other. Behind the second was a figure whose hair gleamed whitely in the dim lighting. It nodded—*she* nodded—as he approached, and the portal sealed itself silently.

"Hanaan zi Ekroz," she said. Her voice was even and clear, with the natural authority of one who can rule worlds with a whisper. "You have taken great liberties with protocol to get here. And great risk to your own reputation."

He bowed his head in formal acknowledgment of her words and her station. "I am aware of that, Officer . . ." He let the sentence trail off suggestively, waiting for her to provide a name or title by which he might address her. But she did not.

"Your news is worth it."

"I think so."

"We shall see."

She came around the desk and held out her hand. He put the chip into it. She was tall, even for an Azean, and moved with a strange and silent grace. What little lighting there was had been angled so that he could not see her face. Of course. He noted white hair plaited into a crown of twisted braids, an expensive designer jumpsuit, and a crescent moon necklace that glittered at the hollow of her throat when her movements caught the light. All else was shrouded in shadow.

"Tell me all," she commanded.

So he did. Not hesitantly. Hasha knew he'd rehearsed this speech often enough that he could give it in his sleep, and after a hundred repetitions his faith in his work was unshakable.

His discovery. His investigation. His conclusions.

Afterward there was silence. She fed the chip to her own computer and reviewed his data. It took a long time, but she offered him no seat to wait in, nor even a nod of encouragement.

He waited.

At last she looked up at him. The light flickered briefly across her eyes as she moved, but not long enough for him to see their color.

"You are saying . . ." she said it slowly, as if tasting each word, "we have a traitor in our midst."

His heart pounding, he nodded.

"You understand the implications of this."

Again he nodded.

"All those at the level you speak of are Azean. Bred for loyalty. As you and I were."

"Yes."

"To say that an Azean would betray his people is to say that those programs failed. It is to make a lie of thousands of years of genetic science, and everything that we understand about the human brain."

"Yes," he said quietly. "I know that."

She gazed at the file again. Her face was like a statue, etched in planes of darkness.

"How many have seen this?" she asked finally.

"You mean the raw data? Or my own work?"

"Your work."

"No one, until now. I didn't know who to trust." He edged sideways a bit as if to point out some key point in the display, but his angle was insufficient to read it. "The raw data's there for anyone to find, of course, but it took an analytic leap to connect all the cases into a coherent pattern. In their natural format they are just . . . failures."

"But together—?"

He drew in a deep breath. "Every one of them benefited Braxi in the Great War. Every failure this Organization has had, which it has *accepted* as failure, has had that effect. Sometimes not for years to come. But every single one, eventually." He could not help his voice trembling slightly as he spoke, if only from excitement. The scope of the treachery was enormous . . . as was the scope of the effort required to uncover it.

"You are suggesting," she said quietly, "that one of our race—an Azean—would sell out his own people to the enemy."

"I regret that. But yes. I am."

She stood, behind the desk, and stroked her chin with one hand. Long nails glittered in the dim lighting. "And that he has planned well."

"Oh yes. Oh yes. The planning . . . meticulous. No one looking for something like this would ever find it."

"And you would do what is necessary to help . . . clean this up."

"If I'm needed." He spoke with what he hoped was suitable humility.

Her other hand dropped to her belt. "I'm glad to hear that. Azea needs its loyal servants."

She raised her hand and faced him. He found that he was staring into the working end of a weapon. It took a moment for it to register. His mouth opened and closed a few times, but no words came out.

"Azeans," she said quietly, "do not betray their Empire."

"But . . . but . . . the files. . . ."

"No one will find them again. Thanks to your hard work. You've saved us much trouble by providing this analysis, zi Ekroz. A window of data that we now know how to close." She smiled faintly; it was a cold and predatory expression. "Of course you will help us with the rest of it, won't you? We'll need to know who you shared this with, where there are other copies that must be excised . . . but I'm sure your brain will part with those facts for us, once we shut down the cognitive centers. We're rather good at interrogation, yes?"

He struggled for words. The longer ones escaped him. At last he forced out the only one he could mouth. "Why?"

She shook her head ever so slightly. The crescent pendant at her throat glittered. "Only in entertainment vids does one get an explanation before one dies, zi Ekroz. I'm sorry, but this being real life . . . I haven't the time."

The stun was quick and efficient. The body only twitched once while falling.

"I do thank you for your help though," she noted.

My home will not be a nation, for nations have failed me.

My home will not be a planet, for planets are too fragile to endure.

My home will not be any place that men can find, for what men find they can too easily destroy.

Rather my home will be among those who share not only my strength but my weakness, not only my dreams but my nightmares, not only my purpose but my pain.

They are my family in spirit, if not in blood, and where they gather, I shall call that home.

—Anzha lyu Mitethe

TWENTY-ONE

"**S**ISTER?"

Zara opened her eyes. It took her a moment to remember where she was, or even who she was. These days it was often like that. Between the shock of all that had happened to her recently and the fact that she sometimes picked up dreams from the ship's other occupants, it occasionally took effort upon awakening to focus on just what reality consisted of, and to sort out which memories were her own.

This day it was even harder than usual. A psychic pressure she had felt building in her brain for the last few Standard Days seemed to have taken root right behind her eyes. She rubbed her forehead, wincing, as if that could banish it. It didn't.

"Come with me. I want you to see something."

She cocked an eyebrow at Rho's tone but rose obediently from the bedfield. Her sister waited while she pulled on a simple jumpsuit, ran a sonic scrub over her teeth, and did a cursory brushing of her hair. The preparations were done quickly but they gave her time to absorb all the emanations that were coming from her sister, and she tried to apply her fledgling skill to interpreting them. Above all else she sensed impatience . . . which only made her want to take longer getting ready. It always took her a while to get her psychic bearings when she awoke, and she certainly didn't want to be confronting the unknown until that had been accomplished.

Finally she was ready to go. The strange psychic pressure in her skull was even stronger than it had been when she first woke up; as she exited she reached for the packet of white powder which lay beside the bed. But Rho put out a hand to stop her.

"Not now. Trust me."

Gods knew she'd been practicing what Rho taught her every waking hour, desperate to be free of dependence upon the drug that would shut it all down. She'd proven moderately adept at shutting out the normal mental chatter from the ship's small crew, and even dodging the occasional bolt of anxiety that was focused in her direction. But this pressure which had been present for the last few days, this alien presence that throbbed behind her eyes, defied all her efforts to banish it. Only the drug shut it out completely, and Rho had made it clear what the dangers were of relying upon that too heavily.

She let Rho have her way, and left the bedchamber without its comfort.

She could tell as soon as she entered the corridor that *something* was happening. Never mind that the crew was moving about with unusual speed and focus. With her newfound sensitivity she could taste the sense of anticipation in the air, though she couldn't identify its cause.

What's going on? she wondered.

At last they came to the observation deck, and Rho ushered her in. Zara gasped.

Spread out before them on the room-sized viewscreen was a station.

No . . . a ship.

No . . . something else that was neither one of those . . . and both.

It was graceful, as the web silk of spiders is graceful, sweeping lines intersecting support spokes in a breathtaking spiral rhythm. It was dynamic, as the wind is dynamic, parts shifting their position with each moment, forming new alignments, new shapes, relationships. It was alive, as a hive of insects is alive, having become something more than a simple home to the creatures who bustled inside it.

She could taste its life pressing upon her newly awakened senses as she gazed upon it: thousands upon thousands of minds melded into a single consciousness. Here and there an individual spark sputtered brightly, as one mind rose above the others in volume and could be picked out. But that was the exception. Was this what she had been sensing, while they approached? Hesitantly, fearfully, she opened herself up to receive it. The sheer force of it made her stagger back a step. Thousands upon thousands of minds, each broadcasting its own mixture of loves and hates, hopes and fears, hesitations and aspirations . . . emotions swirling together in a vast psychic whirlpool of human consciousness. It was white noise of the soul, screaming out its psychic signature into space . . . and yes, this was clearly what she had been sensing, as the ship brought them closer to it.

"On a natural world it's called the planet-mind," Rho told her. "I'm not quite certain what it is out here."

"They're not . . . they're not . . ."

"Sharing consciousness? No. It's just background noise, I'm afraid. They're as human as you or I in the end . . . and most aren't even aware of the overall effect, until they leave here and suddenly it's gone. You learn to tune it out, the same way you tune out the sound of the engines on a transport."

Zara gazed in wonder at the strange station. Stars shone clearly between its spokes; the ship must have come into normal space again while she was asleep. "What is this place?" she whispered.

Rho's eyes glittered in reflected starlight. "Where else would so many psychics be?"

"But. . . . You said we were going to your homeworld. This is a ship."

"It's many ships. Each part can break off and move independently, if need be. In the early days it was necessary fairly often. Now . . . few can threaten us."

Focusing on it now, Zara could make out the boundaries of individual starships, nestled like insects in the great, swirling web. Some were small, the size of pleasure yachts. The largest was almost station-sized, and could have contained a compact city. Support lines and travel conduits had been woven into a surreal tapestry about them, that seemed to pulse with motion as first one, then another small ship shifted in its berth.

"Welcome to the homeworld," Rho told her.

Zara put her hand to the viewscreen as if she could not quite believe its image. For a moment she couldn't come up with words. Finally she said, inadequately, "No star?"

"No."

"Not even a fake one?"

Rho shrugged. "There are other stations without them. Diplomatic stations in the War Border rarely have them."

As a Mediator Zara knew the importance of a natural environment. The human mind hungered for the trappings of its place of origin and did not fare well when they were lacking. That's why ground leave was regularly enforced for any personnel serving on starships or stations for extended periods of time, and in places where that was not possible much effort was expended in seeing that pseudoplanetary vistas were provided.

Anything else, it had been shown, made humans . . . unstable.

"People go to diplomatic stations for business," she said quietly. "They don't live there."

"Zara." Rho's voice was firm; her hand on her sister's shoulder turned her to face her. "You're planetborn; these things seem natural to you. Not to the people here. So much of what you've been taught that humans need to thrive is just window dressing for the tourist industry. As long as there's light available in the right wavelengths, as long as the shift system mirrors the human circadian rhythm—"

"You're planetborn too," she said quietly. "Sister."

With a sigh Rho let her hand fall to her side. "Not since the day we were separated. This has been my home since childhood. My motherland, if you will. It was designed to house a refugee people and keep them safe. That matters more than any sun."

"And trees? Do you have trees?"

"A few small gardens, probably. Private things, nurtured in private quarters. I doubt there's anything large."

"*You* don't have a garden, do you?"

"No need." She smiled faintly. "Half my time is spent on one planet or another. And I've been in enough lousy weather that an artificial homeworld is a very nice thing to come home to."

Zara bit her lower lip, wondering if it was time to voice the question she had thus far not dared to ask. Finally she ventured, "Rho . . . what is it you do, exactly? You've hinted at it but never really told me."

"Ah." Rho gazed out at the station for a moment in silence. "I was wondering when you would ask that."

"I was wondering when you would offer."

Rho shook her head, smiling faintly. "We make quite a pair, don't we?"

Zara drew in a deep breath. "That . . . what happened on the planet . . . that was your work?"

Rho nodded.

"How?"

Rho glanced sideways at Zara, an odd expression on her face; was she worried about how Zara would take her revelation? Finally she said, "I'm a Hostilities Specialist. I go down onto primitive planets—technologically primitive planets—and do an analysis of cultural flashpoints. Beliefs, traditions, taboos, racial tensions, whatever exists within that particular culture with the potential to inspire fanaticism and violence. Then I . . . fine-tune them."

Zara said it calmly, though she didn't feel calm inside. "You insert Braxins."

"In that case, yes. Religion is a very effective tool, I've found. And

myths are an easy thing to add, when you have people who can manipulate the dreams of your subjects." She paused. "I was rather
pleased with the way that one turned out."

"Sculpting hate," Zara said softly.

Rho's eyes narrowed. "It's more than that."

Zara said nothing.

"A single Braxin comes to the planet. The locals must identify him,
distinguish him from other humans like yourself—and for a nonhuman species that's the hardest part to guarantee, believe me—and take
immediate offensive action. All this from a planet that has never had
contact with the Holding, or had any Braxin visitors before." She
paused. "Nothing we told them honestly about the Braxins could ever
have resulted in such a perfect response. The words of aliens are always doubted. The words of gods and demons are not. Getting it all
right . . . it's an art form."

She whispered it: "Why?"

Rho looked at her. There was a hint of darkness in her expression
that made Zara's blood run cold. "Why, what? Why is it an art form,
to fine-tune the development of a primitive culture? Or why we
would work so hard to prepare a welcome for Braxi, out here in the
middle of nowhere?"

"That one. The second." She looked out at the station again, tasting
its . . . what had Rho called it? . . . its *planet-mind*. Dark, it was so dark,
she could sense it now. It reflected back the emanations that Rho gave
off and magnified them, allowing her to give them a name. What were
these people, so immured in hatred that even their psychic signature
was saturated with it?

She had assumed when she reached the psychic conclave she would
find people much like herself, save that they had been trained to control their power. Now, with a shiver, she realized that might not be the
case.

"Because the Empire failed to contain them." Rho's surface emanations had changed; even Zara, untrained as she was, could sense the
difference. The mention of Braxins brought emotions boiling to the surface of the Shaka's mind that were as dark and as cold as anything Zara
had ever sensed. "Because when it could have forced the Holding to its
knees two hundred years ago it failed to do so. It chose another course.
And so it was left to us, Azea's forgotten soldiers, to finish the job."

Rho waved at the darkness beyond the viewscreen, her gesture en-
compassing all the light-years beyond it. "Out there, in that emptiness,

are worlds that Braxi intends to conquer. The Holding's master plan was laid out centuries ago in the Schedule of Conquest, and they haven't deviated one iota from that plan. Their mathematicians plotted probability curves for each sector, of how many human and non-human civilizations would likely be there, down to what the technological learning curve of each was likely to be—and the Holding plotted out its future accordingly, so that they might conquer each new nation before it gained the military capacity to stand up to them.

"Our Founder attempted to skew the curve by bringing high technology to a planet that might not have been able to stand up to them otherwise, so that by the time they reached it, it would be a worthy opponent for them. But her work was discovered, and that planet has paid the price. Now . . ." She gazed out at the distant night, and Zara knew that in her mind she was seeing all the planets that it contained, all the civilizations and future campaigns that were obscured by its midnight vastness. "We move with great care, always. Our agents travel to the primitive worlds that Braxi intends to conquer centuries down the road, and we plant the seeds that will make them its enemy by the time it arrives. Braxi's hunger for expansion will be its ruin . . . and by the time it realizes what we have done, it will be too late. They will be ringed about by our work, and they will suffocate."

"They'll just destroy them," Zara said. "A planet that won't bow down to them . . . they'll just obliterate it and move on."

"Some will be destroyed," Rho agreed. "And some will fight back. But one thing is certain . . . Braxi will find no rest, nor any easy source of supplies, once it expands far enough to encounter our handiwork. Then . . . then, if the Azeans are smart, they will take that moment to attack the heart of the monster, forcing the Holding to collapse inward upon itself. . . ."

"And if they don't?"

Rho's eyes flashed in the starlight. "They will," she said. "If we have to return to the Empire and take control of the people making those decisions . . . they will, my sister."

It took effort for Zara not to say anything further. If it were anyone else reciting those words with such fervor, anyone else whose mind was glowing with such hate and such hunger for conquest as Rho's did now, Zara could accept it. But this . . . this was her sister. Her *twin*. In all their genetic essentials they were identical . . . and therefore in all their potential they must be, likewise. To stand beside Rho, to hear her speak of the destruction of innocent civilizations so casually, so cold-bloodedly, was to ask herself, *could I have been this? If the psychics had stolen me away as well, is this what I would have become?*

"Azea will not fail us again," Rho promised.

Zara nodded weakly, shutting her eyes. The planet-mind throbbed inside her head. If she could have turned back the hands of time at that moment she would have done so, even if it meant being lost and confused on Chandra for the rest of her life. At least there she had never questioned her course in life. Once a diplomat, always a diplomat. It was in her blood, she had thought. Part of her nature. What she was born to be.

Now . . . she was not so sure.

What are you, my sister? What have you come to be, in this place? What am I?

The telepathic touch in Rho's brain was light, the mental equivalent of someone knocking gently on a door. With a sigh she shut her eyes and opened her mind to it. She expected a Hasai to be calling her, or perhaps a Communicant doing the telepathic equivalent of switchboard duty for some less skilled psychic, but she knew the minute full contact was enjoined that both of those guesses were wrong. The mental signature, haloed in gold and vibrating with absolute power, was unmistakable.

~*Shaka-Rho*, the Lyu thought to her.

It took all the self-control she had not to remember her last feelings about the woman . . . feelings of resentment that bordered on treason. No well-trained telepath would be rude enough to dig around for such things without invitation, but that didn't mean they wouldn't be heard loud and clear if she forgot herself and actively remembered them.

~*You have found your sister*, the Lyu thought to her.

~*Yes.*

~*And?*

Rho envisioned Zara for her, knowing the ruling telepath would pick the images out of her mind. A cascade of impressions accompanied it.

~*(Eerie resemblance)*

~*(Disturbing nonresemblance)*

~*(Like but not like)*

~(Weakened by Azea)

~(Concern over whether she can accept the Community's ways)

~(Nascent affection, disturbing in its own right because of the nonresemblance)

The Lyu absorbed it all silently, thoughtfully. Finally she thought, ~I have seen your report to the Hasai, about her Awakening. It is . . . disturbing.

~(Agreement)

~You're sure you're not mistaken? The power didn't manifest until recently?

~I'm sure.

~So late in life . . .

~There are no others on record like that, are there?

~Not as she reports. Sometimes the early stages are subtle enough that the condition isn't recognized until later. But we're speaking of a few years' delay at most. Not anything like this.

~She has great value, then.

~In combination with yourself, Shaka-Rho, yes.

She ignored the attendant compliment-thought. ~I am concerned for her . . . I think she's afraid . . .

~Of what, Shaka-Rho?

She drew in a deep breath. It was an instinctive body-reaction, irrelevant in a world where communication no longer required breath, but on a primal, wordless level it was calming. ~Of becoming no more than a laboratory animal to us.

~We're all laboratory animals, Shaka-Rho. Myself included. You know that.

She shut her eyes and carefully put a damper on her own emotions, so that they would not be accessible in surface communication. If the Lyu delved deeper . . . well then, then they'd have Telepathic Etiquette to argue about, in addition to what Rho was feeling. ~Yes. Of course.

~So we have been since the beginning. Individuals in our own rights, yet also pieces of a great puzzle. You have served that cause since you came to us; you understand its importance.

She formed the thought with deliberate formality. ~Of course, Lyu.

~In time your sister will come to understand that. In the meanwhile, I am sure the Hasai will have many questions for her. No doubt some will wish to explore her mind directly. Do you think she'll object?

~(Hesitation) I think that will depend on how it's presented to her. Right now the Community seems more alien to her than many other species she's known. The goals we pursue mean nothing to her yet. Some are . . . distasteful *to her.* She clamped down hard on those memories, refusing to let them into her foremind where the Lyu might access them. Much strangeness might be accepted, given Zara's alien upbringing, but if the depth of her attachment to the Braxin were known it could make her transition into the Community very awkward. *~The reasons would have to be carefully explained. In time I think she'll accept them.*

Hopefully the Lyu wouldn't push Zara too hard. Right now Rho wasn't all that sure her sister regarded the psychics as her own people, and she might not respond well to the kind of authority they took for granted.

~Tell me about the Braxin.

Startled, Rho thought, *~Sorry?*

~Your Braxin prisoner. Tell me about him.

So she did. It was easiest just to open up her mind and let the Lyu share her memories, from the first moment she had seen him alongside her sister on the planet to the last time she had met with him in his cabin. Well . . . not *all* the memories. Not the end of that meeting. One could gain a good enough understanding of the situation without sharing the few things that were . . . private.

When she was done, and the Lyu had mused privately upon all she had shared, the leader thought to her, *~Interesting.*

~Zara insisted his life be spared. I saw no reason to destabilize her further at that time so I agreed.

~A Braxin can have value.

~For information, yes. In fact, when the first moment's destructive impulse had passed she had realized that her people were better served by having a live Braxin to experiment with than by her leaving his corpse behind on the planet. A pity.

The connection with the Lyu flickered for a moment; there was some thought the telepath did not wish to share. *~For information. Yes.* There was a long pause. *~Perhaps for other things as well. We shall see.*

~Lyu?

~ —Later, Shaka-Rho. Later. There are some things I must discover first. Some things the Hasai must unearth for me. Then we shall know what is . . . possible.

She bowed her head mentally. *~As you wish, my Lyu.*

The sense of telepathic linkage faded . . . but not before one final thought had crossed the vast distance between them, birthed in one mind and placed into another: a final farewell.

~I will take care of the Braxin. . . .

"Tathas?"

He looked up when she spoke. Not before that, Zara noticed. Did he think when the door opened it would mean unwelcome company? His expression was grim but a thin quirk of a smile played about his lips as he recognized her. It was hard to read the emotion behind it with the mind-dulling drug in her system, but it seemed to her the smile was more dry than humorous.

"They let you come see me alone?" He shook his head in mock amazement. "Not afraid I would rape you, or destroy your psyche, or . . . something?"

"Would you?" she asked softly.

He shrugged. "I could overpower you and take advantage of the portal being unsealed. Make a break for freedom."

"Yes," she said quietly, "you could do that."

"Wouldn't do much good, would it?"

"I'm afraid not."

"Good sport, though." He wiped a tangle of hair back from his eyes. "They're not as omnipotent as they like to believe, you know."

"And you're not as afraid as they'd expect."

He shrugged. "Fear is nature's motivator, no more. Channeled properly, it's as likely to lend a man strength in battle as to send him running to a place of safety. Your people have forgotten that; mine haven't."

There was silence, then. Her fault. She had come to say something, hadn't she?

"I did all I could," she tried at last. "I told them you saved my life."

A faint expression, perhaps a smile, flickered about his lips. "You told them I was worth saving."

She nodded.

"And they answered that I was a Braxin."

She blushed slightly in embarrassment, but nodded again.

"Don't mind it. My people would have said something similar, if the situation were reversed. Though without the fear, of course. My people do not *fear* Azeans."

The words were out before she could stop them. "Not even psychics?"

He stared at her for a long, long while in silence; his expression was unreadable. Had she gone too far, offended him in some way that was beyond repairing?

"They are human," he said at last. "Strip away the power, the conditioning . . . the arrogance . . . and at their core they are the same as we are, neither more nor less than human. Subject to the same instincts, fears, and hunger for survival as any other members of the species. Just . . . armed better." Again he shrugged, this time more stiffly. "That's my theory, anyway. I doubt I'll get a chance to test it out. Too bad. Would have made a good tale for the telling, back home."

Despite herself she smiled. "Psychic tales popular back home, are they?"

A brief light of something that might have been warmth flickered in those cool green eyes; it bothered her that her heart skipped a beat, to see it. "What a curious woman you are," he said. "Surrounded by everything you should fear most, and handling it now like it was just another day at the job. And now you're here, assuring me you did all you can to help me . . . when you know and I know that such words mean nothing to anyone involved in this, and cannot change my fate. So why do you say them?"

She blushed more fiercely and tried to look away, but his eyes held hers. "I thought you should know."

"You *wanted* me to know." His voice was soft, perhaps even gentle. (Was "gentle" a word you could apply to a Braxin? A day ago she would have called it impossible.)

It's just professional curiosity, she thought. *A new race to study up close, notes to take, conclusions to draw. It's what I was trained to do.*

He rose to his feet with feral grace, like a cat uncoiling from repose. He took a few steps toward her, closing the distance between them, and she did not back away. He reached out a hand to her face and touched her, soft as breath, upon the cheek: just a single finger. Was it only the Braxaná who considered hands the ultimate erotic zone, or was that all the Braxins? Suddenly she couldn't remember. His index finger traced the curve of her lower lip, a touch so gentle it would not have disturbed the wings of a butterfly. It shook her to the core.

"Remember this." His voice was low but strong, like a chord of music just below the threshold of sound, that thrummed in the flesh. "Remember that once I held something very precious and very fragile in my hands . . . and all the while your people waited with bated breath for me to shatter it, so they could know that they were right about my nature. And I did not." His hand dropped away from her— slowly, so slowly. "Remember that," he whispered.

She tried to mouth words—any words—but they were stuck in her throat.

"Good luck with your people, Zara." He said it quietly, in a tone so rich with sincerity she could not doubt him. "May you find the home you seek among them. If that's what you want."

She whispered it: "May you find your way home too, Tathas."

A flash of emotion sparked in the depths of those Kesserit eyes, too quick and too ephemeral for her to read its nature. Courage? Fear? Anger? All three combined? For the first time since coming she regretted her decision to take the mind-drug before coming. If only she could taste his thoughts directly, perhaps she could understand him.

"Not blessed likely at this point," he told her. A dark smile flickered across his lips. "But thanks for the sentiment."

Any man can adapt, when circumstances demand it; Nature has designed us to be unequalled in this arena.

The question is, can he adapt fast enough?

—Zatar the Magnificent

TWENTY-TWO

THE BODY LAY draped across the bedfield casually, almost peacefully. Van'si wasn't fooled. She had seen such things before, often enough that she knew to check for the rise and fall of the chest, drawing breath for life, before coming to any conclusions.

There was no movement. At all.

How many was that, now? Five? Six? She'd lost count. The others had died in twin pools of blood, or with evidence of chemical mishap lying somewhere nearby. This one . . . this one seemed to be merely asleep, and peacefully asleep at that. Death had come to her as a seducer rather than a ravager, whispering promises of freedom even as he gentled the life from her body.

It didn't take her long to discover the cause of death; the H'karet's computer warned her of it as soon as she tried to enter. *0% oxygen,* it cautioned. Apparently the woman had been skilled enough in environmental control to get the room's atmospheric programs to do the job for her. It would have been a slow death, as the one gas vital to life had been filtered out of the room by equipment designed for other things, but it would have been a gentle one. And there was no sign that the woman had had second thoughts about it while she waited.

With a sigh Van'si set the room to restore an appropriate atmospheric balance and took a temperature reading of the body to determine the time of death. Habit. It didn't really matter when the woman died, did it? Only that she had, by her own hand . . . and that Van'si was the one who would have to tell the Pri'tiera.

If there was one part of her job as Mistress of his House that she hated more than any other, it was that. But for as long as the young Pri'tiera kept making these foolish attempts, there really was no other course possible. He had not yet adjusted to his condition, nor come to terms with the effect it must have upon his relationship with women. Someday he would, she told herself. Someday he would accept what he was, and what his condition demanded of him, and make his peace with it. Like his father had, and that man's father before him. And Zatar the Great, whose terrible curse ruled over them all.

She had served his father for many decades, and served him well. As his Mistress—and by extension, some would argue, the Mistress of all of Braxi—she had been entrusted with the management of his House, the key codes to the H'karet, and a few precious hints about the secret of his line. More than that he would never give her. Perhaps that was a wise choice. She had realized in time what he was—a woman of her acumen could not fail to do so—but even the Braxaná social codes, which made it anathema for a Mistress to betray her patron, might be stressed to the breaking point, were that truth to be put into words.

Easier to pretend it was not real. Easier to tell herself that his family's "curse" was no more than a predilection toward mental instability which they chose to hide from the outside world through this eccentric isolation. Easier to indulge his whims, strange though they sometimes seemed, and not allow herself to think about what was behind them. Certainly there were enough things to keep her occupied, what with running the single most powerful House in the Holding. Enough places and people to focus on that she never had to face the truth head-on and speak its name.

It was better that way, surely.

When the oxygen level in the room was back up to normal she entered it, prodded the cooling flesh of the body with a wary finger, and then noticed a small wad of plastic in one of the woman's hands. The dead flesh was just starting to stiffen, and it took her some moments to work the sheet loose from her grip. When she did she smoothed it open and looked at the words written on it before crumpling it up again and throwing into the trash chute.

I will not serve a monster, the woman had written.

The Pri'tiera would not take this well.

With a sigh Van'si smoothed her clothes and asked the H'karet to locate him. He was in the observation deck . . . as usual. He had spent a lot of time there lately, as if somehow gazing out upon Braxi could make him part of the Mistress Planet in spirit, rather than an exile trapped in this floating sarcophagus of a satellite. For a brief moment she felt sympathy for him, and she hated herself for that. Sympathy was a weakness, and his father would not have tolerated such an emotion in any of his staff. But this Pri'tiera wasn't the man his father was. He never would be such a man, she thought.

She had long since ceased to feel angry about that, or frustrated, only . . . resigned.

He had kept her on as Mistress when his father died. Of course. One did not discard such a skilled servant lightly . . . least of all when one was a boy barely past the age of Inheritance, ill-equipped to go searching for a purebred Mistress on one's own. She had stayed on out of loyalty to his father, but had little hope that the son would ever fill his gloves. And no hope whatsoever that she would ever establish with him the kind of relationship she'd had with his predecessor, that strange and subtle intimacy which could exist between a man of power and his Mistress.

With a sigh she summoned servants to clean out the room and deal with the body, and made her way to the observation deck. Best to just tell him now and get it over with. Maybe in time he would come to trust her judgement enough to let her inspect his women before they were brought to him, so that she could weed out the ones who were obviously too weak to handle the situation. His father had done that, and then taken the traditional precautions, and it had worked well enough. But for some reason, though he accepted her counsel in all other things, this young Pri'tiera was loath to let her counsel him on sexual matters. And thus nearly a century of accumulated family wisdom was cast aside in favor of a boy's uncertain instinct.

He will learn eventually, she told herself. *Or else he will burn himself out in short order, trying to be something he is not.* What would the Holding become in that case, with no clear heir to the Pri'tiera's throne, and a Council full of Kaim'eri ready to fall upon the leaderless government like carrion-birds upon a fresh corpse? It was something she tried not to think about.

He would adapt. He had to.

The portal of the observation deck was closed. She gave it her name and waited. A moment later the barrier faded and admitted her.

"Van'si." He was alone, as usual. Who would he have kept company with if he had wished it otherwise? The staff of the H'karet was terrified of him. The Kaim'eri did not pay social calls on their leader. Any Braxin who came into his presence wanted something, or feared something, or maybe just resented him for having such absolute power over his life. Another man might overlook such things, but the

Pri'tiera was denied such a luxury by his unique condition. How did you seek out human company, when all of their hatred was pouring directly into your brain?

Again sympathy stirred within her; again she crushed it.

I am Braxaná. You are Braxaná. There is nothing to be gained by indulging in weaker emotions.

He looked at her for a long moment, then said simply, "The girl."

She nodded.

"Was there . . . any word? Any reason given?"

"No, my Lord."

His expression was impassive. No pain could lance through such a mask. "She seemed stronger than the others. I had hoped . . ." He sighed heavily, and then slowly turned back to study the panorama.

She bowed and was about to leave when his voice stopped her. "Van'si."

"My Lord?"

His voice was quiet. "You bore my father a child."

She carefully steadied her own voice before answering. "Yes, my Lord."

"After proper Seclusion. Yes?"

"Of course, my Lord."

"And you did that . . . how?" He turned back to face her. His black eyes were hungry, so hungry; one could drown in his hunger if one wasn't careful. "Are you so much stronger than all these others, Van'si? Was my father so much different than I am? Or did he rely upon alien sciences to procreate? Help me to understand."

Against her better instincts she felt her expression harden. "Your father would not have betrayed tradition like that, Pri'tiera."

"Then you shared physical intimacy. And survived it. While the ones I have chosen are dead." He exhaled sharply. "Explain."

She drew in a deep breath before responding. "We took drugs. Recreational narcotics. As a result . . . I have very little memory of any details, Pri'tiera. I'm sorry."

He must have known that, of course. It was no secret. Surely his father had told him.

"Drugs," he whispered.

"You could do the same," she said quietly. "Just enough so they didn't really understand what was happening. Or remember it later. I could arrange it for you."

He gazed at her for a long moment before finally turning away.

"Thank you," he said. His voice was a cold thing, devoid of emotion, as he turned back to gaze upon the Mistress Planet overhead. "I will think on it."

But you won't do it, she thought. *You want a woman to know what you are and accept you for it . . . and that you will never have.*

She was suddenly angry at him, furious at his maddening stubbornness—but she was also Braxaná, and Mistress of a Great House, and that set strict limits upon what emotions she might express. Oh, his father would have welcomed her anger, savoring the honesty of it. But this Pri'tiera—this *boy*—would only be unnerved by such a display, and maybe come to doubt himself more than he already did. Which was something none of them could afford.

With a sigh she forced herself to look calmer than she felt, and took one last look at him before exiting the chamber.

All the fate of Braxi rests upon your shoulders, she thought. *Do not fail us, Pri'tiera.*

In theory, the power of a psychic is a simple thing. It is simply Communication, taken one step further than mere words and flesh would allow.

In practice it is the deadliest weapon in existence, for it can circumvent all the natural defenses of a man, and lay bare secrets he would never willingly reveal.

—Anzha lyu Mitethe

TWENTY-THREE

Tathas awoke from a dead sleep to find someone shaking him. The room was dark but when he moved to turn the light on a slender hand stopped him.

"No." It was Zara. "They're watching you, " she whispered.

His warrior instincts served to have him fully alert by the time she had finished her sentence. "What is it? What's wrong?" He realized only a nanosecond later that she had just given him a direct command, but in the heat of the moment it seemed a very small thing. Utterly unlike her, though. She was usually more careful.

"It's all gone wrong," she whispered. "I'm so sorry, Tathas. We've got to go."

He grabbed up his shirt from the formchair nearby—they'd given it to him at her insistence—and moved to follow her. He hadn't undressed completely to sleep since he'd come onto this ship, sensing perhaps that an emergency might overtake him at any moment. It paid off now in how fast he could be ready to move, shrugging on his shirt as she unsealed the portal.

"Follow me," she whispered, and because she seemed to be doing him a favor of some kind he didn't make a fuss about her language . . . but what had made the normally respectful Mediator suddenly so blind to his traditions? If he was a Braxaná he'd be imagining the spirit of Ar descending upon the small ship by now, drawing strength from her dominant phraseology. Superstitious fools! He didn't believe in divine intervention himself but it was still an uncomfortable thing to tolerate such casual commands from a woman without correction or comment. And it weakened the bi'ti, which was the core of the warrior's strength, to do so; that was simple scientific fact.

Zara led him through the darkened corridors of the ship, narrow hallways that barely cleared his shoulders. Her exaggerated silence might have been well and good for guerilla action on the surface of some planet, but how much did it matter here? Couldn't half the people on the ship hear their thoughts anyway, and look in on them mentally whenever they wanted?

"This way," she whispered, and because it wasn't a direct command he followed her.

Dark. The ship was so dark. It made the corridors seem even narrower than they were, downright claustrophobic. He felt as if there were eyes on him, many eyes, watching and taking notes on his every move. Was that just his paranoia, or was someone really watching him? With a ship full of psychics he couldn't be sure of anything.

She brought him to a large chamber stacked with uniform crates. A docking bay of some kind. In the dim emergency lights he cocked an eyebrow at her, asking the obvious question.

"You need to go."

"I can't escape them," he said quietly. "You know that. Why do you think I've endured imprisonment here; because I like it? Everyone on this ship can sense where I am and what I'm doing. Getting in another ship won't change things."

She looked him straight in the eyes, with a coldness that made the skin on the back of his neck crawl. "They're going to kill you, Tathas."

For a moment his heart stopped beating. Only a moment. Then blood flowed to his brain again and he could think.

"You're saving me." It was a question.

"You saved me."

Warrior's debt. It was a simple enough equation that he could accept it. "That still leaves the question of what good it will do to flee. They'll have no trouble following me, yes?"

Her eyes were hard and cold. "Only if they live to do so."

He opened his mouth as if to speak . . . and closed it again, silently. Not that it wasn't a bad idea overall, and one he'd thought of. But it was hard for him to believe that this soft little diplomat had come up with it on her own, much less was willing to set it all in motion.

"Your sister is on this ship," he said quietly. "Would you kill her too?"

Pain, it seemed, flashed briefly in her eyes. "Sister in blood. That's all."

He just stared at her. Wishing for once he could read her thoughts.

"She's alien to me, Tathas. They're all alien to me, at their core."

He said it softly. "And I am not?"

The cold gaze eased a bit. "Not like they are," she whispered.

Sounds echoed behind them, back the way they had come. Footsteps? "Come on," she said. "Quickly." Again the cultural error of commanding him directly. Had the stress of the moment compromised her normal cultural sensitivity? Or did she feel that because she was saving his life she had the right to address him in such a forbidden manner? A Braxaná would have stopped her then and there, risking death rather than accept those few words as they were spoken. As for Tathas . . . he discovered in that moment that he was not willing to throw away his life over the declension of a verb. Though all the gods of the human worlds knew that for blasphemy of the worst order.

Let Ar show up and argue about the matter if she feels like it.

She led him to a tiny vessel tucked away against the belly of the ship. The air lock was sealed but apparently she had whatever codes were required to open it. "Inside," she commanded him. "Quickly." The noise outside was getting louder, and yes, it clearly was footsteps. There were sounds of running, too, which was a very bad sign. Obviously someone *had* been watching him, and the alarm had already gone out: the Braxin was escaping.

He wondered if Zara's sister knew she was there with him. Would it make a difference to her if she did?

He wanted to just get inside the ship and leave. He wanted that to be all there was to it. This alien woman, Azea-born, was willing to kill her own kin to set him free and he'd be a fool not to accept it. Never mind why she was doing it; that wasn't his concern. His people needed him to return to them, and this was the first step in making it possible. Only an utter weakling would question such an opportunity, or fail to take it as soon as it was offered.

My people . . .

He was Viak'im. A leader of men. Not only because he had been stronger or faster than his father, but because the elders of the tribe had considered him a fit ruler for them all. If he had not been they would have given him poison before his duel, and thus guaranteed that the older man won.

A leader of men.

He blessed the Absent Gods under his breath, but made no move to get into the escape vessel. Instead he took her by the shoulders and looked deep into her eyes. Never mind that the footsteps were coming closer now. Never mind that he could hear the cries of those approaching.

"Blood of her blood, flesh of her flesh." His tone was quiet, even, belying the danger of the moment. A ruler's tone. "Are you sure this is what you want? When you look in the mirror tomorrow, when this is over, will you be able to bear what you see?"

She put her hands over his, gently, and removed them from her shoulders. "There will be no mirror," she whispered. "Now go."

Understanding came to him, cold as a Braxin winter. "You can't stay behind."

"Someone has to blow up the ship."

"Zara—"

"No. It's my choice to make. Now go!"

He might have stayed to argue but just then his pursuers came into the bay. That left only one option which didn't lead to his immediate death, and he took it. Ducking into the air lock, he gave his orders to the ship's computer even as he sealed the door behind him. The lights on the ship came on. The engines stirred to life. By the time he got to the bridge and dropped into the pilot's chair the vessel was thrumming with life, ready to head out into the darkness, far away from any source of imprisonment.

He took it there. Without hesitation, without second thoughts. And when he cleared the station and it blew up, sending its occupants back into the Void that had birthed them, he felt no regret. Such was not a Braxin emotion. Nor sorrow. Only a dark elation that he was on his way once more, heading toward that prize which might win him an end to his banishment . . . and revenge upon the tribe that had sent him there.

But when he was sure that no one on the ship had survived to follow him, and that no outside agency was about to arrive to compromise his bid for freedom, he put the small vessel on autopilot and sought a private space within its confines. He found it in a small lounge just behind the bridge. There he stilled his soul, and waited until the wild beating of his heart had become something more leisured and regular . . . and then he offered up to Zara's spirit, in accordance with Kesserit tradition, his thanks, his respect, and wished her whatever manner of afterlife best suited those Chandrans who died with courage.

To make a sacrifice for what one believes in, even if it is such a foolish thing as love, is an act of greatness by any standard.

Tathas awoke from a dead sleep when a slender hand covered his mouth. He realized by its touch that it was not an enemy, which angered him. Was he not enough of a warrior to know that when you were surrounded by enemies, you always awakened in silence?

Another hand flicked on the light, at its dimmest setting. It was enough to see who stood over him, her green eyes warning him to silence.

K'teva.

Here?

When she saw that he was fully awake and understood the situation, she let go. He mouthed her name but didn't voice it; a question.

"I've been following you." Her voice was a whisper so soft that even here, inches from her, he could barely hear it. "When I saw *they* took you . . . I had to act."

She was dressed in black, all black, tight-fitting clothes that outlined her body in hard, clean lines. Her hair was tied back into a functional queue but a few strands had escaped that effort, and they wisped about her face like a fine black veil. She had never looked better to him, nor had he ever been more glad to see her, but he found it hard to believe she was there. He started to ask her questions but she put a warning finger to her lips and gestured toward the door.

Into the darkness of the psychics' ship she led him, through corridors so narrow it would be hard to fight in them if he had to. How had she gotten here? Every time he tried to think about it his mind shied away from the question, as if something inside him knew he wouldn't like the answer.

"They'll sense us," he warned in a whisper.

"They won't," she whispered back. "I've taken care of it."

He watched her back as they moved through the silent ship. The years had given him familiarity with the movement of her hair, the sway of her body, even her footfall . . . and all those things were right, down to the most perfect detail. The woman before him was no imposter, but the real K'teva.

Then why did this whole scene feel so wrong?

She led him to a large chamber filled with crates. A strange sense of déjà vu overcame him then, so powerfully that for a moment he could neither move nor speak. Had he dreamt of this place? His rational mind said that he had never seen it before, but on some gut, primitive level it was familiar to him.

And there was danger here. He could smell it. More danger than he had ever faced before, and a kind of danger that could not be answered with something simple like a sword. He didn't know where the knowledge of that came from, but the sense of it was so strong that for a moment he couldn't move, but stood frozen in the bay like an animal who'd just caught the whiff of hunters.

—*(people all around, all around, hungry watching watching watching)*—

"They know I'm here," he whispered. Instinctively he reached for his weapon, only to remember it had been taken from him days ago, when he was captured—rescued?—on that planet with Zara. "They're watching."

"You're wrong." Had her expression darkened? It was hard to tell in the dim bay lighting. "No one knows we're here."

~*more sensitive than one expects from a Braxin*

She was wrong.

~*or just paranoid*

He knew it. Somehow. Just like he knew that he had been to this place before, and . . . what? What memory was just beyond reach of his mind, and why couldn't he access it?

There was a small ship tucked away in a corner of the bay. The air lock was open, inviting them to enter. K'teva scanned the whole of the bay to make sure no surprises were there and then gestured for him to go inside. He did, and expected her to follow. But instead she stepped back far enough for the air lock to shut behind him; obviously she had no intention of getting into the small ship with him.

"K'teva?"

"I'll see they don't follow you," she promised. Her expression was cold and strangely distant; something about it chilled him to the soul.

"You can't stay here."

"Our people need you, Tathas. More than they need me."

The sense of wrongness that had been in him since he awakened was a roaring in his ears now, that drowned out all thought. He struggled to make sense of it, to determine the source. That was at the heart of his current danger, he knew it instinctively. Determine *who* or *what* and you would know *why*.

"Someone has to blow up this place," she said.

No Braxaná as capable as K'teva would sacrifice herself so casually, he knew that. She should be climbing into the ship by his side, taking her chances, daring the universe to catch them both. That was the Kesserit way.

In the distance he suddenly heard shouts and footsteps . . . crew members running to catch up to them, to take him prisoner once again. K'teva glanced in that direction and then back to him; her green eyes glowed in the darkness. "Go, Tathas. Put as much distance between yourself and the psychics as you can. Anything else is suicide at this point." When he didn't move, but just stared at her, she urged, "This quest was doomed from the start, you know that now—"

He stepped forward, out of the air lock, and was before her so quickly she didn't have time to step back. He grabbed her tightly by the upper arms—noting as he did so that her flesh felt just as it should, and that her warm, familiar scent was like a drug to his sex-starved senses—and demanded, *"Who are you?"* Not whispering now; her language had given the game away. "Why did they put you here? Is this some kind of test—"

—*(abort abort abort)*—

Darkness.

It was good to be back on Braxi, Tathas thought. Even though he hadn't gotten to see much of the home planet before they had whisked him away on a transport. But the few minutes of real gravity he'd experienced, on the only planet in the universe that truly mattered, had done much for restoring his spirit.

It had been a long trip home. Too many checkpoints, too many petty bureaucrats who'd insisted on checking with the Central Computer System to confirm that the terms of his Wilding now allowed for his return. One hadn't checked at all but had simply decided to take matters into his own hands. A fatal error. Would the Braxaná hold it against Tathas that he had killed some fool on his way home? Surely in the face of the other accusations against him that would be deemed a trivial offense.

Woe betide the man or woman who got between him and his destination now.

He tried to remember the face of the man he had killed but couldn't. The whole journey home was like that, as if the memories were not real at all, but a story playing out in his brain. Very strange.

Now . . . now he was on a transport to the H'karet, with such treasure in his keeping that even the Pri'tiera would be moved. At first it had worried him when he had gotten the invitation to see the mysterious leader alone, but he knew that while the Braxaná were notoriously lacking in any commitment to true justice, they were equally notorious for keeping to the letter of the law when it came to their own tribal traditions. And it would be a defilement of the Wilding for the Pri'tiera to do anything other than receive him, receive his offering, and—if it satisfied the terms of the custom—let him go free.

~envision the offering . . .

He leaned back in the transport's padded seat and started to think about the gift he had brought for the Braxaná leader—the culmination of all his efforts in the Outlands—but his warrior instinct warned him that this was no time for reflection. The gift he had brought was safe in a back chamber, there would be time enough to see it later . . . and to see the Pri'tiera's face when he received it.

~stubborn —

~very —

~could be forced —

~maybe later—

And then, he thought, when he was free to walk the Braxin streets again, when there was no price on his head . . . then he would make them pay. The Pri'tiera first, then all the others of his blessed race. First they would pay for the humiliation his people had suffered for centuries; that was just an appetizer. Then the grand feast of suffering would come, to pay them back for the murder of his tribesmen and their elders. He would find what Kesserit remained on the planet and he would mold them into an army such as the Holding had never seen before, and then they would strike against the Pale Ones in such strength that none could stand before them. For the rulers of the Holding made a good show of barbarism, but in truth they were weakened by eons of luxury and self-indulgence, while his people . . . his people were a sword honed by eons of hatred, readied for that one strike which would avenge all past indignities and set the balance of power right again.

—(hunger for details, hunger for information)—

The transport stopped. He took a second to gather himself together, to make sure the hatred that burned inside him was safely hidden from all observers. So it had been for his whole life, living this god-blessed subterfuge in order to survive. And look where it had gotten him. The elders of his tribe were dead, survivors scattered, and he now had permission to attend the Pri'tiera as a penitent sinner, begging for his master's forgiveness.

He growled low in his throat as the portal dissolved, but his expression was as impassive as ever. That's what came of a lifetime's practice. Deception was second nature to the Kesserit, and may the absent gods help the Braxaná if it ever was allowed to falter.

There were two guards outside. Even here, even now, the renegade Kesserit was not to be trusted. "This way," one of them said, and they let him fall in between them, matching his step to their own military stride.

He had never been inside the H'karet before. He tried to look around as they passed through it, but the details were strangely insubstantial. As if he were watching an entertainment piece that was not quite in focus. A strange dread shivered cold inside his gut, when he noticed that. Surely it meant nothing. Surely.

~hold on to the emotions this time, don't want to lose this one like the last

They marched until they came to a matched set of doors, of a barbaric design that swung on hinges. Tathas waited while one of the men pulled them open for him, noting the relief carvings that covered both, depicting vast battle scenes as well as more private conflicts. He saw a few images of men subjugating women and that seemed strange to him. It wasn't an artistic motif common on Braxi, nor was it one he had heard the Braxaná had a taste for. He tried to look more closely but the door blurred in his vision as it swung further open, and he was ordered inside.

~careful, careful, details must be right
~we have no research on such things
~if you can't draw them from his memory, then don't use them at all

The audience chamber was large and dark, its details lost in shadow. The only light within was fixed upon the man in its center. No, not a man; a boy, or little more than a boy, whose stark white makeup and stylized facial hair could not disguise his true youth. *So young*, Tathas thought, *and yet you rule us? What strength can you have in you, what wisdom, that the Braxaná would allow this?*

He bowed. Nothing else would be acceptable. "Pri'tiera."

"So. You return to us."

"As I promised."

"And you bring us?"

"What I promised, Great One."

"Indeed." The boy's black eyes narrowed as he regarded Tathas. The hatred in them was undisguised. "And I have your reward, Kesserit."

He stepped back, far enough that Tathas could now see what lay at his feet, half in light and half in shadow. A body. A woman's body. A body he knew.

He cried out—a mourning cry, a warrior's cry—and his shout filled the chamber, echoing from the distant walls like the howl of some maddened beast.

"Did you really think you would escape us?" the Pri'tiera asked him. "Any of you?"

K'teva lay still on the floor between them. The life must have only just bled out of her, for her lips were still tinted the fresh rose of life and her eyes were shut gently, as if in sleep. Tathas knelt by her side and took up her hand—still limp, still soft, not yet stiffened in the finality of death—and trembled. Emotions that he had no for name for flooded his brain. Then came the ones that did have names. Grief. Rage. Determination. Hate.

You have pushed us too far, Braxaná.

He stood. His expression was impassive, and gave no warning of the maelstrom inside his heart.

I cannot unseat all your people, without my tribe behind me . . . but I can and will cut off the head of the monster.

There was no warning. One moment he was standing still before the Pri'tiera, as if he feared to act, and the next he leapt across the space between them. The Braxaná pulled some kind of weapon in a startled attempt at self-defense, but Tathas struck it aside easily as he slammed the weight of his battle-hardened body into the boy's own.

Young, his warrior's soul assessed as he bore him to the ground, *muscular but not well-trained, and clearly not prepared to fight for his life.* Good, that was good. The rage was pouring through his veins like molten lead and he had no desire for a good fight, just for the kill. He would rip the boy's throat out with his teeth if he had to, and howl in triumph like a beast on the Blood Steppes howling at the moon. Never mind if they killed him afterward. He knew how the Braxaná mind worked, he knew that in taking down their leader like this he was dealing a death-wound to their pride, and that pride was everything in their government. The death of their precious figurehead would weaken the whole, and whatever Kesserit remained on Braxi would know that sign for what it was, and move against them—

Never mind that he would not live to see it. Never mind that within seconds now the guards would be upon him, dragging him off their leader's body, to beat him to a bloody pulp in punishment for making them fail in their duty. Some things mattered more than a single life.

There will be revolution, he thought, as his hands closed about the Pri'tiera's slender neck, driven by the strength of a madman. He could feel bone shift beneath his grip, and he slammed the boy's head back against the stone floor, twisting it to one side with all his might. *Revolution long overdue, you god-blessed tyrants. Do you know how many Braxins remember the days when tribal identity was the pride of every warrior, not merely the possession of an inbred elite? Do you know how many have secretly prepared for this day? The whole of this planet will vomit you up for what you have done to us, until the very gods are moved to applaud.*

He could feel bone snap beneath his hands even as guards grabbed him by the arms and tried to drag him off the Pri'tiera's body. But he kept banging the boy's head back against the cold stone floor as the rage poured through him, a tidal wave of black emotion that became grief, became sorrow, became. . . .

~*Is more needed?*

~*not our choice—*

~*getting harder and harder to control—*

~*he has a strong mind—*

~*stubborn mind—*

~*recommend further study. Unparalleled opportunity—*

~*should capture more Braxins. See if this is typical.*

~*tribal hostility has great potential—*

~*universal sentiment?*

~*this is an unusual specimen—*

~*the Lyu says to bring him to her—*

~*we should run more tests—*

~*orders are orders—*

~*maybe when she's done with him we can run another sequence.*

~*maybe—*

~*shut down now?*

~ *Yes.*

. . . .

To have control over the life or death of another human being ... that is the ultimate measure of power.

To exercise it, without restriction or remorse ... that is the ultimate indulgence.

—Zatar the Magnificent

TWENTY-FOUR

THE ROOM WAS all stone and metal, unyielding, cold. Glistening tiles of Andalask marble were underfoot, fitted so closely that a drop of water could not have squeezed between them. Walls were surfaced in wafer-thin slices of U'lu schist, that glittered like stars against a sea of pearly gray. Sculpted seats of florentined metal were clearly intended for art rather than comfort, and the matching table held upon it a decanter of Aldousan swept-crystal with two glasses to match. The glass was more fragile than the rest of the room but equally unliving, its substance drawn from the melding of rock and heat rather than organic substance.

K'teva looked over the room with satisfaction and checked one last time to see that the security array was working properly. It was. There was only one thing left to wait for, then, and that was not in her glove.

She was quiet on the outside—as always—but inside her heart was pounding in a fevered expectation. Part fury, part determination, part . . . a strange hunger, that rooted itself in the same parts of her flesh which were normally reserved for pleasure.

You thought I wouldn't find out, didn't you? Her words addressed a man not yet present except in her imagination, and fixed upon him with such rage that if he had been able to sense even a shadow of her mood he would have stayed many systems away from her. But she was Braxaná—more so than he, at least—and knew how to keep such things hidden, until the end.

Until tonight.

It had taken her most of her spare cash to outfit the room properly, but it would be worth it. It was the kind of room that most purebred Braxaná had tucked away in their mansions somewhere, though theirs were probably more subtle in design than hers was. Theirs had to be. The people they dealt with knew the implications of such decor, and their enemies might be hesitant to enter such a space if it were not well disguised.

Would her visitor read the signs right, would he know? *Maybe I should have put out a few pillows,* she thought. A natural fiber rug on the floor might even add to the moment, if positioned properly. Perhaps she should have provided one.

The portal chimed.

Too late now.

She walked with measured calm to the front portal, took a deep breath, and opened it.

The man on the front step was dressed in Central style, but the clothing sat ill upon him, as if he was used to something else. Little wonder. It was probably rare that such a man came into the Holding at all, and she doubted this one had ever been as far as the B'Saloan system. She'd wondered, when she invited him, if he'd be willing to come at all.

"Lady." He bowed. "You wished to see me."

She nodded and stepped aside, clearing the way for him to enter. "You've done well for me, Silkar. I thought we should speak."

"Your ladyship honors me."

How easily the honorific came to his lips. It never ceased to send a shiver through her, to receive that title which the first class took for granted.

She indicated a hallway and let him precede her. She'd left the door open at the end of it, and he took the cue readily enough. Any man who worked for a Braxaná woman learned how to figure out what she wanted, without orders needing to be given. That was as much a part of their culture as the social codes which prohibited her giving him a direct command.

She followed him into the stone-and-metal room and shut the portal behind her. His heavy synth boots, scuffed from years of wear, echoed dully on the marble floor as he took up a position at the far end . . . almost as if he knew where she wanted him.

"I wish to know what you have learned," she said.

He looked perplexed. "You've had my report, Lady—"

"In person." She smiled. "It would please me."

He hesitated. She could almost smell his brain churning out a chemical cocktail of suspicion and doubt. He had, indeed, reported his findings to her already. So why had she called him all the way here, to the Mistress Planet, to meet with her personally? *Let him wonder,* she thought. Anticipation thrummed hotly in her veins as she turned to the small table, lifted the decanter, and poured two round-bellied glasses full of the deep red Central wine. Were her hands trembling just a bit? She steadied them as she lifted one glass for herself and offered him the other. He took it.

She touched hers to her lips but did not drink.

"It's like I told you, Lady." He took a quick drink from his own glass, swallowing it like one might a cheap Border ale, instead of a fine Central vintage that probably cost as much as he made in a year. "No one's seen hand nor glove of your Kesserit for a while, but rumor has it he went off with a bunch of freelancers, and them with none too good a reputation." He drank again, deeply, emptying the glass. "I've got some information on them—and their possible future targets as well—but you have all that, Lady, it was in my last report, so I'm sorry . . . I assume you want something more than that?"

She smiled in what she hoped was a disarming fashion. "Perhaps some new information, Silkar. Something that wasn't included in your report."

He looked perplexed. "All the information I gathered on the Kesserit went out to you promptly. That's the deal, isn't it?"

"Yes." She said it quietly. "That's the deal."

"Did it not get through?"

She put her glass on the table. It was still full. A casual step put her in a place where the table was between them . . . and other things as well. "I would like you to tell me of the others, Silkar."

His brow furrowed. "Lady?"

"Others you report to."

His expression tightened ever so slightly. Another might have missed it, but she was used to the Braxaná and knew how to watch for such subtle signs of expression. "I don't understand," he said quietly. He put down his own glass, now empty. "I've got other jobs, if that's what you mean. You're not the only one wanting information from the Border, and I haven't made any agreement not to sell it—"

"You made an agreement not to sell *this* information though, didn't you? Not to anyone but me."

A muscle flinched along the line of his jaw. He said nothing.

"Who are the others, Silkar?"

"I've kept to our bargain."

"—because you see, I have other spies. And they tell me that there are some men on my home planet who know my business. More of it than they should."

He said it quietly. "That's not my doing."

"Isn't it?" She took a step backward and looked him over. "They tell me otherwise. They tell me that the things these men know could only have come from one person. What's the matter, Silkar?" Her eyes narrowed, as hard and as cold as the stone surfaces surrounding. "Didn't I pay you enough?"

She saw his eyes skitter about the room, marking its only entrance—behind her—and perhaps even searching for things that might be used as weapons. *Too late for that,* she thought. He was like a wild animal caught in a trap, who had only realized that it was that. But she was of the first class by virtue of her half-Braxaná blood, and he was not. For him to lay a hand on her in violence was an offense punishable by death. She could taste the knowledge of that as it lay heavy in the room, could see his tongue lick nervously at the corner of his mouth as if he shared the sensation.

"Tell me whom you report to," she said softly. She had fallen into the speech mode of Seduction, which made her choice of words doubly offensive. "If the information is useful I may spare your life."

He was about to speak, most likely in anger—no Braxin male could fail to take offense at such a direct command from a woman—but even as the words were ready to leave his mouth a sudden stabbing pain in his stomach robbed him of his voice. His hand went to the site of the pain and for a moment he looked more perplexed than afraid. Then his eyes caught sight of the two glasses on the table—his empty, hers full—and when they turned back to her they no longer contained puzzlement, or even fear . . . simply horror.

"You shouldn't have betrayed me," she purred.

He lunged for her, but she was ready. One fingertip's touch to a hidden control brought up a force field that divided the room in two, transforming the short distance between them into an impenetrable barrier. He struck it with such force that she could see his palms reddened as the barrier absorbed the energy of his momentum, but he was beyond feeling such peripheral damage. Pain was churning in his gut now and raw animal terror was drowning out all rational thought in his brain. Screaming invectives at her, he beat upon the barrier. It was a primitive instinct, doomed from the start, but the human hindbrain knew nothing of force fields, only desperation and fear.

And then the Black Death became fully active.

It churned out of his stomach directly, eating through flesh and clothing alike. A black, roiling mass more sentient than mere poison,

a thousand times more horrifying than any stable life form. It churned
out of his abdomen, his chest, and even his mouth, spilling over the
confines of the flesh which had recently taken it in, devouring everything it landed on.

Silkar screamed. It was a primitive, inhuman sound, voiced by a
creature whose higher instincts had been drowned out by terror. He
fell to the ground and clutched at his stomach in agony, but there was
no flesh there any longer—only a black mass of poison that seethed as
it spread, devouring every bit of organic material within reach. It had
gotten on his hands and now they were being consumed, bloodstained
finger bones jutting out as the flesh was dissolved first, then even the
bone crumbling as it, too, was digested. His body began to convulse as
it died, death-spasms casting bits of flesh and poison to all corners of
the room.

A thick wad spattered wetly on the force field right in front of
K'teva's face, the poison seething with hunger as it fell to the floor
inches from her feet. She took a step backward instinctively, fascinated, horrified. She had read of the Black Death, of course, and had
learned the details of its application when her black market contacts
obtained it for her, but to see it in action . . . that was another thing.
Her intellectual facilities assured her that it could not reach her
through the force field, but the animal part of her, ruling over that part
of the brain where lust and fear were regulated, was not so sure.

And then, as quickly as it had begun, it was over. The convulsions
ceased, and the few remaining fragments of flesh—his legs, mostly—
lay still. The seething blackness slowed, then stilled, and finally became inert, its surface dulled and cracked as it died. All around the
room, the bits of poison that had been scattered by his struggles likewise went inert where they had been cast, and did no damage to the
room surrounding them. Of course. The Black Death could only digest
organic matter; stone, metal and glass were immune from its hunger.

A Braxaná would have known that.

She stood there breathing heavily, drinking in the heady elation of
the kill. It was like nothing she had ever experienced before, a
strangely sexual rush that left her flesh aching for other acts, living
acts, as if to counterbalance the dance of death she had just been part
of. She wanted to savor the feeling as long as she could, before the
cleanup began. Because of course, there would be cleanup. Not just of
the room itself. Unlike the Kaim'eri she had no right to kill a man just
for annoying her, which meant there would have to be special

arrangements made. She had set them all in motion before Silkar had arrived, of course, but it would behoove her now to confirm them all, and to make sure no rival had stuck a thorn in her glove while she was . . . indulging.

She looked down at Silkar in wonder, while the heat of arousal slowly leached from her veins. *He betrayed me. He died for it. I made it happen.*

She let the force field disperse. The smells from the other half of the room filled the small space with the stink of fear, and of dying. Tonight it was the scent of her triumph, as sweet to her nostrils as the bouquet of the finest wine.

Tonight, K'teva thought, *I am truly Braxaná.*

To have an enemy worthy of one's respect ... that is a prize beyond measure. What is a lover's touch compared to such a thing? Love is but weakness shared, trials halved for being met in tandem. While a skilled enemy provides stimulation, challenge, and ultimately growth for all those who test their strength against his.

—Anzha lyu Mitethe

TWENTY-FIVE

VOICES WHISPERING
Semisentient memories
Synapses plucked like instruments, by remembered hands
Past present future mingling
Thought is the symphony, its movements measured in generations
What was given? What is kept? What has changed?
What is mine?
What is true?
What is mine?
Lives overlapping
Memories tangled
Breathe deeply and they fade one into the other, all the borrowed
lives, all the injected pain, grafted to this current life like scar tissue over
a livid wound. . . .

The Lyu was sane.

For a long time she hadn't been.

Such things were to be expected, when the throne of the
Community passed from one to another. So it had to be, when
the one who had borne the position before initiated full mental
contact with her successor—communion without reserve, communion without defense, until the very boundaries of identity
were put to question—and poured her memories into her, making her Lyu.

Memories. Foreign lives. They scurried in her brain like insects, tripping over synapses as they did so. The lives she remembered were not whole, of course, nor were the memories
necessarily coherent. Only the most volatile images survived
such a transfer, and each Lyu that had contained them had left

her own mark upon them. The oldest memories were the most impure, for having been passed through so many brains, while the more recent ones spoke of incidents and people so familiar to her that sometimes it was hard to sort out which memories were her own, and which were implanted.

In such a flood tide of input the soul struggles like a drowning man.

It had taken Irela five Standard Years to find her center again, and to submerge the foreign memories into her own subconscious so that her conscious mind could function again. It had taken her another five to learn to draw upon the foreign memories at will, without becoming lost in the wonder and fear of what she had become. It had taken her yet another five to become the composite creature that the Lyu must be, in which all these things were a natural process, so that she no longer had need to question the source of every thought, the veracity of every memory.

Now, as she paced the golden audience chamber, memories stirred. Dark tidings rising up from the depths of her as if from a lightless sea. These were ancient memories, among the oldest she carried, and the thought that she might thus be accessing the mind of the Founder herself was a terrifying one. Those memories, more than any other, bordered on true insanity.

Braxin
Braxaná
ENEMY
Don't trust
(Hunger, all-consuming)
I have ruined him!
Your golden age is ended, Pale Ones
Taste the fate they meant for me
(The flavor of desire. The touch of consummation.)

The Founder must have been truly mad, the Lyu often thought, or else the passing down of her memories through so many brains had distorted them enough that she seemed mad now in false retrospect. Certainly the current Lyu could make no sense of the storm of conflicting instincts which accompanied every Braxin image from Mitethe's memory, nor imagine how a human being might contain such a maelstrom of emotions and still appear to be sane.

They were bringing a Braxin to her now. The mere thought of it set her deepest borrowed memories to stirring, and sent an unnamed heat coursing through her veins. She had never seen a real Braxin before.

Never tasted the mind of one of the Enemy. Never had one before her, in her physical presence, so that she might touch him with her special senses, exploring those depths which had given birth to the darkest of legends among her people.

Shadowy presences within her stirred hungrily, anticipating.

This Braxin—this *Tathas*—had been searching for psychics. The Hasai had plucked that fact from his mind, along with the information that it wasn't for the usual motives of power or vengeance, such as one might expect from a Braxin. What a curious thing. Did he have some latent psychic ability perhaps, newly manifested, that had made him flee in fear from his people to hers? It wasn't impossible. There was at least one bloodline among the Braxaná that had given birth to a psychic strain; it was reasonable to assume there might be more, as yet undiscovered. If so, if that was why he was here, the breeding potential of it was truly stunning. Though she wasn't sure how well the Community would receive the thought of Braxin DNA being injected into its carefully nurtured gene pool.

But whatever will make the psychic strain stronger must be done, she thought. That was the first tenet of the Community, the Law they were all sworn to follow.

The second Law was that Braxi must fall. At any cost.

~Mistress?

She paused in her reflections to accept the tentative transmission. *~Yes?*

~He is here.

Memories that were not her own rose up in a tidal wave along with their attendant emotions, compounded by the life experience of all her predecessors: so strong, this response to the simple presence of a Braxin! She drew in a deep breath and forced them into the background of her mind, accepting only those few tendrils of recall which would feed her the information she wanted. The fact that she had mastered such techniques years ago didn't mean that a particularly powerful stimulus might not upset the whole balance. One always had to be careful.

She sat on her golden throne, smoothed her golden robes into their most perfect folds, and settled the precious keepsake of her rank between her breasts with a hand tipped in golden nails. The vial was cold to the touch, as always.

Then: *~Send him in.*

A few seconds passed in silence, then three figures entered the far end of the chamber. The two guards were both men, she noted; no doubt a deliberate choice. The third man, walking between them, was of a race she had never set eyes upon before in this life, though the memories she had absorbed from her predecessors offered up images from times and places when the others had, as well as a melange of shared hatred so intense that it took all of her skill to absorb it without showing sign of it to anyone. Far, far more than political hatred; even as she tasted it in her mind she wondered at the source of it.

They had chained him to a bar not unlike the yokes used on working animals on primitive planets. A force field could have held him more securely, but no doubt they had wanted the primitive drama of it as a means of humbling his proud Braxin spirit. The weight of the bar across his shoulders, the chafing of manacles that bound his wrists to it, the frustration of not being able to drop his arms by his sides, or gesture with them as he spoke . . . these were things done by primitive peoples to bring their enemies down to the level of beasts.

It hardly made him helpless, she observed. Oh, he was unlikely to get out of this chamber alive, and he'd never make it off the homeship, but if he swung that bar the right way he could certainly take out both his guards before either one knew what was happening. He probably knew it, too.

So much for humility.

She reached out to his mind and tasted his forethoughts. Hatred, of course, and the fury of a caged beast . . . but those were to be expected. He was almost at the breaking point, she noted; probably driven there by the Hasai's experiments as much as anything which came before. One of her imbedded memories stirred to life at the thought of that, relishing the thought that he might indeed snap, and have to be brought down like the beast he was, right in front of her.

My presence before him is the ultimate insult, she thought, *for I am the embodiment of all that his people revile. A woman commanding not only men, but an entire nation. If he could, if he dared, he would rip me to pieces with his bare hands, for I am a thing that goes against Nature in his eyes.*

"Take off the chains," she commanded.

No! The word came into her brain with stunning force, screamed out by nearly every fragment of borrowed memory in her psyche. *He'll kill you!*

But then up from the abyss there rose a whisper, softer than all the others, darker than them. Such was its nature that all the others seemed to fade before it. *Yes,* it said. *Do it. You cannot control this one while he wears a woman's chains.*

She trembled inwardly, sensing the source of that particular memory, its age, its madness. It was not often she accessed the Founder's memories directly, but when she did it always left her shaken. Thank Hasha there were two other lives between them, who had filtered the woman's memories through their own minds before passing them on. She wasn't sure she could have handled Anzha lyu's memories directly.

Though her successor did, she reminded herself.

By then the chains were coming loose, and the bar was removed from the Braxin's shoulders. He glared at his captors but made no move to hurt them. Or her. When the last of the shackles had been removed he rubbed his wrists to restore their circulation, but his eyes never left hers.

Deep green eyes. A startling color.

She nodded for the guards to move back a few steps. They weren't happy about the order but they obeyed.

Then she stood. She was a tall woman in her own right, and the dais her throne rested upon made her taller than him by several heads. The blood-red feathers of her headdress rustled softly as she tasted his surface thoughts again. Calmer this time. Better.

You cannot force them to do what you want, a dead Lyu remembered. *You must seduce them.*

Or threaten them, another recalled.

But do not command them directly, the first one remembered. *For then he must defy you.*

She gestured for him to come closer. After a moment he did so. She stepped closer to him, to the edge of the dais, close enough to feel the heat of his body against her own skin, and to catch the scent of male defiance that hung in the air about him like mist.

~You see, she thought to him. *~I do not fear you.*

He stiffened for a minute as the alien thoughts inserted themselves into his brain, but he didn't panic. Very good for a Braxin, she thought. Normally the telepathic invasion of their brains by a woman was enough to blunt the edge of their pride, but this one wasn't flinching.

And then he thought back to her, *Nor I you.*

That it was a bluff went without saying; she could taste his fear behind the words. But he did it without letting the fear show, which was more than most Braxins were said to be able to manage.

Interesting.

His skin was pale but not without color, a pleasing olive undertone; his hair was dark brown and as wild as a beast's mane. His beard was cut in the Braxin style but it hadn't been trimmed in some time, giving him a faintly disreputable air. He was an attractive man, with strong shoulders and a hard, well-muscled body . . . but he lacked the surreal beauty of the Braxaná tribe, just as he lacked their coloring, and their notorious obsession with physical perfection. A Braxaná in confinement would have trimmed his beard if he had to pluck out every stray hair by hand.

"Why have you come here?" she asked.

The green eyes were steady. "I think you have to ask the one called Rho about that."

Her expression hardened. "You were looking for my people even before she found you, I know that. Why?"

A pause, then. She could sense the flurry of thoughts inside him, but didn't intrude further. He was coming to terms with just how much information they might have lifted from his mind without his awareness, and it would take a few moments for him to assimilate that.

"I sought information," he said evenly. It was a good evasion, true enough to pass inspection, yet revealing nothing. How quickly he had learned the rules of this new universe, she mused, and how quickly he adapted to them! She remembered Braxin prisoners taken by her predecessors who had not lasted nearly as long, nor borne themselves with such confidence in her presence.

A worthy enemy, one of the Lyu-memories whispered. A flutter of admiration accompanied the thought. And something darker, that stirred like a chill serpent in the depths of her shared soul.

"Tathas," she said quietly. "It's the end of the road now, you understand that? Others have danced around your secrets for fear of doing permanent damage to your mind, for they knew I wished to see you in your natural state. So they have not done all they could have to you, only gained those essentials of knowledge which we must have to arrange this interview. But now you are here, and after me there is no one. You can provide the information I seek, or I can take it from you. I would much prefer the first—"

"Why?" the Braxin demanded. "Why not just wring my brain dry of secrets and have done with it? If you have that power."

Because you may be a useful tool, she wanted to say. *Because the Hasai found in you such sentiments that I believe I can use you for our purpose, if you prove malleable enough.*

But instead she said only, "Because we may wish to send you home."

That clearly stunned him. He started to open his mouth but no words came forth. She opened her mind to his and sensed the doubts that were skittering across his surface thoughts: *What would they gain from such a move? Do they mean to program me to serve them somehow? Do they expect me to spy for them?* But he was a man of control and voiced none of them.

"I assume," he said slowly, carefully, "that if you meant to do such a thing, it is because it would serve some purpose for you, not out of concern for my affairs."

"Perhaps our purposes in some things are the same."

A dry smile creased his lips. "I doubt that."

She took a step back from him, then turned away from him to face the throne. She took two steps with her back to him before she turned to sit down and was facing him again. It was a challenge and he knew it. How was his Braxin mind reading such a gesture? As a sign of trust? *I have allowed you to stand here with dignity, surely you would not harm me.* As a sign of confidence? *You know the price of moving against me in this place. You would not dare do so, even when faced with such temptation.* His expression was unreadable, so she reached out to his mind for the answer.

You have balls, he was thinking.

She managed not to smile.

The Founder's memories whispered to her: *You have won the first battle.*

He bowed his head ever so slightly, a token of respect to her rank. She had enough knowledge of his culture to understand that he was stressing its bounds to do even that much. "What is it you desire of me, Mistress of Psychics? What is the price for this . . ." He smiled faintly. ". . . ticket home?"

He said it lightly but she could taste the hunger in him. The bait had been swallowed.

"You are Kesserit," she said quietly.

The green eyes glittered. "Yes."

"Which means what?"

"It is a tribal designation. My people once ruled in Nasqua, and briefly held the Kast'ran Reaches. That was before the tribes were amalgamated under Harkur."

And under Viton, the Founder's memories whispered to her.

"And under Viton," she said.

The green eyes darkened.

"Do you hate the Braxaná for that?"

"No," he said quietly. "I don't hate the Braxaná for *that*."

"But for other things."

A muscle twitched along the line of his jaw. "You ask for the weaknesses of my people. What do you offer in return?"

Her eyes narrowed. "I give you an opportunity to cooperate. Do you forget you are a prisoner? We can take the information we want, if you will not offer it freely."

With a faint smile he shook his head. "No. You can't. I will tear apart the mind of anyone attempting it, if I must drive myself mad in the process . . . and then you will have nothing, Mistress of Psychics. Ask your interrogators, if you like. Ask them if they got one piece of information from me that amounted to betrayal of my people." A faint smile quirked his lips. "Ask the one called Rho what happened when she pushed too hard."

He has balls himself, a dead Lyu noted. *If not wisdom.*

The Lyu nodded inwardly. That was what Rho had said as well . . . while her mind had blazed with a hatred greater than any the Lyu had seen in her before. Whatever this man was, he left his mark on those who got too close to him. "You're very arrogant, for one surrounded by enemies."

He chuckled. "The Kesserit are always surrounded by enemies. Today it's a ship full of female psychics. Tomorrow—"

He stopped himself, but not in time; the thought came through loud and clear to her telepathic senses. *Tomorrow it will be the Braxaná.*

"Tomorrow," she said evenly, "depends upon your cooperation here."

The smile faded from his lips, but not from his eyes. "Of course."

"There's no record of independent tribal activity on Braxi for eons."

"Yes," he agreed. "There's no record."

"There's no record of any tribe called the Kesserit being active during that time."

"No, there isn't." The green eyes alone blazed with fury; the rest of him was so steady it might have been the weather they were discussing. "The Braxaná outlawed all acknowledgement of tribal identity, outside their own circles. Any historian daring to mention that another tribe remembered who and what they were would have been deemed a traitor to the state and executed."

Memories rose up in him then, sparked by his own words, and she could see his jaw clench as he sought to keep the illusion of control.

She reached out to touch his thoughts and images flooded her brain, hot and seething and painful as a fresh wound.

—sword in hand, standing before the crowd of his people, drinking the elixir of the Elders—

—fighting for his title on the blood-slicked stage, pride of the Kesserit tribe—

—Braxaná cutting down his people, his faithful and brave people, while he launches himself at them in battle-rage, ready to die rather than ever submit to the hated Pale Ones—

The cold snake whispered, *Use the rage. Mold him into a tool with it. He will serve us.*

"Your tribe has retained its identity," she said.

"Yes."

"Have others?"

He shrugged, even while his mind confirmed it.

"And they hate the Braxaná as well."

His expression hardened. "Harkur sought to create one nation. In the name of that nation we abandoned the ancient ways and accepted his vision of the future. Then he handed the keys of the Holding over to the Braxaná, who have ruled it since. Is that what you want to know? That a few remain who resent that transfer of power, and its cost in tribal blood? That should be no surprise."

No surprise that it occurred, she thought, *but serendipity that a key player has been delivered into our hands.*

I have use for you, Kesserit.

She shut her eyes for a moment, focusing her senses inward. Deep, deep within her own mind she went, to that dark and fearsome place where the most alien memories nestled. She needed them now, enough to brave the sea of emotions that surrounded them.

Are you sure? the dead Lyu whispered. *I have been there. It is not a good place.*

Nothing is worth that, the other assured her.

Deep, deep inside. Past the barriers she had set in place, to protect her from the madness of the Lyu's shared consciousness. Past the barriers she had absorbed from her predecessor, erected to do the same. Past the work of *her* predecessor, into whose brain the ancient madness had been poured directly . . . Elis the Mad, whose brain had cracked from the assault and who had spent nearly two decades lost in the maelstrom of someone else's emotions, before she finally managed to assimilate the memories of her maker.

Beneath that . . . beneath that was a strata of memory and experience so saturated with violent emotions that one could not access facts without absorbing them. Into that sea of emotion she dove, knowing that what she sought could only be found at the heart of it.

(Frustration)

(Fury)

You have undone all my work!

A roar of despair engulfed her, monstrous in its intensity. She absorbed the self-hatred that had driven her line to the edge of suicide once, ten, a hundred times . . . all of those memories bound up together in one blazing firestorm of despair. Elis the Mad, trembling as she held a dagger against her wrist, too weak—too strong?—to make the cut. Anzha lyu Mitethe, trembling as she held a dead lover in her arms, knowing that her own power had consumed his life . . . screaming fury at the forces which had made her what she was, determined to defy them—

—watching an entire planet die, her fault, her fault—

—planting the seeds of destruction in the one she hated most and watching him survive it—

—impotent fury raging at the universe—

Inwardly, she screamed. It was a terrible, voiceless sound that could be heard by everyone except the man standing before her. All over the homeship Receptives cringed and dropped what they were doing, desperately muttering the keys to Disciplines as they fought to shut out the agonized sending. Telepaths blinded by pain alerted their ships to the need for possible flight, not knowing what had prompted the cry. While here in the audience chamber of the Lyu the Braxin stood quietly, even calmly, unaware of anything that went on beneath the surface of the physical universe.

Damn them for their blindness, their arrogance, their strength! Irela reeled as the ancient memories poured into her, along with emotions so raw and powerful she could barely contain them. Velvet black eyes—predator eyes—gazed deep into her soul, sparking such primal response in her that she could hardly breathe. *I will destroy you!* a memory screamed. Braxaná eyes, coldly dispassionate, gleamed at her like black diamonds—repellent, enticing, maddening. *I will cause you such suffering that at last my hunger for vengeance will be satisfied,* she remembered promising. But it wasn't enough. It was never enough. Each new Lyu had taken the ancient memories and twisted them, adapted them, given them new strength. New hunger.

Not enough to torture one man. Not enough to weaken his people.

Not enough even to seed the whole galaxy with defeat for his nation, so that no matter where the Braxins went they would find themselves reviled and rejected, and all their imperialistic plans would end in catastrophe. In the end the Enemy had proven stronger than expected, and had risen above the trials she had set him, to establish a line that ruled the Holding. The blood of the first Pri'tiera still prospered in the fourth generation. It ruled. It had triumphed.

She knew its weakness.

She knew what she had to do.

Slowly she opened her eyes and gazed at the Braxin before her. He was a tool, no more. All human beings were tools, that the gods of war used and discarded as they saw fit. The generals of this war had made her what she was, had provided her with training and purpose, so that when a moment of opportunity came that the battle might be rejoined she would know it for what it was, and not shirk her duty.

Her voice was quiet as she spoke again . . . at least to his ears. "You would move against the Braxaná if you could."

"Is that a question?"

"No. It is no question." In fact it had been, but his mind had already answered it. "We know your desires, Kesserit, for they showed in the dreams you were given. Our Hasai are experienced in interpreting such things."

"Then." He spread his hands casually, but the intensity of his gaze revealed it for a subterfuge. Every sense he had was fixed on her, every brain cell working overtime to anticipate her next move. "What next?"

"I am . . . curious. Are you not concerned that if the Braxaná fell the Holding would collapse? Revolutions are rarely peaceful."

Tathas' gaze hardened. "Are you asking if we fear Azea? I know what strength lies hidden beneath the surface of our society. We won't falter long enough for them to take advantage of it."

"And internally? You don't fear other things . . . civil war, perhaps, if the Braxaná are weakened?"

Would I admit it to you if I did? "There are enough tribal leaders ready and able to take over. Disruption is unavoidable, but in the long run . . . the Holding will survive."

You're lying, she thought. *I can taste the lie. There's a part of you that wants the chaos—hungers for chaos—believing that those who are best suited to lead will arise in such a time and their competence will be proven.* How alien the Braxin mindset was, with its casual acceptance of violence! It was nothing to this man if millions died in the turmoil of a weakened

Holding, if the end result was a more powerful ruler coming forth. No, even more: it was *good* for millions to die, for war was a competition that weeded out the weak. The more brutal the exchange of power was, the more likely it was that the strongest candidate would persevere at the end of it.

Perfect, the most ancient memories whispered. *He is perfect.*

She steepled her fingers thoughtfully and pretended to study them, while all the while her telepathic senses were reading him on levels he could not even imagine. "And if I gave you the means to bring down the Braxaná?"

His mental aura blazed but his voice was steady. His self-control would have done a Braxaná proud. "Why would you?" he demanded.

"Our Founder . . . did not like the Braxaná."

"Your Founder," he said quietly, "is long dead."

Is she? she thought. *Are you so sure of that?* "Is a prisoner of war demanding to know our motives?"

"No," he said. "But you'd blessed well come up with a bit more convincing argument that you can strike down the Braxaná from out here . . . otherwise, quite frankly, this is all rather meaningless. No offense to you, Mistress of Psychics—" his bow of respect was ever so faintly sardonic "—but I can name a hundred men better placed than you and better trained than you, who pitted everything they had against the Pale Ones and lost. Or do you think psychic power alone will give you the edge? One telepath will succeed where whole armies have failed?"

"No, Tathas." A faint smile curled her lips. "Not a telepath."

"Your Founder played those odds and failed."

No, my proud Kesserit. She hasn't failed . . . yet.

She stepped down from the throne, down the steps of the dais, close enough to stand in his personal space once more. He didn't back away, or even flinch. Of course not. No Braxin male would give ground to a woman, especially one in power. How predictable they were. . . .

She drew a finger up to the neckline of her tunic and traced its edge down to the inner curve of her breast, with a gold-tipped nail. She could see him following the gesture, could taste his instinctive male response to the suggestiveness of it. Deep within her décolletage her medallion of rank rested, golden filigree with a frosted vial suspended in its center. This she touched, and lifted from its resting place just far enough to draw his notice. "Do you know what this is?" she whispered. Softly, for the sexual tension of the moment required softness.

He gazed at it for a moment and then said, "Stasis field. Independent, from the look of it." He looked up at her eyes. "You wear strange jewelry."

"Do you know what's inside this, Tathas?" She waited until his eyes lowered to the medallion again and stroked it lovingly. "DNA. Samples taken from the Founder, before she died. The last remains—and complete genetic record—of Anzha lyu Mitethe."

She could feel the shock of it inside him as she spoke the name. The hunger that attended it. Yes, her Hasai had been right; *this* was what he had wanted so badly, to cross half a galaxy searching for it. To complete a quest begun nearly two hundred years ago, when Braxi's first Pri'tiera had vowed to mix his bloodline with that of Harkur the Great. But he had failed to find a descendant of that famous line. Likewise his progeny had vowed the same, and failed in turn. There was only one known descendant of the great Braxin ruler, and by the time her heritage was made known she was out of Braxi's reach forever.

Understand a Braxin's desire, Anzha lyu had written once, *and you can control him.*

Was not the essence of the woman preserved in those precious double helixes, as much as in the memories she had bequeathed to her successors? Between the two of those things it might truly be said that Anzha lyu Mitethe would never die.

Generations of Braxins had sought her seed. Generations had failed to claim it.

She knew its value.

"You would rather have found a woman, wouldn't you?" She allowed a note of scorn to enter her voice. Let him fear that she had revealed his prize only to deny it to him. "That's the custom, isn't it? To abduct a woman and bring her back to your homeworld, to be raped at leisure by the Pale Ones—isn't that what you came for?"

With effort—great effort—he forced his gaze away from the medallion, and met her eyes once more. The turmoil within him was visible now; no mere Braxin could hide such things from a telepath of her skill.

"What do you want?" he said. His voice was low and barely controlled, the mix of emotions behind it so complex she couldn't pick any one out.

"As I said." Her voice was a whisper, soft and seductive. "Our purposes in some things may be the same. What would you say, for instance, if I told you I had the means to destroy your Pri'tiera?"

"I'd ask why you haven't used it before now."

"Ah," she said. "You see, there's the catch. I've had the means . . . but not a delivery system for it." The smile left her face. "That's what you would be, Tathas."

For a long time he said nothing. She could sense his thoughts racing—weighing risk, appraising options—but she didn't eavesdrop. Now that she was proposing a formal alliance, it would have been rude.

The thoughts settled. The green eyes glittered with hatred—but not for her, she thought. For a man far away, who was infinitely powerful . . . and infinitely flawed.

"Tell me what you have in mind," he said.

All acts of man have their proper time and place . . . including revolution.

—Zatar the Magnificent

TWENTY-SIX

"**B**OTTOM LINE: HE'S a child." Kaim'era Samar's voice dripped scorn as could only be done in a language where the speech modes of disdain, superiority, and intolerance could be combined.

"He is Pri'tiera," Tezal answered in the Basic Mode. *It is enough.*

A servant ducked into the room quickly, set down a tray of glasses half-filled with wine and an ornate decanter also half-filled, and left even more quickly. Tezal had once noted that the speed of a servant's exit from a room was directly related to the power of the men inside it, and this was no exception.

Samar, Tidir, Katur . . . and himself. All Kaim'eri. All Elders. Perhaps the most senior of the current Council, certainly the most powerful in influence. The servant didn't know all that, of course. He just saw four men wearing medallions of the Kaim'erate and decided it was best to be somewhere else . . . fast.

You would think I regularly abuse my servants, Tezal thought, bemused as always by the fear his rank engendered in the lower classes. Then again, the right to kill any human being for any cause, with full sanction of the law, was no small thing.

Katur reached for a glass and then settled back to sip from it. "His age is irrelevant. We let him ascend to the throne and now we have to deal with that. —This is very good, Tezal. What is it?"

"A Kasindran vintage. I'm told the source flowers only blossom once every twelve Braxin years."

"Foreign. Ah. That figures." Tidir took a glass as well and sipped from it speculatively. "One thing to be said, Tezal, you are an impeccable host."

"You honor me."

Samar leaned back, steepling his fingers as he did so. In the Mode of Contemplation he said, "It seems to me, the issue is not what *we* think of him, but what the least intelligent Kaim'era thinks of him. Or perhaps better stated . . . the most impulsive."

Katur looked at him sharply. "You think someone might try to . . . remove him?"

Samar snorted. "I think half of them would give their Houses for it, if they thought it could be done. And I'm not so sure I wouldn't be among them." He claimed a glass and drank deeply from it, draining the contents in a single deep swallow. "You and I both know how much real power the Kaim'erate has lost since Zatar pulled his coup two centuries ago. His children were savvy enough to defend the throne when it could have been pulled out from under them. But this boy?" He leaned forward and poured himself another glass. "He's still Pri'tiera only because there hasn't been a concerted effort yet to unseat him. It's only a question of time."

"And that is what we're here to talk about, isn't it?" Tezal said quietly.

"You agree with Samar?" Tidir asked.

"That sooner or later someone will try to unseat the boy? Yes. Though I don't necessarily share his view that the effort will succeed. Thus far our young Pri'tiera has proven unusually . . . adaptable."

"Not to mention no man can stand up to him, face to face,"

"Yes, well." Samar finished his second drink and set the empty glass aside. "Obviously only a fool would opt for direct confrontation."

"But fools there are aplenty, unfortunately, and with our population as small as it is, it's not unthinkable that some of them have been . . . successful."

"Been made into Kaim'eri, you mean."

Katur's eyes gleamed. "Just so."

Tidir chuckled darkly. "I can think of half a dozen offhand that I wouldn't trust with the datacodes to a lavatory, much less a Great House."

"And I imagine they're scheming now," Tezal said quietly. "Which is precisely the problem."

He leaned forward and claimed the fourth glass for himself. He held it up against the light and swirled it slowly, enjoying the play of colors in its depths.

"It's not necessarily a bad thing," Samar said. "And if a fool does it, then a fool will die for it . . . and we will be here to claim what is left."

"*We.*" Tezal gazed at his wine a moment longer, then brought the glass to his lips and sipped from it. "How much is said, in that simple word. Will all the Kaim'eri vie for his throne, do you think? Or will some argue we are better off returned to the older ways, when we all ruled as equals?"

"Does it matter?" Tidir asked.

"Oh yes." He regarded the other Kaim'eri over the edge of his glass. "I think it matters very much."

"The question is not whether there are men who would use the opportunity to seek their own advantage," Katur said, "but whether all would do so at once, and to disparate ends."

"Chaos," Tezal said quietly, "is something we cannot afford right now."

Samar snorted derisively. "Chaos is inevitable when power shifts."

"There was none when Zatar declared himself Pri'tiera."

"That was different. He had prepared for years, for such a move. He had the right backing and his opponents were isolated—"

"Exactly." Tezal's expression was grim. "He prepared. So I ask you all, do you see signs now of any Kaim'era preparing to claim a leadership role? Or re-establish the Kaime'rate as ruling oligarchy?" When there was no answer he said in the mode of disdain, "Please, do we have to pretend we don't watch each other?"

"I see many who might move if the opportunity arises," Tidir said. "I see none who are in position to do so successfully."

"Exactly. Chaos. Which is fine and good on the Blood Steppes, for a handful of Braxaná warriors, but for us? Azea would move in on us the instant such a state was even hinted at, and I do not see us in position right now to repel such a move."

"Not to mention that now it appears we can't even trust our own." Samar's expression was dark. "They took Kaim'eri Laran away last night, you know. Something about conspiring with Azeans."

"I'd like to see evidence of that," Katur muttered. "And it had blessed well better be good, if the Pri'tiera's people are moving against one of us."

"Courier capsules," Tidir told him. "Half a dozen, my people tell me, and all of Azean manufacture. They found them on his estate—"

The door opened. It was B'Seth. She nodded an apology to the visiting men and then said to Tezal, "You have a message."

He waited for her to hand it to him, but she just waited. After a moment he nodded his understanding and got up to leave. "If you will excuse me, Kaim'era, I will only be a moment . . ."

She did not speak until they both had left the room and the door had shut securely behind them. "Please forgive me, my Lord, I know you don't normally wish to be disturbed while in meeting—"

He waved the apology short. "I assume if you did so you had good reason. What is it?"

She handed him a letter. It was small and square and had been folded so that one couldn't peek inside without breaking the seal.

"From one of your . . . informants," she said.

Hardcopy communication. That meant something that couldn't be committed to any form of transmission, even the most secure. He nodded his approval that she'd done well by her actions, turned away from her, and pressed his finger to the seal. The chip inside scanned his DNA, was satisfied, and broke open.

Inside there was only one line. It was scrawled in the handwriting of one of his Border agents, and when he read it Tezal drew a breath in sharply.

T is coming home.

Seek allies in unexpected places, and you may find yourself with unexpected strengths.

—Anzha lyu Mitethe

TWENTY-SEVEN

"*Y*OU ARE GOING WHERE?"

Rho doesn't meet her sister's eyes, but that doesn't stop her from absorbing her emotions. Confusion, frustration, anger . . . a tendril of thought that cries out, you have brought me here and now you abandon me! Rho winces and absorbs it all, refusing to erect those mental barriers which might protect her from the torrent of emotion, or even dull its edge. She deserves this.

"It's an unprecedented opportunity," she tells Zara. Knowing even as she does so that no one raised outside the Community can truly understand what this means to her, or to her people. Least of all Zara, who so clearly does not share their visceral hatred of the enemy. "Something we've waited centuries for. Not merely to dream of Braxi's destruction, but to set it into motion—"

"And no one else can do this? No one else can throw away their lives for this cause, it has to be you?"

With a sigh Rho takes her sister's hands in her own. So like her own, she muses, yet they contain an energy so alien to her. She would give her soul to have had more time to explore the difference.

But some things matter more than personal happiness. Surely even Zara can understand that!

"I'm the only Shaka who is fluent in Braxin," she tells her. "No one else can manage the journey, much less the subterfuge that may be necessary at its end."

"And your death?" There are tears in her eyes now. "That's required, also? The Holding can't be destabilized if you don't die?"

"Zara." She says it softly, so softly, hoping that her sister will pick up on the false calm in her voice as opposed to the turmoil in her soul. "My death won't forward the cause at all . . . but it's the most likely aftermath, isn't it? I can hope for circumstances that will allow me to get safely out of the Holding after my job is done, but reality is that's not likely." She pauses. "I'd rather go in facing that, prepared for it, than trying to deny it."

"And your value to your Community? This . . . twin thing?"

Your *Community*, Rho notes. *Never* Our *Community*, or even The *Community. Zara could live among the psychics for a hundred years and she would never feel like she belonged. Sometimes Rho even sensed an unspoken admonishment behind her sister's words, as if being a part of the diasporic nation somehow made Rho responsible for its excesses.*

We are soldiers in the greatest war that humankind has ever known, *she thinks.* That's what the Founder intended us to be, it is what we were trained for, it is the core of our identity. Each of us part of a vast campaign that spans the generations, hungering to be the one person who will set in motion the final assault. Hungering to see this thing to its end.

I can be that person. That's what they've offered me. How can I explain to you what that means? How could I refuse such an opportunity? My spirit would be black with despair for the rest of my life, knowing that I had failed the one thing I was made for. You can understand that, can't you?

"They know all about my life," Rho says quietly. "They'll still have you. All the rest is a thing for scientists and databases, that doesn't require my presence."

Zara squeezes her hands, so tightly the grip is painful. Rho can sense her trying not to cry, trying to be worthy of the strength she sees around her. Mad strength, terrible, insane strength, that would throw away a human life just when it had the most to live for. Rho can taste the words of condemnation forming inside her, but they aren't voiced. It's the same choice Rho would have made, had their positions been reversed.

At last Zara says, in a voice both wounded and tender, "This campaign of yours. It's more important than I am?"

"It's more important than I am," Rho says quietly. "That's what matters most."

Alien environment. Tiny cabin. Uncomfortable bed; something solid? Engines thrumming distantly.

For a moment Rho just lay on her bed and stared overhead, trying to remember where she was and how she had gotten there.

Then she did, and she winced.

No helping it now. We do what we must.

It was a primitive cabin with a primitive bed and her back ached with primitive pain as she got up from it. Still that was nothing compared to the irritation of who she was travelling with. The ship the Lyu had given them was way too small for two personalities such as theirs, and the strain of it was beginning to become intolerable.

The Lyu had someone check on her every downshift, of course. This far out that was still possible. Rho didn't know how she would deal with things when her contact with the homeworld was cut off and she was . . . well, not alone. Worse than alone. With one of *them*.

The Lyu had said, *He serves my need.* And would not listen to her protests.

That's great, Rho thought. *Only if we don't kill each other before we get to the Border I will be very surprised.*

With a sigh she cleaned up, threw her old garments into the recycler and accepted new ones from the ship's outlet. The question of what to wear was a thorny one. The first day she had dialed up a neck-to-ankle jumpsuit two sizes too large; she figured she was damned if she was going to offer any kind of sexual display to the man who had mentally raped her. Then she realized that by making such a choice she was only confirming his power, so she ordered up something that almost dared him to come at her. *Try it,* she thought, *I can and will kill you.* But his dry smile, utterly maddening, made it clear that her motives were totally transparent, and that for as long as she let his presence dictate her attire, the game was his.

Damn him to hell.

So now she just wore her usual clothing. Hasha help him if he made one move toward her.

You still alive? the Communicant asked her every downshift, when she checked in. And after she confirmed it always came a question that both amused and irritated her: *Is he?*

Thus far he was. Thus far.

Don't place bets on tomorrow.

The ship was small, an older model that had served as guest quarters when it was attached to the homeworld. From the way it vibrated at high speeds Rho would have guessed its hull was held together by adhesive tape, with pieces of its engines culled from junkfields throughout the galaxy. But Tathas had said that anything more substantial would have drawn suspicion when he returned to the Holding, and the Lyu had agreed. So here Rho was. Sleeping on a slice of solid matter that didn't change its shape when she shifted position, and locked in this nightmare of a flying prison with . . . *him.*

She called up a breakfast bar from the commissary outlet, engaged in her morning constitutional of wondering if it was even worth leaving her room, and then did so.

The corridor was narrow, claustrophobic even for her. The thought that he was larger and it would be even more uncomfortable for him brought her some slight comfort.

Tathas was in the control room. Of course. You could tell when a man had spent most of his life on a planet, he didn't trust the ship to fly itself. Or maybe he just worried about what would happen when the adhesive tape started to peel off.

He looked around to her as she entered. He had shaved much of his face, she noticed, and trimmed the narrow beard that remained to traditional Braxin specifications. He'd cut his hair too, though not well. *Should have let me do it,* she thought. Then she reconsidered: *Me near him with a blade in my hand . . . bad idea.*

"Morning," he said. As usual, he insisted upon that planetbound phrase even in a place where there was no sun to mark the passage of time. It was one of the many annoying things about him. "I was just about to get you."

Something in his tone of voice made her suddenly wary. "Trouble?"

"Far from it." With one hand he waved toward the viewscreen, which displayed a sector of space not unlike every other sector of space they had passed through. Black sky, a sprinkling of stars, pretty much the usual display for augmented travel. The computer provided it to take the place of vistas which the human eye couldn't interpret. "Welcome to the Holding."

Her heart skipped a beat, choosing to clench into a knot instead. She hated herself for having that reaction. "Are we inside, then?"

He shook his head. "Not yet. The Border's right ahead, though, and I've just picked up the first customs beacon from K'solo. Should be dropping speed in less than a shift, barring complications."

"Such as what?"

"Hard to say. I've only made this trip once, remember?" He checked a readout on the control panel. "Rumor has it security inspections are stiff for incoming vessels. That's why I made sure we had a ship that would raise no questions. Something a lone exile like myself might conceivably have gotten hold of." There was an edge to his voice, Rho noted, accompanied by a brief but razor-sharp emanation of resentment. He hated playing these games as much as she did.

Well that was something they had in common, anyway.

"We really need the inspection?" she asked. "Space is a pretty big place, I can't believe they can account for every ship coming in and out of the Border."

"We need a starlane assignment to travel legitimately. Without it we're just a rogue ship, and anyone who wants to can take us down with no interference from the law. We could possibly manage to scrape by without clearance in this region, but as you get in closer to the Central System the odds of slipping past all the authorities gets awfully small. And what the authorities don't catch, independents will; any ship traveling as a rogue is fair game, and believe me there are those who hunt them, both for sport and for profit. Besides," he added, "you forget, our purpose here is legitimate. My own safe return is guaranteed by Braxaná law. As for you. . . ."

He rooted around under his seat for something he had obviously stowed there. When he found it he threw it to her, suddenly enough that she almost dropped it.

It was a bracelet. Heavy. Opulent, in a marginally tasteless sort of way.

"What in all the human hells is this?"

"Token of ownership."

For a moment she couldn't speak. Then, finally, she forced the words out. "As in, you *own* me?"

"I'm afraid so, Shaka-Rho." A faint hint of a smile flitted across his lips; if it had been any more overt she might have killed him for it. "From here on out you are my property, by Braxin law."

"Go to hell."

"—And if you give me orders again I will strike you. Though not for the pleasure of doing so, I assure you. Merely to help you remember that such a mistake could be deadly once we're out in public."

She let the bracelet fall from her hands and said between gritted teeth, "I am not your *property,* Braxin. In public or anywhere else."

He shrugged. "As you wish." He turned back to the control panel. "I'd suggest you review the Social Codes before we arrive, then, so you know when and where you are required to submit to men. I'd also suggest you put that baggy jumpsuit back on; it's less likely to draw attention than what you have on now. Although, to be honest, there are men who are drawn to clothing like that, as it signals a reluctant partner." He shook his head. "Not my taste, but who am I to criticize?"

Rho growled low in her throat.

He didn't smile, but it clearly took effort, which was almost as maddening. "I just forwarded a copy of the Codes to your cabin reader. I assume you want to read it in private."

She hissed softly but said nothing. After a moment she picked up the bracelet. "You couldn't have found something more . . . subtle?"

"Thick enough that a dress glove can't be put over it. That's the custom. Thank the Braxaná for it."

He rose from his seat and headed toward the door, but not before he stopped in front of her and tried to chuck a finger under her chin, a move that would have seemed affectionate had they not both known how much she wanted to kill him.

"You're in my world now," he told her. His eyes burned with a strange fire that she had not seen in them before. "I suggest you come to terms with that before we land. A mistake in the port could be fatal."

"I won't make a mistake," she growled. But by the time she finished the sentence he was already gone, leaving her with a fresh dose of fury and no way to vent it.

Damn him. Damn him, damn him, *damn* him!

It was too easy, Tathas thought.

Too easy.

Not that it shouldn't have been easy, right? He'd followed the law to the letter when he left the Holding. He'd respected it when he was gone. He was coming back now with a woman in tow who would appear to be the price of his return from exile, and there should be no reason for trouble anywhere along the way, going home. Right?

Too easy.

The trouble was that there were Braxaná involved. Nothing with them was ever what it seemed. Logic warned that the easier this trip seemed to be, the more danger he was probably in.

Of course, between him and the killer psychic woman it was likely they could take down most enemies . . . but that meant new risks. Any hint in public that she was more than she seemed, and they could have the whole station coming down upon their heads.

He'd warned her, of course. *Don't use any psychic ability once we disembark. Don't whisper to me even in secret about things you feel, because any corner might contain spies. Don't underestimate how much my people hate psychics, or what kind of violent reaction you might get if you show them even a hint of your power. Strangers have been killed for less.*

Bringing her home to the Central System was not unlike carrying a live bomb in one's hands . . . a bomb so sensitive that it might go off if you breathed wrong. Much as he appreciated a challenging battle, that was not the kind of weapon he would have chosen.

But that was all right. He had other moves prepared. Thing*s* even she didn't know about. *Never walk into a room full of Braxaná with only one way to get out,* wasn't that how the saying went?

I have a new saying for you, he promised them. *Never take on the Kesserit in battle unless you are ready to lose.*

Easy or hard, he would have his vengeance.

The customs station at K'solo was surrounded by a swarm of ships. They were mostly commercial barges, Rho noted, giant shells that could act as stations in their own right, studded with portals that looked like glaring eyes. From a distance they looked like a giant herd of beetles fighting over a morsel of food. It was hard to see what was receiving their attention until Tathas got instructions for wending his way between them, to a berth that was outfitted for smaller ships.

She could feel her heart pounding in her throat as they started their descent through the field of giants. This close to the station she could pick up the sentience of the people on board it, and while truth be told it wasn't much different in tenor from the mind-chatter of any other station, the knowledge that it was Braxins she was listening to made her heart clench in a mixture of dread and elation. All her life she had studied the enemy, so that she might set traps for them amidst the stars. Now she was about to walk among them unarmed—as much as a Shaka was ever unarmed—pretending to be part of their twisted society. Pretending to *belong* to one of them.

It was a great subterfuge, the only problem being . . . how much could she trust Tathas? She knew how much he would gain from betraying her. The Holding would welcome a psychic to dissect and a mind like hers to break for secrets, enough for that gift alone to win him passage home.

The Hasai had reassured her on that point. The Lyu had reassured her on that point. *His hatred of the Braxaná overwhelms all other motives,* they had said. *It will drive him.*

They had better be right.

The bracelet chafed on her wrist, as much as the Braxin chafed on her mind. She could taste his own tension in the back of her mouth now and it wasn't helping matters at all. Disciplines only worked so well when you were with a person who associated you with the quest that was causing him tension. His fears, finely honed, dug their way into her mind like molten barbs, and the best of her mental exercises could hardly dull their heat. For the hundredth time that shift she reached for the packet of pills tucked into her clothing, pressed white powder that could blissfully drive all his Braxi thoughts from her head. For the hundredth time, her hand stopped just short of taking them out. She had never wanted to shut down the part of her mind that was open to alien thoughts more than now, but something in her gut rather than her brain warned her this was not the right time. To go without her power was to be truly defenseless; one had to have a better cause than irritation to enter such a dangerous state.

"We're in," her Braxin "owner" muttered. "Now it starts."

"You anticipate problems?"

"I anticipate nothing. Including success." With a final glance to the fuel readings he shut down the flight display. "Always safest that way."

There would be an inspection, of course; no private vessel would be granted clearance into the Holding without authorities first making sure it carried no contraband. Or at least making sure that they were paid properly to overlook the contraband. Since the tiny ship carried nothing illegal and Tathas was applying the proper bureaucratic lubrication, he had said they should be safe enough. He sounded confident, but that was because leaders were taught to sound confident to their people; but she could sense the strain of it on his psyche, the trigger-taut tension that infused every cell of his body and every synapse of his mind.

He is doing it for my sake, she realized. *Denying his fears to give me courage.*

Damn him. It was almost enough to make her like the man.

"We'll need more fuel," he said. That was a given. They'd known when they left the Community that the small ship couldn't carry enough to sustain them all the way to Braxi. Better to fill up now, at the Border, than risk drawing attention closer in.

"Will we have to leave the ship?" she asked. It was a more more polite question than *Can I get away from you for a while?*

"Doubtless." There was a strange look in his eyes for a moment, then; thoughts flashed through his mind too quickly for her to pick any of them up clearly. "Though I'll be staying nearby. You can go explore if you feel like it." He glanced toward her bracelet, and that maddening half-smile flickered across his lips once more. "No doubt you will find enough to amuse yourself if you wander off alone."

Damn him.

With a sigh of resignation she sat in the other pilot's seat and watched him bring the small ship in. They were offered an air lock that had clearly seen better days, but it functioned well enough to affix them to the weathered station. Rho reflected briefly upon the fact that an immersion dock would have been better; then she could have walked around the ship to see if any of the tape was peeling off. But. When you're invading an enemy's space to destroy its leadership, you make do with what you've got, right?

It was when they disembarked that she felt the first twinge. Nothing specific, just . . . something wrong.

She looked up at Tathas. He was busy talking to one of the port authorities, who was entering information on a computerized tablet as they spoke. Biting her lip, she kept her silence. He had told her how important it was that she not even hint at her power, and he would not welcome a warning with so little information behind it. With a sigh she leaned back against the wall of the reception bay, feigning fatigue so that others wouldn't guess why she wanted its support. Shutting her eyes, she let her mind wander out into the distance, seeking the source of that passing unease.

. . . not find what's hidden in the hull, please!

. . . blessed bribe better be enough, or next thing he'll find is a stun in his gut!

. . . just over the Border and I'm safe!

With a sigh of frustration, she gave up. The station was so rife with random hostilities that picking out one wisp of thought to focus on was nigh on impossible, even for one of her skill. At least the odd feeling, whatever it was, wasn't focused on the two of them. She'd know it if it was; thoughts that were focused on you were like spotlights shining in your face, impossible to miss.

A few more port officers wandered into the dock, conferred with their superior, and headed toward the ship. Rho could sense a sudden crest of tension in Tathas as he waved them inside. Now *that* was interesting. Could it be he had contraband on board after all? She noted that he was carefully staying close to the outer wall of the dock. Did he want to be close to the ship, or just not want to leave enough room for anyone to slip behind him? If the latter it was probably reflex; a lifetime of breaking Braxaná law, he had told her, taught a man to always be prepared for trouble.

Two workers showed up at the far end of the dock, and began to load cargo pallets onto a gravitic pallet for transportation. Halfway though the job, another came to help them.

The feeling of wrongness was still there. Stronger now.

She moved closer to Tathas. He was busy in some kind of negotiations with the port authority; the snatches she caught sounded like some kind of bribery to rush through normal procedures. She saw him glance up at the workmen once or twice, and she could taste the tension in him like a tightly coiled spring, but thus far there was no overt sign of trouble.

She reached out to taste the tenor of the officer's mind. Tension—killing tension, murderous tension—combined with fear, and a clear sense that he was in over his head.

She reached out to taste the workmen's minds. They were not focused on their work, but on something else. Something close to her, but not her.

Tathas?

As the realization hit, the wave of hostility focused upon her Braxin companion became clear to her. No, there was no one in the station planning to harm the *two* of them . . . their target was Tathas and Tathas alone. To them she was as inconsequential as the ship behind him, or the floor beneath his feet. Their focus had been so tight that she had all but missed it.

All of them were in on it. The officers, the inspectors who were inside their ship, the workers . . . every single one of them sent here to greet him, to surround him, and to see that he never left K'solo. There were guards waiting outside as well, in case something went wrong in the dock. They didn't know why someone powerful wanted him dead or captured—she couldn't tell which—but they'd do their job anyway.

A feeling of sickness welled up in her gut as she realized just how completely they had been surrounded. And she had no way of warning him. This close to their enemies she dared not even hint at the truth of the situation; they'd move in before Tathas had time to absorb any cryptic message. Yet he had to know. He was wary, but not wary enough. He knew there might be trouble, but he surely had not anticipated a targeted assassination attempt his first minutes within the Holding. Who had even known that he was headed here, to arrange such a thing?

She had to warn him. But how?

Voices were coming from inside the lock now; the inspectors had done their job and were leaving the ship. They hesitated at the portal, going over some notes they had taken inside. They were near enough to be at Tathas' side in a heartbeat, and if the port official stepped out of the way the workers at the far end of the dock would have a clear shot at him.

She moved closer to Tathas and did the only thing she could.

She took his hand. Affectionately.

He looked down at her in surprise.

She squeezed his hand and smiled at him, hoping it was the way that a piece of property normally smiled at its owner, in this crazy part of the galaxy.

She could feel recognition of the gesture's meaning shoot through him like an electrical current. *Something is so wrong. Something is so very wrong that I'll even pretend I like you. Sorry I can't tell you more.*

He squeezed her hand back momentarily, an equally silent acknowledgment. Then he turned his attention to the business at hand. But she wasn't fooled. She could feel the warrior's tension soar in him, and to be this close to it was intoxicating. Suddenly she found herself strangely elated at the thought of trouble. The two of them against whatever forces K'solo had mustered; wasn't that a challenge worth meeting? His spirit cried out its defiance on levels only she could hear, and his confidence surged through her veins like a drug.

Tathas moved suddenly, She saw Tathas grab one of the inspectors and whirl him about until he was slammed to the Kesserit's chest, pinned by Tathas' arm, a human shield. The motion had been so fast, so utterly without warning, that none of the men in the bay had time to react to it. The port officer tried to duck out of the way so that others could fire at Tathas, but his mind broadcast his intent a nanosecond before his muscles responded and she short-circuited the message, inserting her own instead. Stumbling like a zombie, his face a mask of horror as he found himself yanked about by invisible puppet strings, he lurched toward Rho and Tathas just far enough to put himself in the line of fire as they moved.

Sure, Tathas had told her not to use her power, but he wasn't the prince of *her* tribe, was he? Unlike Tathas, the officer was an easy conquest. His inner mind recognized the nature of the assault being launched and collapsed in terror, leaving her in near-total control of his flesh. Thank Hasha, finally, a Braxin who responded to psychic assault like he was supposed to!

"Come on!" Tathas yelled.

She sent a last spearhead of thought into the officer's brain, trying to freeze up his muscles long enough to keep him in position, blocking the line of fire. She hoped. The power was still new to her and she hadn't had much practice using it in combat. The officer began staggering like a drunk whose left foot had been nailed on the floor; evidently one half of his brain was more resilient than the other. As it was he made a perfect shield for both of them, and she came about toward the air lock prepared to join Tathas in whatever combat was necessary there.

As she turned she saw the free inspector drawing a weapon, apparently willing to shoot his own comrade if that was what it took to bring Tathas down. What a price someone must have been offered for the Kesserit's head! Her mind still dazed from the herculean effort of controlling the officer, she settled for a more primitive weapon this time . . . her knee. Driving it high, with all the power of her body behind it, she rammed it into that part of the man's anatomy that Braxins were proudest of. Not just her strength, but all the weight of womankind was behind her, and she felt her knee hit hard enough to crack against the pelvic bone behind his softer flesh. The man doubled over and began to vomit so swiftly she barely had time to get out of the way, and she spared only a nanosecond to savor the sight before darting through the air lock and into the narrow confines of the ship.

She'd thought at first that Tathas would drag the captive inspector inside as a hostage, but when she saw him empty-handed realized at once there was no point in that; an underling who got in the way would simply have been sacrificed by his fellows. Braxin honor. The sweat of exertion began to stream from her brow as Tathas quickly closed the outer lock, then the inner, sealing them both so that no outside security codes would unlock them. The Community had prepared for at least that much trouble before they'd left the homeworld, she knew that, and the ship's solid armor was infinitely stronger than it looked. Which would buy them all of . . . oh, maybe two minutes.

She dashed into the control room, prepared to separate the ship from its berth, so that they could make a run for it.

"NO!" Tathas cried.

Startled, she fell back. He pushed her out of the way and made sure the controls hadn't been touched. "They were in here. They'll have entrapped the ship, somehow. Probably linked to the systems that would let us take flight."

She felt her heart chill. "Then what do we do?"

"Figure out what they did and undo it," he muttered. "Very, very fast." He sat down in the main pilot's seat and began to feed instructions to the ship's computer. She didn't understand half the codes, but watched in silence as some kind of security array splayed itself across the status screen. "It has to be something simple, they couldn't have had time for anything more . . ." The waves of tension rolling forth from him were like a riptide; it was hard in her current dazed state not to get lost in them.

A noise sounded from the vicinity of the air lock. Something mechanical. "They'll try to break in," he said. "And I can't raise the protective field to stop them, until I know that system's safe." A bead of sweat broke out on his pale brow, matting the dark hair to his forehead as it began to trickle down to his neck. "Bless them! Where is it—"

A horrible shriek rent the air then: metal against metal. The whole ship shook. She didn't need to read his mind to know that there wasn't much time left. Even if he figured out what the inspectors had done to the ship, the force fields wouldn't come on and the ship wouldn't move once the air lock had been breached.

Heart pounding, she turned and was preparing herself to take control of whoever broke into the ship, when he reached out suddenly and pushed her into a corner. "There! Stay there! Out of sight!" he ordered.

Out of sight of what—?

He stood in the center of the chamber then, and ordered the communications system to attend him. How strong he looked in that moment, how confident! Not desperate at all, but like some wild, barbaric creature that drew its strength from battle-frenzy.

"Central Computer!" he said sharply. "Augmented signal, emergency priority. This is Tathas, son of Zheret. Returning from the Wilding with object of great value to the Braxaná, *priceless* to the Pri'tiera. Requesting communication access to the Pri'tiera, direct, immediate. I am currently under assault in the K'solo system, object will be destroyed if assault is successful."

There was silence then. Rho blinked as she tried to understand.

"That was all?" she asked. "Toward what end?"

"The System will decide," he said tightly. "Even now it's collecting data on our current situation, the legal history of my Wilding, the Pri'tiera's past priorities in such affairs . . . all the details that could possibly impact its analysis of my message . . . it will decide how quickly my message goes through to the Pri'tiera, and whether there's an intermediary involved." Something impacted against the hull; the whole ship shivered. "If it's the latter, I don't think we're going to make it. Then of course there is the issue of whether the Pri'tiera will respect the message, or not want his day interrupted by a *commoner*." She could briefly taste the wave of hatred that accompanied the word, but it was drowned out an instant later in the torrent of raw hostility coming at them from outside the ship.

The screen remained dark.

The vibration on the hull continued. The screeching of metal against metal echoed through the narrow corridors. The small ship's flooring shook beneath Rho's feet. Briefly she wondered if the invaders would bother to try to take her captive, and if so, whether death was not a preferable alternative.

Then—suddenly—all was silent.

A moment later, the screen lit up again. It was perhaps the longest moment in Rho's life.

The display was not a full one, but tight-focused; some kind of portable communicator rather than a console. It showed a man's head and little else. A man's? No, a boy's. The face was surreal, sculpted in planes of gleaming white, like polished stone rather than flesh. Its beauty was surreal as well, the kind of beauty possessed by great works of art rather than living creatures. Black hair curled about the whitened face in perfectly formed crescents, evenly spaced, that mirrored the obsidian blackness of his eyes. Every feature was perfect in its size and placement, the arch of the fine jet brows sweeping into an aquiline nose of perfect proportion, above lips that, if they had been a fraction thinner or fuller or wider or more pursed, would have detracted from the perfection of the whole. Yet despite all the paint and powder which had been applied to it, despite the surreal inhumanity of its visage, it was a boy's face only, and not a man's. No paint could disguise that truth.

"I would say that this had better be worth my time, or you will die for it." The voice of the Pri'tiera, like his countenance, betrayed his youth, but the timbre of absolute authority was clear in it nonetheless. "However, the System assures me you are about to die anyway, so I will refrain from stating the obvious."

"My Wilding is completed." Tathas' voice was strong, self-assured, but Rho could sense the tension inside him, like a wild animal's hackles rising at the scent of a rival. "Braxaná law guarantees my right to return."

"It guarantees your right to try, and that the Holding won't officially hunt you down for it. Nothing more. If you've made personal enemies, they are not our business." A black-gloved hand dismissed the subject with a short motion. "Is that all, Tathas? I didn't interrupt my day for a philosophical debate."

Tathas reached into his tunic, then, and pulled forth a small object.

Rho gasped—then quickly covered her mouth, hoping the sound had not been heard.

It was a stasis vial, of the type used to preserve small tissue samples. But not merely a vial from a lab, no. The remnants of a golden filigree frame still clung to its frosted surface, evoking memories of its regal owner. Rho had gazed upon that vial during many formal occasions, fixing it in her mind as the focus of her heritage, her history, her hopes. Now it had been set into an open container made of cruder stuff, with some kind of mechanism on the top. Tathas held it up where the Pri'tiera could see it clearly, depressed the button that was on top of the mechanism . . . and held it down.

"You know what this is?"

"I assume from your dramatic posturing, a dead man's switch. You are most theatrical, Kesserit, but I grow bored, which is dangerous for you. Why should I care if you live or die? You have—" he glanced off-screen to consult a chrono "—two hundredths to make your case strong enough to interest me."

"In this vial," Tathas said quietly, "is the genetic material your family has sought for generations."

You can't have that, Rho screamed silently. *You can't!*

"DNA samples from a direct descendant of Harkur the Great," Tathas continued. "Preserved with meticulous care from the moment of her death." He turned the vial so that its frosted surface caught the light. "This is all there is, Great One. One precious sample, from which a new generation might be born. Your blood and his, commingled. Has that not been the dream of your line, since the time of Zatar the Magnificent? I can make it happen . . . assuming I live to get it to you. If I am killed before I can do that. . . ." He glanced meaningfully at the hand that held the button depressed. "Then it will be lost."

It took every ounce of self-control Rho could muster for her not to throw herself at Tathas at that moment. Was it truly fitted with a dead man's switch that would destroy the sample if he released it? Good, then her work would be easy. And if the damn thing blew up and killed them both, that was a price worth paying.

The substance of our Founder will not be fouled by your race! she swore.

But his hand warned her back, almost as if he knew what she was thinking. Trembling with frustration, she remained crouched out of sight. *I can kill you from here,* she thought. *I don't need to touch you. Remember that.*

"You're a long way from the Central System," the Pri'tiera said. "Do you propose to remain awake for the entire journey?"

"That's my problem, not yours."

"And you want from me—"

"Safe passage to the Central System. As is my right." He nodded toward the part of the ship where the noises of assault had been the loudest. "You can start by calling off your dogs on K'solo."

"They're not my dogs, Kesserit."

"Their master answers to you. Or his master. This is your Holding, yes?" Rho could hear the scorn rising in his voice. "All men within it answer to you. At least . . . that's what common Braxins are taught. Do correct me if it's wrong."

Despite the boy's control over the impassive mask that was his face, she could see the shadow of anger come into his eyes. "K'solo will not harm you," he said stiffly. "The rest I cannot guarantee."

"Not good enough, Pri'tiera. Not if you want me home safely. Whoever tried to get me here will surely try again at our next stop . . . and like you said, it's a long journey home." He held the vial up to eye level. "An escort. Full protection. For the sake of your prize."

There was a long silence then. Waves of authority and dominance battered at the gates of her mind, more powerful than anything she had imagined the Braxin capable of. If his emanations were this strong, what must the Pri'tiera's be like? For the first time since she had agreed to undertake this mission, she wondered if she would be strong enough to defeat him.

"Very well," the boy said at last. "I will have you joined in orbit about K'solo. My people will lead you home—directly home, of course."

Triumph resonated in Tathas' brain. Triumph, and an almost sexual elation that the duel of words had ended in this victory. "Thank you, Pri'tiera. I am humbly grateful for your assistance." His bow of humility contained only the faintest shadow of mockery . . . but the screen went dark so fast it was probable the Pri'tiera never saw it.

"Tathas—"

He waved her to silence and checked the console. Only when he had confirmed that the communications channel was indeed fully closed did he nod that she could speak.

And he removed his finger from the button.

"You didn't—it wasn't—"

His smile was fierce. "Of course not."

"And the DNA—"

"Is Anzha lyu Mitethe's. Of course." His tone was dry. "Would I lie to the Braxaná?"

He put the vial down on the console, close enough that she could have reached it if she tried.

"Our safe passage is assured, anyway. Not the way I wanted to come home, but at least it's direct."

The console flashed a signal; incoming data. He read the brief message and a smile of dark satisfaction flickered across his face. "They altered the force field array. Good choice. No ship can launch without it. Good thing they got to the air lock before we could try to bring up the 'fields; we'd have blown the ship sky high if we'd tried."

Sky high. What a strange, planetbound phrase that was. Strange as all the other things about this man, alien and incomprehensible. She watched him for a while to see if he needed help, but apparently he didn't. After a few minutes the air lock released them, and he eased the tiny ship out into space once more. The Void, Braxins called it. As if nothing was out there. She remained awake for the half-tenth it took for the Pri'tiera's escort vessels to rendezvous with them, and then, when she finally saw Tathas relax, when she knew from his mental emanations that the worst was over, she slid down to the floor where she'd been standing and . . . maybe slept, maybe just stared into space . . . drifted away, at any rate, into places where Braxin thoughts didn't assault the mind and death-squads weren't waiting around every corner.

~*Shaka-Rho?*

  ~*Yes, I hear you.*

  ~*Is all well?*

  ~*(Hesitation) Yes, all is . . . well. We have escort to Braxi now, I doubt there will be trouble. Until we get there.*

  ~*This is our last transmission to you, Shaka-Rho. (Regret) You're inside his borders now, and we don't know the limits of his power. If we call out to you when you are closer than this, he might sense it and be warned.*

~*Yes. I understand.*

~*(Query/concern)*

~*(Determination/certainty)*

~*You are sure?*

~*I am sure.*

~*Our hopes lie with you now, Shaka-Rho. All the Founder's people pray for your success.*

The gods do not care what we do, Tathas had told her. *It is only man who cares, and man who carves his own fate from the stuff of destiny.*

~*I will not fail you,* she mind-whispered.

~*Hasha be with you, then.*

She remembered the vial. It still lay on the console. Hasha's own essence manifest in the blood of the Founder, or simple Braxin deception? It didn't matter. Odd though it was to discover the fact, she trusted Tathas. He didn't want the Pri'tiera to get hold of that DNA any more than she did.

Trust in his hatred, if not in his spirit, the Lyu had told her.

His spirit was strong. Like wine in her veins, when she had tasted it. The essence still lingered on her lips.

"Hasha be with you as well," she whispered.

Until one has known the hunger for a true equal, one has not known desire.

—Zatar the Magnificent

TWENTY-EIGHT

LONG BEFORE THEY reached the Central System, Rho could feel the Pri'tiera.

Even in the Community he would have stood out, by virtue not only of his raw power but his sheer emotional intensity. Here, in the telepathic silence of the Holding, his thoughts were like screams in the night. They came suddenly, without warning, thunderbolts of hunger and despair and longing that lanced into her brain with enough force to leave her reeling . . . and then they were just as quickly gone again, as the Pri'tiera's mind turned to other things. She couldn't even tell if he was aware of them or not, or whether he had any kind of control over what he was broadcasting. She suspected not. There was a terrible hollowness to all his sendings, a desolation that bore witness to countless nights spent alone, countless cries gone unanswered, a nameless and terrible misery.

They hadn't known the nature of his power, back in the Community. They had only known that his bloodline had been Awakened to express its latent talent two centuries ago, and that every Pri'tiera since then had showed signs of psychic awareness. But no one had been able to get close enough to experience the power directly, or to subject it to any kind of professional analysis. All they knew was that, like his ancestors, he hid the power from his people for fear of his life, isolating himself in the orbiting station which Zatar the Magnificent had built for that purpose.

What they hadn't known back in the Community was how very young he was. The power must have come to him only recently, Rho realized. That would make him dangerously unstable, on top of everything else. And of course, being Braxaná, he had probably repressed any overt sign of his power, perhaps even his own acknowledgement of it . . . which would only make things worse.

She took the mind-numbing drug to sleep, but only then. No matter how bad her waking hours were, she knew that she had to use them to accustom herself to his mental signature before she came into his presence or she would be lost when they met. Her sleep was filled with nightmares about actually touching the man, feeling his power flow through that natural conduit, directly into her brain with an intensity no Discipline could block. Yes, she was Shaka, and had the means to kill him . . . but she was also a Receptive, designed by Nature to absorb the thoughts of others, and no trick of training was going to hold so powerful a mind at bay. Everything she was sensing now at a distance would soon be pouring into her soul—a tidal wave of raw, unfettered emotion—daring her to make her attempt to kill him even while she drowned in the sea of his despair.

She tried not to let Tathas see that she was afraid. He was risking his life to bring her to her target—sacrificing it, most likely—and he had to believe that success was certain, or he might lose his courage. Or so she told herself. It could also have been that the thought of appearing weak in front of him was abhorrent to her, and that she would rather bite her tongue till it bled to keep herself distracted than reveal, for one moment, just how uneasy she was.

He sensed it, though. Or maybe smelled it, like an animal smelled things. For all that his mind was dead to psychic talent, he had an uncanny ability to read people.

"You need to relax," he said.

"I am relaxed," she said tightly.

She was at the pilot's console, checking on the latest starmap. Already B'Salos, the star of the Braxin system, was noticeably brighter than most of the celestial bodies surrounding it.

"I don't think so," he said. And then: "There are ways to help that, you know."

It took her a moment to realize what he meant; when she did she turned on him, speechless for the moment in pure indignation. When at last she found her voice again she sputtered, "how dare you even *suggest—*"

He waved her protest short with a gesture that seemed more bemused than angry. "Please. It's not my fault your people have forgotten what sex is all about, or so linked it to softer emotions in their mind that they have forgotten it has other uses. Lust is rooted in the same part of the brain that generates fear, hostility, hunger . . . these things bleed one into the other, when synapses so close to one another are stimulated . . . where is 'love'? Another biological realm altogether."

He checked one of the small displays—a positional analysis of the B'Saloan system—and then turned to her again. His tone was more curious than challenging, which was the only reason she didn't storm out in rage as he continued. "Have you truly never hated a man, and used him for your pleasure? Have you never known what it was to drive an enemy to the point where he lost control over his own responses, and was helpless in your embrace? Do you truly not understand how those things intensify passion, far more than the gentler emotions ever can?"

She remembered the Braxin who had raped her, half a lifetime ago. Did Tathas understand how deeply and personally she hated the race that had produced him? That if he had tried the same thing that day on the ship, instead of just imagining it loudly, she'd have had his private parts on the wall as a trophy?

"If you're telling me to go screw my enemies, no thank you."

His eyes narrowed slightly. "I'm telling you that you are wound tighter than an atomic coil right now, and any Braxin worth his blood will be able to sense it. Telepathy or no. Is that really how you want to show up at the H'karet?"

"And of course you would be happy to help," she said between gritted teeth. "For my sake."

A faint smile flickered across his lips. "My mission depends upon your state of mind, does it not?"

No, she didn't storm out in rage—because he meant well, damn him—but she stormed out nonetheless. And he was right; that was the part that really burned her. She couldn't go to the Pri'tiera like this; he'd sense in an instant that something was wrong.

So that night she took a pillow and she found a marker and drew a face on the pillow that looked remarkably like Tathas, and she beat it and beat it and beat it until it lay in fragments and she, exhausted, fell to sleep in their midst.

There. That was *much* better.

"They are here, Great One."

They. Not just the Kesserit upstart, but a woman as well. The Pri'tiera had seen her on the security screen while his men searched

the two of them for weapons, explosives, even hidden implants . . .
any manner of thing that might be used to harm the Braxin leader.
There was nothing, of course. Even Tathas, in all his arrogance, wasn't
foolish enough to imagine he could sneak a weapon past the Pri'tiera's
skilled staff so easily.

She was lean and lithe and moved with the grace of one whose
mind and body were a perfectly integrated unit. She was dressed in a
gown of claret-colored velvet that clung to her body suggestively when
she moved, hinting at a sensual nature within that athletic shell. Her
hair was oddly cut in a style that hinted at alien worlds, a strange
fringe of spikes that framed her face like a halo. Her golden eyes were
framed by sweeping alien brows; he had seen that once when she
turned toward the hidden camera. The whole of her was not displeas-
ing, though truth be told she lacked any of the elements he would normally have associated with feminine beauty. Yet even that had its own
appeal. In the stifling confines of this intolerable seclusion anything
that tasted of the exotic was bound to raise his interest, and she was
certainly that.

He didn't recognize what race she was from, which was even more
intriguing, as it spoke of origins beyond the Holding. But that only
made sense. Was that not where the Kesserit had gone, in his search
for suitable breeding material?

*If she is what K'teva promised me . . . if this Tathas has done what she said
he would do . . .*

He didn't dare finish the thought.

The guards flanked the man closely as they entered the Pri'tiera's
chamber, warily, as if they were leading a mad dog. The Kesserit was
of little interest to the Pri'tiera, save as one who might or might not
deliver valued goods; his men would keep him at a safe distance until
that operation was concluded and then lead him away. But the
woman . . . ah, that was a different matter. He thought as he looked
her over that she stiffened a bit, very subtly, in the manner of someone who didn't want their reaction to be noticed. Fear, defiance, or
something else? Normally he could read both men and women with
no effort—little wonder, given the family curse—but she had depths
he could not access so easily. Intriguing.

There were few enough real mysteries in his life that he valued a
new one.

Tathas began to step forward, as if to hand him something, but the
guards stopped him before his foot had hit the ground. They knew the

details of his arrest well enough to understand that he could be deadly even in unarmed combat, and weren't going to take any chances on his getting within arm's reach of the Pri'tiera.

"You may give what you have to my guard."

There was hesitation in the man's eyes, but nowhere else. That was good. It was rare among common Braxins you saw such self-control. No doubt that was part of the reason the Kaim'eri wanted him dead so badly.

You didn't know that, did you? That it was one of my Kaim'eri who was hunting you down on K'solo. I don't know which one yet but I will, soon.

The vial Tathas handed over to the guard was small, the kind of portable stasis container that might be used in a laboratory. The Pri'tiera received it wordlessly and turned it over in his black-gloved hand, noting with some curiosity the fine filigree casing at the top and bottom. As if the thing had been set in jewelry at one point. An odd adornment.

He looked up at Tathas. "Tell me what it is, now, in words no man may mistake. —And be aware I shall hold you to every one of them, Kesserit, and if you lie to me, I shall make you wish that death had claimed you on K'solo."

Tathas didn't blink an eye. "Within that vial is a sample of DNA taken from the Azean Starcommander Anzha lyu Mitethe during her lifetime. Who was, as you know, purported to be a descendant of Harkur the Great, of the Hirinari." He stressed the tribal name slightly, perhaps to emphasize that Braxi's greatest ruler had not been of the Pri'tiera's tribe. "I believe your family has sought this for some time."

A lifetime of veiling his feelings in front of others made it possible for him to mask his reaction . . . but just barely. *Don't be so sure it is what he says,* he warned himself. *Have it tested. Remember that he has no reason to serve you, and every reason to want you dead.*

He focused on the vial again, so this Tathas might read nothing in his eyes. He forced his tone to be casual, even disdainful, as if the priceless treasure Tathas had just described was of little consequence. "And so you purport to give me this to satisfy your Wilding, do you? It's customary to bring a live woman back, not a vial of chemicals."

"And as you see, I've brought that as well."

So. The strange woman was indeed more than a travel accessory. "She is to strengthen the Race?"

"She is for you, Great One." A faint smile flickered about his lips. "What you choose to do with her is your affair."

There was no sign of fear about her, nor the scent of it, but nonetheless he could sense a restlessness in her, like a wild animal trapped in too small a cage. She'd be dangerous under the right circumstances, he thought; that made her all the more interesting.

"And what about her gives her such value that you think it will satisfy your Wilding?"

"That," Tathas said quietly, "I think is best explained by her."

His fingers wrapped tightly about the precious vial (*more precious than you know, Kesserit, but I won't give you the satisfaction of seeing that!*), he nodded toward the woman. "Tell me."

She drew in a deep breath before speaking, as commoners often did when they didn't understand how much emotion that revealed. "Begging your leave, Great One, that information is best delivered to you privately."

The Kesserit looked startled. Interesting. Was she not sticking to the script he had prepared? That alone made it worth the game.

The Pri'tiera nodded. "Take him to his ship. Don't let him leave yet." To Tathas he said, "If your gift is acceptable, you'll be allowed to leave this station alive. Not otherwise. Understood?"

"Yes, Great One." It clearly wasn't the way the man had wanted this scene to end, but what else could he do? The kind of personal escort which the Pri'tiera had sent to him at K'solo didn't come cheap. Let him pay it off in worrying about whether the girl would stick to her script when he was gone . . . and what might come of it if she didn't.

This scene was getting more interesting by the minute.

He took a moment, while Tathas was being led out, to study the stasis vial in his hand. Could it truly be what Tathas claimed, the DNA of his bloodline's infamous nemesis? The one who had unleashed the powers in them that slowly drove them mad, until one by one they could no longer stand living in this world? If so, then he had managed something his prouder and older progenitors had never even dreamed possible. For all their power, for all their decades of experience in Braxaná politicking, the other Pri'tieri had never even dreamed of something like this.

A rush of elation filled his veins to bursting. This was *his* moment, *his* triumph, and it would be *his* mark that was left on the world when blood of the Pri'tiera's line mingled with that maverick Azean bloodline . . . and with the blood of the greatest Braxin leader of all. It was *his* name that would be remembered in the history books as the one that had made it happen. The thought was like wine rushing straight to his head, or the moment of ecstatic release inside a woman.

Ah, the woman. Yes.

"You may speak now."

She looked pointedly at the remaining guards and said nothing.

"You expect me to send them away as well?"

Her voice was a whisper. "Some things aren't meant for lesser ears, Great One."

It was an audacious request and he was about to respond to it as it deserved, when a whisper of awareness flitted across his mind. A sense of Otherness so strong that for a moment he could say nothing at all, to her or to the guards. It was something he had never sensed in another human being before, and so it was reasonable that it took him a few seconds to identify it. When he did it shook him to his very core, and it took all the strength and self-discipline he had not to let his reaction show.

The curse.

She had it too.

"Go," he whispered. Not even looking at the guards as they left . . . only at her.

When they were gone, when the portal was sealed securely behind them—when he had made sure that all surveillance systems in the room were in the *off* mode—he said quietly, "You're a psychic."

Her eyes didn't leave his as she nodded. "That, and a messenger of psychics."

A thrill of fear coursed through his body. It was a purely instinctive response, natural to a people raised to fear psychic invasion of the mind more than any other form of assault. But there was also hunger, and yearning, and whispers of emotions that no Braxaná would ever acknowledge. That those emotions had no names in his language didn't blunt the edge of their power.

"Does Tathas know?"

She shook her head slowly, side to side.

"Does anyone?"

"Only those who sent me."

"And they are who?" he demanded.

"Ones like yourself, who haven't been locked away in a sterile satellite since their childhood. Ones like yourself who weren't raised to fear their own potential. Ones like yourself who have learned how to channel the power properly, how to discipline it to their need . . . and how to silence it, when silence is required." She paused. "You are not alone any longer, Pri'tiera."

His heart was pounding, but he forced his voice to be steady—even cold—as he told her, "You assume much."

"We've heard your voice on the night winds, Pri'tiera. We've felt the touch of your mind, in those places where such things are named. But none were strong enough to answer your call directly, and we didn't have the means to send someone to you safely . . . until now."

"Tathas."

"Yes."

"And does he know all this?"

She smiled, ever so slightly. "It's easy to manipulate a man when you can sense what he desires most. Is it not, Pri'tiera?"

He didn't answer her question. To do so would be to step off a cliff, into an abyss so dark and so bottomless that a man might never stop falling.

But the thought of a woman to whom he might speak of the things no outsider could know . . . that was a heady drug indeed.

"Why have you come?" he demanded.

She cocked her head and studied him for a minute in silence. Was she reading his thoughts even now? The concept was unnerving, but also . . . strangely arousing.

"Your line is strong," she told him. "So very strong. In all our centuries of searching, we've never seen its like. Four generations breeding true to the power, against all odds, and with no genetic manipulation to help it along. Four generations strong enough in their minds to reach out across the vast wastelands of open space in search of community . . . and to be heard. Yet none of the others were as strong as you, Pri'tiera. None have cried out to the stars with your strength, or your need.

"Braxi has given you a rare and precious gift. But it can't give you the one thing you need to enjoy it. Knowledge. Knowledge of how to refine your senses so they serve you best. Knowledge of how to close yourself off from others when you wish to. . . ."

She let the words trail off suggestively. Did she understand what such a gift would mean to him? Not a normal life, perhaps, but something as close to "normal" as a Pri'tiera's life might ever be. Certainly a life away from this prison, where walls of steel and synthetic and the vacuum of space provided physical barriers to take the place of the mental ones he didn't know how to erect.

To touch a woman . . . to be able to touch a woman . . . without one's touch driving her mad . . . he had dreamed of it, yes, and dreamed of a teacher who would make it possible, but he had never truly expected to find one. Much less to have one delivered to him, ready and willing to teach.

It took effort to keep his voice steady as he asked her, "And in return for these services? Something of equal value would be expected, no doubt. You didn't make this trip just for my benefit."

"Not for your benefit at all, Great One." Her golden eyes gleamed. "Rather . . . fair barter. You want knowledge, and new strength for your bloodline. We want knowledge also. And so I have been sent. To teach you what you wish to learn, to bear you children for your Race if you desire . . . and when that is done, and your eldership assured, to take the daughters of our union—which will be mine by Braxaná custom, yes?—back home with me. From them we can learn what *we* need to know . . . and give them a life where they are free to revel in their gift, rather than living in constant dread of discovery."

"And Tathas?" he asked. "What of him?"

She shrugged. "He's served his purpose. It means nothing to me whether he lives or dies." She looked deep into his eyes, then, and he could feel the psychic heat rise between them, mind touching mind with every word. "I made this journey for you, Pri'tiera."

The portal chimed.

For a moment he didn't move. Then he half-turned to the door, his eyes still on her, and said, "What?"

SARAS HAS THE REPORTS YOU REQUESTED.

For a moment he shut his eyes. It took a second for him to switch mental gears enough to remember what report the portal was talking about . . . and to acknowledge that it was something that really did require his attention.

When he looked at the woman again she had unhinged the heavy bracelet on her wrist and was removing it. Tathas' token, no doubt. Her eyes never left his as she did it, nor as she let the bracelet drop to the floor, a meaningless bangle now. She was his.

He wanted to touch her. He wanted to feel with his senses what she had told him in words, that she was a consort fit for his curse, not just another sacrifice. He wanted to feel what it was like to let the power loose, to allow it carry him away, without dreading the moment that the other soul it was pouring into would become overwhelmed by the experience and would shatter like glass in his hands.

SARAS IS WAITING, the portal reminded him.

He was Pri'tiera. Duty came first.

"I am sorry." He said it formally, but he also allowed genuine regret to color his voice. She deserved that much. "Business I must deal with." He walked to the portal; it parted to receive him. Outside there were two guards waiting, too professional to look as curious as they undoubtedly felt. "My men will show you to quarters. I will come to you when I can. We can speak then . . . more privately."

"And our barter?" she asked.

He turned to her, and drank in the sight of her—the promise of her—and let her see that he was pleased with what he saw, on all the levels that she might observe. Did she know enough of Braxaná ways to understand what a rare offering that was?

"If you know enough to offer such a bargain," he said, "then you already know my answer."

Above all else, the Hasai told her, *you must seduce him. You must uncover his fears, his dreams, his desires, and weave a web about him so resonant with his nature that he does not think to question its existence.*

We cannot tell you what those things are. We can only tell you that by the time you are close enough to guess at them, you will be close enough also for him to sense your intentions.

Choose your moment carefully, Shaka-Rho, for once it is chosen, there will be no turning back.

It was over a tenth before he could return to the woman. That was good, though. It would give her time to prepare for him, and to settle herself into her new role as his consort. Besides, after her long journey with the Kesserit, he suspected she would welcome a few moments of solitude.

Or am I just afraid of going to her, of being tested? he wondered.

It was indeed a disquieting thought, that the Pri'tiera whose presence could bring men to their knees might find himself matched by a woman. It had never been an issue with Braxin women, of course; with them it was more a question of how much of his power they could tolerate before their minds snapped utterly. The few who survived him often took their own lives soon after; it had happened frequently enough that he had taken to making sure each new consort had convenient means to do the job. The thought of a woman who not only could survive his intimacy, but who might return for a second helping, was nearly beyond his comprehension.

Yet. Here she was.

There was no denying the heat he felt, contemplating her potential. He tried to focus his mind upon all the things that he'd gain from her teaching—upon all the advantages it would give him in the arena of Braxaná politics—but in fact that was all secondary to the simple primal hunger she had awakened. The family curse had forced him into an isolation almost beyond bearing, and the thought of enduring it for a lifetime was sometimes more than he could handle. Now—at least for a short while—he would not be alone.

Loneliness is a weakness, he told himself. *Need is a weakness. Wanting that which you do not possess, enough to forget who and what you are, is the greatest weakness of all.*

He'd had her taken to the observation deck. He could sense her there now as plainly as if he were gazing upon her in person. She was pacing the chamber beneath a vaulting force field, with the glory of Braxi blazing in the sunlight overhead. As he gazed at her in his mind's eye he realized that he had never in all his years wanted a woman so much . . . or feared taking one so much.

Fear is a valid emotion only so much as it cautions us to be wary, his great-grandfather had once written. *When it stands in the way of our ambition, then we must learn to master it.*

His hands were shaking by the time he reached the portal of the observation deck. He took time outside it to steady himself . . . while wondering if the attempt had any meaning in this context.

Surely a trained psychic could pluck his emotions right out of his mind, regardless of whether or not he displayed them openly.

You don't know the extent of her power yet. You don't know what she's capable of. Make no assumptions and you won't make any errors.

With a last deep breath to steady himself he commanded the portal to open.

She was standing in the center of the room, waiting for him. Sunlight reflected from the planet overhead turned her spiked fringe of hair into a halo, and the claret velvet of her gown shimmered as she shifted her weight slightly. He could sense no emotions in her, none at all, only utter stillness. It was so different from anything he had ever sensed in another person that he knew it at once for the product of her training, a skilled and deliberate veil she had placed between them.

Can you sense my hunger? he wondered. *Or does that same trick which guards your thoughts from being known make it hard for you to hear the thoughts of others?*

He stepped into the room and heard the portal close behind him. "You haven't told me your name yet."

"Rho," she said quietly.

"Rho." He spoke the name slowly, tasting it with his tongue. "You know that men can't lie to me, Rho. I know it when they do."

She nodded.

"If you haven't come here for the reasons you say, I'll know that."

"I know," she whispered.

A fleeting wisp of emotion escaped from her then, but it was gone too quickly for him to identify. So his guess had been correct, then; she wasn't calm in truth, simply controlling how much of her emotional state she would allow him to observe. What an amazing concept! If he could only learn such a skill, there would be no limit to what he could do.

To walk freely among my people . . . to live a normal life . . .

He pushed the thought to the back of his mind. It was an unacceptable weakness to dwell upon such things in the presence of one who could probably read his thoughts. He needed to put her on the defensive and keep her there, at least for the moment, lest she mistake the nature of their relationship.

"Are you afraid of me, Rho?"

It seemed to him she hesitated for an instant. Good. That meant he was treading on ground she wasn't prepared for. Finally she said, very carefully, "Our power is like fire, Great One. Tame it to your purpose and it is a wellspring from which great strength may be drawn. Let it run wild and it can destroy whole worlds."

"And mine is a wildfire."

She didn't answer him.

He took a step closer to her, well within what should have been her personal space. She didn't back away. "And you're here to help me tame it."

"If that's what you want," she whispered.

He reached up a hand to touch her face. She didn't draw away, but something dark flared within her as he made contact. Perhaps even . . . hostile? If so, that would be no surprise. His people had hunted psychics for over a thousand generations, and the power was a death warrant by order of his own government. If he'd sensed anything remotely like warmth or affection in her he'd have known her for a fake.

The fact that she might fear him, and perhaps even secretly hate him, only added flavor to their bargain.

Smoothly, deliberately, he withdrew his hand from her and began to open his glove. His eyes never left her as he split open the seams that would allow him to remove it. To his surprise she reached out to him, took his gloved hand in her own, and began to ease the tight leather off it. Carefully, oh so carefully, her fingers never actually touching his flesh, but so very close to doing so. He found himself holding his breath as she removed first one glove, then the other, then smoothed them out and set them carefully aside. Every motion slow, sensual, enticing. Did she know enough of Braxaná ways to understand what such a gesture meant to him, or was she inside his brain even now, drawing that knowledge from him directly? Could she feel the movement of air across his palms as he did, was she aware of how acutely sensitive human flesh was when it was first released from a day's bondage?

The thought of her being in his mind should have unnerved him, but it did just the opposite. An urgent heat was building in his flesh, more intense than anything he had felt with a woman before. He reached out to caress her face again, this time with a naked hand, to close that circuit of body and mind which was the very focus of all his suffering and hunger—

—and she reached out first and took his hand in both of hers, and touched her lips to the center of his palm—

—and the boundaries of his world gave way, sensation pouring into his brain in a cascade almost too intense to bear. For a moment it was all he could do not to lose himself in its fearsome current, and drown in it utterly. Images swirled through his mind that were wholly unfamiliar, emotions that had no source in his own consciousness. Pleasure and pain coursed through his body, that had no source in his own flesh. Was this what women had felt when they first touched him, when physical contact brought his mental barriers crashing down and the curse poured his thoughts directly into their brains? If so, he could understand why their minds collapsed.

Overhead he could feel the mass of Braxi, not measured in earth and sea and air any more but in the press of human minds against his own. Millions of men and woman hungering, fearing, despairing, hating, struggling for survival . . . he could taste each one of them as if their thoughts were his own, a maelstrom of emotion. Somewhere in the distance the psychic woman moved her lips against his hand and a thousand caresses echoed it, across the surface of Braxi overhead. Heat stirred in his groin and a thousand men overhead stiffened to pleasures of their own, all pouring into him at once at once, a tsunami of human arousal. Was this how psychics normally saw the world, was that what he was absorbing?

Come, her mind whispered. Words without sound took shape deep within his mind, as if they were of his own making. *I will show you our universe. . . .*

Outward he soared, his mind linked to hers. Past the teeming multitudes of Braxi, past the sullen orb of Aldous, out into the very Void itself. It was no longer empty now, that Void, but filled to bursting with the stuff of human thought. Each planet was a caress upon his mind, even as the heat of her flesh was a caress upon his naked hand: each one unique, each one filled with wonder. A symphony of sensation so rich and complex that he could not single out any individual mind, but drank in the whole of it in awe, even as his mind trembled to contemplate its beauty.

Come, she whispered silently. *Come.* It was a direct command, forbidden to her by Braxaná custom, but such things no longer seemed to matter. Eagerly he followed her invitation, drinking in the richness of her vision, drowning in it.

And yes, there was hatred in her. He could taste it clearly now. And he drank that in as well, like bittersweet liqueur, and he let it wrap itself around him like the moist heat of a woman's flesh, even as his mind sought new and greater mysteries in the heavens. She had come to do her duty despite that hatred and so it was just one more thing to savor, in a universe so filled with wonder that a thousand lifetimes would not suffice to explore it all.

Outward, outward their conjoined minds thrust into the universe, awareness strained to the utmost. Was he truly seeing all this through her eyes, or was he merely sharing her own memories of things she had seen in the past? She offered no explanation . . . and it didn't matter. He had spent his entire lifetime starving for such a thing, and to question its source would do disservice to a priceless gift.

I will show you our Home, she whispered.

A brightness appeared on the mental horizon, so distant that at first he had to strain to make it out—then so blazingly brilliant as his mind finally focused upon it that it left him breathless. This was not a world like any other, filled with the scattered mumblings of discordant minds, but a place so rich in power and purpose that he trembled to approach it. Music arose from its surface, wild and beautiful and more than human senses could contain. Yet it was dark in nature, as the soul of an artist is dark, and tortured, as a man's soul may be tortured by tasting more knowledge than a human mind was meant to contain.

Show me, he begged her, and she did.

A nation of psychics born to the power, raised to the power, reveling in it. Children raised to hunger for their Awakening rather than fearing it—teenagers learning of lust and communion with the same eager touch—dreams shared, fears revealed, desires absorbed—and yet there was no gentleness here, nor anything akin to *moderation.* Violent souls, all of them, they filled the Void surrounding them with the clamor of their hatred, their need, their determination. A nation more powerful than any other, and more tormented, and more *alive.*

It was beautiful beyond imagining.

Home, she whispered; he knew that it was indeed home, in the truest sense . . . a refuge for misfits such as himself, trapped between worlds by their power. Borders didn't matter here, nor governments, nor ancient politics. Only this vision which she had shared with him, which was at the heart of the psychic's reality. A vision which his ancestors, for all their power, had never known. Only *he* had been deemed worthy of receiving it.

You are not alone any longer, she had told him.

He trembled, knowing for the first time, without doubt, that it was true. He dove down into the Homeworld's mental aura, feeling its substance refresh his spirit, washing away the years of terror and isolation and making him, for the first time, *whole* . . .

Then suddenly, the whole of his universe seemed to quake. Darkness appeared about its edges, a flickering blackness that threatened to devour the whole like Braxaná poison. Somewhere in the distance his heart clenched tightly, like a fist, and blood pounded in forgotten veins as it tried to make its way to vital organs. Stunned, he struggled to return his awareness to his body, to see what was wrong—

—and he failed, for he didn't know how to get back. Or perhaps she held him fast, and wouldn't let him leave. Pain lanced through a human chest somewhere in the distance; he had to struggle to remember that it was his chest, to remind himself that if something happened to his body his mind would soon follow. That all these wonders he had seen would be lost to him forever if he died.

He tried to return.

She held him fast. Her hatred whipped about him like stormwinds. *This is my duty, Braxin. Not your pleasure. Your death.*

He struggled, but he was in a universe where the rules for struggling were unknown to him, and his surrender to the woman had given her too much power. Above him, below him—surrounding him—the consciousness of the psychic world was like a vast, dark heartbeat, pounding its triumph even as his own heart spasmed in its death throes. Blackness veiled the universe as his consciousness began to sputter. A thousand stars that were not stars burst into life before his eyes, and a thousand real ones were extinguished. The consciousness of all the worlds that he had passed began to bleed one into the other, as he tried to break free of her death-grip upon his mind and return to his body, to save it—

And an image appeared before him. Ghostly in substance, yet blazing with a light brighter than that of any sun. A golden image, of a woman bedecked in golden ornaments, with hair like flame, like streamers of blood, and a stasis vial nestled between her breasts.

And what will you return to? she asked him. Her voice was like the music of the stars, and it flooded his soul with agonizing beauty. *To a world that hates you? To a people that will never accept what you are? To a lifetime lived in the shadow of what you have seen here, knowing that your true family is out here, among the stars . . . and that you can never be part of it?*

Somewhere in the distance a stranger's heart weakened, and the mental fist that was closing about it tightened its grip. The edges of the woman's halo bled out into the darkness as his sight began to fail him. He tried to struggle, to fight for life, but he couldn't find the strength.

What would he be struggling for?

Come to us now, the goddess whispered. *Leave behind that life which has failed you, which has given you nothing but pain. All the might of your ancestors cannot force you to remain on Braxi, if you choose to do otherwise. Come to us, of your own free will. Be with your family. Join with its spirit, forever.*

And he knew in that moment what he was, and what he had done . . . and that there was no turning back.

And the arms of the goddess Ar closed about him like a lover's, and in the embrace of her darkness there was only peace.

Consciousness returned slowly, reluctantly, painfully. Rho's head felt like it was about to explode. For a moment she couldn't remember where she was, and when she tried to the mere act of thinking sent waves of pain shuddering through her mind and body.

. . . not good . . .

Slowly the memory came back to her. Slowly, cell by cell, her body became aware of its surroundings. Her body registered the weight of the Pri'tiera where he had fallen upon her. His flesh was no longer heated by life, but beginning to cool. How long had she been unconscious?

She tried to move, but the effort to send any kind of command to her flesh was too much to bear. It was as if her mind was an open wound, and any effort to do more than simply lie there and observe worried at the edges and set it bleeding anew.

I'm going to die if I don't get out of here.

She laughed, which turned to coughing, which turned to despair. Of course she was going to die. There wasn't any other end this crazy mission could realistically have had; they knew that when she went in.

I thought I'd go down fighting, at least.

Any minute now the guards would realize that their master had been gone too long and would come looking for him. That would be bad. Alternatively, she told herself, he might have secured such privacy for himself that no one would ever come looking, which was not all that good a scenario right now either.

Voices. She heard voices.

She tried to raise herself up, to push the Pri'tiera's dead weight off her. Pain lanced molten through her brain at the attempt and she fell back, gasping. Evidently her brain had done all it was going to do today, and not even the plea that it just do enough to move her body into some place of hiding was enough to convince it to try again.

Voices closer now. This was not good.

She leaned back and shut her eyes. Maybe they would think she was dead. Maybe they would throw her corpse out of the air lock and then all she would have to deal with was the vacuum of space. Easier than this.

The portal hissed open. Footsteps approached. Dread welled up like a knot in her gut. She flinched, expecting the burn of a stun any second, but none came.

And then she heard Tathas speak, in a whisper. "Alive?"

"She is. He isn't."

She opened one eye, and through a field of hazy vision saw . . . herself. *What the hell—?* The figure leaned over her now, short spiked hair catching the light as the claret velvet gown gaped forward over her breasts.

I'm mad. That's it. My mind has finally snapped and I'm seeing things.

"Rho? Rho? Can you hear me?"

Her sister's voice. Her sister? Zara didn't look like that. She, Rho, looked like that. Didn't Zara know which one of them she was supposed to be?

"Better leave that for the ship," Tathas said.

"Zara?" The sound came out of her like a croak, somewhere between the mating call of a Chandran mist-frog and the death rattle of a Haluvalan sloth. Then someone rolled the Pri'tiera's body off her and she could breathe again, which was better. She tried again. "Zara?"

The mirror image of her nodded.

She was dimly aware of someone—Tathas?—searching the Pri'tiera's body and removing something from it. Weapons? Security chips? Souvenirs? It hurt to think. Zara was smoothing her hair, and she couldn't feel her sister's thoughts like she should be able to. Panic welled up in her gut and she had to swallow with all her strength to keep from vomiting it up.

"It's all right," her twin whispered. "Hard part's over now. Only a short while more. Hang in there."

"How—" she gasped. "I left you in the Outlands . . ."

"She came in cargo," Tathas said, crouching down by her other side. "Slept through the trip so you wouldn't sense her presence."

A tiny connection sparked in her brain. "That's why you wouldn't leave the ship on K'solo . . ."

"See?" Tathas said to Zara. "I told you she'd figure it out." He turned back to her. "Brace yourself, I'm going to have to carry you, and we're going to have to move fast. Getting in was the easy part, thanks to your sister, but if we want to get out alive we have to do it before anyone thinks to check on . . . him."

"Why?" she asked Zara, as his strong arm slid behind her shoulders. "This isn't your war. Why risk your life for this?"

"You didn't really think I was going to let you go off and do something this stupid alone, did you?" The tone of the admonishment was gentle. "Tathas thought having your double along might prove useful, if he had to get through the H'karet without you. Not to mention that if you ran into trouble he'd need my talent to find you."

"I suggest we focus on getting out of here right now," Tathas said, "otherwise this may all be theoretical at best."

He was carrying a sword, she realized. A Zhaor, complete with Braxaná inscriptions along the scabbard. She managed a croaking laugh as he picked her up. Souvenirs, indeed.

"The guards . . . let you pass? Because Zara looked like me?"

He was carrying her toward the portal now. The room swayed as she bounced with his motion.

"The guards were confused for a moment," he told her. "That was all I needed."

"That," Zara said, "and having an ally who could sense when and where guards would be waiting."

"That too," he said. "Speaking of which . . ."

Zara shut her eyes for a moment, concentrating, and then nodded." "All clear."

And the portal slid open.

Sometime later there was a ship. And a fight with guards. Or maybe the guards fought before they got to the ship, and Tathas and Zara hid the bodies so that the station's security wouldn't be alerted. The element of surprise was important, Tathas said. Or maybe it was Zara who said that.

She tried to walk on her own but her one attempt didn't last long. Tathas swept her up again after the fight and carried her over his shoulder like a bag of grain. She couldn't argue with him over it; it left his good hand free.

She trusted him.

"What now?" she whispered, when they were inside the ship.

"We get out of the Holding," Zara told her. "That is, assuming his skill and my . . . talent . . . can get us past security." A dry smile flickered about the corners of her lips. "Not that I'd turn down your help, when you're up to it."

"Tathas is . . . coming?"

"Yes," Tathas said, "Tathas is coming. You don't think I'm going to let the two of you try to run this gauntlet on your own, do you?"

She found his face swimming above her own and tried to focus on his eyes. Green eyes, very beautiful. She had never noticed that before. "You have your own battle," she whispered. "Kesserit on Braxi—"

"Braxi is the last place I want to be when the Pri'tiera's body is discovered." He turned back to the pilot's console and made a few adjustments. Rho could feel the vibration of the engines through her spine as they shifted their settings "I'm afraid Braxin space is not a good place for me to be right now . . . at least until the hunt dies down. Don't worry, though. I'll be back." He looked at her. "In the meantime . . . you are both my property, yes?" He grinned. "A man does have obligations to his property."

She would have hit him for that, if she'd been strong enough. Maybe he knew that. Maybe that was why he chuckled softly as he turned back to the pilot's console, and why Zara smiled gently as she took her sister's hand.

She tried to say something—many things—but the effort was too much.

She slept.

The more complex a game one plays, the more important it is to be sure one understands the rules.

—Zatar the Magnificent

TWENTY-NINE

It TOOK ALL the self-control K'teva had not to pace while she waited. The nervousness inside her demanded outlet, and the fact that she wouldn't even let herself wring her hands, or tap her feet nervously against the cold marble floor, only made the tension harder to bear.

This was it. The end. All that she had worked for, all that she had fought for, lied for, manipulated men for . . . all of it was here in the Citadel, waiting for her.

She was certain they were watching her now, though the means was invisible to her. It couldn't have been otherwise. The proud Braxaná would never welcome someone into their ranks who could not hide her emotions at such a time. It was a final test, for the woman who had passed all others.

She would pass this one as well.

She had no idea what the procedure would be, when the Elders received her. Tezal had said only that she was summoned here to meet them, and had left her to guess at the details. Her spies had already told her that Tathas had returned to the Central System safely, not only with a woman for his Wilding, but with a prize whose value (it was said) was inestimable by Braxaná measure. Twice what she had expected of him. For a moment she felt a twinge of regret at using her former consort the way she had, but that was quickly banished by the thought of what she had gained by doing so. Surely if he knew, she told herself, he would understand.

The ultimate prize.

It was cold in the Citadel. If she'd thought about it she would have anticipated that. The stifling layers of grey and black wool that the Braxaná always wore, the thick black gloves and boots and the collars and cloaks and all the sartorial accoutrements of their rank, all those things begged for a chill environment. On the planet's surface they had an image to maintain, and bore with silent discomfort such bodily discomfort as would leave other races gasping. Here, in the Citadel of the Kaim'erate, where only the purest of the bloodlines might gather, there was no need for such subterfuge. Visitors were few and far between, and not likely to be taking notes on Braxaná weaknesses when they were present.

She had dressed in black and grey, not overtly Braxaná in style, but acceptable to their tradition nonetheless. Walking a thin line between the fact that she was not yet one of them and the fact that she hoped to be soon. Not that her own status would change in any legal sense, of course. But at a time when the Pale Ones were seeking the blood of outsiders to strengthen their failing gene pool, a half-breed woman might earn herself a special place as the mother of a Braxaná . . . if the elders saw fit to grant her that right.

You were my Wilding, Tathas. My proof to them that Kesserit blood—my blood—was worthy of inclusion in their circle. Where was he now, her valiant Viak'im? Returned to Braxi, to take up his life anew and struggle to rebuild the tribe? Or betrayed by the same Pale Ones who had sanctioned his Wilding, and removed from the playing field forever? A pang of regret surfaced briefly in her heart. How strong he had been, how brave, and how ambitious! But in the end the only game that mattered was the one the Braxaná played, and that required a willingness to sacrifice everyone and everything in the name of your goals. Loyalty did not win you points in the Great Game . . . and when your blood was only half Braxaná to start with, every point mattered.

She heard a sound from within the meeting chamber, and tried to still the beating of her heart. It was said the purebred Braxaná had senses so acute that they could smell fear, like an animal could. Probably that was part of the reason they dressed the way they did, so their own biochemical cues would be hidden.

The great doors opened.

It was Tezal.

"K'teva, daughter of Xanat." His tone was utterly formal; she might as well have been a stranger to him. "The Elders bid you come to them now, and receive their judgement."

Elders. The word meant a different thing here, among the Pale Ones, than it had among her own people. Kesserit Elders were those whose accumulated wisdom had made them fitting guardians for the tribe. Braxaná Elders were those who had managed to add four purebred children to their tribe's failing numbers. Even the very nature of their status was a reminder to her of how desperate they must be for out-side blood, strong blood . . . fertile blood.

Mine is the blood of fertile mothers and fierce warriors, she thought. *Take my child into your Race and it will strengthen you, I promise!*

The hall was of stark marble, and the floor echoed to the cadence of her footsteps as she went to the place Tezal indicated, at the focal point of the room. The five semicircular ranks surrounding her provided more seats than there were currently Elders; this room had clearly been built in the Braxaná's heyday, and now, in the dusk of their Race, the empty seats only served to highlight their genetic failure.

K'teva could feel her heart pounding as she took her place before them, with no chair or pulpit or even railing to define her space. Just her in this empty, open arena, and the bleached faces of the Pale Ones like ghosts on every side.

"K'teva, child of Xanat." Tezal's voice was cold and solemn, his speech mode one of formality and distance. A reminder to her, that though they had shared a bed, that meant nothing here. Though K'teva was well versed in the many modes of upper-class speech she knew she was no master of the language—few outsiders were—and she strained to the utmost to catch every subtle shift in language and tone, to decipher every layer of his meaning. "You have come before the Elders of the Braxaná to petition for the right to bear a child of our tribe. Such a right is rarely granted, and only to those whose blood is most worthy. Tell me now, what you have done that you feel you merit such an honor?"

This wasn't right, she thought. Where was the Pri'tiera? He was the one who was supposed to present her petition, not Tezal. The prize she had sent Tathas to fetch was something meant for him, not the rest of the tribe.

Succeed and I will be by your side, he had promised her. *Though not an Elder I am the master of all Elders, and they will respect my word.*

There was no helping it, she realized; she would have to manage alone. "The Pri'tiera set a test for me," she told them. "A Wilding to be played out not in the far reaches of space, but in power invoked from the Mother Planet. I was to manipulate another to serve the Pri'tiera, to seek out a prize of great value to Braxi, and to see that he retrieved it."

"And this you did?" Tezal asked.

The room really was cold; she resisted the impulse to wrap her arms around herself for heat. Maybe that was some kind of test as well, she thought. The Pri'tiera had said she would be tested somehow, but he had not told her the process. "Yes."

"So he brought back the prize you sent him after."

"Yes," she breathed.

Surely that was what her informants had referred to. And if not? Then Tezal was weaving a trap with words, testing her somehow. Did he expect her to show doubt, or fear, or hesitation? No Braxaná ever would. Therefore she would not.

Bring on your tests, she thought defiantly. *I have prepared all my life for this; I will pass them all.*

"And it has been delivered?" he asked.

"So it was reported to me."

Tezal nodded; his expression was unreadable. "It is good to know who planned this." His speech mode was an ancient one, that hinted at ice and pain and death. "It is good to know who claims responsibility."

Wrong, wrong, this was all wrong. Where was the safe path in all of this? His manner gave her no hints.

"The Pri'tiera knows the details—" she began.

"The Pri'tiera," he said in the Mode of Finality, "is dead."

The words crashed down upon her like an avalanche. The floor and ceiling spun, and for one dizzying moment it seemed the whole world had gone mad. Just for a moment, and then all was still again. She managed to catch her breath, somehow. She managed to find her voice. She could not stop herself from shaking.

"Dead?" she whispered.

Tezal nodded. "Your *tool* apparently managed it." His speech was in the Mode of Condemnation, chillingly severe. "So . . . *you* brought him here . . . and set him up . . . and sent him after whatever 'prize' he came to deliver . . . is that what we are to understand?"

There was a speech mode of Death, but he didn't use it. He didn't have to.

"I suggested that he seek genetic material. Harkur the Great's—"

He waved her statement short with a brusque gesture. "Your plans do not matter to us," he said curtly. "What matters is what came of it."

She met his gaze head-on, knowing that even now, in the jaws of death, she dared not appear weak. There was still a slim chance this was all some terrible kind of test . . . that the Pri'tiera still lived, that he wished to see how she would handle this challenge . . . she dared not appear weak. "I promised Tathas would seek out and bring back that prize which the Pri'tiera sought. That much was done, yes? I am not Shem'Ar," she said coldly. "I do not command every action of a man. If he chose the course of a traitor when his quest was done, it was not my doing."

"And we are to believe that this one man, all by himself, managed to plot this thing out in its entirety?" He glanced back at the assembled elders as if to let her know that his words were not for her alone, but for them. "Forgive me if I find that a bit hard to believe, K'teva."

There was no safe path. She said nothing.

"If you were not allied to him, then perhaps others were." He tapped the hilt of his Zhaor suggestively as he paced before her, studying her first from one side and then the other. His eyes, once the eyes of a consort, were so cold that she tried to turn away from his gaze . . . but whichever way she turned, he was there. "Perhaps it is your tribe we should blame, for giving him such backing as this assault required. I'm sure there were many Kesserit who helped him. Yes?" He stopped before her, directly before her, and waited until her eyes met his. "Is it your tribe we should blame for this, K'teva? Should we honor you for the strength of your blood and hunt down the last of the Kesserit, that this band of revolutionaries shall not trouble the Holding again?"

He waited for her answer.

The chamber was silent. So silent that her own breathing roared in her ears, as her mind raced to absorb what he was saying. So silent that she could hear the thudding of her heart as it drove blood through her chilled veins, driving desperate thoughts before it.

A choice. He was giving her a choice. Admit to treachery or . . . what? Condemn her people to be killed in her place?

This is the test, she thought desperately. Maybe the Pri'tiera was really dead. Or maybe he had only withdrawn to watch this drama from some secret place. What was it he wanted to hear? What was it that would prove her worth to these callous Elders, who cared for nothing beyond the struggle to maintain their Race?

Or perhaps it was not a test at all, she realized suddenly, but simply Tezal's attempt to give her a safe way out of this situation. The Kesserit were doomed anyway, if not before now, then certainly now. Could she place the blame upon their shoulders and come out of this safely herself? Was that what he wanted her to do, to save herself, to prove to him that the Braxaná mattered more to her than a mere common tribe? Was this all a test to see if she still owed loyalty to the Kesserit?

So many paths to take, she thought, but in the end, only two destinations. She took a deep breath and looked into Tezal's eyes, trying to read the truth there. Black, black eyes, a pair of twin mirrors in which a woman's soul might be tested. She could not read him. She had never been able to read him. It was a gift of the Braxaná, to close the windows to their soul so that no outsider might steal their secrets.

She could not steal them . . . and he would not offer.

It was their way.

"It may be," she said slowly, "that some members of my tribe were involved in this. As you say . . . it would have been a hard thing for him to manage alone."

He sighed, and he shook his head then, and she knew with a sinking heart she had chosen the wrong road.

"Too bad." He said it quietly, in the Basic Mode: *Your mistake speaks for itself.* "The Braxaná have always respected treachery, when it is well managed. Was not our Creator himself a traitor, who betrayed his own Maker? We are his children, and thus it is in our blood that even when a sword strikes at us, we take the measure of the blade . . . and its wielder."

A gloved hand moved to the handle of his Zhaor, black-clad fingers wrapping around its grip. "I thought your blade was sharper than this, K'teva. What a pity. To take down the most powerful man in the Holding . . . imagine how such a woman might be received! Imagine how she might have been courted by Braxaná bloodlines that needed strengthening!"

The Zhaor slid soundlessly out of its scabbard. She found herself mesmerized by its blade, by the play of the chamber's cold light upon its edge. "Instead, you would have condemned your entire tribe to save yourself." He spoke quietly, but with such personal disgust she could not help but cringe. "Are these the genes we should accept into our Race? Would you have us breed Braxaná who would turn against their own blood, and condemn their own tribe for a moment's gain?"

But. . . . But. . . . She tried to mouth the words but nothing would come out. In that moment she had a terrible inspiration, that Tezal was not only the messenger of this judgement, but its originator as well. Did their time together mean so little to him?

It is what you did to another, her conscience whispered. *Is it not?*

In the silence of the room the sudden sweep of the Zhaor was like an arc of sunlight. When the blade impacted the flesh of her neck it was almost silent, its edge so sharp that muscle and bone parted with but a soft squelching sound. The blow was swift enough that her look of horrified surprise was frozen in place as her neck parted. . . . then it fell. Her head hit the ground first and then her body followed, its lifes-blood pulsing from the neck for a few seconds, then slowing to a trickle, then dying.

He looked down at her severed corpse for a moment and then leaned down by its side, to wipe his blade clean on a fold of her tunic.

"I'm sorry, my dear." He stood, and smoothly sheathed his sword. "But in the end you really didn't understand us at all, did you?"

You ask, what is the price of war?

I answer, what is the price of peace?

—Harkur the Great

THIRTY

THE STATION WAS dark, as befit a structure nestled in the middle of the War Border's vast blackness, without planet or star to mark its location. The humming of its motors was barely perceptible as they came to life and stirred the air a bit, creating a simulacrum of a weak breeze. Monitors flashed arcane signals to no one, measuring oxygen content, carbon dioxide, and the thousand trace gases which war stations might contain. *Acceptable*, the mechanical guardians indicated, then faded back into their eternal half-sleep.

Lights came on in one room, then another, following the man who traversed the seemingly abandoned hallways with a steady step. Black leather boots glistened in the lights of the tiny cleaning robots which swept the floors for dust. Black-gloved hands idly brushed the wall, then stopped at the lock to a conference chamber. A small box was raised to the handplate; its display plate blinked *Override*. After a minute the portal dissolved and the visitor passed inside.

It was a conference chamber like any other in the War Border, vast and circular and divided in two by a long table flanked by static chairs. On the far side stood a figure, tall but thin, swathed in a black cloak and hood. Tezal assumed it to be a male, by its height, then remembered as its two slender hands pushed back the hood that the enemy had women who stood as tall as men.

Her skin was golden, a warm contrast to the cold synthetic surfaces surrounding them. Her cheekbones were sharp and high and her white hair was plaited into a crown of twisted braids, in a style he had never seen on an Azean before. Not that he had seen many Azeans in the flesh, of course. A few prisoners, on their way to being broken. An occasional messenger. Direct contact with his counterparts in the Empire meant risk of discovery for both sides, and was something to be avoided whenever possible.

In a voice as soft as the rest of the station was dark, she spoke the code that he would know her by. He responded in his turn.

"You may call me Miranme," she said. "Not my real name, of course."

"A woman," Tezal mused. One eyebrow arched slightly over his pale, powdered face. "That is a change."

Her expression darkened a bit. "You know we don't choose our personnel for your convenience. Or to kowtow to your prejudices. If you don't want to speak to a woman you're free to leave."

Such fire in their females, he thought. Such a waste. Azean men didn't know how to value them.

He shrugged. "I merely note the change."

"You asked to speak to one of rank. I am that."

"That is all that concerns me, then. You may call me . . . Bitir. If you need a name."

The flash in her eyes told him she recognized the derivation of it. *Know me as the Warrior Spirit,* he had told her.

"You take great risk," she said, "coming out to meet in person. And you ask I share that risk."

"Some things cannot be entrusted to transmissions. Even encrypted ones."

A slender eyebrow arched upward. "Or couriers?"

"Couriers can be waylaid. It's happened in the past." His dark eyes narrowed. "Once very recently, as you may recall."

She nodded grimly. Her office had supplied him with the evidence he had needed to make sure that no one learned the true source of the original message . . . or its intended recipient. It was, in many ways, a true test of their alliance, that effort. The memory of it remained the glue that bound conspirators together, when tides of tradition and prejudice threatened to tear them apart.

"You were not detected coming here," she said. A question.

"Of course not." The question was not one of procedure, he noted, but of power. Only men of the highest rank could subvert the Central Computer, erasing all files of a starship's passage. That was as it should be. Only men of power—or women, in the enemy's case—knew of the conspiracy that bound their worlds together. Others might serve it, but they called it other things, and lacked any real knowledge of what they served. Some of them even thought they served the Great War, and that their efforts would help one side win it.

Men always served a cause with the greatest enthusiasm when they were told what they wanted to hear.

He drew in a deep breath, preparing himself. Then: "We have reached a crisis point," he said quietly.

A slender eyebrow arched upward again. There was no other sign of emotion. "Indeed."

"The Pri'tiera has fallen. He has left no heir of sufficient age to fight for his throne."

If she was surprised by the news she didn't show it. "Will you choose one to replace him, then? Or let that . . . experiment . . . end?"

He stared at her for a long moment before answering. Even knowing why he spoke them, the words were hard to bring forth. "The Kaim'eri haven't decided."

"Ah." She exhaled softly. "I understand."

"If the Empire moves against us now—"

"They will be fighting a Holding without certain leadership."

"Precisely."

"And we could win the War."

He said nothing.

"What do you wish, then? A Peace?"

He shook his head. "I doubt you can get one in place before the news breaks. Azea will never agree to one after that."

She nodded. The focus of her eyes shifted elsewhere for a few seconds, shifted nowhere, as she digested his news. Finally she looked back at him and said, "Give us at least a few days, if you can. There's a system on the far Border that can be . . . destabilized. Enough ships committed to that front and Azea would be hard pressed to mount a meaningful assault on the Holding, at least on short notice." She paused. "They will come for you, though, regardless. I can't stop that, in the face of this kind of news. This will buy you a bit of time, nothing more." She paused again. "The blood of a wounded animal is irresistible to predators."

"Time is what we need."

"Then you shall have it."

In the silence, breezes shifted; the respiration of a station drawing in used air, expelling fresh.

"It has been a long time," she mused, "Since the Holding has needed our help on this scale."

He nodded.

"Perhaps not since the time of Zatar . . . when this alliance was founded."

"I don't think things are quite as bad this time as they were back then."

"There are some who believe that if Azea had not been bound by Peace then, we would have conquered you."

He smiled at her coldly. "And that would have been your destruction."

"Of course." She smiled as well, equally coldly. "We are not fools."

"The absorption of the entire Holding as conquered territory . . . think what a dreadful fate that would have been for Azea! The end of your peace and stability forever. No nation can occupy or control that much enemy territory for long. You would have been torn to pieces politically, unable to control us, unwilling to leave us to our freedom. A conflict ten times worse than the Great War, which would never be ended."

"And what of you?" she countered. "More willing to play victorious conqueror, no doubt, but to no better end. How many planets would Braxi have to destroy in subjugation before the rest rose up against you? Our population is larger than yours, our planets more independent. How many starships would you be willing to lose in the battle to dominate them all . . . and how many of the Holding's past conquests would see in that battle a chance to break free of your control at last? Oh, Braxi loves a good war . . . but that wouldn't be a *good* war, would it? It would be the beginning of the end for you."

"It would be a disaster if either side won the War," he agreed. "Which is, after all, the reason we are here."

Silence reigned, thick with thought, with unspoken promises.

"Azea did not move against you after the Great Plague," she said at last. "It will not do so now."

He bowed his head. "I thank you."

"The day may come when similar extremes are asked of you," she warned.

"We have enough people in place. We will do what needs to be done." He paused, then added, "There are enough in the leadership ranks who understand that a *stable* War is required, if we are to prosper."

"If we are *both* to prosper."

"Of course."

He stepped back from the table that divided them, took one last look at her face—if it was her face, and not some temporary construct produced for the sake of secrecy—and then bowed his leavetaking with all the formality of Braxaná custom. "I thank you for coming, Lady."

"And I you." She bowed her own head with the regality of an Emperor. "May we never need to meet again, Lord Bitir."

He turned upon a booted heel and presented his back to her as he left. A sign of trust perhaps . . . or else just acknowledgement of their interdependence. She remained behind a moment after he was gone, musing upon his exit. Or perhaps instead upon the strange politics of a universe that made such a meeting necessary.

Then she drew up her hood over her face again. A faint sparkle beneath her throat caught the light as she did so, a tiny bit of jewelry flashing in the light. Had anyone else been present they might have caught sight of a small silver pendant in the shape of a crescent, before her cloak enveloped it in shadow.

But no else was present, of course.

Alone, in the silence of the station, she made her way back to her starship.

The lights went out automatically behind her.

Glossary

Absent Gods: A belief system of the Braxaná, later adopted by the rest of Braxin culture, that claims whatever gods might have been responsible for the creation of the universe no longer have interest in it and are not actively involved in its maintenance. They regard this as a positive development, noting that creatures with eternal life and nearly unlimited power are not likely to share humankind's priorities or care much about the welfare of a single life-form. In the words of one Braxin theologian, "There is nothing more dangerous than a jaded god."

The Braxaná creation saga as recorded by Davros in the third century is an excellent illustration of this principle, with its chilling images of Taz'hein and Avra-Nim driving human armies to bloodshed simply for their own amusement.

Braxaná regard with scorn any culture that maintains a belief in active beneficial deities, both for their emotional dependency and philosophical shortsightedness, and the phrase "Bless him with an active deity" is regarded as one of the most condescending insults in the Braxaná lexicon.

A.C.: After the Coronation of Harkur (Braxi). The Harkurian calendar was adopted 76 years after Harkur's death to honor the man who unified Braxi and brought it to interstellar prominence. Historians note that it was a Braxaná government which chose to institute the new calendar, and may have done so to placate tribal factions in an era when its own power was less than certain.

Aldous: Sister planet to Braxi, closer to their shared sun, Aldous is made habitable by dense atmospheric components that block out a portion of the sun's radiation, making a human-compatible environment possible surrounding both geographic poles. Believed to have been seeded with human stock in the first wave of transplantation (see **Scattered Races**), Aldous became home to a civilization which was advanced in technology and yet wholly planetbound. Scientists postulate this was the result of cultural evolution in an environment in which neither stars, moon, nor open space was visible, causing human creativity to focus upon more local elements. Those who study the Scattered Races regard Aldous as one of the clearest examples of targeted experimentation, and use it to bolster arguments that the purpose of the Seeding was to study the effects of planetary environment upon social evolution.

Braxi made contact with the human inhabitants of Aldous in the third century before Harkur's reign and quickly established dominance. The inclusion of the lesser planet's name in the full title of the Holding represents its symbolic importance as a satellite of B'Salos, rather than any political or military significance.

Anzha lyu Mitethe: Legendary Starcommander and Functional Telepath of the Azean Star Empire, lyu Mitethe is credited by some historians as having set the stage for the ultimate defeat of Braxi. Unfortunately, the Empire had just entered into a binding Peace with the Holding and was thus incapable of launching the offensives her plan would have required. Enraged by what she saw as the loss of a one-time opportunity, lyu Mitethe stole an experimental starship and fled to the uncharted reaches of space. Some historians believe that she took advantage of **Llornu**'s destruction to gather the psychic community under her own banner, while others note references to her in Braxin intelligence reports several years after her disappearance and speculate that she simply moved to another border, to launch her campaign without Imperial assistance.

The question of lyu Mitethe's true heritage is one that has fascinated genetic historians for two centuries. Though born of Azean parents whose family trees would seem to indicate no input from other Scattered Races, lyu Mitethe expressed a somatotype that was undeniably foreign to that race, and most modern geneticists accept the theory that a recessive gene grouping from some outside source was responsible. Unfortunately, her medfiles were lost when Llornu was destroyed, so these guesses cannot be confirmed. It is noteworthy that within the Holding it is believed she is descended from the

Braxin leader **Harkur the Great**, though how the two races could have exchanged genetic material in an age when there was no contact between them remains a mystery.

<u>Ar:</u> Now regarded as the goddess of Chaos Incarnate, Ar is believed by some scholars to have once been an active member of the Braxaná pantheon, and the deity responsible for the yearly cycle of death and rebirth witnessed throughout nature. Historians trace the change in her aspect to the period following the reign of **Viton the Ruthless**, a result of the deliberate politicization of Braxaná mythology by Viton's successors.

The Braxaná claim that in any situation where a woman commands men the spirit of Ar (Chaos) will be manifest. This is used as the justification for the exclusion of women from all facets of Braxin government, as well as the harshest of the **Social Codes** regarding women's behavior. As with most of the Social Codes this restriction is of least concern among the Braxaná themselves, who admit to admiring strong women, and who long ago developed customs and language to allow their own females to wield considerable power, albeit indirectly.

<u>Avra-Nim:</u> Creator-god and sun-god to most Braxin pantheons, Avra-Nim was the preeminent deity prior to the rise of the Braxaná. Some historians postulate that he was originally the dominant figure in Braxaná mythology as well, and point to the solar nomenclature of the Holding as evidence of this. Others theorize that this was a purely political move meant to facilitate the absorption of other tribes into a greater Braxaná whole.

A failed god whose human creations have long been dominated by his brother's get, Avra-Nim has not been accorded worship in many centuries.

<u>Azean Star Empire:</u> Officially founded in 1,187 Y.E. (the date of the absorption of Lugast's Union of Planets) the Star Empire is both aggressive and exploratory, and today comprises the largest unified territory in known space.

Although Azea has always had titular control of the Star Empire—the Emperor or Empress is required to be of that race—the actual governance of planets was once equally divided between the House of Humans and House of Non-Humans. The Lugastine faction was particularly strong in human politics in the early years, and there was some speculation that the Lugast would come to dominate the Star Empire in fact, if not in name.

In 2,234 Y.E. the discovery of Braxi's **Schedule of Expansion** and ensuing military escalation moved the focus of the Empire to martial affairs, and Azea's genetic advantage in that forum gave them added advantage in political circles as well. By 2,479 it was clear that the Holding did not intend to break off hostilities until the Star Empire was completely destroyed, and a new arm of government was instituted to focus on this tenacious and determined enemy. In 2,481 **StarControl** was given mandate to function as a ruling body of the Empire, thus beginning the so-called "Azean period" of Imperial governance. Despite periodic protests by the non-human membership of the Empire that this move upset the balance of the Empire in humanity's favor, StarControl remains an equal partner in the Imperial government, and is accorded precedence in any situation or region where Braxi is an active threat.

The genetic strength and conditioned loyalty of the Azean people has long been recognized to give that race a natural advantage in military affairs, for which reason the so-called Border Fleet has traditionally been dominated by Azean personnel. In later years it became the custom to restrict service in the war with Braxi to those of Azean heritage, and in 3,571 the Council of Justice was established to rule upon issues of racial heritage and loyalty among that people. While technically an equal partner in the Imperial government, the Council limits its scope to matters concerning the Azean people in particular, and is grudgingly accepted as a nominal fifth Crown in what has become a human-dominated Empire.

Detractors are quick to point out that should the war with Braxi terminate, the need for both StarControl and the Council of Justice would cease to be of Imperial concern, and the balance of government might return to the Empire's original design.

B.C.: Before the Coronation of Harkur (Braxi).

Betrayer: See **Taz'hein.**

Bi'ti: The essence or spirit of the warrior, which is considered the core of the Braxaná identity. It is believed that both men and women possess the bi'ti, and acts of violence which would have been considered unsuitable for women in other tribes are accepted among the Pale Ones as a natural expression of this fierce inner spirit.

Early Braxaná believed that a strong bi'ti could be inherited, for which reason returning warriors were permitted to mate at will with fertile members of the tribe. It was believed that such sexual union would strengthen the woman and all her offspring, lending even to the child of another man the fierce spirit of the warrior. It is this tradition which was later written into law as the Code of Sexual Access, though critics note that in its current form it has little to do with the custom's original form or purpose.

Black Death: Literally translated from the Braxin as "Waiting Death," the Black Death is one of the most deadly and feared organisms in the human worlds. Derived from a life-form originally found on Ekkos IV, the poison has an inert phase, during which it invades its host and lodges in internal tissue, and an active phase, during which it consumes its host for energy, growing so rapidly that witnesses may mistake its advance for locomotion.

In its natural form the Black Death was responsible for the decimation of several human colonies, and its home world was subject to biological cleansing by Zherat in 1,972 A.C. in order to keep it from invading the Holding at large. The controlled strains have been bred to be dependent upon human science for reproduction, and fertile samples are carefully guarded.

The most common strain becomes active 10–40 days after invading its host, usually at a single point of cataclysm. Less common is the so-called "timed dose," which is developed to suit the individual organic template of its host, allowing for refined prediction of its activation schedule. The Black Death has no known cure or treatment, and is 100% fatal to organic hosts. The only hope of survival for a victim is to remove the affected limb before the activated Death can spread.

It is considered a capital offense for anyone but a Braxaná to possess the poison, and research facilities adapting the strains for military use are under tight government control. Nevertheless it is rumored that the Black Market has occasionally seen trade in the Death, and the use of weakened strains by non-Braxaná is occasionally rumored.

Braxaná: Originally a nomadic tribe inhabiting the Blood Steppes of northern Braxi, the Braxaná were noteworthy for their rejection of modern culture and its social compromises, believing that such things weakened the sacred essence of the warrior spirit (**bi'ti**). Attempts to conquer, absorb, or even negotiate with this fierce barbarian tribe all proved futile, and in the 5th century B.C. the Council of Eastern Tribes officially (and grudgingly) ceded them the Blood Steppes in perpetuity, acknowledging that the only means by which "civilization" was going to encroach upon Braxaná territory was by inciting more bloodshed than the land was worth.

It was **Harkur the Great** who first realized the full potential of the Braxaná spirit, and he sought out members of the tribe to serve in his court. The most famous of these was **Viton the Ruthless**, who succeeded him in 86 A.C. Though Harkur never openly proposed Braxaná rule, historians believe that he saw in the so-called **Pale Ones** a possible tool for unifying the other tribes, and his discussions with Viton provided the foundation for subsequent Braxaná domination of global affairs.

Following Viton's rule the Braxaná remained in power, eventually establishing an oligarchy of purebred males, the **Kaim'eri**. All attempts to displace the Braxaná by force or to demand political representation for other tribes have failed, in part because of steps taken to eradicate the concept of tribal identity from common Braxin culture. While not wholly successful, this campaign has made it difficult for any group to use blood-ties or shared history to provide unity in an uprising.

See also **Shlesor**

Braxaná Dialect: Because early Braxaná culture relied upon verbal rather than written records, little is known about roots of the so-called Braxaná dialect. Most linguists are in agreement that its forty-seven speech modes were derived from a language once common on the Blood Steppes, which had ceased to exist as an independent tongue by the time of Harkur the Great.

Linguists agree that in complexity of form and in raw communicative potential the Braxaná dialect surpasses all other human languages. Gaten, son of Vralos, characterized it as "The one human language which no outsider can ever truly master." Forty-seven **Speech Modes** allow for fine communication of social and emotive context, and secondary and even tertiary messages can be imbedded in many simple statements. It is said that a master of the Braxaná tongue can hold several different conversations at once, and true mastery of the language is so highly regarded that Braxaná poets are among the most celebrated of artists. While non-Braxaná rarely use the more obscure forms, most are familiar with the major contextual modes, and the ability to use them fluently in one's speech is regarded as a sign of intelligence and social refinement among the upper classes.

The Braxaná dialect contains a mode which is entirely neutral, and which has been adopted throughout the Holding as the "common Braxin" tongue. Speech in the Basic Mode is said to be acceptable in all social situations, though Braxins of the upper classes may look with disdain upon those who are too poorly educated to make their language more interesting.

B'Salos: The yellow sun of Braxi and Aldous, B'Salos was the focus of worship for much of early Braxin culture, and an assortment of sun-related deities peopled the pantheons of most early tribes.

Central Computer System (CSS): The centralized data storage and processing system of the Holding, among the most complex of its type ever to have been created. The CCS functions as a central clearing house for all information in the Holding, both static and dynamic, and contains subsidiary indexing systems fine-tuned to the needs of a variety of species.

Citadel of the Kaim'eri: A man-made satellite orbiting Braxi, which houses both the great meeting hall of the Kaim'erate and the main processors and storage banks for the Central Computer System.

Communicant: Second highest category of psychic functioning, indicating one who is capable of receiving the thoughts of nonpsychics and transmitting his own to them in turn, with near-perfect comprehension and reliability. As with telepathy there are various grades leading up to that of full Communicant, which reflect varying degrees of power and control. A true Communicant is capable of linking together several minds, as well as subsuming the power of (willing) colleagues to increase his range and sensitivity.

Communicants are rarely capable of complex communication with nonhumans, although those who are gifted in abstract visualization have a natural advantage in this arena.

Community of Mind: The official name for the psychic community established following the Diaspora. Also called the **Tskiri**.

Diaspora, psychic: With the destruction of **Llornu** and the subsequent collapse of the **Institute**, those psychics who survived the disaster took shelter where they could find it. Some remained within the Empire, while most fled beyond its borders. Those who remained behind were initially accepted, as their gifts had always been valued, but it soon became clear that absorbing the mental fallout from the simultaneous deaths of so many of their colleagues had exacted a cost. Patterns of mental instability were noted in many, and the damage done by Psychic-Aggressives as they spiraled downward into insanity was destructive enough that in time the Empire was forced to take action to register, restrict, and finally isolate its psychic population. The result was a second wave of emigration into the reaches of space that lay beyond the pale of either Empire or Holding, as well as a series of daring raids from the outside that freed those whom the Empire had already confined.

Evidence was later uncovered that this mental instability was in fact typical of psychics, and represented a propensity for insanity which the Institute had effectively hidden from the public. This discovery sealed the fate of the psychic community, whose members were now recognized to be threats to the public order regardless of their intent, and who would therefore no longer be welcome to return home.

It is currently not known whether those who fled managed to reestablish some kind of centralized community, or remained scattered refugees along the frontier of the Empire. It is said that even in the Outlands they are regarded with great suspicion, and in some domains it is considered acceptable to kill them upon discovery, as this is seen as contributing to public safety.

See also **Shaka**.

Disciplines: Mental rituals originally designed by the **Institute for the Advancement of Psychic Evolution**, used to control psychic ability. The majority of Disciplines are defensive in nature, designed to protect the integrity of the psychic's mind when dealing with potentially destabilizing influences. Some are voluntary, requiring that the psychic activate a mental trigger to bring them into play, while others are conditioned into the psychic's mind as a last-ditch defensive measure, to be triggered automatically when the boundaries of identity and or sanity are threatened.

It was the development of such Disciplines which enabled the Institute to establish a viable psychic community and to bring what was then a rogue power under enough control to be established as a measurable science. The full range of Disciplines is never discussed outside of psychic circles, and it is rumored that some have been developed which allow for the focusing of aggressive energies against a target.

Endless War: Common label for the series of military conflicts between the **Star Empire** and the Braxin Holding which began in 1,193 Y.E. and have not yet concluded. Some scholars believe this to be no more than an extension of the Braxin/Lugastine conflict, already in its second eon when Azea absorbed both Lugast and her political agenda.

Though viewed in the popular mind as a single unending conflict (hence the name), the War is in fact a series of military and political campaigns punctuated by formal truces. Some of these truces were temporary or geographically limited in nature, while others were meant to conclude, or at least deescalate, the conflict as a whole. Those in the latter class were invariably broken by Braxi to suit her convenience. Despite the proven treachery of their negotiating partner, Azea rarely turned down the opportunity for a Peace, for the Empire had other interests it could only pursue when the War Border was quiet.

Most historians agree that the War came closest to being ended in 12,081 Y.E., when the aggressive military campaign of the halfbreed telepath **Anzha lyu Mitethe** coincided with a **Tsank'ar** pandemic among Braxi's ruling Braxaná class, almost wiping the latter out. Politics interfered, however, and lyu Mitethe soon after fled the Empire and left the War to the politicians who had frustrated her efforts.

First Class: The most prestigious of six formal social class divisions within Braxin society, the First Class includes all purebred and halfbred Braxaná, as well as the children of half-bred Braxaná who serve in Braxaná households. The latter are defined by matrilineal descent only, though several attempts have been made to institute a DNA-based standard which would allow for the inclusion of patrilineal issue.

Freelancer; Freespacer: A term used in systems outside the Star Empire and the Holding for opportunistic mercenaries who have no declared geographic or political allegiances. Freelancers range from small-scale merchants to soldiers for hire, with some working as bodyguards for the wealthiest inhabitants of the Outlands. The word generally has negative connotations, however, and in many places freelancers are assumed to be outlaws or at least the associates of outlaws, and are treated accordingly.

Founder: The title used by the psychic **Community** for **Anzha lyu Mitethe**, who is credited with having gathered many of the fugitives together after the destruction of **Llornu** and enabling them to establish a viable nation in exile. Anzha lyu Mitethe provided the diasporic nation not only with a system of governance but a cryptic and sometimes violent political agenda as well. The latter is sometimes cited as justification in the Outlands for killing psychics on sight.

Functional Telepath (FT): The highest of fifteen ratings developed by the **Institute** for the Advancement of Psychic Evolution, FT status is granted only to those who can send and receive thoughts to both human and nonhuman subjects at will, and with consistent accuracy. The Functional Telepath is required to have mastered all **Disciplines** and to be able to facilitate the mental communication of nonpsychic minds as well. It is to be noted that many psychics may achieve telepathic-level communication without fulfilling all of the criteria perfectly or consistently, and three lesser ranks of Telepathy are also recognized by the Institute.

It has been stated that the long-term goal of the Institute is to isolate the genetic codes required to make functional telepathy available to all humans. However, a series of studies done in '87 suggest that several of the factors involved are not linked to psychic coding, but to personality traits which are part of the Seling Complex, and which cannot be altered without putting larger patterns of mental processing at risk. Former Director Kalu er Tashenin stated at the time that so-called Conditional Telepathy might still be possible for all humans, but less optimistic scientists cite **Communicant** status as the best that can be offered to the human race as a whole.

Great Plague: (See **Tsank'ar**) The Plague of 11,091 A.C. was an endemic of unprecedented scope, which swept through the Holding with deadly force and laid low the last great age of the Kaim'eri. Though the Braxaná are loath to let any outsiders guess at their numbers, genetic historians have speculated that the minimal gene pool of the tribe was fatally diminished at this time, and point to the resurrection of ancient traditions to bring in new blood as the tribe's last-gasp effort to provide the genetic diversity required for the survival of their Race.

Great War: See **Endless War**

Harkur the Great: The single greatest ruler of Braxi, Harkur the Great is credited with uniting the 117 Major Tribes under one international government, and with establishing the Holding as a major interstellar power.

Hirinari by birth, Harkur supplemented his formal education with travels to the far reaches of Braxi, including tribal territories normally closed to outsiders. Though records of his travels are incomplete, modern scholars believe he may have visited the Blood Steppes themselves, and some believe that he witnessed Braxaná customs normally kept hidden from the eyes of outsiders.

Harkur's dream was a Braxi truly united in purpose, a far cry from the conglomeration of warring tribes whose throne he claimed in his fortieth year. Within zhents of his Coronation he had begun what would become the central campaign of his lifetime, focusing Braxin aggressive energies outward, toward the stars. A rapid series of dramatic raids into Lugastine space won him support from the Braxin media, and the benefits to be reaped from cooperative efforts in interstellar warfare soon won even the most warlike tribes to his cause.

Harkur's manipulation of the Braxaná was either his greatest accomplishment or greatest offense, depending upon one's perspective. Without a doubt he paved the way for Braxaná domination of the Holding, believing it to be the one formula sure to keep Braxi united. Whether that unity has been a good thing in the long run, or whether the social cost of Braxaná rule is something no political goal can justify, is a subject hotly debated in scholarly journals outside the Holding.

Hasai: See **Probe**

Hasha: The first human born on Azean soil, Hasha's origins have long been shrouded in mystery. Early records hint that her mother was not among those present at the Founding, and the appearance of a portrait in the Holding that allegedly depicts her beside Harkur the Great implies early contact between Azea's Firstborn and the young Braxin nation. It is to be noted that no authorities from the Empire have been allowed to examine this relic, and some experts there have questioned its authenticity.

Whatever her origin, Hasha's birth was regarded in its time as a sign of divine approval of the Exodus and Founding, and a necessary symbol of hope to a people about to colonize a biologically hostile planet. Myths have arisen surrounding her birth which grant her nearly divine status in her own right, and references to "the Firstborn" appear throughout Azean literature as appeals to a supernatural patroness, much in the manner that lesser gods and prophets are called upon by other peoples.

Hasha's firstborn child was given the subname **Iyu**, a custom which has been maintained down through the ages to memorialize the significance of Azea's first birth. The name is believed to mean "birth" in the language spoken by the Founders.

Holding: The proper name of the territory ruled by Braxi, in its complete form *the B'Saloan Holding under Braxi/Aldous*. Some historians feel that the name is a holdover from the sun-worship of the early tribes, and trace the name of B'Salos back to Be-Nesaal, a sun god prominent in the northern hemisphere. It is said that by naming the interstellar empire after a sun shared by two planets—and perhaps a god shared by many—Harkur the Great hoped to stress the unity of the Holding, rather than encourage competition between the various tribes and factions it contained.

Household, Braxaná: A broadly inclusive term for the property, personnel, financial assets, political ties, and business interests of a purebred **Braxaná**. The key figure in a Braxaná House is its **Mistress**, who generally has control in practice if not in name of all of its Master's assets.

The creation and maintenance of a so-called Great House is the life's work of the purebred Braxaná, and rivalries between Houses are considered by some to be the driving force behind the Braxin political dynamic. While many half-bred Braxaná—the so-called First Class—establish their own Houses, few are of the size or influence that the purebred enjoy.

It is noteworthy that many Braxaná females have their own Houses, although the organization of them is of necessity different than the males', and the service of a **Token Domitor** is required to enable a woman to exercise her power in a culture where she is not permitted to give direct orders to any man.

Human: Full-sentient beings believed to be descended from the human stock of the **Source Worlds**, being no more than 18% divergent from the Standard Human genetic template, and capable of interbreeding with other humans to produce fertile offspring. The term is also used in a more colloquial sense to indicate those who belong to the "human community," and is rejected by some races which might qualify in a purely technical sense.

Because the governments of both the Star Empire and the Holding distinguish between human and nonhuman species for bureaucratic purposes, the issue of human status is subject to continual debate and revision. The requirement that Source World origin be proven beyond reasonable doubt was officially abandoned in '897 Standard, when it was demonstrated that several human worlds had deliberately falsified their archeological records to distance themselves from the existing human political structure.

H'karet: "Place of the Hidden," the second artificial satellite to be set in orbit around Braxi. Originally built by Zatar the Magnificent, the H'karet has served as home for all four Braxin Pri'tieri, providing an unprecedented degree of isolation for the enigmatic dynasty.

Institute for the Advancement of Psychic Evolution: Perhaps the most notorious of Azea's government-financed Institutes, it was established in 10,027 Y.E. with the stated purpose of isolating the genetic sequences responsible for psychic sensitivity, as well as developing a program of training for those classed as psychics. The first goal proved to be an elusive one; it is now estimated that as many as two hundred "trigger sequences" may play a part in causing psychic talent to express, fewer than one hundred of which have been definitively identified. Nonetheless the Institute earned credibility for its quest by establishing a community of well-trained psychics to serve the Empire, and in 11,287 introduced the first **Functional Telepath**.

The Institute was notoriously secretive about its training programs, which led some government officials to protest its increasing budget, as well as its unprecedented autonomy. Rumors abounded of secret conditioning programs, of telepaths with imbedded commands who served the Institute before the Empire, and of psychics trained to function as weapons, skilled in destroying the minds of opponents. Not until **Llornu** was destroyed in 12,080 did it become public knowledge that the psychic condition was directly linked to mental instability, and that the apparent price of psychic sensitivity was inevitable insanity.

Just Cause: Within the **Holding**, reasons which are accepted as justification for a woman's refusing sexual access to a man. Most are derived from Braxaná tribal practices and focus upon the female reproductive cycle: menstruation, pregnancy, and both pre- and post-menarche life stages are considered Just Cause for refusal. Health issues are also considered—the list of conditions which qualify being specifically detailed—and any occupational responsibility which would be compromised by lost time may qualify.

One category of Just Cause which was not derived from tribal practice is that of Ownership. Braxin law states that any woman who has surrendered her sexual independence to one man owes nothing to others. This in fact contradicts the underlying tribal tradition, in which it was considered desirable for warriors to impregnate all the women in the tribe, thus strengthening the women's own *bi'ti* and the children they would bear for their mates in the future. It is postulated that the original intent of the "ownership clause" was to encourage the establishment of long-term partnerships between men and women. If so, the adoption of such laws at a time when gender relationships were in turmoil did not bring about the intended results. Most Braxin men and women lead isolated lives, and the partnerships which qualify as Ownership among the lower classes are generally temporary conveniences. Among the upper classes, whose extended households may easily claim Ownership of those who belong, the question is not quite so pressing, and women who come to serve a great House sometimes bargain for Ownership as part of their contract.

Kaim'era: Originally the title of Braxi's ruler, in later periods one member of the planet's ruling oligarchy. From the roots *kaimras* (leadership) and *tiera* (attributes focused upon an individual). Plural Kaim'eri.

Kesserit: One of the Major Tribes represented on the Council of Tribes in the time of Harkur the Great, the Kesserit were renowned even among the militant Braxaná for their fierceness in battle, as well as maintaining a tradition of succession by mortal combat. They were one of the few tribes to openly protest the Braxaná move to criminalize tribal identity outside their own circles, as a result of which they were targeted and nearly exterminated by the early Braxaná leadership. Some sociologists, noting the absence of Kesserit issues from the public stage after that, have postulated that the tribe was indeed destroyed at that time, reduced in number enough that they were forced to practice exogamy, and absorbed into the greater Braxin population. Experts in tribal culture however are quick to note the unique resiliency of the Kesserit throughout history, and some have suggested that the tribe simply went underground in its attempt to preserve its people and its traditions.

Leadership, Azean: The Azean Star Empire is represented by five Crowns, each with its own sphere of authority. *The Council of Humans* and *Council of Non-Humans* are the oldest government bodies, which together with a figurehead Emperor or Empress (always of Azean blood) governed the early Empire. *StarControl* was later added to oversee military affairs, and the *Council of Justice* to adjudicate matters of Azean heritage and loyalty.

It has been noted by some nonhuman critics that though the original Azean government reflected a plan to divide power equally between two complimentary Councils, Azea's increasing concern with Braxin aggression has resulted in an imbalance of representation in the current system, with four of five Crowns being human by definition. A few extremists have gone so far as to argue that the human rulers of the Star Empire have encouraged the continuation of the Great War to assure continued human dominance, but no evidence for such conspiracy has ever been offered.

Leadership, Braxin: Originally a loose confederation of warring tribes, the early Braxin Holding was unified under **Harkur the Great**, and remained under a single leader for several centuries. That system gave way beneath the pressure of **Braxaná** political rivalries to a formal oligarchy, ruled by a prime number of Kaim'eri.

Two hundred years ago, as the Kaim'eri declined dangerously in numbers and influence, a maverick leader named **Zatar the Mag-**

nificent declared himself the sole ruler of Braxi in the ancient tradition, with the Kaim'eri serving as his counselors. The title of **Pri'tiera** has been borne by him and by three generations after him, establishing the first hereditary monarchy the Holding has ever known.

Llornu: Home planet of the **Institute for the Advancement of Psychic Evolution.** The name is sometimes used as shorthand for the Institute itself. Llornu's research center was destroyed in 12,080 Y.E. by a nuclear fusion incident that killed thousands of psychics and destroyed or polluted the bulk of the Institute's DNA records. The sudden absorption of so many violent deaths into the worldmind of Llornu triggered madness in much of the population, and was responsible for a wave of suicides in the first few days, followed by the mass exodus of psychics from the Empire.

  Though it was rumored that **Anzha lyu Mitethe** was responsible for the assault, historians have come to question whether that was truly the case, and point to later evidence of her involvement in organizing the homeless psychics as proof that they, at least, did not credit such tales.

Lyu: 1) Azean **subname** taken by firstborn descendants of Hasha, establishing a lineage whose members have periodically been called upon for ritual functions within the Star Empire. The last known member of this bloodline was **Anzha lyu Mitethe**, who is believed to have died without natural issue. 2) Leader of the secretive psychic **Community** which was established sometime after Llornu's destruction. The title is believed to have been adopted to honor the memory of lyu Mitethe, one of the **Star Empire**'s most famous telepaths.

Mistress: see **Household, Braxaná**

Outlands: A region of inhabited space surrounding the Star Empire and/or Holding, but not contained within the War Border between the two. Comprised of independent worlds and freelance settlements, answering to no single authority, the Outlands have enjoyed unusual stability due to the Endless War, which keeps the energies of both interstellar empires focused upon each other rather than expansion into Outland space.

Renowned as a refuge for outlaws and political malcontents, the Outlands have a reputation for lawlessness and casual violence. However they are also home to a thriving network of independent worlds and stations, and in some places limited planetary alliances which maintain common law and security.

The Outlands have fallen under Imperial scrutiny in recent years due to rumors that the renegade psychics have taken up shelter there, but thus far no investigations have turned up any proof of this allegation.

Pale Ones: A common term for the Braxaná, which refers to the distinctive coloration of that tribe. Although other pigment-deficient Scattered Races are known, the black hair and eyes of the Braxaná make their complexion seem uniquely colorless by contrast, and the habit in post-**Shlesor** generations of adding white cosmetics to the skin makes the nomenclature reflective not only of tribal appearance but custom.

Plague: See **Tsank'ar**

Pri'tiera: Braxin title which translates to "one who has waited." First granted to **Zatar the Magnificent** upon his ascension to the Braxin throne, the title of Pri'tiera has been borne by his firstborn male descendants ever since.

Probe: Technically a subcategory of Functional Telepathy, Probe status is wrongfully believed by many to be a "higher" level of psychic functioning. In fact, the Probe designation merely indicates the concurrence of Functional Telepathy with specific patterns of cognition that are present in the population as a whole, and does not reflect upon either the strength or reliability of telepathic powers.

Because Probes have advanced powers of abstract visualization they are capable of sending and receiving thoughts in their "pure" form, without need for a verbal or metaphorical framework. This ability makes them particularly well suited to analysis of deep-brain emanations, as well as communication with nonhuman species.

As with other top Institute ratings, Probe status is only granted to those whose performance meets strict criteria of reliability and control, and several lesser grades exist which encompass the same cognitive abilities.

Psychic: Any sentient being who is capable of receiving the thoughts or emotions of another, or of transmiting his own to another subject, without need for material vehicle. Psychic ability ranges from simple empathy (most common) to the full panoply of powers mastered by the Functional Telepath.

While general sensitivity is not uncommon among humans, most find that the power can neither be predicted nor controlled. The Institute devoted centuries to perfecting techniques which could bring psychic sensitivity under conscious control, and among their own ranks the title of "Psychic" was only granted to one who has attained reliable control over their power.

Most Psychics fall into four general categories. Psychic-Empathetics are responsive to strong emotions in others. Psychic-Receptives can receive and interpret more complex thought patterns. Psychic-Aggressives can transmit their own thoughts and/or emotions to others. Psychic-Connectives are capable of initiating a two-way exchange, though not with the accuracy and control required of a full Communicant.

It is rumored there are other categories which deal with more aggressive powers, including legends of the **Shaka**, a much-feared psychic who is said to be able to take control of the bodies of other living creatures and even kill with thought alone.

Scattered Races: Human populations believed to be derived from a single genetic source, spread throughout known space in a past incident known as the **Seeding**.

Humankind is by far the most successful species of those that were Seeded, and is believed to have survived on 78% of the planets to which it was transported.

Scattered Species: Species which were transplanted to other worlds during the Seeding, and which survived the transition to establish themselves as competitors to native life forms.

Of the five, humankind alone has developed interstellar technology. By contrast, the cetacean transplant species has developed low-tech complex civilizations on several dozen planets, and two land-based subspecies are known to exist. Other transplanted species have not distinguished themselves, save by fact of their survival. Scientists postulate that they may have originally been chosen for promising intelligence, but that they were not adaptable enough to rise above transplantation trauma quickly enough to gain advantage over local competitors.

It is possible that more than five species were transplanted during the Seeding, but the remainder may never be identified. Populations which failed to establish themselves would have left behind little or no evidence of their arrival, and would quickly have been subsumed into the native archeological record.

Schedule of Expansion: It is rumored that the infamous Braxin blueprint for galactic conquest had its roots in Harkur's own writings. If so, it did not appear in its final form until centuries later, when the Holding was firmly established as a major interstellar player and the Lugastine Union of Planets had already been absorbed by the young and aggressive Star Empire.

Based upon Sukar's **Schedule of Progress** (below), the Schedule of Expansion was an exhaustive study of known human space, which sought to predict the rise of new interstellar powers both within and without human-charted regions. The Schedule set forth a plan for military expansion which took into account the need to crush such powers in their infancy, as well as a blueprint for manipulating the tides of human progress to weaken and ultimately destroy Braxi's great rival, Azea.

Although Azea was aware of the existence of the Schedule it did not have access to the document itself until 2,234, when a copy was leaked to Imperial authorities. Historians have described this as a "wake-up call" to the Empire, who had apparently not anticipated the full scope of Braxin aggression. Only later would nonhuman critics suggest that it was the Empire's response to the Schedule which guaranteed Azean sovereignty over other races within the Empire, and that perhaps the contents of the document, if not its very existence, should be questioned accordingly.

Schedule of Progress: In 117 A.C., Sukar of Braxi postulated that the rate of technological development of a planet's human population was directly linked to the adaptation trauma it suffered during transplantation. (See **Seeding**). His argument was that human populations which were seeded onto hostile or unstable worlds must waste valuable energies adapting themselves to their new environment, delaying the onset of technological development. Based upon this pattern, Sukar claimed that the Source World for humankind could best be recognized by its early entrance into the interstellar arena, as it alone would have been spared any adaptational delay.

While scientists acknowledge the obvious political bias of Sukar's work (in his time, the only known candidates for Source World status would have been Lugast and Braxi), further study has indeed confirmed his basic hypothesis, that a measurable relationship exists between the environmental conditions of a particular Seeding and the pace of technological development which followed it. Later theoreticians expanded upon Sukar's work, providing a schedule by which one might estimate the time it would take for a transplanted population to achieve the technology necessary for starflight, and a statistical means of predicting how many technologically advanced worlds would arise in a given time and place. The latter study provided the basis for the infamous **Schedule of Conquest**, which predicted that military operations would become more difficult over time, as target planets became more and more likely to have advanced armaments of their own.

Seclusion: The practice by which purebred **Braxaná** guarantee the paternity of their offspring, by isolating the woman from all other sources of human sperm until implantation is confirmed. Seclusion was a practice unknown to the early Braxaná, and became common only after the **Shlesor**, when issues of genetic inheritance and tribal fertility took center stage.

Although modern technology is capable of confirming paternity, such practices are considered unacceptable by the Braxaná, who have showed a lasting unwillingness to subject any part of the reproductive process to scientific "interference."

Seeding: The common name for the past interstellar event in which human stock and that of several other species were transported to a wide variety of planets, and allowed to establish themselves without subsequent aid or interference. It is currently estimated the Seeding took place over the course of 50,000 years, though scientists acknowledge that this figure is an estimate derived from studies in local space, and that future exploration may expand the figure considerably.

The exact purpose of the Seeding is not known, nor is there any clear evidence of what species was responsible for it. Lugastine scientists first suggested the possibility of such an event as early as 178

U.P., when studies first showed that humans from various planets within the Union were similar enough in DNA structure to be able to produce fertile offspring. These results were contrasted with studies of other species, wherein it was shown that even when parallel evolution produced species that were indistinguishable in appearance and/or behavior, disparity in DNA was still marked enough to make them incapable of interbreeding.

Five species are known to have been transplanted in this manner, although scientists acknowledge that more may remain undiscovered. Of those, only humankind is known to have mastered the technology necessary for starflight. (See **Schedule of Progress; Scattered Races; Scattered Species.**) Many human scientists regard the preponderance of human transplantations as proof that the architects of the Seeding were themselves human-derived, and theorize that they wished to study the effects of diverse environments upon the evolution of their own species. If so, then the true Source World for humankind may yet be undiscovered, and the most ancient human civilizations in known space may be no more than the first stage in a vast experiment, whose end has yet to be realized.

Shaka: A class of psychic rumored to be able to invade the minds of others and control them. Reports of the Shaka first began to circulate after the final phase of the psychic Diaspora, and some believe they came into existence when the destruction of **Llornu** fostered insanity in the Institute's most powerful telepaths.

Little is known about the Shaka and their existence has never been confirmed to the satisfaction of Imperial authorities; however they are much feared in the Outlands, where it is rumored they intermingle with "normal" humans for purposes unknown. There are several cases on record of strangers being killed simply because their odd behavior or other quirks made others suspect they might belong to this class of deadly creature. In all cases, legal charges against the assailants were dismissed, courts ruling that such violence was "unfortunate, but justified."

Shem'Ar: Literally "Servant of Ar," the word is used for any woman who invites Ar's attention by dominating the actions of men. Tradition states that when this happens Chaos will begin to erode the rational underpinnings of the universe.

The Shem'Ar is the ultimate taboo in Braxin society, rejected by common culture long before it was proscribed by law. The effect of this taboo is most evident in language, where the circumlocutions required for women to communicate without ever giving men so much as a casual order has resulted in what has been called "the female dialect." (This is notably a lower-class phenomenon, as the upper class Speech Modes offer the means to temper any statement with modifiers that indicate "I mean this only as a suggestion.") While the lower classes abhor the Shem'Ar in all her manifestations, among the upper classes it is not unknown for a perverse sexual attraction to exist. Braxaná claim that this is the vestigial remnant of their warrior tradition, which rewarded women for military domination of men of other tribes, but psychologists outside the Holding suggest that the real reason has more to do with the absolute power of the Pale Ones, and the rare appeal of "forbidden" indulgences.

Shlesor: A program of selective breeding among the Braxaná, believed to have lasted several centuries. The Shlesor was but one facet of a greater effort on the part of the Braxaná to set themselves apart from other tribes, in accordance with the counsel of Harkur the Great:

> *If the Braxaná, or any other single tribe, were to try to rule Braxi for an extended length of time, they would have to set themselves apart from all other Braxins. They would have to create an image so alien to the rest of Braxin culture that no other group could aspire to it, and do it to such an extreme that the image itself becomes synonymous with power. Then and only then, no man would dare to question their rule.*

The exact details of the Shlesor are not known, save that the Braxaná disdained to utilize genetic technology in their efforts, preferring instead the more primitive practice of infanticide to cull undesirables out of their gene pool. By the third century A.C. a change in the appearance and demeanor of the tribe had already been noted, and the writings of Janos in the seventh century made clear reference to the unusual strength, endurance, and beauty which had become characteristic of the Braxaná in his time.

Geneticists note that the tribe was uniquely well prepared for such an exercise. Their breeding customs already allowed for giving preference to the seed of successful warriors, and those who were limited in their progeny rights might still take pride in passing down their **bi'ti** to the next generation. The reliance upon primitive methods had its cost, however, and by the sixth century there were rumors that repeated inbreeding had weakened the tribe in ways that were not immediately apparent. By the ninth century it had been noted that the Braxaná population was failing in numbers, and it is believed that the Shlesor was officially abandoned by the turn of the millenium. Repeated efforts by geneticists to gain the co-operation of the Braxaná in analyzing such changes have resulted in a tribal hostility toward genetic science which remains strong to this day.

Social Codes: Customs derived from the tribal practices of the Braxaná, some of which have since entered the body of Braxin law. The Social Codes were originally a warrior ethic, designed to bolster personal strength and obliterate weakness, both in the individual and in the tribe as a whole.

The Braxaná Social Codes are best known for relegating women to a subservient position in Braxin society, and for mandating their sexual availability in many situations. (See **Just Cause**). Curiously, this infamous custom was not originally gender-specific. Among the ancient Braxaná it was not uncommon for females to take up arms, and those who fought beside their men were equally entitled to H'kanit Sar, or the *Fruits of War*. Those returning from battle, male and female alike, were entitled to take from among the tribe whatever mates they chose, for the needs of the warrior were considered more important than any other social restriction or contract. This not only guaranteed the free flow of sexual energy—which the Braxaná believed was necessary for the health of the **bi'ti**, or warrior spirit—but gave the warriors an opportunity to spread their seed throughout the tribe, thus guaranteeing the strength and fierceness of the Braxaná people as a whole.

Many historians believe that when the Braxaná adapted this practice to greater Braxin society and made it the law of the land, it was meant as a "bribe" to the males of the Holding, in order to win their support. Others are quick to point out that the Braxaná relationship between male and female was unique, and that the law became oppressive only when removed from its proper cultural context. The Braxaná philosopher Durat wrote at length about the custom in 897 A.C., deriding the fact that a law which should have encouraged men and women to establish stable households together had instead become an excuse for isolationism.

Source World: A planet on which human life evolved independently, rather than having been placed there during the Seeding. While no Source World has been confirmed as such, several are considered candidates by virtue of their archeological record and/or placement in the **Schedule of Progress**.

Speech Modes: See **Braxaná Dialect**

Standard: Terminology associated with the planet Zeymour. Measures of time such as the Standard Year were adopted by the Star Empire in 837 Y.E., in order to provide a calendrical system which would not favor any existing planet. Though nonhuman cultures within the Empire periodically protest the "human bias" of the system, the Standard system of time measurement functions throughout the Empire as a neutral foundation for interspecies communication.

Star-: (Azea) A prefix used to indicate any species, organization or event which is associated with interstellar culture rather than a particular planetary base.

StarControl: Technically the branch of the Azean Imperial government responsible for all military affairs, StarControl has as its special mandate management of the Braxin–Azean conflict, in peacetime as well as during active hostilities. As a Crown of the Empire the Director of StarControl answers to no one save the Emperor himself, and in matters concerning the Great War is traditionally granted complete independence.

    While membership in StarControl is not technically restricted to Azeans, in practice it is rare to find humans of another race in any position of authority within the organization. Azeans cite the unique stability of their race as justification for this, while detractors are quick to point out that the establishment of yet another Azean-dominated Crown has political ramifications beyond the range of military affairs. Nonhumans as a rule do not serve in StarControl, believing the obsession with Braxi to be a purely human affair; non-human negotiators have been known to refer to the conflict as "not our war."

Star Empire: See **Azean Star Empire**

Subname: The second name taken by Azeans, inherited through patrilinear or matrilinear descent according to the child's gender. Originally the numbers of Zeymourian ships used during the Exodus, subnames were adopted soon after the Founding to memorialize the planetary migration. They are used today in combination with the chosen name as a form of polite address, the Azean equivalent of "Mr." or "Ms."

The subname "Iyu" is reserved for the firstborn descendants of the line of Hasha.

Taz'hein: The "traitor god" of the Braxin pantheon, Taz'hein was recognized by neighboring tribes under a variety of other names, usually as a lesser god or demon. His destruction of the Creator served as a convenient explanation for why more benevolent gods did not involve themselves in human affairs, and historians note that much of Taz'hein's "worship" was not meant to draw favorable notice from the treacherous deity, but rather to encourage him to keep his distance.

It is not known exactly when the **Braxaná** first claimed a line of descent separate from that of other Braxins, with Taz'hein as their creator, but the myth was aggressively promulgated by **Viton the Ruthless** as part of a greater political agenda to set the Braxaná apart from other tribes. Under Braxaná influence Taz'hein would eventually dominate the lesser pantheons of other tribes, with the Creator relegated to a well-meaning but ultimately failed role in human history.

Token Dominance/Token Domitor: Among the Braxaná, a man who serves as personal assistant to the Mistress of a female-owned House, representing it in legal situations where she cannot. As Braxin law does not permit a woman to give direct orders to men, token male dominance is required in any situation where men must be commanded, or where gender-sensitive negotiations must take place.

Token of Ownership: An item, usually jewelry, signifying the submission of a Braxin woman to the sexual ownership of a man. Such a token is considered **Just Cause** for refusing granting sexual favors to any other male.

While the token of ownership may be of any form and therefore it is tempting for women to lie about having one, the fines for such subterfuge are high and enforcement is fierce. Any man suspecting deception is permitted to demand the identity of a woman's owner, and to make a citizen's arrest if she fails to provide it.

Tsank'ar: A virus native to Braxi, which has spread through the interstellar community to every known human planet. Though the effects of the tsank'ar are usually mild, the virus is subject to episodes of mutation which occasionally produce more virulent and more damaging strains.

Attempts to monitor the virus and provide preventative treatments have proven successful among the human population at large, and lesser mutations of the tsank'ar have been rated by Montesekua's Virology Center as a class IV, and are rarely lethal.

Major mutations of the tsank'ar are cause for greater concern, and Montesekua keeps close watch upon potentially threatening strains. These mutations appear approximately once a century and are known to be particularly damaging to the **Braxaná**, many of whom will isolate themselves during epidemics. The disruption of normal political processes during such a so-called **Plague** provides a rare opportunity for Azean military aggression, and it is said that virologists within the Star Empire watch the tsank'ar as closely as do their counterparts in the Holding, seeking to anticipate the next period of Braxin vulnerability

Tzkairi: See **Community of Mind**

Viak'im: Ruler of the Kesserit tribe. The Viak'im is chosen by ritual combat, overseen by a council of elders who may weight the proceedings in favor of one candidate or another.

Viton the Ruthless: Braxaná servitor to **Harkur the Great**, and the first Braxaná Kaim'era of the B'Saloan Holding.

Little is known of Viton's early life save that he was raised in the Braxaná tribal reaches, isolated from greater Braxin culture and technology. In his youth he made several forays into "civilized" territory, and while numerous romanticized tales have been written of his adventures there, the only acts that can be ascribed to him with certainty are the theft of the Zaldovi tribal relics in 4 B.C. and the assassination of a Brentasi prince in 2 A.C.

Viton came to the attention of Harkur's agents in 5 A.C. and was invited to the new international capital to meet him. His ruthless Braxaná spirit impressed the monarch and he served Harkur as companion and advisor through the duration of his reign. Their discussions of political and social philosophy were recorded by both parties, and have served as inspiration for warriors and politicians ever since.

Viton claimed the throne after Harkur's death in 57 A.C. Harkur's belief that the planet would take issue with Braxaná rule proved prophetic, and at least fifteen separate assassination attempts were known to take place during Viton's lifetime. He remained Kaim'era for nearly five decades despite such opposition, during which time he established the Braxaná so solidly as the power behind the Braxin throne that no man could hope to dislodge them.

Void: Braxin term for "outer space," more specifically the space between star systems. The Void refers not to lack of matter or energy but lack of consciousness, and hearkens back to the belief of many tribes that the universe was originally a vast pool of awareness. Each god born during the Creation drew his consciousness from that pool, until at last there was nothing left but nonsentient darkness.

Periodically cults arise in the Holding which purport to have located or even "spoken to" some surviving fragment of that great Awareness. Although the Braxaná are loathe to act against any such movement for fear of creating martyrs, it is known they keep a close eye upon such groups, and will act if necessary to keep such religious cults from gaining a foothold in Braxin society.

War Border: A region of space situated between the **Braxin Holding** and the **Azean Star Empire** where the majority of battles between those nations are fought. Territory in the War Border frequently changes hands, for which reason colonization is limited, and the majority of business conducted in the Border has to do with exploitation of planetary resources by a mobile freelance community that shifts its interests in accordance with territorial gains and losses, to avoid falling into enemy hands.

The territory known as the War Border does shift over time as imperial strategies play out, and planets which once housed large and complex civilizations within the Empire or Holding have on occasion found themselves in the control of those they once called enemies. Most famous of all of these is the colony of Hakrite, which changed hands 135 times in the 53rd century of the War, and where it is said that the natives kept flags of both nations in their houses, checking each morning to see which one it was appropriate to fly.

Wilding: An aggressive mating custom of the early **Braxaná**, common in their isolationist period, in which a male or female of fertile age would leave the tribe's territory to seek a mate from among surrounding peoples. While exogamy was common among Braxin tribes in order to sustain the genetic health of small populations, the Braxaná practice of mate-abduction, and the fact that they recognized no legal or cultural restrictions upon whom they might claim, made them less than popular with their immediate neighbors.

The practice was supposedly abandoned in the third century B.C, when the developing technology of surrounding nations forced the Braxaná to become more circumspect, but some historians believe that the custom was simply practiced more discretely after that point, and Braxaná females were known to aggressively seek impregnation by outsiders as late as the reign of Harkur the Great. The **Shlesor** put an end to all such customs, and is credited with turning Braxaná mating practices from an inclusive to an exclusive focus.

Y.E.: Year of the Exodus. The current Azean calendrical system begins its year count with the Founding of Azea.

Zatar the Magnificent: One of the youngest Braxaná ever to be elevated to the rank of Kaim'era, Zatar the Magnificent would later establish himself as the figurehead of the entire Holding, and establish his nation's first hereditary dynasty. While the first part of his life was lived in the public eye, with particular acclaim for his outstanding service in the Border Fleet, Zatar retired to a life of solitude soon after claiming his throne, with few public appearances and little direct contact even with his own Council. While many have speculated about the reasons for this hermitage little is actually known, and many ascribe the move to an attempt to create a sense of personal mystique above and beyond the Braxaná norm.

Zeymour: Formerly the third planet in the Azean star system, it is estimated Zeymour is the source for 87% of the material in the Daylish asteroid belt. While Azean tradition blames the planet's inhabitants for its destruction, scientists now believe that the passage of an alien body through the system was responsible for the planet's breakup, either by direct impact or by combination with local gravitic stressors.

Zeymour is regarded as a possible Source World for humankind, mostly due to Azea's advanced placement in the Schedule of Progress. Given the current state of Zeymour's archeological record it is unlikely that sufficient evidence will be uncovered to either prove or disprove this theory.

Zeymophobia: A syndrome unique to starfaring cultures, zeymophobia encompasses several disorders associated with fear of being planetbound. First noted among interstellar scouts on extended missions, Type I zeymophobia most often manifests as a fear of being unable to leave a planet's surface at will; in the most extreme cases this will produce crippling anxiety at the failure of any transportation device or system. Type II zeymophobia entails fear of natural ecosystems, and by extension all environments which are not strictly controlled by human technology. Though the symptoms of both types can be treated, the underlying causes are not fully understood, and sufferers are encouraged to develop a lifestyle independent of planetary habitation.

It has been long noted that zeymophobia is a purely human phenomenon, and several nonhuman scientists have speculated that this is the natural result of the human species "spreading itself too thin" among the stars. Other theorists postulate that it is a vestigial memory of species trauma from the time of the Seeding, and that if the other Scattered Species were of sufficiently advanced sentience similar symptoms would be observed in their populations.

Zhaor: The traditional weapon of the **Braxaná**, worn by members of the first class as a sign of rank, used in dueling challenges between them. The Zhaor blade has a triangular cross-section for two thirds of its length, with the final third being sharpened along both edges. Many styles of guard and quillons exist, the most common being a variety of openwork fashionable in the time of Viton the Ruthless. Early Zhaori were quite opulent, and while later models were fashioned to suit the understated image of the Braxaná, surviving relics from earlier eras still surface at high dress occasions among the older bloodlines, strangely at odds with the stark, colorless clothing that is their backdrop.

The Edict of 1,916 forbade the carrying of any bladed weapon by Braxins of "lesser blood," making the wearing of Zhaor one of the most visible and recognizable signs of a Braxaná inheritance.

Although Braxaná women of fertile age are forbidden to duel they are permitted to wear the Zhaor, as a reminder to all that in ancient times they served as warriors beside their men, and were revered for their fierceness as well as their fertility.

Zhene: The single moon of Braxi, orbiting its mother planet in 17+ Braxin days, and keeping one face toward the planet at all times. Zhene was explored in the second century B.C. and a government base was established there soon after, to be used for scientific experimentation and galactic observation. With the refinement of gravitic science it became possible to colonize the satellite on a greater scale, and in 474 A.C. Zhene was claimed by the Braxaná as a haven for their Race. Zhene is now restricted to members of the First Class and their households, and shines in the night sky of Braxi as a visible reminder of the separatist policies of the Pale Ones.

Zhent: The passage of Braxi's moon through all its phases, or 17+ Braxin days.